10-18-02

The Hostage

To Sally:
Thank you for reading my novel
Mary

THE HOSTAGE

A NOVEL BY

MARY R. DEMAINE

Editor and West Coast Publicist
Genie Lester

PZA PUBLISHING
WHITE BEAR LAKE, MN

PZA PUBLISHING, JUNE 2000
3722 WEST 50TH STREET
PMB #287
MINNEAPOLIS, MN 55410-2016

Published in the United States by
PZA Publishing, White Bear Lake, MN

Library of Congress Cataloging-in-Publication Data
DeMaine, Mary R.
The Hostage/ by Mary R. DeMaine - PZA Publishing
p. cm.
Greek - Homer - 20th century - Fiction

ISBN 0-9673471-1-4

Printed in the United States of America

Set in Palatino
Designed by J. Barniskis

Acknowledgments

This novel would not have been possible without the generous encouragement, insights, and feedback from many friends and colleagues. I wish to thank all of them. My spouse, Dwight, not only critiqued all versions of the text, but made me take time to live, at least occasionally, during the writing. Ron Lyschik read the first draft and made many helpful suggestions. Genie Lester edited the final draft. Her editing led to a number of significant modifications. Rabun Taylor and Marilyn Chiat read the final draft and offered many insightful suggestions. My publisher, Jennifer Barniskis, edited, proofed, designed, critiqued, and never failed to provide encouragement when I needed it.

Foreword

The ancients universally accepted the identification of Homer as the author of the *Iliad* and the *Odyssey* until the end of the second century CE when scholars began to observe inconsistencies in the two poems that led to some doubts. Ancient doubts were intensified in 1795 when a German scholar, F. A. Wolf, published a study in which he proposed, based upon an extensive analysis of the inconsistencies he found in the *Iliad* and the *Odyssey*, the two epics were not the work of a single poet. Rather, he argued, they were a compilation of popular poems recited by a multitude of poets. With this publication, there began a controversy which continues to the present day.

Many modern scholars still subscribe to the ancient Greek belief that the *Iliad* and the *Odyssey* were written by one person. For them, the inconsistencies Wolf found are indicative not of multiple authorship, but the process by which the poems were created. Though the author of the *Iliad* and the *Odyssey* is never identified in either poem, most of the scholars who accept single authorship also accept Homer as the poet. A few scholars modify this assumption to include the possibility there was no actual man named Homer, but rather the name was used to identify some famous poet from the past whose true identity had been lost by the time the epics were recorded.

At least one scholar who endorses single authorship does not accept Homer as the author. Minna Skafte Jensen argues from historical data the poems were first written in Athens under the tutelage of the tyrant, Pisistratus. Traditionally, Pisistratus has been credited, not with the original writing of the poems, but with commissioning an official version of them in the mid-sixth century BCE.

Among the multiple authorship adherents, there are those, like Wolf, who believe in many authors and those who believe in two authors, one for the *Iliad*, another for the *Odyssey*. The latter base their arguments on demonstrable stylistic differences between the two poems. Even the ancient Greeks, who did not question Homer's authorship, recognized there were stylistic difficulties. Those who addressed the problem explained the phenomenon by suggesting Homer wrote the *Iliad* as a young man, the *Odyssey* in old age. Modern two-author adherents do not accept the ancient Greeks' explanation. Instead, they argue it is more probable there were two different authors working a number of years apart.

Even though many scholars disagree as to who authored the *Iliad* and the *Odyssey*, there is, and has been in the past, almost universal agreement that the language of the poems supports their having been created in the area where Ionic Greek was spoken; that is, the southwestern coast of Asia Minor and the surrounding islands. Within the Ionian area of ancient Greece, many cities and islands claimed Homer as their native son. Prominent among the various claims were those of Smyrna, Ios, and Chios.

Smyrna's claim to be Homer's birthplace is summarized in the writings of Pseudo-Plutarch, who claimed to have gotten his information from Aristotle. According to Pseudo-Plutarch, during the Ionian settlement on the island of Ios, a local woman became pregnant by one of the gods. When her belly began to swell, she got embarrassed and went from her hometown to a small village on the island. There, she was captured by pirates who eventually took her to Smyrna and gave her to the king of Lydia. The king, in turn, gave the young pregnant woman to his friend Maion, who fell in love with and married her. When the young woman's labor pains began, she happened to be standing near the Meles River. Soon after, on the bank of the river, she gave birth to a son, whom she called Homer. She died after the birth. Maion, who had no obligation to the baby, nevertheless took this half-divine child into his home as his son.

Ios also claimed to be the birthplace of Homer. The Ios claim involved the most important oracle center in Greece, the Sanctuary of Apollo at Delphi. According to the Delphic legend, Homer himself went to Delphi to inquire about the place of his birth. The answer the oracle gave to Homer was, "Happy and ill-starred-for you are of both fates—you seek your fatherland. But you have a motherland and not a fatherland. The island of Ios is the fatherland of your mother, and it will receive you when dead. But, be on your guard against the riddle of young boys." This answer not only incorporated the famous legend of Homer's divine birth at Smyrna, but also drew upon another well-known legend about Homer in ancient Greece, that he died because he couldn't answer the riddle of a young man, sometimes portrayed as a young fisherman.

Chios' claim to Homer did not include any integration with the legends from Smyrna or Ios. Instead, the basis for the Chios claim was familial continuity. For several centuries after the alleged life of Homer, there lived on Chios a group of poets called the Homeridae. These poets specialized in reciting from the *Iliad* and the *Odyssey*, and, at times, wrote poetry of their own and attributed it to Homer. While some scholars, ancient and modern alike, have accepted the Homeridae as descendants of Homer, many of their colleagues point out there is absolutely no evidence to support a familial connection between Homer and his later followers on Chios.

The Greeks had three theories as to when Homer lived. One group, represented by Hecataeus and Eratosthenes, thought the poet was contemporary with the ancient Greek dates for the Trojan war, and thus, dated him to about 1200 BCE. A second group, which included Thucydides and Herodotus, concluded that Homer lived well after the Trojan war. Herodotus (484-425 BCE), reckoning backwards from his own life by generations, dated Homer to about 850 BCE. The last group, whose views were characterized by Theopompus, placed Homer at about 700 BCE.

Most modern scholars, whether they theorize one, two, or several poets, accept a date for the recording of the *Iliad* and the *Odyssey* in the eighth Century BCE—usually the second half of the century, sometimes as late as the end of the century. Further, those who follow the theory that the stylistic differences indicate different recording dates for the *Iliad* and the *Odyssey* usually date the *Iliad* earlier than the *Odyssey* by several years. Jensen, whose theory was discussed above, represents an exception among modern scholars. Since it is her contention that the *Iliad* and *Odyssey* were recorded under the direction of Pisistratus, her date for the recording of the poems is around the middle of the sixth Century BCE.

While the recording of the *Iliad* and *Odyssey* is undisputed fact, the method used by the poet or poets to record them is as problematic as the other facets of the study. Although at times in the past it has been proposed that the epics were created as written poetry, almost all scholars now agree, as the form of the poems suggests, that they were most probably created orally and had a long history of oral dissemination before they were written down. Here the agreement ends.

Some scholars contend that the poet or poets who recited the *Iliad* and *Odyssey* were illiterate. Their argument is primarily based upon the research of bards in the former Yugoslavia undertaken by Milman Parry and Albert Lord. The scenario often presented is one in which the poet or poets recited from memory while a literate scribe, most likely under the patronage of some wealthy individual, recorded. Other scholars argue that the oral poet or poets responsible for the *Iliad* and *Odyssey* would have been literate. They project a situation in which the poet or poets recorded the epics without the assistance of a trained scribe.

Most scholars seem to agree that some form of correction or rewriting was done after the initial recording. If the poems were not recorded under the direction of Pisistratus, as Jensen contends, they most certainly were edited.

Lacking specific information about Homer did not deter the Greeks from portraying him. Both in literature and in the plastic arts, he was consistently portrayed as a blind, elderly man. Many explanations have been offered to account for the association of blindness with Homer. Some argue it is based upon the assumption that the blind poet portrayed in the *Odyssey* was really a self-portrait of the poem's author. Others suggest that there may be an association with a blind poet among the Homeridae. Still others have advanced the idea that there may have been some connection between the blindness and the name Homer. In Greek, Homer means hostage. In some instances in ancient Greece, the blind seem to have been referred to as hostages. Thus, a poet named Homer or hostage, could be understood to be blind.

In sum, after centuries of research, we have accumulated only one fact. The *Iliad* and *Odyssey* were written down. In their present form, each of the epics consists of twenty-four books written in dactylic hexameter. While interesting and informative and, at times, highly imaginative, the results of all attempts to determine exactly who wrote the two poems, when, where, and how they were written, must be, in the final analysis, classified as fiction!

My story parallels the approach to historical events taken by the historian, Herodotus, as described by Jeremy McInerney in his Teaching Company lectures about ancient Greek civilization. According to McInerney, Herodotus viewed history as research, but he thought it was much more important to tell a good story. In my story, I adhere to the facts as closely as possible, but with the clear knowledge that only the facts we have found are in Homer (and his somewhat later fellow writer, Hesiod). The remainder of the "facts" that scholars use to recreate the period are really extrapolations from the much later historical periods and from archaeological discoveries. Both are open to interpretation.

Two of my interpretations that may be questioned are the story's portrayal of women and slaves. Later Greek writers suggest that women were totally powerless. They were expected to literally stay within their homes. The historian, Thucydides, quotes the great Athenian leader, Pericles, as having described the perfect woman as being one who is never talked about, whether it be for her virtue or its opposite. She is one who stays home and performs her family duty without complaint or greater expectations.

Yet the literature suggests that the Greeks were certainly willing to entertain the idea of strong, self-willed, even evil women having existed. Medea killed both of her children to punish her husband Jason for having abandoned her to marry the daughter of the king of Corinth. She was not punished by the authorities, but went instead to Athens with Aegus, the king. Clytemnestra, wife of the greatest Mycenaean king, Agamemnon, killed her husband upon his return from Troy. She was not punished for her deed by any public authority. She was punished by her son who murdered her in revenge when he grew up.

Later Greek laws and precedents seem to have kept women under the control of a male member of their families at all times. Yet the *Odyssey* suggests that precedent may have been more amorphous during earlier periods. Even though Odysseus' father lives on his son's estate during his ten-year absence, it doesn't seem to be the father, but Odysseus' wife, Penelope, who has the right to make the decision about her fate. The suitors who come daily to the estate, where they sit around eating Odysseus' wealth, do not make their appeal for Penelope to take a new husband to Odysseus' father, but to her. Although she doesn't have the power to send them away or stop them from squandering the estate (neither does her father-in-law), she does have the power to put them off for ten years with trickery. The example of Penelope seems to me to open up the possibility that all women living during the Homeric period weren't always totally subjected to male authority.

Slaves, like women, had no power in the historical ancient world. Further, there seems to be no written evidence to suggest that the concept of slavery was ever questioned. On the contrary, Aristotle argued that slavery was a natural and desirable state, and McInerney points out that even those slaves who wanted freedom probably expected to own slaves themselves once freed. Thus, any change wasn't a question of eliminating slavery, but of changing one's status as a slave.

Should we assume that no individual on his/her own ever questioned the morality of slavery because the individuals who wrote down their thoughts never questioned it and Aristotle even defended it? It's impossible to say without written records, but it seems plausible to speculate that it might have happened since we do have precedents for serious questioning of societal mores. Elizabeth Vandiver, in her Teaching Company lecture series about the *Iliad*, points out that the withdrawal of Achilles from the battle at Troy comprises a rejection of mores of his society, even a questioning of his world's paradigm of what it means to be human. Much later, we find Socrates questioning how life should be lived. Significantly, we would know nothing of his questioning had it not been for his pupil, Plato, since Socrates wrote nothing down.

Even if the evidence we have for individuals questioning the mores of their societies opens the possibility that there could have been individuals who questioned the morality of slavery, the leap from questioning slavery to action is a great one. Was an aristocratic-led slave rebellion on a small-scale possible? It seems improbable, but we do know that in the fourth century Theban strategy for containing Spartan power included freeing Spartan serfs, the Messenian helots, returning them to their ancestral home, and founding a city for them to live in. We also know that the Spartans controlled their helots very strictly. Were their actions preemptive? Or did unrecorded memories of past rebellious incidents exist?

There are many more questions than I have touched upon in this short discussion. I do not pretend to have the answers, but like Herodotus, I have done my research and I do have a story to tell...

Part I

One

"Please!" Nicias pleaded, suddenly frightened. "Let's turn back."

"What in the name of Zeus for?" Philocleon stretched onto his tiptoes to get a better view of the immense foreign ship anchored in Poseidon's sea at the bottom of the cliff.

Nicias shuddered. What was it about the ship that frightened him? The way the sea gulls were frantically circling the deck? The strange shape of the prow? The snake-like tear in the sail? By themselves, none of these things seemed very ominous. Still, his fear persisted and grew stronger. "You've got to listen to me," he insisted, as he searched desperately for some way to curb the unexplained agitation he felt. "That ship's carrying disaster. I'm sure of it."

"I'd say it's more likely to be carrying boys." Philocleon examined the ship carefully again. Finding nothing to convince him he should be frightened of it, he edged toward the steep path leading to the harbor below. "I heard men talking the last time we were at the port. They're expecting a Phoenician ship carrying slave boys for the Laurion silver mines."

"Are you sure they were expecting boys?" Nicias' throat tightened with each word until he was sure he would strangle. Though he fiercely wanted to turn his back forever to the ship, he couldn't force even the smallest part of his tall frame to move. Terror-stricken, he stood and stared, his feet and legs so heavy they seemed shackled to the limestone crag, his hands hanging like boulders at the ends of his arms.

"Father," he whispered, closing his eyes to shut out the horrid memory that was appearing before him. After more summers had come and gone than he cared to remember–everything–from the breath hissing out of his father's bleeding mouth to the sinister grin on the captain's face–everything–was still as vivid as if it had just happened.

He saw his father trapped at the olive press by three Cretan slave traders, yelling frantically at him to run to the house. But his legs had not moved. He had stood there paralyzed with fear while the captain put a sword through his father. Nor had he been able to move when the captain pulled a stone from the olive press and came toward him. The stone had come smashing down on his right foot, but he had barely felt the pain. He had already been shocked into numbness by his father's death.

"What is it?" Philocleon asked, suddenly aware that Nicias was groaning. "You're as pale as an albino mare."

Nicias searched Philocleon's face somberly, his rich brown eyes darkened almost to black with agitation. "I feel a little sick," was all he said, afraid any discussion of the horrid flash into his childhood might unleash more of what lay hidden in his mind. Worse, too many times unwanted flashes into his past had ended with even less wanted flashes into the future. It was enough that the ship frightened him. He didn't want to know why.

"It's the heat," Philocleon decided as some of the color came back into Nicias' face. "Next time we'll take the horses." Hiking straight down the cliff was much faster than meandering back and forth on the horse trails, but Nicias wasn't young anymore and lately his foot had seemed worse.

"It's not the walking that's bothering me. It's that ship," Nicias said, trying one more time to keep Philocleon from going to the port.

Philocleon stood for a moment debating whether he should continue or turn back. Though Nicias was a slave, Philocleon did not for a moment question his ability to see into the future. After all, he had saved Philocleon's father from a savage death with one of his uncanny visions. But today Nicias wasn't making any sense. "What is it about the ship that's frightening you?" he asked, examining the vessel from prow to stern once more. "To tell you the truth, it doesn't look any different to me than the other foreign ships we've seen."

Nicias didn't answer. He couldn't. He did not know what was frightening him and he wasn't willing to search through the hidden recesses of his mind to try and find out.

Convinced by Nicias' silence that his dark mood was caused by exhaustion and not the ship, Philocleon stepped onto the steep harbor path. "If we stay here much longer, I'll miss all the excitement."

Nicias examined the sky. Helios had ridden his chariot of fire only a short distance, but fiery light coming from the sun god was already beating down so mercilessly both men were soaked with sweat. He pulled a wineskin from his traveling sack and offered it to Philocleon. "Thirsty?"

Philocleon shook his head, sending beads of sweat splattering from his black curly hair onto his broad shoulders. He wiped his face with the skirt of his tunic and waited for Nicias to speak, his usually calm olive brown eyes beginning to sparkle with impatience. Why am I waiting, he wondered. Now that I have seen the summer and winter solstices pass eighteen times and Nicias is no longer my pedagogue, I don't need his permission to go to the ship. Still, he waited.

"Go ahead," Nicias finally said, realizing from Philocleon's determined gaze that he would never convince him to turn around. "But please be careful."

"I will," Philocleon promised. Then, pretending his iron dagger was a bronze sword, he charged down the cliff fighting fiercely against one imaginary Trojan hero after another. He was in a chariot and so were his enemies. His friend Patroclus was at his side.

During his last trip to the Sounion port, he'd heard the older men talking. They said, in an age of heroes no longer remembered by any man, the Greeks were not just herders and farmers as most men were now, but fearless warriors. They had defeated the powerful kingdom of Troy in the most glorious battle ever fought. Every hero returning to Greece had his ships filled with gold and silver and slaves.

The oldest man in the group insisted Greece would be great again if only the young men would walk in the path of Achilles and the other Greek heroes of the Trojan war. Philocleon had never seen a chariot, and he had no idea where Troy was, except that it was somewhere across the Aegean. It didn't make any difference to him. He firmly believed he was destined to be one of the heroes who would make Greece great again.

With a final victory cry, he jumped off a boulder, caught himself on a branch, swung his legs over a second boulder, and dropped to the bottom of the cliff. He ended his heroic battle with a final flourish of his sword as he raced to the port and made his way into the crowd that was gathering at the ship.

"Make way for Heracles," a voice boomed from the line of oarsmen filing through the crowd.

One of the tallest men Philocleon had ever seen stepped out of the line, balancing an amphora on his shoulder. The man lumbered over to a small boy. "Stand back or you'll find this amphora on your foot." The boy didn't move. He was too awed by the size of the man and his voice.

Reaching out and pretending he planned to snatch the boy, the colossal oarsman leaned forward, causing the enormous two-handled jar on his shoulder to waver. Philocleon ducked instinctively with the rest of the crowd and stepped backwards. The laughing oarsman juggled his load back into balance and pointed at the boy again. "Get the nets," he bellowed toward the ship, "and we'll snare ourselves a deck swabber."

The boy edged around Philocleon and tried to disappear behind his legs.

"Here." Philocleon grinned, handing the child a wineskin someone in the crowd had passed forward. "Offer him this."

The ship's captain, a man whose build was as strikingly small as the oarsman's was colossal, stalked from the deck onto the gangplank and threatened the people gathered around the oarsman that if they didn't get away from his ship, he'd take his whip to them. He shook his fist at the oarsman. "You drop that amphora and you'll see what it means to be a deck swabber."

Grinning, the oarsman leaned his head back and started emptying the wineskin.

"A bronze piece says he can't do it," someone yelled.

"Two says he can," someone else yelled.

Philocleon was sure the men betting for the oarsman would win, but he was too anxious to get a closer look at the ship to wait and find out. Chanting, "drink it down," with the other men, he skirted the group gathering around the oarsman and made his way toward the gangplank.

Ever since his two Assyrian tutors had told him about their sea voyage from Ionia to Athens a few months ago, he'd dreamed of being a ship's captain. Now, walking toward the ship, he imagined himself standing on the deck ordering his crew out to destroy some ferocious enemy of Greece.

He found it hard to believe the comic little man on the gangplank could actually be the captain of this ship. He'd always assumed captains of foreign ships were tall men with athletic builds like his. The few he'd seen had been.

At the foot of the gangplank Philocleon watched an oarsman unleash a man tied to the whipping post. With the speed and power of a trained wrestler the man broke away when the oarsman tried to retie his hands behind his back. He darted around the sail and headed for the gangplank.

"Stop him," the oarsman yelled.

Someone lunged, bringing the man to the deck. He struggled, kicking and hitting with powerful blows, but one oarsman after another piled on him until he was totally pinned. Two oarsmen brought him up from the bottom of the pile by the hair and pulled him backward halfway down the gangplank to the captain.

Cursing, the captain muttered something Philocleon couldn't hear, and the two shoved their captive toward the bottom of the gangplank. He stumbled, caught his balance, stumbled again, and fell into Philocleon, knocking him backward into the crowd.

"I'm sorry," the man said, springing effortlessly to his feet, holding his hand out to help Philocleon up. "Captain's a little upset. I didn't hurt you, did I?" He continued to glance over his shoulder to make certain none of the captain's men was coming after him.

"What happened?" Philocleon asked, still a little stunned from the unexpected fall. "Why were you thrown off the ship?" Now that they were facing one another, he could see the man wasn't an oarsman. His face wasn't weathered as it would have been had he spent his life at sea, nor was the hand he offered callused from hard work.

"I was thrown off the ship for borrowing a bit of the captain's wine supply," the stranger answered. He punctuated his remark with a vulgar snap of his arm toward the ship. "Filthy man doesn't know how to reward a poet properly."

"Bu, but...what does that have to do with you?" Philocleon was shocked. The man looked much too scrubby to be associated with a poet, let alone act as his protector.

"Sir. I am the poet I was referring to." The man dramatically brushed the dirt off his filthy tunic.

A poet? This unkempt man who had seen the solstices pass only a few more times than he had? Philocleon couldn't quite believe it. But then, he reminded himself, he'd only heard about poets, he'd never actually seen one. "How is a poet properly rewarded?" he asked.

"He should be offered wine as a gift after he has recited, not forced to steal from the kitchen to soothe his parched throat." The stranger rubbed his throat as though it ached.

Philocleon was both amused and intrigued by this outrageous man. He decided to challenge him. "Sing us a line and I'll buy you as much wine as you like." He held up the leather bag hanging around his neck and shook the bronze pieces in it to prove he could keep his word.

The stranger placed both hands on his hips and bowed from the waist. He was enjoying the sparring as much as Philocleon. "Yours is a challenge I can't but accept." He raced to one of the carts winding its way out of the harbor, climbed onto the back, and feet astride, arms out, announced he would recite.

With the purest voice Philocleon had ever heard, the stranger began his singing by imploring the beautiful muse, Calliope, to come to him with perfect verses. Moments later, his grey-brown eyes glowing passionately, he recited for his audience the saga of how the handsome Trojan prince, Paris, visited the great Greek prince, Menelaus, fell in love with, and kidnapped, Menelaus' beautiful wife, Helen. How Agamemnon, lord of all the Greeks, and brother of Menelaus, led thousands of men to Troy to destroy it and bring Helen back to Greece.

Just as the Greeks reached the shores of Troy, the stranger stopped singing and jumped off the cart. Philocleon no longer doubted this man was a poet. Even more important, he was a poet Philocleon decided he had to know. The saga he had just sung told the story of how the Greeks' war against Troy began. This man obviously knew all about the Greek heroes of the past. Weaving his way through the crowd that had gathered he excitedly joined the clamoring for more poetry.

"Not until I have quenched my thirst," the man insisted.

"I'm no Cretan. I keep my word," Philocleon told him. "I

promised you wine and you will certainly have it, but first I'd like to know your name. Mine is Philocleon."

"Remember the gift you promised me and I will tell you my name." The stranger threw his head back, letting his greasy golden brown locks fall where they would and laughed with total abandon, his eyes dancing with mischievous delight. Philocleon laughed too, though he had no idea what they were laughing about. "Follow me," he said when their laughing had subsided into friendly grins.

He led the stranger toward the portico through the labyrinth of stalls the fishermen's wives were cleaning. Soon, the stalls would be filled with the night's catch, if there was one. At the moment, the strong smell of stale fish left both men holding their breath.

They circled the last stall, climbed over the torn nets thrown behind the market, and entered the spice bazaar. Stepping gaily over and around spices piled on leather napkins, they made their way through a multitude of peddlers dressed in bright colors, sitting side-by-side, gossiping in languages neither man could understand, their spices saturating the air with rich odors.

Philocleon reached the portico first. He waited while the stranger wandered from one peddler to another, tasting, smelling, arguing. At last a bargain was struck. The stranger took a small container of frankincense and left a bronze ring that had adorned his finger when they'd entered the spice market.

Together again, the two men meandered along the wooden colonnade that supported the thatched portico roof on the sea side, stepping in and out of the shade, playfully dodging around peddlers and oarsmen, passing without interest the long row of wattle and daub shops built at the back of the portico until they came to the taverns.

"This one," Philocleon said, stopping in front of his favorite tavern. He entered, ordered two drinking bowls filled with wine at the bar, and handed one to the stranger. "Now, what is your name?"

Clicking his wine bowl against Philocleon's, the man answered, "Homer."

"To Homer," Philocleon called to the noisy crowd that filled the tavern, many of them men he knew and liked though he'd been told enough times by his father it was a disgrace for a man of his breeding to frequent the same taverns as merchants and freedmen.

"To Homer," came from the back of the tavern. Lamachus lifted his bowl.

"He's a wine merchant," Philocleon told Homer, more pleased than he'd expected to be introducing the poet to the men in the tavern.

"Then he's a good man to know." Homer lifted his bowl in return.

"Is Homer buying us wine? Is that why we're drinking to him?" a slurred voice rumbled from the floor. Creon, a good-natured Athenian who'd always had too much of Dionysus' nectar, as he liked to call it, crawled up onto his hands and knees and held out his bowl in supplication to Homer.

"If you'd labor once in awhile at something besides begging, you'd be able to buy your own wine," Philocleon teased, flipping the smallest bronze piece in his leather bag into Creon's bowl. As Creon staggered to the bar, two men Philocleon recognized from the port came into the tavern. "Ask him to recite," one of them said, standing next to Philocleon.

"Help me up on the bar," Homer told the two men without waiting for Philocleon to ask. A glance at the crowd told him this wasn't going to be the kind of audience he'd gotten used to in Ionia, but they all seemed to have leather bags jingling with bronze hanging around their necks. Surely, some of them would part with a few pieces if he sang well. And, no doubt about it, with Philocleon at his side, he'd get a meal and plenty of wine before the night ended.

"To Homer," Philocleon repeated, handing up a bowl of wine.

As always, Homer began his reciting by imploring the beautiful muse, Calliope, to come to his assistance. The only thing in life he truly feared was being forsaken by this wonderful muse who'd saved him from a life of poverty with her gift of memory.

Within moments of his earnest supplication he felt the tingling of excitement throughout his body that he knew to be the sign of the muse. Without hesitation, he began. The verses that came to him were those of Helen's abduction by Paris. And so he sang it a second time, listening to his voice as he recited, certain his singing could rival that of Apollo.

"More," voices demanded from all directions when the saga ended. Looking around, Homer saw that the crowd listening to him not only filled the tavern, but also covered much of the portico. "Does anyone have a lyre?" he asked, thinking that with the gathering crowd he might do better than gain a few bronze pieces. The owner of the tavern sent his slave to get one. "It's yours," he told the poet when he handed up the instrument. Smiling, Homer took the lyre and sang again, this time of the untimely death of Zeus' own son, the Trojan hero, Sarpedon.

Nicias arrived as Homer began the saga of Perseus. He waved at Philocleon but didn't bother to stop. Instead, he went directly to the tavern frequented by slaves, ordered himself a bowl of wine and sat down, propping his foot on his traveling sack. The evening breeze had already cooled the stone benches, bringing with it the smell of ripened fruits and vegetables from the stalls crowded into the marketplace below the slaves' end of the portico. Waving, he called to one of the vendors he knew to bring over some figs. He took the figs, and turning his back to the sea, made a pledge to stop thinking about that ship.

The tavern boy was handing a third bowl of wine to Nicias when the lamplighter started placing small ceramic pots of fire around the portico. Entranced by the dancing flames, Nicias forgot his pledge to himself and turned toward the harbor. The ship was moored directly in front of him. Before he knew what had happened, he was staring at it, horrified. Instantly his peace of mind was gone. His heart started to race again. Knots formed in his stomach. Frantically, he stood and called to one of the young errand runners waiting by the portico. "Hey, do you know Trygaeus?"

The boy walked over. "What's he look like?"

Nicias held his hand out at shoulder height. "About this tall. Kind of fat with bushy grey eyebrows and beard. He drives one of the supply wagons."

"He got a foot like yours?"

"The same." Nicias winced.

"I know him."

Nicias tossed the figs he hadn't eaten to the boy. "Tell him to meet Nicias at the olive oil shop with his wagon."

He waited until the boy disappeared into the crowd before he threw his traveling sack over his shoulder and worked his way through the fruit and vegetable vendors to the small portico. Built closer to the sea when the main portico got too crowded, it was mostly filled with wine and oil merchants, their amphorae stacked so precariously high in the small rooms that Nicias feared to go inside.

At the door to his favorite merchant's shop, he ordered two amphorae of olive oil, then spotting Trygaeus, waved him over, turning again to the oil merchant when Trygaeus had come with his wagon. "You got any amphorae with the tops broken off?"

"Four or five."

"I need two." He loaded two amphorae filled with olive oil onto Trygaeus' wagon, put the two broken ones beside them, and climbed up next to Trygaeus.

"Wine?" Trygaeus pulled a wineskin from under his seat.

Nicias took a long drink, feeling better now that he was doing something about getting away from the Sounion port.

"What happened that you came looking for me?" Trygaeus asked. "I thought we were meeting at the tavern to eat before we went for supplies."

"Nothing. I just wanted to get started," Nicias lied.

Taking the wineskin, Trygaeus grinned. You never got anything from Nicias until he was ready. He backed the oxen away from the portico. "They for salt?" he asked, pointing his whip at the broken amphorae in the back of the wagon.

Nicias nodded.

Trygaeus maneuvered his oxen through the marketplace and onto the seacoast road. Letting the animals take their own pace to the salt ponds once they were on the road, he searched through the sack under his seat, finally finding two pomegranates. He peeled one open and handed the other to Nicias. Eating slowly to try to fool his stomach into thinking it was getting enough, Trygaeus turned to the conversation he'd been waiting to have with Nicias since shortly after his last trip to the port.

"I have a surprise for you," he said.

"What is it?" Nicias couldn't stop his voice from quivering. He knew from Trygaeus' tone, he had news of Bromia.

"A driver who came to work the port is from Sparta. Says he's sure he's seen your Bromia at one of the estates where he delivers salt. He's going back after the harvest festival. If you want to send a message, he's willing." He nudged Nicias. "Course, I told him I didn't think you'd be interested."

Nicias tried to speak, but his voice failed. After so many seasons had passed, was it possible he'd actually found her? Giddy, he took a long drink of wine and handed the wineskin to Trygaeus with shaking hands.

"We can't be certain it's Bromia," Trygaeus said, looking away toward the sea, pretending he hadn't noticed how nervous Nicias was. "We've been wrong before. But this time it seems likely we're right."

Nicias only nodded agreement. He didn't trust that he could speak without his voice cracking. Was it possible? He ran his thumb and forefinger nervously down the sides of his mouth several times.

"I guess I'm a little excited," he finally managed to say.

Trygaeus smiled. "I hadn't noticed." He patted Nicias on the arm. "No need to hurry. We'll talk when you're ready."

Nicias nodded.

"When you're ready," Trygaeus repeated as they reached the salt area.

Nicias slipped from the wagon and limped to the numerous earth bridges that separated the salting area into ponds. He passed the first set of ponds on the closest bridge, checking the water carefully. It had never ceased to amaze him that sea water could be turned into salt.

The water in the first ponds was brought directly from the sea by channels. It was here that most of the water evaporated, turning first bright red and then pink. Years ago he'd asked the salt-maker what made the water change color. The salt-maker had explained it was little things growing in the water when it came in from the sea that turned it red. When these things died, the water turned pink. It didn't make sense to Nicias, but he figured the salt-maker probably knew what he was talking about.

The pink water with all of its dead things was channeled into another set of ponds where it was left until it crystallized into salt. Nicias took one of the bridges to the crystallization ponds. After some searching he found the salt-maker in one of the ponds shoveling salt into skin bags. He took a pinch of salt and tasted it. "Seems a little bitter."

The salt-maker pointed to another pond. "Try that one."

The salt there tasted better. "I'll take two bags from this one."

Brushing scum from his legs, the salt-maker got out of the pond. "Did you get the amphorae?"

"Two. Like you said."

"Good." Motioning for Nicias to follow, the salt-maker walked over to the pond Nicias had chosen, squatted down and ran some brine through his fingers to test it.

Nicias followed him. "How do I use it?"

"Simple. Fill the broken amphorae with water and set 'em in the sun. Put a little bag of brine in the top of each one. Shake the bags up every once in awhile during the day and fill 'em when they get empty. Keep doing this until no more brine will dissolve. When that happens, drop an egg or a small dried fish in the amphorae. If it floats, you're ready for pickling. You got many pigs this year?"

"None on the estate, but Hipponous is planning to do some wild boar hunting. I'd guess a couple of skins will serve."

The salt ordered, Nicias worked his way back to the wagon, reexamining each set of ponds. When he'd helped the salt-maker load the skins, he climbed up next to Trygaeus.

"Fish stalls next?" Trygaeus backed his oxen around and headed back toward the marketplace.

"I'm not stopping for fish," Nicias answered, trying to sound casual. "Let's pick up Philocleon and get out of the village while it's still cool."

"Are you sure?" Trygaeus looked Nicias over carefully. Not once in all the trips Nicias had made to the village to buy supplies had he gone home without fresh fish. Trygaeus had seen Hipponous furious when he thought the fish wasn't fresh enough. What would happen when they turned up without any fish? "Something's really wrong when you decide to go home without a visit to the fish stalls. Is it all this talk about Bromia?"

Nicias shrugged. "I'm just too tired."

"I don't believe you!" Trygaeus knew full well Nicias was lying. He'd never skip buying fish because he was tired. Not knowing what else to do, he made a halfhearted attempt to tease Nicias into talking. "Tired? You? Come on. You're the only man I know who's celebrated Persephone's return from Hades thirty-five times without aging." He patted his own big paunch affectionately. "You're as firm and strong as a man half your age."

Nicias smiled. Trygaeus had a way of making him feel better no matter what. It had been the same when they were two scared kids on the slave ship. "Did you hear where that big ship in the harbor came from?" he asked gingerly.

"Ionia."

"Philocleon said he thought it was a Phoenician ship."

"Nope. Ionia. I know 'cause I was there hauling cargo for the captain."

"Did you notice anything strange about the ship?"

"Nope. Just your usual cargo ship with your usual nasty captain. Stingy too. Tried to cheat me after I'd done his hauling. Why do you ask?"

"I don't know. It's just a feeling I had when I first saw it."

"That ship have something to do with your not going for fish?" Trygaeus knew about Nicias' premonitions.

Nicias took a long drink of wine to avoid having to explain and changed the subject. "Do you suppose Bromia looks the same as she did when she left?"

"Who can say?" Trygaeus knew it wouldn't do any good to ask Nicias about the ship again, curious as he was. "Look at my wife. She used to be a pretty little thing. Now she's as mean and ugly as they get."

"What did you expect?" Nicias smiled. "She's had to put up with you, hasn't she?"

"Just ask my sons who got the best of that bargain," Trygaeus joked. "You sure you don't want to go to the fish market?" He hoped Nicias would change his mind by the time they reached the market-place.

"I can't help wondering," Nicias said more to himself than Trygaeus, "how many children we'd have if we'd been able to marry."

"Why do you suppose Hipponous sent her away?" It was a question Trygaeus had pondered many times.

"I don't know. He sent me here to buy supplies. When I got back, she was gone."

"I bet the old cock was jealous."

"Hipponous never knew about Bromia and me."

"You kept it from Hipponous?" Shaking his head in disbelief, Trygaeus pulled his oxen to a halt at the main portico. "You go for Philocleon. I'm going for some fish," he announced. "I'm not in the mood to listen to Hipponous' complaining."

Nicias nodded, knowing Trygaeus would go whether he wanted him to or not. Feeling somewhat relieved, knowing they were almost out of the port, he searched through the tavern until he found

Philocleon slumped over an empty wine bowl. Homer was sitting on the floor in front of him, still reciting.

"I'm not leaving without Homer," Philocleon said when Nicias finally got him onto his feet.

"But you know how angry your father will be. He's forbidden me to even let you go near that tavern," Nicias pleaded.

"Listening to Homer is like listening to Apollo himself," Philocleon persisted. Homer had grown in Philocleon's eyes from a great poet reciting the deeds of heroes to a hero himself as quickly as Night had spread blackness over the port. He could no longer see any difference between his new friend and the ancient Greek heroes – Achilles, Patroclus, Odysseus... "My father will be happy I invited him when he hears him recite."

Nicias sighed. "Your father won't be happy. Believe me. He'll be furious."

"You could tell him Philocleon insisted against your will," Homer suggested. "Then you'd be out of trouble."

"It won't help," Nicias muttered under his breath. Neither would standing there arguing.

"What do you mean it won't help?" Philocleon asked.

"Nothing," Nicias answered, trying not to think about how angry Hipponous was going to be. "Can you stand?" he asked Homer.

With help from Philocleon, Homer got onto his feet. Together they staggered out to the wagon, Homer strumming his lyre, both of them singing.

"He's teaching me the saga of the Trojan war," Philocleon told Nicias as they climbed onto the wagon.

"Should I sing you the saga of Perseus again?" Homer asked Philocleon.

Philocleon nodded, but fell asleep before Homer had even begun singing. Homer leaned his lyre against the side of the wagon and fell asleep next to Philocleon.

"Who's that?" Trygaeus threw a string of fresh tuna for Hipponous into the back, put a smoked one for himself and Nicias on the seat, and climbed up.

"A poet Philocleon met."

"That'll make Hipponous happy," Trygaeus muttered to himself.

"You don't have to tell me."

Trygaeus maneuvered his oxen though the marketplace toward the road that meandered up the cliff Nicias and Philocleon had climbed down that morning. He planned to ask Nicias more about the poet when they got onto the cliff road, but never got the chance. Nicias was asleep before they left the marketplace.

"I guess that means there's nothing left for me to do," he informed the sleeping Nicias with a grin, "but wait until you're awake again." He broke off a piece of the tuna resting on the seat between them.

Nicias woke with the first appearance of rosy-fingered Dawn in the sky. They were nearly home. As always, the arrival of Dawn brought memories. But this time they were memories he'd worked hard to keep vivid in his mind, not the unwanted glimpses of his life on the slave ship.

He saw himself as a boy in Argos crawl onto his father's supply-laden wagon, settle down on a bag of wheat and fall sleep under the dark mantle of Night. He didn't stir until his father touched his shoulder and pointed to Helios. Even now, when the appearance of the sun god gave him nothing to look forward to except hard work, Nicias still felt cheered by the first sight of his chariot.

Trygaeus handed Nicias the one small piece of tuna that was left. "I saw you smile. Must have been dreaming about Bromia."

Nicias smiled again. "No. I was thinking about my father."

For the first time since he'd recognized Trygaeus in the Sounion port tavern eight winters ago, he wanted to talk about the time they spent together as slaves. "On our way to the port we saw that big ship from Ionia coming into the harbor. Philocleon said he'd heard it was carrying boy slaves for the silver mines. It started me remembering. Do you ever think about the slave ship?"

"Never! At least I try not to."

"For many summers now I haven't thought about those horrible men, but today everything in my past seems to be coming back to me." Nicias' words came haltingly. "Ever since we saw that ship, I've been thinking about my kidnapping." He turned slowly and looked at Trygaeus, his eyes dull with pain. "I'll never forget the look on my father's face when he fell at the captain's feet. It wasn't so much a look of dying as of unbearable sadness, like he knew what was going to happen to me."

Trygaeus sighed gloomily. "The captain and his men didn't kill my father. They grabbed me when I was swimming alone. But, what's the difference? I never saw my father alive again. I spent so many seasons working as a slave before I earned my freedom, both my father and mother were dead when I was finally finished with slavery."

"My mother's dead by now. I'm sure of that. But sometimes I wonder about my sister – if she's alive, if she's married, if she has children." Thinking about his sister made Nicias feel a little better. "My sister was as cute as a newborn cub when she was small. Tiny, always wanting to crawl up on your lap and cuddle. But as prim and proper a child as you'd ever want to meet. Arrogant, too."

"I've at least got a reminder. One of my sons looks just like my father." Trygaeus glanced at Nicias.

Reluctantly Nicias let the image of his sister sitting on his lap fade from his mind. "Your sons are fine boys." He knew how proud Trygaeus was of his sons.

"You should have a son of your own." It made Trygaeus furious to think of Nicias still being a slave after he'd served Hipponous faithfully for so long. "I just can't understand it. You've been a loyal slave. You've worked hard. Why won't Hipponous free you?" He didn't expect to get an answer from Nicias. He'd asked the question before. Never had Nicias answered it.

Nicias lowered his voice. "He's afraid." For some reason – the ship, the remembering – he wanted to unburden himself.

"Afraid of what?" Trygaeus couldn't imagine Hipponous being afraid of anything.

Nicias hesitated. He looked into the trees framing both sides of the narrow path they were following. Were the Erinyes out there? Would they punish him? For watching when it was forbidden? For telling what he'd seen?

Trygaeus repeated his question. "What's he afraid of?"

"The Erinyes."

"Who isn't afraid of the Erinyes?" Trygaeus shrugged.

Nicias made sure Philocleon was sleeping. "But, Hipponous has real cause to fear them."

"What has he done?" The question left Trygaeus trembling with fear, though he was curious enough to repeat it when Nicias didn't answer.

Nicias continued to examine the trees, trying to decide whether he dared repeat what he knew. At last, unable to control his desire to unburden himself any longer, he leaned so close to Trygaeus their heads almost touched. "It all started with Calonice," he whispered.

"Philocleon's mother?" Trygaeus whispered too.

Nicias nodded. "Hipponous and I were out in the barn delivering a colt when it happened so I didn't actually see anything. I only know what Calonice's slave, Kynna, told me afterwards. Calonice had gone to her room. She was near to having Philocleon and she was very sick. Besides, it was hot. She called Kynna to come to her. Kynna came and bathed her in cool water and she seemed to be better but not enough for Kynna to want to leave her alone, so Kynna sent one of the cook's youngsters to fetch a clean peplos. The girl got one from a stack of laundry just brought into the house. When Kynna opened the peplos and wrapped it around Calonice, a snake slid out of one of the folds and slithered across Calonice's belly to the floor."

"Oh, Zeus. What could be worse for the unborn than that kind of an omen?" Trygaeus shivered.

Nicias nodded knowingly. "We heard Calonice's scream inside the stable. It was horrible. High pitched like some kind of a trapped animal. We dropped the colt we were delivering and ran to the house. Calonice was sitting on the floor babbling the way children do who aren't right in the head. Hipponous carried her to her bed. By the time Night had blackened her room, she was crying – soft desperate sobs. She sent for me and when I got there, she threw herself at my feet and begged me to tell her what the snake omen meant. I couldn't. I didn't know." He looked down at his hands. How he wished he'd been able to help her.

"How did the snake get into her peplos?" Trygaeus asked, his skin crawling. He was deathly afraid of snakes.

"It must have slithered in when the laundry was drying on the rocks by the stream."

"Poor Calonice." For the first time since he'd met Hipponous, Trygaeus felt a little sorry for him too.

"When Helios had driven his chariot across the sky three times, Calonice told Hipponous she wanted to see the sibyl of childbirth in the hollow at Corinth. He thought she was too weak to make the journey and refused. But she insisted, crying and begging whenever she talked with him. Finally, he relented. He told me to prepare the carriage. The three of us left for Corinth as soon as the carriage was ready.

"Calonice was so pale when we got to Corinth she looked like she could die then and there, but she wouldn't rest. Instead, she insisted on buying a votive statue of the Mother Goddess in the market and walking along the suppliant's footpath to the sanctuary. I took the horses to the stable and followed after them. When I got to the hollow, Calonice had already gone inside. Even though I knew I would be punished with death if I got caught watching the secret ritual, I saw that Hipponous was going to watch, so I hid outside the entrance and watched too."

Trygaeus gasped. "You watched the secret ritual of the Mother Goddess?"

Nicias nodded.

Both men waited, barely breathing. Had the Erinyes heard them? What would they do?

"And?" Trygaeus whispered when nothing happened.

"There was a sibyl of the Mother Goddess sitting by a spring inside the hollow," Nicias continued, remembering the scene with horror. "She scared me more than anyone I've ever met."

"More than the captain of the slave ship?" Trygaeus was suddenly so nervous, he couldn't keep himself from talking. "I remember how I used to shake when the captain would stagger across the deck with that whip in his hand, torture beaming out of his beady eyes."

Nicias thought for a moment. "Yes. I think she frightened me more than the captain. You always knew with the captain what he was going to do. But with the sibyl, there was no way of knowing."

"Hard to believe she could be more frightening than the captain," Trygaeus argued, "since you always knew the captain was going to beat you." He touched a scar on his arm lightly. Suddenly, he felt angry. "Why did you make me remember all this?"

"I'm sorry. I won't say anything more. I shouldn't have burdened you with my troubles."

Frightened as he was, Trygaeus knew from the way Nicias sat staring straight ahead that his friend needed to talk. He gathered his strength. "You were telling me about the sibyl."

"Are you sure you want to hear it?"

"I'm sure."

Nicias took a deep breath. "I remember the sibyl's eyes more than anything. They were as hollow and black as the cave – sunk into her wrinkled face like two sticky mud holes. She'd lost most of her hair. All she had left were yellowish grey clumps here and there. She smelled, or else it was the cave, like a rotting animal. I felt like I was facing the entrance to Hades' underworld when I first saw her."

"Dear Zeus," Trygaeus whispered.

"When Calonice saw the sibyl, she put the little terracotta votive she'd bought at the old woman's feet. It was a statue of the Mother Goddess with her arms held out in front of her. Calonice stood and held her arms out exactly like the arms on the statue, bowed, and said something like, 'Earth sends up fruits, so we praise Earth, the Mother.'

"It was then I first realized the sibyl was surrounded by snakes. She was dressed in a black cloak that covered her whole body, even her arms and legs, so it was hard to see at first, but when she leaned forward toward Calonice, what I thought was part of the bedrock turned into a mass of slithering snakes. There were snakes all over her black cloak. Every time she moved, they started to slither around on her. She slid this claw-like hand through a slit in the cloak. Aaaaaaaaeeeeeeeehhhhhh."

"What's wrong?" Trygaeus screamed. "Did you see something?" Frantically he searched the trees. "We're going to die, aren't we?" He shook Nicias who was sitting motionless staring at his hands.

"What's going on?" Philocleon attempted to sit up, but fell back down too dizzy to move.

"Nothing," Trygaeus answered, nearly hysterical. "You can go back to sleep." He shook Nicias again. "What is it? What did you see?" he whispered, watching to make sure Philocleon fell asleep again.

"The ship," Nicias stuttered. "T...T...The ship."

"What ship? I don't know what you're talking about." Trygaeus grabbed Nicias' arm.

"The ship in the harbor. When I saw it, I had this horrible feeling of disaster, but I didn't know what made me feel that way…until now." Nicias licked his dry lips. "The tear in the sail."

"What tear? You aren't making any sense."

"There was a snake-like tear in the sail. Boreas' breath blew the sail when we were standing there. It came apart at the tear. Helios' light came through the tear. It made me feel exactly the way I felt when I saw the sibyl's yellow hand coming out of that black cloak. Oh, Father Zeus, protect us. I was right. We shouldn't have gone to the port. It's the revenge of the Mother Goddess that ship was carrying."

He covered his eyes with his hands, thinking he could somehow stop his mind if he closed his eyes. It didn't work. He kept thinking anyway. Did the flashback to his childhood mean the revenge would be death? No. It was too horrible.

"Revenge on who?" Trygaeus asked carefully.

"Hipponous. Who else?"

Trygaeus felt relieved though he was still frightened. "Are you sure it's Hipponous?"

"I tried to tell him," Nicias whispered, his breath coming in short spasms. "Over and over, I said. You must be careful of the revenge of the Mother Goddess, but all he said was he wasn't afraid of the..." his voice dropped to a whisper so low Trygaeus could barely hear him, "afraid of the old hag."

"He called the Mother Goddess a..." Trygaeus refused to even think the word, let alone say it.

Nicias nodded and went back to his story. "After Calonice had placed the votive of the Mother Goddess on the ground, the sibyl told her to drink from the sacred spring. Calonice cupped her hands and filled them in the spring, but just as her lips touched the cold water, she broke into a violent shiver. She dropped the water and fell on her knees in front of the sibyl, begging help from the Mother Goddess.

"Hipponous was as frightened as Calonice. I heard him whisper he knew the shivering was an omen of death. He threw himself on his knees and swore an oath to the Mother Goddess. He promised, if the birth was auspicious, he'd return and dedicate a silver statue of the Mother Goddess at the hollow."

"But how would promising to dedicate a statue of the Mother Goddess make her want to send the Erinyes for revenge? I'd think she'd like to have a statue dedicated at her hollow."

"What was that?" Nicias bolted upright.

The two men listened. It came again, a low howling from the trees. And again. Trygaeus finally recognized it. "It's a wolf." He patted Nicias' arm.

Nicias looked once more into the back of the wagon to make sure Philocleon was sleeping. "The day Philocleon's birth began, we took every precaution."

"But you haven't answered my question," Trygaeus interrupted.

"Why would the Mother Goddess punish Hipponous for giving her a silver statue?"

"Just wait. You'll see." Nicias continued. "When the birth came, I placed pine pitch on all the doorways. Hipponous sent for midwives from all of the surrounding estates. They came, each with a bag of herbs. Every one of them had children of their own but, as is mandatory, they were all beyond childbearing age."

Nicias began to hurry, feeling it would somehow be less terrible if he told it quickly. "After the midwives went into Calonice's room, we waited while the shadows passed from the front to the back of the house. Finally, the head midwife came out of the room and asked for Hipponous. They talked in low voices. I didn't hear what they said, but afterwards, they went together into Calonice's room and when Hipponous came back out of her room, he told the midwife to bring him the baby as soon as it had been purified with a bath. Afterwards, he went into the dining hall. I had never seen Hipponous so pale.

"Not until every lamp in the house had fire in its belly did the midwife come out of Calonice's room with Philocleon. Hipponous ran around the hearth with him three times, named him, and gave him back to the woman. Then he instructed me to bridle two horses. We rode out to the hut where his silversmith lives, picked up a statue of the Mother Goddess the old man had made, and left for Corinth.

"By the time we reached Corinth, Hipponous seemed a little mad to me. Instead of dedicating the silver statue of the Mother Goddess at the hollow as he'd promised, he went to a tavern. I couldn't get him to stop drinking. Eventually, he made so much noise and got into so many fights, the ruling council of Corinth ordered him out of the village. When we left, he took the statue of the Mother Goddess and threw it into the Corinthian gulf."

Trygaeus was utterly shocked. "No man except a mad man would treat the Mother Goddess that way."

"When I realized what he was going to do, I tried to talk to him. To remind him what the Erinyes do to those men who break their oaths to the Mother Goddess. I repeated it many times, but he wouldn't listen. He just kept insisting he was not afraid of the old..." Nicias couldn't bring himself to say it again.

"The man is a fool," Trygaeus said, thinking to maybe ingratiate himself with the Erinyes, should they be listening.

"It's the only time I've ever seen Hipponous ignore his responsibility to any of the gods or goddesses. Since the day I first met him, he was always overly concerned that he follow the rituals perfectly." Nicias shook his head. "Even though he still insists he isn't worried about the Erinyes' revenge for the Mother Goddess, I know he fears it. He calls me whenever he has a dream he can't understand or if he sees the birds fly in a way he thinks is peculiar. This is why he will never free me. He wants me near him always to interpret the omens."

Neither man spoke again until they neared the estate, Trygaeus afraid of what their conversation might bring on them, Nicias paralyzed by his need to fight against the thought that the Mother Goddess really meant to take revenge.

As they turned onto the path leading from the main road to Hipponous' house, Trygaeus asked the question that was foremost in Nicias' mind. "If you find Bromia and Hipponous refuses to free you, what will you do?"

"I've been thinking about that," Nicias answered. But before he had a chance to say more, Hipponous' hunting dogs came racing down the path barking ferociously at the oxen.

Trygaeus tightened the reins and talked gently to his oxen while Nicias grabbed the whip and snapped it at the leader of the pack, a dog Hipponous called Wolf. If he could keep Wolf back, they'd be all right. The other dogs wouldn't attack without him.

The oxen bolted off the path. Cursing Hipponous and his bloodthirsty dogs, Trygaeus jumped from the wagon and grabbed the reins at the animals' heads. "Come on. Just one more hill."

They had one steep climb to go before they rolled onto the flat stretch of ground the farm buildings sat on. He could already see the roof of the house, a majestic stone and timber building Hipponous had constructed in the trees on the southern end of the farmyard. Two stadia to the north of the house was the stable with Hipponous' newly built kiln sitting in front of its eastern end. The storage buildings they were headed for sat in the trees to the west of the stable.

"Come on, boys," Trygaeus urged. "You'll be safe as soon as we get to the storage bins." Once, when Hipponous wasn't home, he'd taken a whip to the dogs back there. Since then, they'd shown no inclination to follow his oxen beyond the stable.

Two

Crouching down to less than half of his height, Hipponous pushed through the kiln doorway. As soon as he got inside, he brushed his thick brownish-grey hair from his forehead with both hands and went to work testing the sturdiness of the kiln by running his fingers over the circular mud-brick wall and tapping the ceiling. Bending into an even more strained position to measure the stoke hole, he called out, "When are you planning to fire some pottery?"

Egyptus put the clay pot he had been trying to finish all morning back on his work-bench and rinsed his hands. He covered his agitation with a forced smile as he walked around the kiln and stuck his head inside the doorway both to reply and to find out what Hipponous was checking this time. Surprised by the comic sight of Hipponous' hefty frame squeezed into a space barely big enough for himself, the potter snickered out loud quite unexpectedly.

Hipponous twisted around and scrutinized Egyptus to see if he'd really heard what he thought he had. The potter stood there looking at him with open amusement, his entire dark-skinned face drawn into a smirk. "You have exactly one horse's whinny to wipe that grin from your face," Hipponous informed him, doubling his fist. "Or I'll do it myself."

"Sir, I assure you I am not smirking!" Egyptus backed away from the doorway as Hipponous came through it. He met Hipponous' angry olive brown eyes for only a moment before he turned his own dark eyes modestly toward the ground. Frantically, he searched through his mind for a way to save his skin.

As Hipponous grabbed his arm and started to twist it, Egyptus suddenly remembered. A few days ago Nicias had told him how afraid Hipponous was of offending the gods by some lack of propriety. "Wait!" he said. "I was standing here smiling to protect you from the fury of the great Egyptian god, Horus." Reverently, he lifted his hands toward the sky.

Hipponous stopped where he was. "And just exactly what is it that makes you think I need protection from Horus?" he asked through clenched teeth.

"In Egypt, we believe that a man who steps into a virgin kiln before water blessed by Horus has been poured into the stoke hole will be severely punished. I was standing here smiling to distract Horus. I was hoping the great Horus would be so occupied with my happiness, he wouldn't notice you were in the kiln."

"You're lying," Hipponous hissed. "Ever since you arrived at my estate you've told one fantastic story after another. I've never heard of any such thing as Horus blessing water for a stoke hole."

Egyptus shook his head as if in disbelief. "I don't mind what you do." He shrugged. "But I'm an Egyptian and I would never, never, never, go into a virgin kiln without first pouring blessed water into the stoke hole." He covered his face with his hands and pretended he was asking the blessing of Horus.

Hipponous silently called for Zeus to protect him. He really didn't believe Egyptus. But still, who could know for sure what an Egyptian god required. Too afraid of Horus to step back into the kiln, but determined to save face, he began an exaggerated inspection of the doorjamb. "I asked you when you were planning to fire."

"Just as soon as Nicias gets back," Egyptus answered.

"From the sound of the dogs, Nicias is back." Hipponous bent over and examined a rough spot in the mud-brick floor just inside the doorway. He rubbed the spot smooth with his sandal and then, unable to find anything else wrong with the interior construction, started circling the kiln testing the mud plaster finish on the exterior by tapping it.

"You're right. He is back." Egyptus followed Hipponous wondering whether the inspection would ever end. "I can hear him yelling at the dogs."

"Don't you have anything better to do than trail around behind me like a lost puppy?" Hipponous snapped, turning heatedly toward the potter.

Egyptus thought about pointing out that the work he had to do was sitting on his workbench at the back of the kiln where Hipponous was headed, but he changed his mind and went instead to wait for Nicias and Trygaeus. Still smiling to himself, he watched the wagon roll onto the clearing at the far end of the yard. He waved and called to Trygaeus, hoping the arrival of the supplies would distract Hipponous before he'd had too much time to think about Horus and the stoke hole.

Waving in return, Trygaeus turned the oxen off the main trail and followed a path across the yard. He tethered his animals under a shade tree and waited for a chance to get a close look at Hipponous.

Nicias slid to the ground. "When are you planning to fire?" he called to Egyptus.

"When Night has perched and taken flight again," Egyptus called back. Grinning, he motioned for Nicias to come to the kiln. He couldn't wait to tell him what had happened.

"Who's with Philocleon?" Hipponous demanded, coming around the side of the kiln.

Egyptus shrugged. "Here comes Nicias. You can ask him." It took all of his effort to keep from laughing when he turned and saw that a big splotch of water had been spilled on the front of Hipponous' tunic. So that was why he didn't want to be followed around the kiln. He'd gone to the back to pour water into the stoke hole.

"I'd rather ask Philocleon," Hipponous informed Egyptus, pushing past him, scrutinizing the stranger sleeping next to his son. The man's filthy appearance told Hipponous his son had squandered his time in the village drinking in one of the taverns again. He'd thought things would change when Philocleon passed into early manhood, that he'd come to understand it wasn't proper for an aristocrat to drink in taverns, worse, to pick up and bring home every flea-infested peddler he met. But obviously the boy hadn't learned anything. And what about Nicias? Hadn't he given him strict instructions about this sort of thing? He shook Philocleon. "What is that?" he asked harshly, nodding toward the stranger.

Philocleon opened his eyes slowly and looked at the man shaking him. Gradually he realized the man was his father. They must be home. He sat up carefully, held his breath to keep from throwing up, then fighting off dizziness, crawled off the wagon and stood next to

Hipponous. He shook his head to clear it.

"I asked what that is." Hipponous repeated impatiently.

"A poet. His name is Homer," Philocleon answered, self-consciously smoothing his wild curls so they circled his forehead in a flat row as they were supposed to. He'd planned to go to the barber in the village but hadn't made it.

"The pup looks more like a deck swabber than a poet, and not a very good one at that, or he'd at least have earned enough to buy himself a clean tunic."

Philocleon brushed off his own tunic, tried to get the pleats to hang straight again. "We spent the day in the—" he paused and searched for a way to admit he'd been in a tavern, without saying tavern, "—a wine shop. His tunic got dirty there, at least for the most part."

"Take him back with the wagon," Hipponous instructed Trygaeus, flipping his hand toward the poet in a manner suggesting he was talking about a bag of barley rather than a man.

Trygaeus nodded, wondering how a man who had so certainly brought the fury of the Mother Goddess on himself could still be so arrogant.

Deciding to ignore Trygaeus' wide-eyed staring even though he found it aggravating, Hipponous turned and started back toward the kiln calling for Nicias. He wanted an explanation.

Philocleon ran after him and caught him by the arm. "Wait. If only you'll listen to him recite, you'll change your mind. I swear every aristocrat in the village came to hear him. They cheered endlessly and begged him to sing again whenever he even paused."

Hipponous turned back toward the wagon and examined the stranger again. "What are you staring at?" he snapped at Trygaeus.

Trygaeus looked at the ground. "Nothing, sir."

Homer sat up, thought about telling Hipponous he was no longer interested in Philocleon's invitation to visit the estate, but changed his mind since he had nowhere else to go.

"Ask Nicias if you don't believe me," Philocleon continued. "We even had to move out to the portico to make room for everyone who wanted to hear him. Besides," he grappled for something that would convince his father, "think of how men will gossip if you send him back to the port village without at least one night's hospitality. I invited him in front of everyone."

Hipponous studied his son. Philocleon knew how proud he was that all over Attica men talked of his generosity as a host. "Why would you want to do something so ridiculous?" he asked. "Isn't it enough you've asked this peddler to the estate? Must you also insist on making your invitation public gossip?"

Philocleon relaxed. Hipponous' voice had betrayed him. The words were harsh, but the tone of his voice told Philocleon his father was more intrigued than angry. Quickly he continued, "The way men were crowding around him, I was afraid if I didn't get our invitation out, someone else would ask him and we'd be too late."

Hipponous thought about it. Philocleon, with all his studying, should certainly be able to judge the man's poetry. If he really was a good poet and if all of the village aristocrats had actually come to hear him, it might be advantageous to have him around for a banquet.

Sensing further softening in Hipponous' attitude, Philocleon called to Homer, "Come and meet my father."

Homer jumped from the wagon, grabbed his lyre and went over to stand before Hipponous. Under better circumstances, he would have insisted on going back to the village. But things being as they were, he might as well stay. The captain had not only thrown him off the ship, but the buzzard had seen to it he had none of his belongings when he left. All he had to his name at the moment were his tunic and sandals and the lyre the tavern owner had given him. "I am most grateful to be here," he said, smiling at Hipponous in spite of the snubbing he'd gotten.

The pup isn't stupid, Hipponous decided. He has no intention of returning to the village unless he is forced. Looking the poet over carefully, he said to Philocleon, "I'll think about it," and walked off toward the stable.

Whether he had developed horse sense to accommodate his name, 'Hippo' for horse, 'nous' for sense, as his father had maintained, or had been given the right name by some act of fate as his mother had believed, all his life, Hipponous had felt better making decisions about a man once he had seen him ride a horse. The way a man mounted, handled the reins, took the terrain – these things said something about him. After he'd seen Homer on a horse, he'd make his decision.

At the stable entrance, Hipponous paused as he always did and whispered an entreaty to Poseidon to protect him while he was riding. Inside the barn he called out for a slave.

"Up here," a voice answered from the rafters. "There's birds nesting in the thatch."

"I want you to bridle three horses for riding," Hipponous called up.

The slave came down a rope ladder carrying a nest. "Wind blew some of the thatch off this spring. I didn't see it 'til I heard chirping. Take a look," he held the nest out toward Hipponous, "some bird made herself a nice little home in the hole." He tossed the nest out the door calling to a mother cat sunning herself at the back of the barn. "It ain't good having the critters in the barn. The chirping makes the horses nervous." The cat bolted past him and pounced on the nest.

"I'll ride Pegasus," Hipponous said, his tone making it clear he had no interest in the birds or the hole in the thatch. "Philocleon can take the bay mare." He walked down the center of the stable looking over the well-bred horses tethered on either side of him along the lengthy walls of intertwined branches. "And the white stallion for our guest."

"Yes, sir." The slave rushed off to bridle the horses. He wanted to ask Hipponous about repairing the thatch, but he'd learned long ago not to ask questions when Hipponous wanted something done. Of course, when the thatch wasn't repaired and Hipponous noticed...

Hipponous took the reins from the slave at the barn door and led the horses to the supply wagon where Philocleon and Homer were waiting for his decision. "It's a disgrace," he told Homer throwing the stallion's reins to him, "the way the men of Greece have lost interest in fine horsemanship."

He threw the reins from the bay to Philocleon, mounted Pegasus and galloped off, circling behind the stable, past the storage buildings to the trail that led to the north. Jumping ravines and dead trees, ducking branches, and trampling small bushes, he raced to a deep ditch at break-neck speed along the most treacherous trail he knew.

Homer understood he was being challenged. Not much different than it used to be with grandfather, he mused bitterly. Always having to prove myself. He slipped the leather strap of his lyre over his right shoulder, under his left arm, swung gracefully onto the stallion, and galloped off, following Hipponous without difficulty to the ditch. When he saw that Hipponous had stopped, he urged his stallion forward and made a dangerous jump over a boulder at the ditch's edge, just barely pulling to a halt before his stallion skidded over the bank.

Hipponous felt the thrill of the jump as surely as if he'd made it himself. Still breathing heavily from the excitement, he called gaily to Homer when he'd stopped, "You ride like a young man who has had many seasons of training." It was obvious from the way the poet rode he wasn't the peddler Hipponous had assumed he was.

Homer turned his stallion around and rode back to where Hipponous waited on Pegasus.

"Tell me the name of the father who taught his son to ride so well," Hipponous said, as they watched Philocleon gallop around the boulder Homer had just hurdled.

"Zeus," Homer answered, grinning sardonically. Spurring his stallion forward, he rode past Hipponous, trotting north along the western bank of the ditch. His mother, who'd died when they had only celebrated the harvest festival fourteen times, had insisted up to the day of her death his father was Zeus, come to her disguised as a shower of gold the same way he'd come to Danaë. 'You see,' she'd always say as she stroked his golden brown curls, 'most of the gold Zeus brought went into your hair.'

He'd believed her...right up to her death...which was when he got his first rude awakening in life. He and his grandfather had barely burned her funeral pyre when his grandfather had informed him the fine golden locks his mother had been so fond of had not come from Zeus, but from a blond-haired barbarian who'd caught her alone in the trees.

"Did you say Zeus?" Philocleon asked, trotting up behind Homer.

"Zeus!" Homer answered again, urging his stallion into a gallop.

Exchanging surprised glances, Hipponous and Philocleon galloped after Homer, watching him race up to a fallen tree trunk or a boulder with the fury of a wounded lion, then jump the stallion over it with the nimbleness of the three graces. By the time they had caught up to the poet, Hipponous was so impressed with Homer's horsemanship, he had decided to forget about the poet's rude unwillingness to give an account of his lineage.

"Have you ever hunted wild boar?" Hipponous asked as he looked Homer over from head to foot, taking in the fine tone of his muscles, his strong hands. "Philocleon and I will be needing a third man on a boar hunt." If this poet hunted as well as he rode, he'd make the powerful third Hipponous needed.

"Of course," Homer answered. Though his grandfather had taught him to ride at his mother's insistence, he had never taken him along on a boar hunt. Still, Homer reasoned to himself, he'd sung the saga of the Calydonian boar hunt so regularly, he would surely know what to do.

"Maybe we could use you as our third," Hipponous said making it clear with his tone of voice he was suggesting, not inviting. He liked the way the poet sat on his stallion. Firm. Confident. If he turned out to be as fine a poet as he was horseman, there would be a place for him on the boar hunt.

"I would be honored should you decide to take me along." Homer smiled to himself. It seemed as if his daring ride had served its purpose. Even if he wasn't invited to join the boar hunt, he'd won the old man over. There was little doubt he would have a place to sleep when Night descended.

Hipponous, feeling pleased, galloped Pegasus out in front of the other two horses. He rode alongside the ditch to the pastures on the northern ridge where his sheep and goats were grazing. Steering Pegasus into the first herd of goats he came to, he sent the animals scattering and selected the friskiest of the lot for eating. He ordered the herder to deliver it to the house. "And tell Nicias to send two or three of the older boys out with invitations to a banquet. Have them inform our guests that when we've dined, they will hear one of the finest poets in Greece recite."

Hipponous sauntered Pegasus back to the two young men. He was already beginning to feel the thrill he always got when he'd thoroughly outdone his aristocratic companions. "And, this poet friend of yours," he joked with Philocleon. "Are you sure he'll recite for us after the banquet?"

"Will my drinking bowl be ever filled with the gift of Dionysus?" Homer held his hands out toward the endless rows of grapevines that spread into the valley below the ridge as far to the west as he could see.

"Filled and with the finest wine in all of Greece," Hipponous bragged. The vineyards had come to him as a part of Calonice's dowry. He was more than a little proud of the wine his grapes produced.

"Then, after the feast I will show you how bravely the Greeks and Trojans fight when those wild ladies of Dionysus, the maenads, revel on my tongue."

Hipponous laughed loudly. "He's as quick with words as you," he teased Philocleon.

"Wait until my head has cleared of wine," Philocleon in turn teased Homer. "Then, we'll see which of us can split trees with his sharp phrases."

Homer laughed too, but offered no retort. His was a talent of memory, not twisting phrases. "Where now?" he asked, prancing his stallion around impatiently.

"To the house to plan the banquet," Hipponous answered, trotting off toward the farmyard. Philocleon and Homer followed him through the lower pasture where he kept his cattle and oxen, across the road leading to his silver mines, and finally into the hollow where he kept his bee nests.

The beekeeper was at the door of his shack as soon as he heard horses on the trail. Seeing it was Hipponous, he went out to meet them. "You coming for honey, sir?" he asked, grabbing hold of Pegasus' bridle to steady him when Hipponous stopped. "I got me a new bucket full just this morning."

Hipponous' eyes glided from the fresh welts on the beekeeper's arms and chest to the bee nests in the hollows of the rocks. Agitated from the beekeeper's intrusion, the bees were bunched so thick around their nests they looked like clusters of grapes hanging in mid-air. About to tell the beekeeper they'd just come through on their way back to the house, it suddenly occurred to Hipponous it would be interesting to see how Homer reacted to a new challenge. He unpinned the silver fibula holding his mantle together at the shoulder and tossed it to the poet. "This fibula goes to the man who brings us back a honeycomb."

Homer caught the fibula, but he didn't race to the bee nests. Instead, he sat dead still on his stallion and stared angrily at Hipponous.

"Father, I don't think..."

Holding his hand up to quiet Philocleon, Hipponous slid from

Pegasus. Grinning smugly, he pulled his mantle from where it had fallen on Pegasus' rump when he undid his fibula. He threw the mantle to the beekeeper as he headed for the stone bench where the bucket of fresh honey was sitting. "Bring the honey when you return the mantle," he ordered the beekeeper, dipping his fingers into the honey and licking them. Nodding his approval, he picked up the bucket and held it out to Philocleon. "Try some."

Philocleon shook his head. "Father. I don't think a guest should be asked to..."

"But I have asked him," Hipponous answered, eyeing Homer.

"It's a good time for honey," the beekeeper explained to no one in particular as he tied Pegasus to a tree branch. "The flowers are nice and sweet."

Homer appraised the fibula, a carefully made silver knob with a thin pin attached to the underside. He turned it over in his hand, tossed it into the air to feel its weight. Mentally calculating the value of the fine piece, he examined the bee nests, then the welts on the beekeeper. Red and festering, they reminded him of the cuts and bruises, broken bones, and whiplashes, he'd endured trying to please his grandfather.

"Well?" Hipponous was tired of waiting. His eyes darted impatiently between Homer and the bee nests.

Homer held up the fibula. "To the man who brings back a honeycomb. That's what you said, wasn't it?" He'd made up his mind a long time ago he'd prove himself only once to a man. As far as he was concerned, he'd already done it for Hipponous.

Hipponous nodded. "That's what I said."

Homer threw the fibula to the beekeeper. "It's yours if you bring us a honeycomb."

The beekeeper was stunned. He'd never held a piece of silver in his life. Just knowing it was there in his hand sent tingles up his arms. Soon his entire body twitched with excitement. He ran to Homer. "You must be Hermes himself," he said, kissing the poet's hand. "How else could a poor man like myself fall into such luck." He bowed to Homer and clutching the fibula to his chest raced toward the bee nests.

Hipponous was on his feet the moment the beekeeper caught the expensive fibula. "You cocky bastard!" Fury radiated from every pore in his body. He was not accustomed to any type of defiance.

This kind of audacity was unthinkable. Under any other circumstance he would have answered the pup's insolence with the use of his whip, but with all the important men he'd invited to the banquet, bragging he had a poet who would recite, he was trapped. Seething, he smashed the bucket of honey to the ground and walked over to Pegasus.

Homer met Hipponous' hateful stare with one of his own.

"Medusa's curse on you," Hipponous hissed at the poet. Saying no more he mounted Pegasus and ripping the reins loose, rode over to a stunned Philocleon. "See to it he leaves when the banquet is finished."

The beekeeper dropped the honeycomb he was holding when the bucket of honey hit the ground. He ran back toward the shack. Idiot, he said, hitting himself on the chest with his fist. Why didn't you see what was going on? The stranger was using you to make a fool of Hipponous. Now, you'll pay with your hide. The ecstasy he'd felt racing to the bee nests turned into anguish. He knew the whip of Hipponous.

He hurried back to the front of his shack, but Hipponous was already gone when he got there. In a panic he threw himself on the ground in front of Philocleon. "Please sir. Don't whip me. I'll give back the fibula."

Philocleon stared at the beekeeper lying prostrate in front of him. "I don't understand. Why are you worried? You haven't done anything wrong." He wiped his forehead and arms with the skirt of his tunic, wishing he could somehow wipe the fierce pounding that had begun in his head away with the sweat.

The beekeeper raised himself from the ground. It was his turn to stare. Was the boy a madman or was another joke being played at his expense? "I'll be in for a whipping sure," he repeated. A bee sting was starting to swell in the middle of his forehead. He felt of it. "It'll be the smallest welt on my body soon," he wailed, pulling aside the shoulder of his tunic to show Philocleon the scars from his last whipping.

"Why would you be whipped?" Philocleon asked. The persistent wailing of this man whose swelling forehead was making him look more and more like some strange creature with a horn at the center of its head was beginning to exasperate him. "You've done nothing."

The beekeeper scrambled to his feet. He could see the boy was going to be of no help. "What difference would that make to Hipponous?" he asked and ran back to his shack.

Homer, feeling guilty the slave might be punished for what he'd done, tried to intercede. "It's my fault," he said to Philocleon. "I should never have given him the fibula."

"You don't really think my father would have him whipped when it wasn't his fault?" Philocleon asked of himself more than Homer. He knew Hipponous had his slaves whipped. He'd seen it happen often enough, but he'd always assumed the slaves who were whipped had done something to deserve it. Now he wasn't sure.

Homer grinned sarcastically and wondered how Philocleon had managed to stay so naive, but he didn't say anything. Looking through the shack window he could see that the beekeeper was putting his belongings into a sack. He considered telling Philocleon, but decided against it.

From his position Philocleon couldn't see into the shack and he didn't move to confirm for himself what Homer's sideways glancing and fidgeting suggested was happening. Instead he sat thinking. If the beekeeper was planning to run away, it was his responsibility to tell his father. He knew that. Yet, it didn't seem right for the man to be whipped when it wasn't his fault. Besides, if his father hadn't been trying to goad Homer, none of this would have happened.

Finally, exhausted with the whole thing, he made up his mind. One slave more or less on an estate the size of his father's wouldn't make any significant difference anyway. Better to let the beekeeper escape, if he was willing to take the risk, than to punish him for something that wasn't his fault. "It's hot," he said to Homer, turning his back on the beekeeper's shack. "Let's go to the sea and cool off."

At the sea's edge Philocleon pulled off his tunic and dove in, swimming hard, trying with each broad stroke to put the beekeeper's shack out of his mind.

Homer followed Philocleon into the water. He wanted to talk with him about what had happened, but his way of talking was with his lyre and a poem.

As the chariot of Helios dropped below the treetops, Philocleon swam to the shore. He waded out of the water and dropping his tanned body on the bank, propped his head with his tunic, closed his eyes and tried to make some sense of his feelings. The awe he'd felt toward Homer in the tavern had blossomed into full-blown admiration at the bee nests.

Not once in his life, even when he knew he was right, had he stood up to his father the way Homer had at the bee nests. What's more, he'd never seen anyone else face up to Hipponous the way Homer had. He applauded him intensely for it in spite of the guilt it made him feel about his father.

Homer dove once more before he swam to shore. Determined to recapture the frivolity they'd shared before the bee nests, he grabbed his lyre and, picking the largest sunflower he could find, pushed the stem into a shrub next to Philocleon's head. He arranged the flower so that it stood upright as if in a vase and, strumming his lyre, sang for Philocleon.

"Once, when the world was very young, a beautiful water nymph fell in love with Helios. In the beginning, the sun god loved the water nymph as much as she loved him, but soon after, he came to love another. Heartbroken, the water nymph sat on the bank of the river and pined, her face turned always toward Helios. From the time he rose until he had crossed the sky and disappeared, she looked at no other thing. One morning, after many days of sorrowing, the water nymph's limbs took root in the ground and she became a sunflower, her face turning on its stem so as always to follow the handsome sun god."

Philocleon opened his eyes and smiled. "Is this your water nymph?" he asked, pointing to the flower Homer had placed in the bush.

"Yes," Homer answered as he pulled the flower out of the bush, "and I've named her Calliope."

"Calliope?"

"When I recite she brings the verses to me. She is my Helios. My love has never been turned from her for a moment. If she were to discard me, I would pine like the water nymph until I wasted away to nothing."

Philocleon closed his eyes again, thinking he could not bear to see Homer leave after the banquet.

Homer put his lyre down, pulled the sunflower off its stem, and made his way down to the sea. He dropped the sunflower into the water and watched it float away. "See it," he said to Philocleon when he returned. "The floating prison of Danaë."

Philocleon rolled over on his stomach and, resting his chin on his elbows, prepared to listen. He knew the story of Danaë and Perseus must have some special meaning for Homer because he had recited it twice in the village tavern. He thought about asking Homer what its meaning was for him, but before he got the chance, the singing began.

"Danaë," Homer sang. "She was a most beautiful woman. When she was still very young, her father inquired of an oracle whether he would have a son as well. The god answered that Danaë's father would have no son. Instead, it warned, his daughter Danaë would have a son who would deprive his grandfather of his life.

Afraid, Danaë's father locked her up in a subterranean chamber. But, unhappily for her father, Zeus had already seen the lovely Danaë. Pouring himself through her roof as a shower of gold, the wily Zeus visited Danaë. She soon found herself with child. When he was born, she named him Perseus."

Unconsciously, Homer ran his hands through his golden brown hair. As a child he'd often begged his mother to convince Zeus to visit her again and bring him a brother. Looking now at Philocleon, he thought they would have made great brothers. "Do you have any brothers?" he asked.

Philocleon shook his head. "No sisters either. You?"

"Neither," Homer said taking his lyre in hand again.

"Perseus had watched the winter rains come and go four times in the chamber before Danaë's father heard him playing. He brought forth his daughter and grandson, locked them in a chest and cast it out to sea. The chest floated until it was found, far from Danaë's home, by a fisherman who took the mother and son to his king.

"The king was a very fine man. He treated them well. Perseus grew from a boy to a man. But when he was a man, the king's brother, determined to have Danaë for his wife against the will of Perseus, tricked the young hero into a foolish boast. Perseus promised to kill a terrible monster who had the power to turn men into stone by looking at them."

"Medusa," Philocleon sang with Homer.

"Perseus hid after his boast to kill Medusa, but Hermes, the trusted messenger of the gods, found him. He gave Perseus the winged shoes from his own feet and Athena's shield. Thus armed, Perseus went to kill Medusa. He approached her under the black wings of Night. With his sword, he cut off Medusa's head while she slept, using her reflection in Athena's shield to guide him, so as to avoid looking directly at her and being turned into stone.

"From the drops of blood that fell from Medusa's head into the earth sprang the winged horse, Pegasus. Athena caught Pegasus and tamed him. Afterwards she presented him to the muses. He has belonged to all poets ever since that day."

Finished with the story of Danaë and as always overwhelmed with sadness by it, Homer put his lyre down on the earth next to him and pulled his knees up, wrapping his arms around them. He rested his head on his knees and sat a long time watching the water. Loneliness overtook him as it often did when he thought of his mother. "When I was a boy, I named my horse Pegasus. He galloped so fast, I just knew he could fly. When I had celebrated the fall harvest for the fourteenth time, I ran from my home, thinking to fly away with him."

"What happened?"

"I had to sell him to buy passage on a boat," Homer smiled sadly. "I floated away instead, without Pegasus." He picked up a handful of pebbles and started tossing them one at a time into the sea.

"Didn't your father come after you and force you to return home?"

Homer snorted and threw the remainder of the pebbles into the sea. "On the ship I met a poet who earned his keep traveling from city to city reciting the sagas of the Greek heroes. He needed a servant. I hired on, finding places for us to stay, food and drink, running errands, making arrangements for performances on the surrounding aristocrats' estates whenever we got into a new village. In time he began teaching me to recite the sagas. Soon I could sing them as well as he could. Then I started to work on my own, traveling and reciting."

"How did you end up on a ship in the Sounion harbor?" Philocleon was intently curious.

Unwilling to tell Philocleon anything else about his past for fear it would come back to the question of his father, Homer picked up his lyre again, played and sang. "There once was a fountain filled with the purest of water. The young Narcissus came upon the fountain. Bending over to refresh himself with a drink, he saw a most handsome young man in the water. Overwhelmed with longing, he brought his lips down to the water to give the man a kiss, plunged his arms into the water to embrace him, but the young man disappeared in a ripple of waves each time Narcissus touched the water. He begged the young man to stay, but it was no use. At last, consumed with desire, Narcissus left the water, pined away and died."

Finished, he turned to Philocleon and smiled, a little shyly, Philocleon thought. "When the poet was first teaching me his sagas, he used to joke I was the poet's Narcissus, consumed with a desire to hear my own voice endlessly."

"Was he right?"

"Yes." Homer laughed. "And now," he stood and pulled his tunic over his head, "I must return to the house and sleep a little or I'll certainly disappoint you at the banquet."

Philocleon stood too, pulling his tunic over his head as he followed Homer toward the bank above. From the position of Helios in the heavens, he knew he should already be in the room of his tutors. He would have to hurry.

At the top of the bank both men mounted their horses. The joy they had known in the village returned. Leaning forward to pull the reins free from the bush where he had tied them, Philocleon challenged Homer playfully. "My father always calls his most prized horse Pegasus. He says when Athena tamed Pegasus, she gave him to one of our ancestors, not the muses. The ancestor bred the winged horse to his finest mare and thus began the line of purebred horses my father still raises." He raced off toward the house, showing his horsemanship now that his head had finally cleared of wine.

Homer raced behind him, calling, "Your father had best beware laying claim to a horse that belongs rightfully to poets."

"I don't think he's likely to worry," Philocleon replied when Homer caught up to him at the edge of the yard. "He says our family has the special protection of Athena."

"Family? You said you have no brothers or sisters. I've heard no mention of a mother," Homer joked. "I thought you must have been born full grown from your father's head like Athena from Zeus." He imitated the birth of Athena by popping his hand away from the side of his head.

"My mother died when I was born." Philocleon said quietly. "Grandmother says she was beautiful and kind, everything I could have wanted in a mother. I wish I had known her. What about your mother? What was she like?"

"The most wonderful woman you could imagine. But she died when I was a boy."

"What about your father? Who was he?" Philocleon hoped to find out why Homer had told Hipponous his father was Zeus.

"Zeus," Homer answered again, urging his stallion into a gallop around Philocleon toward the stable, determined to put an end to the questions.

Inside the stable, they dismounted and handed their horses over to the slaves. Homer made up his mind as they walked to the house, he'd try to make up with Hipponous at the banquet if he could, for Philocleon's sake. Philocleon, on the other hand, had already begun to plan how he would convince his father to let Homer stay after the banquet ended.

Leaving Homer with a slave he'd instructed to care for the poet, Philocleon rushed to the room of his tutors, two Assyrian scribes Hipponous had hired to teach him reading and writing, geography and mathematics. He found both men seated on their silk covered couch at the far end of the room reading aloud from a papyrus text. As usual, he was slightly overwhelmed by the sweet fragrances that wafted toward him from the two of them as he walked up to the couch.

"Where have you been?" Na'id-Assur pointed his jewel-covered hand at the window without looking up. The wooden lattice that filled the opening when it was hot, sat propped against the wall under the frame. "You remember." He smoothed his thick, black hair. "We begin the lesson precisely when Helios rides below the top of the big shade trees."

Philocleon nodded, then looked for and found his favorite chair behind a small table near the window. He brought the chair back to the couch, placed it beside the ivory table in front of Na'id-Assur and sat down. "I'm sorry. I didn't realize Helios had traveled so far in his chariot."

"How can I ever teach you to read if I can't even teach you to come for your lesson when you're supposed to?" Na'id-Assur asked, placing the papyrus text on the ivory table in front of him with his right hand, tipping his forehead into his left hand.

The forehead gesture was supposed to mean he was angry, but Philocleon knew he wasn't. Na'id-Assur loved dramatics and he never got truly angry. "I promise it won't happen again," he assured the Assyrian.

"Let's hope not." Content he'd sufficiently disciplined Philocleon, Na'id-Assur reached over and picked a ceramic pitcher off of the table. Separating three drinking bowls from the stack that stood next to the pitcher, he filled them with beer. It had taken forever, or so it seemed to him, to teach the estate cook how to ferment beer. Still, with patience, he'd taught the man. He handed one of the bowls to Philocleon, another to his plump friend.

Qurdi Marduk took the bowl from Na'id-Assur and wiped his forehead and neck with a silk handkerchief. "In the palace we had slaves to fan us, you remember?" He picked up a small silver dish from the ivory table and fanned himself with it, sighing.

"We also had a harem to take care of." Na'id-Assur took the dish from Qurdi Marduk and placed it back on the table. He turned to Philocleon. "The king had more concubines than seeds in a pomegranate. All of them bored and demanding with only a handful of us to see that they got what they wanted. That is what I remember."

Qurdi Marduk nodded, but didn't bother to answer. Instead, stimulated by Na'id-Assur's analogy, he posed his first mathematics question of the day to Philocleon. "If the king had a vineyard with thirty-one rows of vines in it and fifty-two vines in each row, how many vines would he have?"

Philocleon got up from his chair and went to the cupboard next to the door. He searched until he found a stylus and his writing board. Using his thumbs, he pressed his last lesson out of the beeswax spread on the ivory board, returned and sat in front of the men again. Cutting the numbers into the wax with his stylus, he multiplied thirty-one by fifty-two. "One thousand six hundred and twelve," he said when he'd finished.

"Very good." Qurdi Marduk shook his head in approval. He'd been hired to teach mathematics, Na'id-Assur, reading, writing and geography. Philocleon was proving to be an astute student.

"My turn," Na'id-Assur said to Qurdi Marduk, rubbing his hands together with delight at the idea that he, who had trouble tallying the total number of rings in his jewelry chest, could come up with a mathematics question. Leaning forward as he always did when he was pleased with something, he put his hand on Philocleon's shoulder and asked, "And, if the king had one-third as many women in his harem as he had vines, what would he have?" When he was finished, he leaned back against the couch, poked Qurdi Marduk in the ribs.

"A lot of fun," Philocleon answered, his eyes twinkling with the joy he felt at being able to twist words with his tutor. The three men laughed. Na'id-Assur poured each of them another bowl of beer. He took a sip and dabbed his lip with a silk handkerchief. Neither Na'id-Assur or Qurdi Marduk had a beard, though Na'id-Assur had some fuzz on his upper lip he referred to as a moustache. Most of the Greek men Philocleon knew, wore beards, but no moustaches. Once he'd thought about growing a moustache, but after watching Na'id-Assur forever dabbing at his, he'd changed his mind.

"So," Na'id-Assur continued, twirling his beer around in his bowl, "I see our pupil has been out grinding his wits to a sharp point on a stone."

"No wonder he didn't see Helios' chariot of fire drop below the shade tree," Qurdi Marduk added. "Sharpening those wits must be very hard labor." They all laughed again.

While the two men sipped more beer, Philocleon divided one thousand, six hundred and twelve by three. When he had the answer he looked up. "It looks like he'd have about five hundred and thirty-seven women..."

Qurdi Marduk prepared to correct his student.

"And, one-third wit," Philocleon finished, attempting to produce a second laugh.

It worked. Both men broke out laughing again. Na'id-Assur slapped himself on the top of his thigh as he always did when something really tickled him, sending a gush of beer out of his bowl. The beer splashed into the lap of Qurdi Marduk, causing the fine silk tunic he was wearing to drape between his legs, forming a wet frame around his undersized member. The sight of the small member against the man's huge thighs made all three of them laugh again.

Philocleon had never heard the word eunuch until he'd asked them one day how, with all of the women in the harem, they'd managed to keep from stealing a little of the king's fun. They'd explained only eunuchs worked in the harem. Then they'd explained what a eunuch was.

Taking his turn with the clowning, Qurdi Marduk jumped up and pulled the silk away from his legs, took large folds of it in his hands and pulled the full-length tunic up so that the hem barely reached below his knees. "Now, look what you've done," he admonished, pushing his voice even higher than its normal pitch. "You've messed up my gown. Call the king. I'll have you flayed for this," he squealed, prancing around the room in imitation of the woman who'd been in the king's harem the longest. She'd grown extremely querulous from sitting cooped up in the palace with nothing to do but wait for the king.

Just as Philocleon couldn't imagine a man letting his manhood be taken from him, something that both Na'id-Assur and Qurdi Marduk seemed not to question, he couldn't imagine one man having three hundred women, all waiting for him. And the palace they described, hundreds of rooms filled with exquisite silver and ivory furniture, it seemed impossible to him.

While Qurdi Marduk changed his tunic, Na'id-Assur posed the last mathematics question, whispered to him by Qurdi Marduk while Philocleon was dividing the vines into thirds. "If the king decided to give every women in his harem a basket of grapes and each basket held six clusters with one thousand, six hundred and twelve grapes on them, how many grapes would each of the women receive?"

Philocleon figured, then refigured his answer. Finally, convinced he was right, he answered. "Nine thousand, six hundred and seventy-two."

"Exactly," Qurdi Marduk said, returning in a bright yellow silk tunic. Unlike the Greeks who wore wool and linen, the two Assyrian men wore only silk, brought with them when they left the harem. Qurdi Marduk smoothed his brown curls and sat down again. Unconsciously, his hand went for the silver dish. Soon he was fanning himself with it.

"Time to put these away." Na'id-Assur gathered the drinking bowls and returned them to the cupboard. He pulled out several writing boards, returned to the couch, and put one of the boards on the table in front of Philocleon. On it he drew a general outline of the area around the Mediterranean Sea. "Let's try a little geography before we get too silly."

The lesson in geography always revolved around the two men's travels. Each day there would be a new story and with it, new places to identify. He began, "We came to you from Assyria, two scribes trained in the court of the Assyrian king. I was born in Assur, a great city on which river?" He was reviewing yesterday's lesson.

"The Tigris," Philocleon answered, first pronouncing the word, then pointing to it on the beeswax map, finally writing it down on his writing board.

"Not one, but two great rivers run through Assyria. What is the name of the second river?"

"The Euphrates." Philocleon continued to point and write each time he answered.

"Is the Tigris east or west of the Euphrates?" Qurdi Marduk asked.

"East."

"What is the name of the kingdom to the south of Assyria?" It was Na'id-Assur again.

"Babylonia."

"In which city in Babylonia was Qurdi Marduk born?"

"Babylon."

"What is the name of the kingdom to the south and west of Assyria?"

"Phoenicia."

"Still farther south and west?"

"Egypt."

"What is the name of the great sea that lies to the west of Assyria?"

"The Mediterranean."

"Where are we now?"

"In Greece."

"What lies to the west of us?"

"Across the sea to the west, the cities of Sparta, Argos, Olympia, and farther to the north, Corinth, Delphi, and Thebes."

"To the east?"

"Across the sea, the Ionian Greek cities."

"To the north?"

"Athens."

Qurdi Marduk took over from here. "Now we will return to Assyria and our story. When Na'id-Assur had seen the spring flowers come and go nine times and I seven, Na'id-Assur was sent to a priest in Assur, I to a scribe in Babylon to learn how to read and write. While we were busy studying, our fathers were busy sending gifts to the king. Soon, due to our fathers' generosity, we were selected to serve the king. We went to the palace to live. There we met and became great friends. In the palace we saw many wonderful things."

"What did you do in the palace of the king?" Philocleon interrupted.

"Whatever we were told to do. We ran errands, delivered messages, entertained the king with our stories along with the other boys who were chosen to serve in the palace. When the king didn't need us, we studied with the palace interpreter who translated and spoke Greek for the king. The interpreter taught us your language. We planned to become interpreters of Greek ourselves, but instead, we were assigned to serve the harem."

"Why?" Philocleon asked.

Na'id-Assur and Qurdi Marduk looked at one another with surprise.

"One does not ask why of the king. One does as one is commanded to do," Qurdi Marduk answered.

Na'id-Assur continued, pleased with his pupil's interest. "Vassals of the king would send gifts to the palace. Among these gifts came many unusual creatures, such as lions, elephants, crocodiles, deer, gazelles, wild asses, leopards, bears and two-humped camels." He indicated Philocleon was to write out the names of the animals as he spoke them.

Philocleon paused at gazelle. He couldn't remember how to spell it. "J-E-G. No. G-E-G. I can't remember," he finally said.

Na'id-Assur took the stylus and wrote gazelle in large letters. Philocleon repeated the word three times, rubbed it out with his thumb and did it again. "I have it," he said.

"When the king returned from battles," Qurdi Marduk continued, "he brought with him much booty – gold and silver vessels from Urartu, carved ivory furniture from Syria, faience figurines from Egypt, purple dyed cloth from Phoenicia and many wonderful fragrances and spices from the east.

"After we had worked for the king for many seasons, he went on a major military expedition to the west. Since he decided to take some of the women in the harem with him, we too went along. The king attacked and captured some cities, but most of the cities we went to surrendered without a fight."

"Why?" Philocleon asked, surprised that strong men would surrender without a battle.

"Why? Because the king sent agents ahead of the army to spread the rumor a disobedient governor who had just been caught in the mountains by the king's troops had been skinned alive and his skin hung in the mountains."

"Was it true?" Philocleon doubted it.

"We weren't there," Qurdi Marduk answered. "But there are many who insist it was true." He shrugged. "With that king, anything was possible."

"When we left Syria," Na'id-Assur continued, "we went on to Phoenicia. Tell me the important cities on the sea coast."

"Byblos, Sidon, and Tyre." Philocleon placed x's on the map where each city was located as he named it.

"When we were in Sidon with the harem and the king had gone down the coast to Tyre, we saw our opportunity to escape all those bickering women. We told our overseer the king had sent us a secret message. He wanted us to bring some important documents down to him at Tyre. The overseer didn't believe us, but he was too afraid to stop us. After all, if the king had really sent us a message and the overseer had refused to let us deliver the documents, his life would have been in danger when the king returned. So, under the pretense of taking the documents he wanted to the king, we packed all of our things in several trunks, took all the gold and silver we could find in the harem treasury, and boarded a ship."

At this point the story always varied, depending upon which cities in Greece they were teaching Philocleon to locate. "First, our ship went to a large island northwest of Sidon." He drew an island on the map. "It is called Cyprus."

"Cyprus," Philocleon repeated.

"That's right." Na'id-Assur spelled the word for Philocleon, had him repeat it. "From Cyprus, we traveled west, arriving at?"

"Another island?"

"Yes." Qurdi Marduk drew Rhodes on the map. "This island is called Rhodes." He spelled it for Philocleon and asked him to repeat it.

"Last, we stopped at one more island, farther yet to the west, and a little to the south. We told you about this island a few days ago. Do you remember it?" Qurdi Marduk asked.

"Crete." Philocleon wrote the word, proud of himself.

"From Crete, we made our way to Ionia."

"Why did you go to Ionia?" Philocleon asked. "I'd have gone to Egypt."

"There are many Ionian Greeks who trade with the king of Assyria," Qurdi Marduk explained. "They paid us well for our knowledge of Assyrian and Greek. In fact so well, we planned to stay in Ionia until an Athenian trader came into port. He offered us even more bronze than the Ionians to interpret for him in Athens. Of course, we went with him but our job didn't last long. Your father came along and convinced us to come here and tutor you."

The story always ended in Athens. The number of places he had to identify was shorter than it usually was because Philocleon needed to get ready for the banquet.

"Your next lesson, we will review the cities in Ionia," Na'id-Assur said, putting his stylus down on the ivory table. "For now, we must stop the geography lesson and go on to your reading lesson." He leaned forward and rubbed his hands together. "We have something very, very special for this lesson. We are going to tell you the story of the great priest-king, Gilgamesh."

"Was he a Greek?"

"Certainly not! Gilgamesh was created by the gods when the world was still in its infancy, to be king of Uruk."

"From the heavenly sun god, Shamash," Qurdi Marduk added, "Gilgamesh was endowed with perfect beauty and from Adad, the powerful storm god, he was given courage. When the two gods were finished, they gave to Uruk one of the strongest, most handsome kings known to mankind."

Na'id-Assur bent over and wrote Gilgamesh in the beeswax on Philocleon's writing board. Philocleon repeated the letters after him. Then, he put his writing board down and waited for his teacher to begin.

Na'id-Assur picked up the remaining writing boards he'd brought from the cupboard and showed them to Philocleon. "We often heard the saga recited and Qurdi Marduk saw it written on clay tablets in Babylon before he went to the king's palace. We've written what he can remember down on these boards for you."

"But," Qurdi Marduk said, "before we begin the story, we want to put a riddle to you, as always." He stood and locked his hands together behind his back. "It will be your responsibility to consider this riddle while Na'id-Assur is reading and to answer it when he is finished. The riddle is," he paused, rolled up onto his toes, leaned forward for emphasis. "How was it possible that Gilgamesh both died and gained immortality?"

"It's not possible," Philocleon said before the story had even begun. "I understand the word, immortal. It means that a man lives forever. If he died, he could not have been immortal."

"Ah, so you are willing to give up so easily?" Qurdi Marduk teased. He pulled a stool from beneath the couch, sat down and, propping his golden-slippered feet up on the stool, leaned back and prepared to listen.

"Remember," Na'id-Assur told Philocleon, "learning to read words means nothing unless you learn to use the words to reason."

Philocleon loved this time of his lesson most. Always, before they told him a story, Na'id-Assur and Qurdi Marduk posed a riddle he would have great difficulty answering. Always, he complained and insisted no answer was possible. Always, he became so interested in the riddle by the time the story ended, he couldn't rest until he had figured it out.

"Remember," Na'id-Assur repeated, "learning to read means nothing unless you learn to use the words to reason. Now reason and answer our riddle." He leaned back and propped his feet on the stool next to those of Qurdi Marduk. "As I told you before, Gilgamesh, the young king of Uruk, was very strong. But he was also a little like you, I'm afraid: unruly." He chuckled and held up his hand to quiet Philocleon who was just about to defend himself. Then, taking up his boards, he read.

"Gilgamesh was such an unruly king it wasn't long before his people were praying to the gods for relief from his cruelty. When the gods heard the prayers of the people, they felt pity. To Aruru, the goddess of creation, they said, 'You created Gilgamesh. Now you must create his equal. Together, the two men can go from Uruk and leave the people in peace.'

"Aruru, obeying the commands of the gods, dipped her hands in water, pinched off clay and threw it into the wilderness. Out of the clay came the wild man, Enkidu. The untamed Enkidu lived in the wilderness with the wild beasts, innocent of the ways of man, until he met up with a prostitute. He fell in love with her and she showed him her womanly arts. Sadly, when Enkidu left her and returned to the wild beasts, they ran from him.

"Desperate, Enkidu returned to the prostitute. She took him to Uruk where Gilgamesh was king. When Enkidu entered Uruk, the people gathered round and rejoiced. 'He will protect us from the king,' they said. When Gilgamesh came to the center of town to take his pleasure with the new bride before her husband, Enkidu stood before the bride's house and blocked passage to Gilgamesh.

"Gilgamesh grabbed Enkidu and they wrestled. Grappling like bulls, they fought until Gilgamesh planted his feet and with a firm turn, threw Enkidu to the ground and held him there. When Gilgamesh had won, his fury abated. 'Come', he said to Enkidu. There is no other man like you in the entire world. We must become friends.'

"No sooner had Gilgamesh and Enkidu sealed their friendship than Gilgamesh told Enkidu he wanted to go to the Land of Cedars where he would cut down the cedar trees and build a monument to the gods. The eyes of Enkidu filled with tears. 'In the Land of Cedars dwells the protector of the trees, Humbaba,' he told Gilgamesh. 'Surely it would be dangerous to fell any of his trees.'

"Gilgamesh answered him. 'Only the gods live forever. For mankind, the seasons are numbered. I will cut down the cedar and build a monument to establish an everlasting name for myself. Even if I am defeated by Humbaba and die, men will remember me. They will say, Gilgamesh was killed by Humbaba.'

"So the two men strapped on their swords and took up their axes. Deep in the Land of Cedars, they fought with Humbaba and killed him. When they returned to Uruk, Gilgamesh called for a festival to celebrate his great victory. At the festival, the Goddess Ishtar fell in love with Gilgamesh and commanded him to be her consort. Gilgamesh refused and Ishtar sent the Bull of Heaven to destroy him. But the Bull of Heaven did not destroy Gilgamesh. Instead, Gilgamesh and Enkidu killed the bull.

"Ishtar was so angry when she learned what Gilgamesh and Enkidu had done, she demanded of the gods that Enkidu die. Enkidu fell ill. He continually grew weaker until when Gilgamesh touched the heart of his friend, it no longer beat. Gilgamesh cried out. 'Enkidu. My friend. My brother. What is this sleep that has come over you?' Wailing he veiled Enkidu like a bride and caused all the people of Uruk to lament.

"Weeping for his buried friend, Gilgamesh roamed over the land. 'When I die, shall I not suffer the same fate as Enkidu?' he asked. 'But I am afraid of death, he said, 'so I must go to find Utnapishtim, called the Faraway, and ask him about everlasting life. For he has entered the assembly of the immortal gods.'

"He took his axe in his hand. He strapped on his sword and he traveled to the cabin of Utnapishtim. 'Why is it that you are sad?' Utnapishtim asked.

'Should I not be sad?' Gilgamesh asked. 'My friend Enkidu is dead. He has turned to clay. Shall I not one day also lie down and not rise again?'

"Utnapishtim answered, 'Only the gods live forever. For mankind, the seasons are numbered.' But taking pity on Gilgamesh as he left, Utnapishtim said, 'I will reveal a secret of the gods to you. There is a plant at the bottom of the sea with prickly horns. If you take it, though it pricks your hands, you and whoever eats the plant will stay young forever.'

"Happily, Gilgamesh fixed heavy stones to himself when he got to the sea and let them drag him to bottom of the water. There he found the thorny plant and he took it and started back to Uruk to give it to all of the old men in the village. But during his long journey Gilgamesh became tired. He saw a pool of cool water and went down to bathe in it. Deep in the pool, a snake smelled the fragrance of the thorny plant. While Gilgamesh bathed, the snake rose out of the water and snatched the thorny plant.

"When Gilgamesh learned what had happened, he sat and bitterly wept. 'For nothing have I toiled so long,' he said. 'I have toiled for so long and now the snakes snatches the thorny plant from me that will keep men young.' Weeping, he returned to Uruk.

"Lamenting his sad fate, Gilgamesh looked over everything he had built when he reached Uruk. Then, weeping, he sat down and engraved the story of his journey on a stone. As was his destiny, when the end of his life drew near, Gilgamesh laid himself down and did not rise again. Now, he lies buried in a tomb."

"Well?" Qurdi Marduk asked when Na'id-Assur stopped reading.

"I don't understand," Philocleon answered. "Gilgamesh died. How could he be immortal?"

Neither Na'id-Assur nor Qurdi Marduk answered him. They only smiled.

THREE

Alcmena leaned forward and grasped the arm of her slave as soon as he turned the donkeys onto the path through the trees surrounding the back of Hipponous' house. "I'm getting off here. Daemones will go on to the house alone." She brushed a crumb from Daemones' thin grey beard and smoothed the hair on his nearly bald head. "You haven't forgotten now, have you?" she asked gently.

"No. I haven't forgotten." Daemones didn't even try to hide his agitation. "I'm supposed to bring Philocleon to the family crypt." He pushed her hand away. "And I haven't forgotten you have been reminding me all the way over."

"I'm sorry. It's just that you sometimes forget things lately."

Daemones continued to scowl, but said no more. It wasn't her reminding him so often that upset him; it was knowing she was right. He did forget things. No matter how hard he tried, he forgot things, got things mixed up.

She got down from the cart, thought about reminding him once more, but changed her mind. "Bring the cart back here when you've dropped him off," she instructed the slave. "As soon as I'm finished, I'll want you to take me home."

"Will Daemones be returning with you?"

"No. After you take me home you can return and wait for him. I'm sure the banquet will last until Dawn rises to her throne." She stepped back from the cart and waited until the two men had disappeared around the side of the house. Then pulling her shawl tightly around her head and shoulders, she walked to the crypt, a small cave in one of the limestone outcroppings at the back of the trees.

Daemones' slave pulled his horses to a halt at the front of the house. "I don't see any other carts," he informed his master, getting down and helping him to the ground. "You must be the first man to arrive."

Daemones looked around. The slave was right. Good. That would mean he'd be able to talk with Philocleon. "Remember," he said, moving away from the cart so the slave could turn it around. "No gossiping with Hipponous' slaves when you return tonight. Hipponous must not know Alcmena was here."

The thick wooden door at the entrance was closed when Daemones got there. As he stood, deciding whether to knock or wait for one of the slaves to pull the door open for the banquet, he examined, as he always did when he stood at the entrance to Hipponous' house, the huge wooden frame that held the door. As though drawn by some inevitable force against his will, his eyes followed the line of the frame upward to the lintel. The grotesque carving of Medusa spilling out of the wood, her head crawling with hideous snakes, made him cringe with fear. Frightened by Medusa's penetrating stare, he made up his mind to knock.

A slave opened the door. "Good evening, Sir. Hipponous is in the courtyard." Daemones walked past the slave down the corridor that connected the entrance with the interior courtyard.

At the end of the corridor under the opening to the courtyard stood the Altar of Zeus, a huge limestone slab. In spite of himself, Daemones was always as impressed by the walk down this corridor as he was repulsed by the entrance. He paused before the altar. "Father Zeus," he implored, picking up the ceramic pitcher left on the altar for libations after he'd purified his hands with water, "if ever before you have listened to my entreaties and did me some honor, so one more time bring to pass that which I ask for. Help me to persuade Philocleon." He poured wine from the pitcher onto the ground in front of the altar.

Hipponous was giving instructions to his cooks at the far end of the courtyard when Daemones first saw him. He waited until Hipponous had sent the cooks back to the kitchen before walking over to him. Having given up pretending affection for his former son-in-law when his daughter died, Daemones made no attempt to make even polite conversation. Instead, he abruptly demanded, "Where is Philocleon?"

"He'll be here shortly." Hipponous could see Daemones was nervous. What was it? Always, there was something.

Daemones scanned the richly decorated columns that supported the opening into the dining room. "I see you are still living quite nicely on Calonice's dowry," he said sarcastically.

He didn't object to Hipponous bedding Philocleon's nurse Bromia after Calonice died. Many men bedded their slaves. What he objected to was the way Hipponous treated Bromia. Like a wife instead of a slave.

When he'd learned about Bromia, he'd demanded that Hipponous turn control of Calonice's extravagant dowry over to him until Philocleon had matured enough to oversee it. Hipponous had offered instead to marry Philocleon to Alcmena and Daemones' granddaughter, Scapha. Daemones had accepted, knowing he couldn't enforce his demand anyway. But he hated Hipponous for it.

"And, his bride to be? How is she?" Hipponous asked, stifling what he wanted to say by reminding himself Philocleon would soon have all of Daemones' land if he kept his feelings about Daemones and Alcmena to himself.

Daemones glared at Hipponous. It enraged him when Hipponous ignored his remarks about the dowry. At least he could act like he was sorry for what he'd done. "Scapha looks more like our dear little Calonice every day," he answered stiffly.

Hipponous didn't even try to hide his impatience. All the old weasel ever did was talk about his little Calonice. As though talking could change anything. "If you'll excuse me, I see there are other men arriving," he said and walked away across the courtyard to greet his many guests. It seemed, as he looked around that almost all of the surrounding estate owners and their sons had come to the banquet, as had a number of the aristocrats from the village at Sounion. If Homer turned out to be the poet Philocleon said he was, the evening would certainly be successful and his reputation as one of the finest hosts in Attica maintained and enhanced.

Daemones waited until he saw Philocleon enter the courtyard. He waved and Philocleon came to him. Except for Philocleon's build, which was tall and athletic like his father's, he seemed to Daemones to look more like his mother every day. He had her gentle olive brown eyes and soft, curly, black hair, her smile. In fact, his resemblance to Calonice was so striking it might have been a problem if she had lived. After all, those women were always suspect who had sons that didn't look exactly like their fathers.

Philocleon, still excited about his lesson, kissed his grandfather on both cheeks and hugged him. "I'm sorry I wasn't here to greet you when you arrived Grandfather. I was finishing my reading lesson." Looking over his grandfather's head, he examined the group of men gathered at the center of the courtyard to see whether Homer was with them. "He must still be in his room," he mumbled to himself, not finding the poet among the other guests.

Daemones slipped his hands behind Philocleon's head and pulled it toward him to gain his full attention. He kissed his grandson with affection on both cheeks. "We have missed you at the estate. You haven't been over to visit us lately."

Philocleon started to remind his grandfather he'd been there just before the last rain, then changed his mind. He took the old man's frail hand and smiled. He could see his grandfather was agitated, the way he always got when he was trying hard not to forget something. His memory seemed to be getting worse every day. "What is it grandfather?"

"Come with me to the family crypt."

"What?" Philocleon asked, surprised at the strange request. "But I can't just now. I have to help father with the banquet."

"Just for a moment, please." Daemones clutched Philocleon's arm and tried to pull him toward the door.

"Why do you want to go to the crypt?"

"Please!"

Philocleon started to say no, but couldn't do it. "All right," he sighed, unable to face his grandfather's disappointment. "I'll come with you, but we can't be gone for very long. I have to be here to help father greet the guests." He took Daemones' arm and pulling a burning branch from the fire as they passed the hearth, led him out the door, around the house into the forest to the small cave his family had used for generations to store the ashes of their clan.

Keeping the branch in front of him for light, Philocleon took his grandfather into the damp crypt, stopping at the stone bench his father had set up in front of the burial amphorae. He waited for Daemones to sit on the bench before he bent down on one knee in front of him, and pushing the unburned end of the branch into the soft ground at an angle to illuminate the old man's wrinkled face, asked, "Now, what is it that's so important it couldn't wait?" He hoped his grandfather wouldn't notice the impatience in his voice.

"He didn't want to talk to you. I did." Alcmena stepped out of the shadow created by the shelf that held Calonice's ash urn.

Startled by the unexpected intrusion, Philocleon whirled around to stare at his grandmother. "What are you doing here?" he asked.

She held out her small hands and waited for him to come to her.

He looked from her to his grandfather trying to understand what was happening. "What is she doing here?" he asked Daemones.

Alcmena lifted her extended arms slightly higher. "I came here to speak with you. Maybe," she paused, pulling her shawl tightly around her head, "I shouldn't have come."

Philocleon, somewhat recovered from the surprise of finding her in the crypt, went to her, took both of her hands, kissed them, hugged her and kissed her on both cheeks.

She clung to him. "I'm sorry if I've displeased you. It's just I so needed to talk with you."

Philocleon led her to the stone bench and helped her sit down. "You didn't displease me. You surprised me. Grandfather didn't mention anything about you." Suddenly, he remembered his grandfather. Daemones was standing, staring at the amphora holding Calonice's ashes. "Grandfather," Philocleon said gently. "Come over and sit down with us."

Daemones did as he was told. When he was seated, Philocleon took the hands of both of them, two of theirs in one of his and held them in his lap. "Now," he said, leaning over to kiss his grandmother's grey head, "What is it you have to tell me?"

"Actually," Alcmena began, avoiding his eyes, "I didn't come to tell you anything. I came to ask for something." She squeezed Philocleon's hand tightly. "Give me your word – here, over your mother's ashes, you will marry Scapha."

Philocleon started to laugh, but looking into her pained olive-brown eyes, which had turned to search his face, he stopped. "Do you mean to tell me you came all the way over to our estate and hid in the crypt to ask me to pledge myself to Scapha? Grandmother, you know I'll marry Scapha. You have my father's oath."

"Your father's oath isn't worth the shit his horses leave," Daemones blurted out, pulling his hands out of Philocleon's.

"Grandfather," Philocleon said patiently. "You mustn't say things like that. Remember what I told you?" When his grandfather was agitated the worst things came out of his mouth.

"You wouldn't say that if you knew how he treated your mother." Daemones scrambled clumsily to his feet. "Whether you want to believe it or not, your father would use or sell anybody, no matter who it was, if he could gain from it." Overcome with anger, he stormed out of the crypt.

Used to his grandfather's outbursts, Philocleon put his arm around his grandmother. She was so small, it was like holding a wisp of wind in his arm. "I'm afraid he's getting old, Grandmother."

"What he said is true," she said, now looking straight into Philocleon's eyes, tears gathering in her own. She reached up and lovingly straightened one of the curls on his forehead. "You must try to understand."

"What is it?" Philocleon brushed a tear from her cheek. When had she grown so wrinkled?

"It's about your mother. She was all I had."

"I know." He still didn't understand what she was doing in the crypt.

"In my family, the women always had trouble with babies. My sisters and aunts – all of their babies either died at birth or were born with defects. Me, I was different." She pulled away from Philocleon. "I had one healthy baby after another from the first year I was married. One after another, they came." She sobbed and fell against Philocleon again.

"What do you mean you had one child after another?" Philocleon was so surprised by what she said he wondered if her mind had begun to fail the way his grandfather's had. "Mother didn't have any sisters or brothers."

Her voice barely audible from the pain of remembering, Alcmena continued. "He came." She breathed deeply to try and calm herself. It was so important to make Philocleon understand.

"Who came?" Philocleon asked gently.

"Your grandfather. After each baby was born he came and took it from me."

"Why?" He knew many babies were exposed, but he didn't know his grandfather had done it.

"I had girls and he wanted boys. My girls, he carried, each and every one up to the ridge and left them."

"But, Mother?"

"By the time your mother was born, I wanted to die. All my babies. Dead. When your grandfather heard it was another girl, he came to my room and told the midwives he wanted her. I cried and begged, but he took her anyway, just like the others. But this time I had already made up my mind. I would die with my baby. I got out of my bed, bleeding and weak, and I followed him. When he put her down, I went over and lay down beside her." Alcmena suddenly smiled. "She was so beautiful. Black hair like yours. Olive brown eyes. She was crying from hunger. I gave her my breast. For the first time after so many babies, I gave one my breast. It's impossible to tell you how happy it made me."

"What did grandfather do?"

"He stood there for a long time. Then he said he was going to take her from me. I told him he would have to kill me. At first he didn't believe me, but afterwards he did. When he reached for her, I bit his hand. He threatened me and even hit me in the face, but I wouldn't let go of my baby. When he saw it was useless to try to persuade me, he left us both in the mountains. For the rest of that day we lay side by side, Calonice and me. By dark your grandfather had relented. He sent one of the slaves up to get us; and when we returned, he took little Calonice into his house."

Philocleon found his grandfather's cruelty toward his mother difficult to accept. "But grandfather talks all the time of how much he loved mother."

"At first he resisted her, but she was so beautiful and so full of life, and spunk too, his resolve didn't last beyond her first year. Soon, he loved her as much as I did. Before we knew it, the season for Calonice to marry had come. We agreed to marry her to your father. Soon you were on the way. When you were about to be born, she became very, very sick." Twisting the pleats of his tunic with a vehemence only hate could produce, she blurted out, "In her sickest moment, your father decided to take her to Corinth. I tried to tell him she was too sick and weak, but he wouldn't listen. After she came home from Corinth, she went to bed and never got up again."

"What was wrong with her?" Philocleon had asked his father about his mother's death, but Hipponous had always refused to talk about it with him. Now, he thought he was beginning to understand why.

"I don't know. All during her pregnancy she was sick, but after she'd gone to Corinth, she got much worse. When finally you had been born, she started to bleed and nothing anyone gave her could stop the bleeding. I don't know why.

"As soon as your father had named you, he got on his horse and went to Corinth. There he celebrated your birth while your poor mother suffered with no husband to comfort her. When he came home, she was dead. He buried her, and before her ashes were cold, he had another woman in his bed."

"Who?" Thanks to his grandmother, Philocleon had always felt protective of the mother he'd never known.

"Your nurse, Bromia."

"Bromia. Why?" Anger toward his father began pulsing through him.

"Because he never loved Calonice. He only married her for the dowry."

"Did she love him?"

"Very much. She so wanted to marry your father, I convinced your grandfather to give all of our vineyards, many goats and oxen, and much of the silver from our treasury as a dowry." She clutched Philocleon's arm. "She was my only child. I wanted her to be happy."

"I know." He'd often heard his father brag about how well he'd done with the dowry.

"When Calonice died and he took Bromia to his bed, we asked that the dowry be placed in the hands of your grandfather until you became old enough to control it so your father wouldn't be able to use it up. Your father refused. Instead he promised to marry you to Scapha. Lately we have heard, he has been taking you around to the estate owners and introducing you. Some say he plans to break his oath to us and marry you to someone else."

"Why would he do that?" Philocleon asked. "Anyway, he's never mentioned marrying anyone else to me."

"We've heard he's already used up Calonice's dowry except for the vineyards and that he is in need of another dowry. You know Scapha is not truly our granddaughter even though that's what we call her. She is the youngest daughter of my dead niece. We couldn't force your father to keep his oath."

Philocleon hugged his grandmother tightly, partly to comfort her, but as much to comfort himself. He felt totally overwhelmed. There were suddenly so many things about his father he didn't understand and didn't like. Undeserved beatings of slaves. The inexplicable, cruel goading of Homer at the beekeeper's. Now this. Deserting his mother on her deathbed. Treating a slave like a wife before he'd even mourned properly. Stealing his grandparent's dowry. "Grandmother. Why didn't you tell me this before?" he asked, feeling intense pity for the burden she'd been carrying by herself for so long.

"Because I am afraid of your father," Alcmena answered. "You must understand, your father is a very strong and cruel man and your grandfather is not the man he once was."

"Why did you decide to tell me now?" He wished with all his heart she'd hadn't chosen to tell him right before the banquet.

"Your grandfather said the banquet tonight was to introduce you to more estate owners. I became afraid. If your father...and you didn't know...I'm worried for Scapha."

Philocleon smiled just a little. "The banquet isn't to introduce me to estate owners. I met a poet at the port in Sounion. It's to honor him."

"Are you certain?" Alcmena felt foolish.

"Yes, I am." Philocleon pinched her cheek just a little, playfully, then turning serious again, gently took her to the amphora where his mother's ashes were buried. He filled a silver cup with wine kept near the amphorae for libations and got down on his knees before his mother's amphora. "As Athena is the protector of our family, I swear I will marry Scapha." He poured the wine on his mother's ashes trying not to think about his father celebrating in Corinth while his mother lay dying.

Alcmena dropped, sobbing, beside him. She kissed his hands, his feet. "You're a good boy, Philocleon."

Embarrassed by his grandmother kissing his feet, Philocleon stood and pulled her to her feet. "You mustn't worry any longer, Grandmother." He hugged her. "I'm a man who keeps his oaths. You believe that, don't you?"

When she stopped sobbing, Philocleon put his arm around her and walked her outside. He helped her into the cart and ordered her slave to take her home. If women had been allowed, he'd have taken her into the banquet with him. She looked so lonely and fragile sitting there in the cart. "You must not worry," he repeated. "Nothing will stop me from keeping my oath."

Trying to sort out all of the things he'd just heard Philocleon waited for the cart carrying his grandmother to disappear in the trees. "Come," he said gently to Daemones when they could no longer see the cart. "I have to return to the banquet."

At the entrance to the courtyard, Philocleon called one of the slaves. "My grandfather isn't feeling too good. Make certain you watch over him." He kissed Daemones on both cheeks and, trying to ignore the pain he felt at the back of his head, walked toward the end of the courtyard where he'd left Homer when they'd returned from the stream.

Immediately upon their return, Homer had stripped off his filthy tunic, thrown himself on the clean, white fleece covering his bed and fallen asleep. Memories of straw mats filled with lice at the bottom of the ship gave way in his dreams to the luxurious bed he'd left in Ionia. He woke, feeling exhilarated.

Sitting up, he saw that his soiled tunic had been replaced with an elegant linen tunic made at the household looms. The garment lay on a carved wooden table placed next to his bed while he slept. On the table, he also found fine leather sandals and a mantle made from the skin of a panther.

As he reached over to feel of the panther skin, a servant who had been waiting for him to awaken came to his bed. She took him to the terracotta tub at the far end of the room. There she washed him and rubbed him down with oil. Afterwards, she formed his golden brown hair into a long strand of curls at the back of his neck.

Homer returned to his bed and sat on it, barely noticing the slave slipping the fine tunic over his head, straightening it, and quietly leaving the room. He was certain the clothes were a gift from Philocleon. When he'd met Philocleon, his thoughts had been exactly this. To get a free meal or two, a soft bed, some clean clothes. Why then, did he feel so sad about having to leave after the banquet?

He picked up the panther skin and, as he was trying it around his shoulders, he saw Philocleon coming across the courtyard. "What do you think?" he asked at the door. "Fit for a meeting with 'Father' Zeus himself, wouldn't you say?" He spread his arms to show Philocleon how handsome he looked in the mantle.

"I'd say." Philocleon tried to recover his earlier enthusiasm. It was gone. Lost in the tears and sadness of his grandmother. "But we have to hurry. I want to introduce you to father's guests before it's too late."

"Is something wrong?" Homer could see Philocleon's mood had changed. He dropped the panther mantle on the bed.

Philocleon smiled, unwilling to spoil Homer's fine evening of poetry. "No. I'm fine. Just a little tired from the lesson. After the banquet, I'll tell you all about it." Saying no more, he took Homer around the courtyard, introducing him to Hipponous' impressive guests, wondering each time he introduced the poet to a man who had a daughter if Hipponous had talked with him about marriage.

As Philocleon and Homer spoke with the last group of guests, Hipponous was informed by his cooks that the meal was ready. He instructed his slaves to take everyone to the dining hall, an ornate room situated directly across the courtyard from the altar of Zeus. Unlike the other rooms that opened by small doorways onto the courtyard, the vast rectangular dining room with its central hearth was separated from the courtyard by nothing more than a row of elaborate columns.

The guests were taken to couches covered with ornately decorated coverlets and pillows. Each man had his sandals removed and his feet washed. Finally, the slaves brought low marble tables and placed them in front of the couches.

Hipponous opened the banquet with an invocation to Zeus in the center of the courtyard. "Great Father Zeus. If ever you have smelled the smoke from my offerings, and if it pleased you, send your wisdom upon this house and its guests." From a sack of barley brought to him by Nicias he spread grain in honor of Zeus and asked for his protection.

Satisfied the invocation had gone perfectly, Hipponous had the kids he'd chosen that afternoon brought to him. Ceremoniously he examined them for flaws, turning each around twice so his guests could observe the perfection of the animals. With elaborate gestures he held the animals' heads back and slit their throats. He cut the best pieces from their thighs using a dagger made of silver, wrapped them in fat, and had the slaves place them on the spit for Zeus.

The remainder of the kids he ordered the slaves to roast for his guests. While the slaves cut the meat, he had Philocleon mix one of his finest wines with water in a silver-mixing bowl. Two slaves carried the bowl to the dining hall, and Philocleon filled two-handled goblets and gave one to every man.

Sitting among his guests waiting for the meat to roast, Hipponous bragged incessantly about Homer. If he was going to have to put up with that imprudent poet for the night, he fully intended to make the most of it. Homer, for Philocleon's sake, pretended to be excessively pleased with the bragging.

As was his custom Hipponous served the roasted meat himself when it was ready while Nicias passed baskets filled with honey cakes and bread and Philocleon poured more wine into the goblets. A parade of kitchen slaves brought greens to the dining room: cucumbers spiced with vinegar and wine, onions, garlic, olives, and greens covered with ginger, rue, pepper, honey and dates. When the greens had been placed on every table, the slaves returned to the kitchen for fruit and cheese. From baskets filled with grapes, pomegranates, fresh figs, and thick wedges of goat's milk cheese, they served the guests. As soon as they had left the dining hall, Hipponous poured a libation to Dionysus and invited everyone to eat, noting to himself how many of his guests were already remarking on his generosity.

Nicias brought a mixing bowl of the choicest estate wine to Hipponous at the end of the meal. Elaborately, Hipponous mixed the delicate wine with water and had Philocleon fill the goblets of his guests once more. As always, they responded by raising their goblets to the most generous host in all of Greece.

Hipponous in turn responded by inviting Homer to take the honored place at the center of the room.

"He's the greatest poet in the Aegean," Philocleon slurred, his tongue thickened by the volume of wine he'd drunk.

Homer walked to the center of the room and sat. Nicias brought him his lyre. He took it and called most earnestly for the beautiful muse, Calliope, to bring him her wonderful verses. As he sat waiting for that familiar surge of excitement that told him the muse had come, he saw Hipponous audaciously grinning and nodding to his guests, acting as if they were the closest of friends – as if he hadn't called Homer a bastard.

As he thought about being called a bastard, Homer's body tensed with hatred and anger. When the verses he was waiting for came to him, they were the saga of the ferocious quarrel between Agamemnon, leader of the Greeks, and his bravest warrior, the brilliant Achilles, during the Trojan war.

Quite naturally, Homer saw Hipponous as the arrogant Agamemnon and himself as the wronged Achilles. The entire wrath he'd felt at the beekeeper's shack vehemently pulsed through him into the poem. He began his saga by telling his audience the Greeks had awarded the daughter of Chryses, Apollo's priest, as his booty after they'd fought and won one of the fiercest battles of the war. Even though the unhappy father had gone to Agamemnon when he learned the fate of his daughter and offered a most handsome ransom to the king for his daughter, the unreasonable and selfish Agamemnon had refused to return her.

Enjoying the revenge he was about to recite as though it were his own against Hipponous, Homer continued. He told his audience the angry priest went to Apollo and begged for revenge against the Greeks. Granting the request of his priest, Apollo struck the camp of the Greeks with his deadly arrows. Men died one after another of the plague until, certain they would die to the last man, the Greeks called for one of their seers.

Agamemnon's refusal to return the priest's daughter, their seer told them, was the cause of their defeat. Achilles was the only general, Homer informed his spellbound audience, who dared to demand Agamemnon return the priest's daughter. Agamemnon agreed after a fierce argument, but he took the woman Achilles had been given by the Greeks as his booty in revenge. Insulted and angry, the brilliant Achilles withdrew from the fighting.

Using his verses to cut through the silence he'd created as swiftly as a blacksmith's newly forged sword, Homer enumerated with the joy of a victor the sad defeats of the mighty Greeks by the Trojans following the withdrawal of the brilliant Achilles from the fighting. Hero after hero fell, wounded or dead, until finally, Homer ended his singing with the wounding of an Attic hero, whom he begrudgingly named – to keep his promise to be nice to Hipponous for Philocleon's sake – Hipponous, stubborn in battle.

So awed were the men listening to Homer, not one of them moved when he ended his singing and sat recovering for a few moments with his head bowed. The only sound in the dining room was the soft moaning of Philocleon and Homer's own exhausted breathing – until the poet raised his head. The moment he moved, all the men in the room were on their feet cheering.

"To Homer," Hipponous yelled, pushing his way though the crowd, his full chest bursting with pride.

"To Homer," someone repeated, "and to Hipponous – stubborn in battle."

Hipponous raised his goblet. "To Homer's joining Philocleon and me on the boar hunt." He tipped his goblet toward Homer and then toward Philocleon.

Philocleon refused to even look at his father. Instead, he raised his goblet to his grandfather.

Daemones raised his goblet in return before he kissed Philocleon on both cheeks, whispering, "It makes me happy to know my grandson has such a fine companion. Surely, Achilles could not have been very different from our Homer." He clamped a bony hand on Homer's shoulder. "Well done, my son," he said and left the hall.

When his grandfather was out of sight, Philocleon wobbled to his feet and lifting his goblet, proposed a toast of his own. "To Achilles,"

Goblets clinked all over the room. "To Achilles."

Philocleon turned and faced his father. "To Achilles and his belief that the vilest man on the earth is one who breaks an oath." Achilles had said it of Agamemnon. Now, he was saying it to his father.

Not quite understanding what Philocleon's toast was about, but understanding it was intended to embarrass him, Hipponous stood when it was finished and started toward his son to find out, but before he got to Philocleon's couch, one of the other silver mine owners from Laurion stepped in his path. "Where are the dice?" he asked, draping his thick arm over Hipponous' shoulder.

Hipponous shook the man's arm from his shoulder and sent Nicias for the dice. He'd seen Daemones bend over and say something to Philocleon. What was it the old weasel had told his son? "He'll push me too far," he muttered and poured himself another goblet of wine.

Nicias returned with the dice and handed them to Hipponous. "I saw Daemones wander into the women's quarters," he whispered. "I'm going to fetch him."

"Don't bring him back here. Take him to his cart and see to it he leaves." Hipponous threw the dice across the table to the silver mine owner.

Daemones finally figured out where he was when he recognized Calonice's room. How many times had he cursed standing there on her wedding day with the others, cheering as Hipponous escorted her into this room. "You weren't ready for marriage," he said to the room of the dead Calonice. "And he never wanted you, anyway, just the dowry. I should have kept you home with me longer."

As he stood sorrowing, a strong hand grasped his shoulder. "Come. I'll take you to your wagon." Nicias gently took the arm of the thin man and guided him out of the women's quarters.

"You have no idea what it was like…my daughter with that brute," Daemones lamented. "It would have been better if she'd never married."

"But then you wouldn't have Philocleon," Nicias reminded him.

Daemones nodded, but he didn't feel comforted. "Why didn't you ever marry?" he asked Nicias. "Surely there must have been one woman willing to marry you, even with that foot."

"I would never want my son or daughter brought up as a slave," Nicias answered. There was more to it than that, but it was not for him to tell Daemones. Not only would Hipponous never have agreed, it would have been dangerous to even ask him. Learning that a woman, even a slave, preferred a crippled slave to him, was not something Hipponous would have tolerated.

"Is it so bad, being a slave?"

"Hipponous has treated me decently. I have no complaints, but neither have I any freedom." How many springs had passed since the first night Bromia had come to him. He had awakened thinking something was crawling on his cheek. He'd brushed his cheek, but it hadn't gone away. Then, he had opened his eyes and there she stood, her long beautiful brown hair dropping gently on his shoulder, brushing his cheeks lightly. I would have come sooner, she'd whispered, but Hipponous demands me whenever he is here. It was the first he had known about Hipponous' use of Bromia.

He helped Daemones into the cart and woke his slave. From the house, they heard Hipponous call. "Make sure he doesn't come back into the house," Nicias reminded the slave, slapping the rear end of Daemones' horses to get them on their way.

When Nicias reached the house, Hipponous was demanding the cottabus candelabrum. Nicias found it in the storeroom and brought it to the dining hall. There he set it up, fastening the long narrow shaft into the center of the three-footed base with a leather thong. Once the shaft and base were assembled, he handed Hipponous the bronze disc. Hipponous fitted the hole in the center of the thin disc into the top of the shaft. Using both hands he balanced the disc. "Who'll try first?"

A young man from one of the neighboring estates whom Hipponous called Snail because he came in last in every competition, emptied his drinking goblet down to the last few drops. Placing his fingers in one handle of the goblet and being careful not to move more than his forearm, he flipped his final drops of wine at the disc. They missed completely and fell onto the bottom of the candelabrum. He was applauded with catcalls and hissing.

Peleus volunteered next. He had the distinction of being the only man at the banquet who'd ever beaten Hipponous in horse racing. Even though the race had taken place many winters ago when they were both young men Hipponous still felt the defeat as keenly as he had when it had happened. If Peleus hadn't turned out to be one of the wealthiest men in Attica, he'd never have seen the inside of Hipponous' house.

Peleus threw the few drops of wine left in his goblet at the disc. The wine dropped on the disc, but the sound was poor and the disc moved only a short distance down the shaft.

Elated, Hipponous emptied his goblet. "Obviously, we need men for this task." He tossed his wine drops and they landed perfectly, making a good sound when they hit the disc, sending it sliding to the bottom of the candelabrum. Cheers came from everyone watching.

Peleus bowed. "You were lucky."

"Send in the hetaerae," Hipponous said to Nicias as he filled his goblet and drank all of the wine down without breathing.

"We can't stand for this," Peleus' son insisted to his father. He emptied his goblet and when Hipponous had replaced the disc, tossed his last drops of wine. They hit the disc and it fell to the bottom of the candelabrum. All of the young men cheered and Peleus proposed a toast.

While Peleus prepared to make a second toss, a fine-boned young hetaera entered the dining hall followed by two older hetaerae, one with a lyre, the other with a flute. The older women played soft, erotic music on their instruments while the younger woman danced. She wore a nearly transparent purple peplos made of silk. Fastened at both shoulders with gold fibulae, the sheer gown fell in great waves from her shoulders to her tiny, gold-girdled waist, then swept to her thin ankles. In her hand she carried a muffler of white fur. She touched the muffler to the men's faces as she danced around the room.

"Forget the cottabus," someone yelled. Laughing, Hipponous put the candelabrum to the side and turned with the rest of the men to watch the beautiful hetaera dance. It wasn't long before he could feel himself swelling. He looked around and saw that almost every man in the great hall felt the same way he did. He snickered. They could wish as much as they liked, but it was his banquet. She would be his in the end.

The dancing continued, the white muff racing from face to face. Tunics heaved. Young and old men alike, moaned, exploded. Recovered. Exploded again. Everybody begged the beautiful young woman for more, and she obliged them with dance after dance, each more revealing and exciting than the last.

As the dancing continued, she returned more and more often to dance before Homer. He played his lyre and sang to her. Then, when Dawn opened the gates of heaven for Helios, she took a set of dice out of her muffler, kissed them, and handed them to the poet. "Are you as lucky as you are handsome?" she asked.

"What's the prize?" he asked in return.

"I am."

Homer took up his lyre and sang a love song to her. Someone took the lyre from him and sang a song learned from the oarsmen at the port. More wine was passed all around. Homer kissed the dice and held them up to the hetaera. "The man with the lowest number has to drop out each time," she said. He tossed a five.

The dice went around and came back to Homer. One of the silver mine owners from Laurion dropped out.

Homer winked at the hetaera, kissed the dice, threw them again. Eight. Philocleon dropped out.

Repeatedly the dice were thrown, one man dropping out each time, until only Homer and Lycon, who'd barely begun to grow a little fuzz on his face, remained in the game.

"He won't even know what to do with her if he wins," one of the older men groaned.

"You're right there," Hipponous said. He held out his hand and instructed Lycon to give him the dice. Reluctantly, the young man handed them over to his host.

"Let her decide who she wants," Philocleon insisted, "if you aren't going to let Lycon play."

Homer, determined to keep his promise to be courteous to Hipponous for Philocleon's sake, shook his head. It was too obvious which man the dancer would choose. He kissed the dice a last time and threw them across the table. Everyone who still could stood up to see the number.

"Eleven. He got an eleven," Philocleon yelled. He slapped Homer on the back, weaved, almost fell.

Hipponous spit on the floor for luck, shook the dice vehemently, leaned forward, and threw. He understood the odds.

Again, bodies crowded around the table.

"A three." Philocleon slapped Homer on the back again. "The best man won," he said to Hipponous, emitting a deep-throated laugh that almost sounded like a cry.

Homer stood up and held his hand out to the hetaera. She took it and together they left the dining hall. Hipponous got up too, planning to stop them, but Philocleon pushed the man next to him into his father. Hipponous fell back onto his couch not realizing what had happened. Giving Philocleon a nasty poke in the ribs, the young man quickly grabbed Hipponous' goblet and filled it with wine. "I'm sorry I bumped into you," he said, handing the goblet to Hipponous. He turned to the other guests, "To Hipponous." They raised their goblets to their host.

Hipponous struggled to his feet. "Nicias, we need more wine," he bellowed. While the goblets were filled, he started toward the door. He'd paid for the hetaera and he meant to have her.

Philocleon stepped forward as his father passed him. "Where are you going?"

"To find the hetaera I paid for."

"But Homer won her."

Hipponous looked at his son incredulously. "So what?"

"You agreed to the rules of the game. You gave your word."

"Medusa's curse on my word. I paid for the hetaera and I intend to have her." He pushed past Philocleon.

"So, as usual, your word isn't worth the shit your horses leave," Philocleon yelled after him. "You couldn't wait until my mother's ashes were cool to bed my nurse either." He felt himself starting to cry.

Hipponous stopped and stared at his son. Since when did his own flesh talk to him that way in public. He knew where that 'shit his horses left' came from. Daemones had used it often enough. "I'll break that old weasel's head in two the next time I see him," he informed Philocleon and staggered forward.

With practiced eyes the dame of the three hetaerae watched Hipponous weave toward the courtyard, reeling and tripping over couches and men. Unnoticed, she slipped around the outer edge of the couches and intercepted him. "Here, let me help." She took his arm and steered him to a couch placed near the colonnade. Gently pushing, she tried to get him to lie on it.

"Leave me alone," Hipponous snapped, pushing her away. He swayed and fell to one knee.

She helped him up onto the couch. "There, there," she soothed him, gently massaging his shoulders. "Why don't you tell me what's wrong. You look like a troubled man." She'd spent her life with men. She knew instinctively when they had something they wanted to get off their chest.

"It's that old weasel. He's been poisoning my son against me."

His tongue was so thick she could barely make out the words, but she pushed on. As long as she had him talking her young hetaera was safe. "What old weasel?" she asked.

"Calonice's father."

"Calonice?"

"My dead wife."

"What did her father tell your son?"

"How should I know?" Hipponous felt furious at her incessant questions. "I wasn't there. Now, if you'll get out of my way, I'm going to find that hetaera I paid for." He tried to stand, but couldn't. "Nicias, where are you?" he yelled.

"Look, why don't you just rest a moment. Get your breath. Then I'll find this Nicias for you." Gently, she picked his feet up and put them on the couch, then sat down on a footstool next to him and massaged his chest. "Tell me about Calonice."

Hipponous fell asleep and woke again. He sat up and looked around, trying to remember where he was. Staring at the woman on the footstool, he asked. "Who are you?"

"I am one of the hetaerae you hired to sing and dance tonight."

He looked across the room, but he couldn't focus on anything. Everything was swirling. "Get me up," he demanded. He lay down again. "I'll put a spear through that absent-minded old buzzard," he said.

"Why don't you tell me about it. You'll feel better," she encouraged him.

"I hate remembering. Remembering is for idiots like Daemones." He lay for a moment. "Bring me some wine."

The hetaera returned with a goblet filled with wine. She helped Hipponous drink. When he'd finished the wine, he grabbed the goblet out of her hand and threw it across the room. "And my own son talking to me that way. I wanted children, many children. I never remarried because Calonice begged me not to. She wanted to make certain there would be no chance of our only son's inheritance being contested. Now he criticizes me for taking some comfort in his nurse during those long dreary, lonely years. Medusa's curse on him."

He tried to get up again, but the last goblet of wine had taken its toll. His head spun so relentlessly when he sat up, he lost his balance and fell back onto the couch. "She did something, I'm certain of that," he mumbled.

"Who?" the hetaera asked.

"Bromia. I wanted to have children. Bastard sons and daughters wouldn't have had any claim to Philocleon's inheritance, but she never got pregnant. I'm sure she did something, but she denied it, even when I had her beaten."

"Where is she now?"

"I sent her away." Hipponous looked at the woman, tried to remember who she was, but couldn't. "Leave me alone," he said closing his eyes.

When the hetaera was sure Hipponous was asleep, she found a fleece and covered him. Looking around the room, she slid her hand under the fleece. Assured that no one was watching, she closed her hand tightly on the silver ring Hipponous wore on his smallest finger and pulled it off. Deftly, she dropped the ring into the pocket hidden among the folds of her peplos. Without looking back, she walked across the courtyard, outside to the carriage to wait for her hetaerae.

Four

Awakened by the insistent chirping outside his window, Nicias rolled onto his back and stretched his aching legs. Too tired to do much else, he sat up and lōoked out the window. Helios had already ridden high into the heavens. Moving slowly to the edge of the bed he watched the laundry slave's three children struggling to get a cart heaped with soiled chair coverlets down the path to the stream. Any other day he'd have gone out to help them.

Reluctantly, he dropped his feet onto the floor, stretched, rubbed his chest and head. The air was hot and heavy. Egyptus will be happy, he thought, pulling his tunic over his head. The potter maintained that pottery never turned out right unless it was as hot outside as inside the kiln.

He grabbed his sandals and made his way down the portico to the kitchen. There hadn't been time for him to eat during the banquet, and he was starved. Three slaves pushed ferociously past him at the kitchen door carrying heaping baskets of wheat loaves from the oven out back. "I'd like a loaf for myself and one for the potter," he told the first one.

"Take a look at all those mouths," the old woman muttered, pointing her thumb over her shoulder toward the courtyard. "Before long, they'll be up demanding to be fed. It'll take all the loaves we got."

"Looks like everybody who came to the banquet decided to stay," the woman following her grumbled. She handed Nicias a hot wheat loaf. "From the noise we heard, I'd say we'd best avoid Hipponous."

"Is he up?" Nicias asked, surprised. It wasn't like Hipponous to be up after a long banquet until Helios had ridden beneath the trees.

"How long have you been living here?" The woman gave him a disgusted look.

"You were talking about avoiding him," Nicias answered defensively.

"I didn't mean he was up. I'd be surprised to see him on his feet before the chickens have roosted. I meant he'll be horrible when he does get off that couch."

"Especially since we heard the poet got what the old fox wanted," someone added from the kitchen, giggling loudly.

Nicias heard a nasty slap. One of the women screamed. "Shut up. If he hears you, we'll all be whipped." It was the cook's voice.

"Leave her alone," someone else yelled.

Afraid their fighting would wake Hipponous and he'd be forced to stay in and help serve the morning meal, Nicias slipped out the back door. He looked for Egyptus as soon as he got around the corner of the house. The potter was already loading his greenware into the kiln. Nicias limped quickly across the lawn, anxious to help with the firing in spite of his exhaustion, thinking how much more interesting his life had been since Egyptus had come riding up in his cart, and announced he'd found clay on the estate and was willing to split the profits if Hipponous would let him build a kiln and sell pottery from it.

"You planning to help or sleep?" Egyptus dropped a wad of wet clay on Nicias' foot. Although Nicias had helped him unload his kilns many times, this was the first time he'd had time to help with the firing. "I've already got the kiln half loaded."

"Help," Nicias answered, embarrassed he'd been so lost in his thoughts he hadn't noticed Egyptus walk up to him. "Seems I do a lot of sleep walking lately."

"I'm not surprised." Egyptus took the wheat loaf Nicias held, dipped it in wine and gave half back to him. "You've seen the four seasons pass too many times to serve at Hipponous' banquets until Night hands the heavens over to Dawn."

"You don't have to tell me. I already know it. Maybe you could tell Hipponous," Nicias suggested going for a stack of green pots.

"Maybe I should tell him that Horus doesn't approve of how he treats you," Egyptus suggested, grinning. He took the pots Nicias handed him and walked into the kiln. "I still have to laugh when I think of Hipponous all scrunched up in the kiln." Chuckling, he stacked the pots, deftly placing fired sherds around each one to keep them from touching.

Nicias grabbed a handful of toy carts and held them inside the doorway. "I still can't believe you dared to do such a thing to Hipponous. If he ever finds out you tricked him..."

"He won't find out unless you tell him. Besides, I hear he has other things to worry about. A kitchen slave told me he got into a fight with Homer over one of the hetaerae."

"The kitchen slaves are always full of gossip. They threw dice for her and Hipponous lost."

"I wouldn't especially want to be Homer when Hipponous wakes up. I'd say he's about to be tossed off the estate."

"I don't think so."

"Are you serious? After what happened at the beekeeper's shack, and now the hetaera. Are you telling me Hipponous likes Homer?"

Nicias handed Egyptus a stack of plates. "No, I think he hates Homer. But right after Homer had recited and Hipponous saw how impressed everybody was, he announced Homer would be going on a boar hunt with him and Philocleon. I heard one of the merchants from the village say Hipponous had even hinted to him that Homer was planning to invent a verse or two about the boar hunt. I don't think Hipponous is likely to go back on his invitation now. Not after so much bragging in front of everyone."

Egyptus laughed. "So the old rooster trapped himself with his bragging. I like that."

"I wish Homer was leaving."

"Why? What have you got against the poet? He seems nice enough to me."

"I've got nothing against him. In fact, I like him and he seems to be good for Philocleon, but I'll feel a lot better when he's gone." Nicias told Egyptus about the torn sail on the Ionian ship. "I can't seem to rid myself of this feeling something terrible is about to happen."

"But what does Homer have to do with the torn sail?"

"He came from that ship."

Egyptus shrugged. "My guess is Hipponous will throw him off the estate as soon as he gets a chance and your worries will be over."

"I wish I felt as sure about that as you."

"You're a worrier by nature. I'm not."

"It's not just Homer and the ship I'm concerned about," Nicias continued thoughtfully. "Something's happened between Philocleon and Hipponous. At the banquet, Philocleon said things to Hipponous that...I've never heard him talk to Hipponous that way before."

Egyptus examined the contents of the kiln and deciding he had enough pottery for a firing, stepped through the doorway. "What did Philocleon say?"

"I was on my way to the kitchen and with the noise, I couldn't hear exactly what either of them said. It had something to do with Calonice."

"Who's she?"

"Philocleon's mother, but she's been dead for years. Anyway, it's not so much what Philocleon said that frightens me, but the bitterness and anger I could hear in his voice. I know Philocleon. Something terrible had to happen for him to act that way."

Egyptus started filling in the kiln doorway with damaged and broken pots. "Well, if I were you, I wouldn't worry too much. My guess is they'll patch things up. The one person Hipponous does seem to actually care about is Philocleon."

Nicias nodded, but he remained unconvinced.

When he had the doorway completely filled, Egyptus patched in the gaps with fresh clay. Satisfied no heat would escape, he made a small opening in the center of the filled-in doorway. "Take a look. I'll watch the fire through here."

Nicias looked through the peephole.

"I think you should come with me when I leave the estate," Egyptus said when Nicias stepped back from the peephole. "I know the idea seems sudden to you, but I've been thinking about it since you came back from the village. There are just too many strange things going on here and living under the control of that conceited rooster is no life."

"Where would I go?" It was a question Nicias had asked himself many times. "And where would I hide when Hipponous came after me?"

"Bromia is in Sparta. You could go there."

"But where would I go after that? We'd have to live, and I'm not trained in any craft."

"You've told me about your family in Argos. I could take you there."

"What happens if I don't have any family anymore?"

"We'd think of something." Egyptus opened a leather bag hanging around his waist, pulled out a scarab, pressed it into the clay above the peephole, stepped back, raised his hands and head toward the sky, "Come to us, Athena, and hold your hand over our oven."

"Why are you asking Athena?" Nicias was surprised. "Why not the Egyptian gods of your people?"

"My father was Egyptian, but my mother was Greek. I petition the gods of both people. Besides, there's no need to ask Horus' blessing. He already gave it."

Nicias shook his head. "If Hipponous ever finds out you lied about Horus, you'll be in more trouble than a bird trapped by a cat."

Egyptus shrugged and stepped up to the peephole. "Let's get started. Put some kindling into the stoke hole and start the fire. Then add wood, but not too much at first. Otherwise, we could have an explosion."

"What happens if it explodes?" Nicias asked as he walked around the kiln feeling a little frightened.

"One of the clay pots blows up and spreads itself all over the other pots, and I have to start over." Egyptus watched through the peephole until Nicias had the wood burning, then he walked around to where Nicias stood. "Will you at least think about coming away with me?"

"Yes." Nicias smiled at Egyptus, always teasing and joking and telling fantastic stories, acting like he didn't care about anything or anybody, but underneath it all, one of the most kind-hearted men ever to walk under Zeus' blue sky.

Egyptus waited for Nicias to say something more. "Is that all you have to say?"

"I'll think about it."

Egyptus returned to his peephole. "Don't think too long. I don't plan to be here forever." Silently, he implored Horus to give Nicias the wisdom to run away with him.

"Are we past the point where the pots could explode?" Nicias called around the kiln some moments later. "I wouldn't want anything to happen to the pots." The possibility that all the pottery could be destroyed worried Nicias. Egyptus had worked from the moon goddess Selene's fullness to her waning into a crescent to make them.

"I think we're all right," Egyptus answered. "And we could use more wood if it won't interfere with your sleep."

Nicias wiped the sweat from his face and chest. "It's too hot to sleep, if, by some whim of the gods, you hadn't noticed." Quickly, he pushed two large branches into the stoke hole. He'd been so busy worrying, he'd forgotten to add wood. "How's it look?"

"It won't be long," Egyptus replied, stepping back from the peephole to cool himself a little. "The fire's almost up to heat." Pushing the damp hair that had fallen onto his forehead out of his face, he returned to the peephole. A few moments later he saw the color of red he wanted. "That's it," he called to Nicias. "Let's take a rest."

By the time Nicias came around the kiln, Egyptus was already sitting in the shade. "It's a good omen when it's hot like this," he explained as he handed the wineskin to Nicias.

"Where did you ever hear that heat is a good omen for firing pottery?" Nicias sat next to Egyptus and took a drink.

Egyptus folded his hands behind his head and leaned back. "Where I heard it."

Nicias smiled. It was Egyptus' standard answer to everything.

Before long, Egyptus was grinning at Nicias. "When I was in Egypt," he said. "I saw a man make a cup like those you just put in the kiln, only you could see right through it."

"Was it made of pottery?"

"Nope." Egyptus opened the leather sack around his neck and pulled a small pouch from it. "I got these from the man who was making the cups you could see through."

Nicias opened the bag. It was filled with colored beads. He took several out and examined them. Some he could see through, others he couldn't. "I've seen beads before. Everybody has. What do they have to do with cups you can see through?"

"They were made by the same man." Egyptus grabbed the pouch out of Nicias' hand and laughed. "First he put sand, then limestone rocks ground up, then salt into a pan he had sitting over a fire. He kept stirring, and the next thing you knew there was this soft stuff in the pan. He took it out and made beads and cups."

Nicias thought a great deal before giving his usual response,

"Not possible." He folded his arms and looked at the potter. The worst thing about Egyptus was knowing for sure the man didn't make things up, except for the story about Horus he told Hipponous. No matter how outrageous his stories, they always turned out to be true, like when he told him the Egyptians buried their dead kings under mountains made as tall as the sky. At first he had doubted Egyptus, but he'd asked Philocleon, and he'd said it was true. But cups a man could see through?

Egyptus got up and looked through his peephole. "That's it," he informed Nicias. "I can add whatever wood I need from now on by myself. I won't need you until it's cool enough to take the pots out. You look tired. Why don't you go back to the house and sleep a little."

Nicias stood and started to leave, but he turned around and came back to the potter. "Cups you can see through made from rocks and sand! You've got sand in your head." He ruffled Egyptus' sweaty hair affectionately. "You'd have to have watched the spring flowers bloom a thousand times to have seen everything you claim to have seen. How many festivals have you seen anyway?"

"Enough."

"I'd say."

"Go get some sleep." Egyptus waved him away.

Nicias turned to leave, but before he'd taken a single step, Hipponous walked up to them. "I just got a message from my cousin, Merops," he growled at Nicias. "He'll be here for the boar hunt by the time Selene is full again. As if that isn't enough good news, his messenger said he's bringing his twin sons with him. I expect you to have everything ready for the hunt when he arrives. Find Philocleon and tell him to start testing the horses."

FIVE

Hipponous paced back and forth in front of the house only glancing down the trail to the main road when his back was turned to the slaves grinding thyme on the threshold. He pretended to be watching for Philocleon. No one, not even a slave was going to know he could be made to wait by his cousin, Merops.

He turned suddenly toward the house. Unnerved by his pacing, two slaves sat watching him. "What are you staring at?" he snapped.

"Nothing, Sir."

"Get back in the kitchen, both of you." He pointed at the one closest to him. "You. Bring me some wine."

Turning in the direction of the trail again, he hissed, "I should have expected as much." Merops had promised to get to the estate as soon as Dawn appeared in the sky. He still hadn't arrived and Helios had already dropped below the big shade trees.

"Here is your wine, Sir." The young slave kept her eyes firmly focused on the ground as she held out the bowl of wine.

Hipponous took the wine bowl. "Now get out of here. "With one gulp he emptied the bowl and threw it on the ground. Dealing with tradesmen might have made Merops wealthy, but it certainly hadn't taught him any manners. But then why would it? An ox couldn't be taught manners!

It was nearly impossible for Hipponous to accept that he and Merops belonged to the same clan – by anyone's standards, one of the wealthiest in Attica. For as long as the clan had existed every member had invested his wealth in land. That is, every one except Merops. Behind the backs of the other clan members, Merops had talked their great-grandfather into giving him the land that was to have been divided among all of them at the old man's death. Then he sold it and bought a ship.

When they found out, the clan members had rallied and made plans to punish Merops. But their plans had failed. The agreement was in order legally and their great-grandfather, old and feeble but still excessively proud, had supported Merops' spurious legitimacy claims.

Worse, Merops had bought his ship when the larger towns had begun establishing trading colonies. Through the kind of luck only Hermes could bring a man – no one in the clan would ever admit it could have been anything but luck – Merops had convinced a group of merchants to give him sole rights to carry their goods between the mainland and the colonies.

When the clan members heard about his trading plans, they laughed, thinking they wouldn't have to punish him after all – his own foolishness would. No one in the clan thought at the time these colonies would survive. Not only had they survived but they'd grown, both in size and in number. Merops' one ship had turned into a fleet of seven. He, a rogue who had cheated his own great-grandfather to get the price of a ship, had become the wealthiest member of the clan.

Merops' message had surprised and worried Hipponous. All it had said was Merops was interested in trading one of his ships for one of Hipponous' silver mines. He would come with his twin sons to look at the mine. Afterwards Hipponous could accompany them back to the port of Athens to inspect the ship. If they agreed on the terms, the arrangements could easily be drawn up in Athens. "By the way," Merops had ended his note, "while we are visiting, my twins would like to go on a boar hunt."

Hipponous had answered saying he'd talk, nothing else. More than any other member of the clan he'd put his faith in land. Still, it was a fact. He was not selling nearly as many horses as he had in the past. For some reason the land didn't seem to be producing as much as it had in the past either. All in all, it was the silver mines that kept things going. And two of the mines had been emptied. A ship could make the difference between remaining one of the wealthiest clan members or turning into a poor relative.

The outline of a cart in the far distance interrupted his thoughts. Determined not to let Merops find him waiting, he hurried from the house to the salt amphorae across the yard where Egyptus stood watching Nicias test the brine. "You know," the potter was saying to Nicias, "Egyptians don't cremate their dead kings. They rub their bodies with salt and incense, wrap them in linen, and bury them under those slave-made mountains of stone I was telling you about."

Before Nicias could protest the potter's latest story, the three men's attention was abruptly jerked from the two salt-filled amphorae to a cart racing toward them across the yard. Straight through the barnyard fowl it came, sending birds flying and running everywhere.

Dogs, stirred by the squawking, came suddenly from every direction. They barked and nipped savagely at the wheels of the cart and the horses' hoofs, chased and killed as many of the birds as they could reach, and sent the untethered donkeys grazing by the stable kicking and braying toward the trees.

With a loud yell, Merops brought the horses to a halt. He jumped off the cart and swaggered toward Hipponous. He might be short and fat, but he knew how to present himself. Shipping had taught him that. He grabbed Hipponous and planted sloppy kisses on both of his cheeks. "Cousin." Pursing his lips in a mocking smile, Merops pulled Hipponous toward him, stuck his fat cheek in Hipponous' face and waited for it to be kissed.

"Cousin Merops." Fighting down repulsion, Hipponous brushed Merops' cheeks lightly.

Waving his arm so the hanging fat quivered under Hipponous' nose, Merops pointed toward his twin sons sitting in the cart. "Grown a bit since you last saw them, eh?"

Born the same season he acquired his first merchant ship, he had named them Castor and Polydeuces, after the ancient twin heroes of the Argonaut expedition. A good omen, he'd told his wife, since the Argonauts Castor and Polydeuces were worshiped throughout Greece as the patron deities of seamen. He had assumed Polydeuces, like his famous namesake, would become a boxer, while Castor, wanting to emulate his famous namesake, would breed and raise horses. Instead, both became boxers. He couldn't resist bragging. "They'll be boxing for Athens at the next games in Olympia."

Hipponous sized up the twins. The winter rains had come and gone six times since he'd seen them. While they were short like their father, their training as boxers had left them taut and muscular.

There was no trace of his mushy fat on either son. As to which twin was which, it was impossible to decide, not because they had been born with exactly identical features, but because perpetual battering had reduced the features on both of their faces to almost identical precipices of scars and jagged noses.

Hipponous waved somewhat unenthusiastically and waited for the twins to get down from the cart and to come over to greet him. Neither of them moved. Arrogant just like their father, he decided, with the manners of tradesmen. But then, hadn't their aristocratic father turned into a tradesman? Fine, if they wanted to act like common tradesmen, he would treat them accordingly. They could put their own cart away. Flipping his arm in a vaguely obscene manner, he pointed toward the stable. "Put the cart behind the stable and the horses inside." He turned back toward the amphorae to examine the brine.

Grabbing the reins and whip from seat where Merops had left them, Castor lashed the horses ferociously. They bolted, galloping around the open space between the house and the stable, the cart flying behind them. On a whim, he steered them to the eastern end of the stable, straight through the pottery workshop, smashing everything sitting in the path of the horses' hoofs and the wagon wheels.

"No!" Egyptus ran toward the kiln.

"What's this? A craftsman raising his voice to an aristocrat?" Polydeuces took the reins from Castor. He turned the horses around and galloped back to the kiln. With his riding whip he sent every stack of fired pottery he could find crashing to the ground.

Hipponous stood, his mouth fallen open from shock while the cart disappeared behind the stable. Quickly the shock gave way to anger. Raging, he turned to demand an explanation from Merops, but his cousin was already walking toward the house complaining loudly that he hadn't been offered any wine after his long journey.

Merops wanted to laugh, but he didn't. It wouldn't be prudent to add blatant ridicule to the insult his sons had just delivered to Hipponous. Besides, he didn't want to distract Hipponous' anger from the problem at hand. Either he had to accept the damage the twins had done without complaining or he had to take the side of a craftsman over that of an aristocrat. Even better, aristocrats who were boxers.

Hipponous followed Merops to the house feeling more wrathful and more impotent with each step he took. By all aristocratic codes he should have already thrown all three of them off the estate. But if they went, so did his chance to recover his wealth with Merops' ship. He had no choice but to endure.

Stopping at the door intent upon reestablishing his authority, he turned to Nicias. "Wine. Now. In the courtyard," and to the stable slaves, "get to work immediately or you'll feel the sting of my whip."

Egyptus grabbed one of the branches he and Nicias had stacked for a firing and ran toward the stable as soon as it became clear Hipponous planned to do nothing to punish the twins.

"No," Nicias yelled and hobbled as quickly as he could to intercept the potter. "Don't do it. You'll just get hurt." Panting, he caught up to Egyptus and taking a firm hold on his arm, said, "Don't do it. Please. Can't you see they're the kind of men who will hurt you?"

Egyptus stopped, but he didn't put the branch down. "Let them try it again when I'm standing here with a club," he told Nicias, his deep brown eyes fierce with anger.

"Listen to me. You are no match for those two. You'll only get hurt." Nicias held Egyptus' arm until he could feel the tension wane. "Let's go back to the kiln," he said when Egyptus finally dropped the branch. Pretending he didn't see the angry tears gathering in the corners of the potter's eyes, he led him to the kiln, got him to sit down. "Stay here. I'll be back as soon as I've served the wine. We can decide what to do about the pottery then."

Hipponous called for one of the slaves to spread silk coverlets on couches for himself and Merops. Determined to observe social propriety to the utmost degree so as to not give Merops the impression he'd been upset by the incident outside, he ordered his cousin's sandals removed and his feet washed.

"Please seat yourself, my dear cousin," he said waiting for his own feet to be cleaned. Appealing silently to Zeus to give him the patience to endure, Hipponous waited for Nicias to bring the mixing bowl. If only he could get through the boar hunt without killing one of them, which was what he felt like doing at the moment, Merops and the twins would have a played out mine shaft while he would have a ship.

Taking the mixing bowl from Nicias without waiting for him to mix it with water, Hipponous filled a bowl and handed it to Merops. "My finest estate wine." He poured himself a bowl and raised it to his cousin. "May Poseidon keep the sea calm whenever your ships are sailing." Smiling, he imagined himself on the deck of his new ship, Merops standing at the bottom of an empty mine shaft. After all, any man could see if a ship was fit, but how many men could tell when a mine was no longer productive?

Merops raised his bowl, drained the wine, and handed the bowl back to Hipponous. His dear prig of a cousin looked pale. Could it be he was suffering from shock? Well, that was what happened when you were dealing with someone who didn't intend to be pushed around.

"Another wine?"

Merops accepted a second bowl. "May that celestial artist, Hephaestus, abide always in the hands of your silver craftsmen." He clinked his bowl against that of Hipponous. He chuckled to himself. If that over-stuffed phallus of a cousin wasn't so afraid to lower himself and talk with tradesmen he might have learned all the trade agreements he'd made with the colonies had been bartered away from him by Phoenician traders. The ship's only function by fall would be dragging Hipponous' goats down from the mountains along his ditch.

Nicias refilled both drinking bowls. "To the boar hunt." Hipponous clinked his bowl against that of Merops' and drank it down immediately. Becoming the wealthiest member of the clan had certainly made Merops arrogant. Too bad this contest wouldn't be won by wealth, but by brains, a word that was undoubtedly as foreign to Merops as the language of the Egyptians.

"To the boar hunt," Merops returned, lifting his bowl. His dear cousin looked so smug. Perhaps it would be wise to remind him they were both old men. It would be up to their sons to decide the fates of their families. And what about Philocleon? Was the boy tough like his father? "I haven't seen Philocleon," he informed Hipponous, smiling maliciously. "Is he here? I'm so anxious to learn whether he has grown into a strong young man after his father."

"He'll be here soon."

"My sons aren't a thing like me." Merops faked a disgruntled sigh. "They are both terribly mean."

So that was the reason for the boar hunt. They were planning to test Philocleon. "Philocleon has grown, too," Hipponous assured Merops. "Right now he is in the mountains with one of the finest poets in the Aegean." It was his turn to brag. "Not that you, busy with your tradesmen, would ever have time for poets."

"I find pedants more interesting personally." Especially, Merops laughed to himself, the one who had told him there was a movement about to turn silver into trade pieces which would no doubt make the silver mine he was getting even more valuable. "But I'm certain you would have no interest in the prattle of pedants."

"You're quite right. I would not." Hipponous was beginning to feel the wine. "I don't suppose you're hungry?" He examined his cousin's big belly and snickered sarcastically.

"As a matter of fact, I am." Lifting himself slightly from the couch, Merops released a torrent of gas built up from his last meal, spilling wine on the expensive silk coverlet below him in the process. He settled back down and smiled at his cousin.

Hipponous smiled in return though he was seething with fury. He poured more wine. He would not be forced to lose his temper.

Merops took another bowl of wine from Nicias.

Catching his breath when the stink got to him, Hipponous snapped at Nicias. "Get us something to eat."

Nicias hurried to the kitchen and returned with fruit, grout, and cheese. He put it on tables in front of the two men and refilled their wine bowls again.

"Please." Hipponous gestured toward the food and turned to again Nicias, "Tell one of the slaves to set up tables for the twins and Philocleon and Homer." He took a chunk of cheese. Wouldn't Merops be surprised if he knew Philocleon was taking reading lessons. It hadn't been easy with so few men around who could read. But, thanks to his finding the Assyrian tutors, Philocleon would soon join those few men in Greece who were literate. With Philocleon's knowledge of reading and geography and his cunning, their wealth would soon surpass that of everyone in the clan. "To our sons." He held his bowl up to Merops.

Nicias motioned for one of the other slaves to watch over the food and wine as soon as he had filled the drinking bowls yet another time. He hurried out to the kiln and without saying anything dropped to his knees next to Egyptus who sat on the ground aimlessly picking up the broken pottery.

"I'm putting the clay that can be reused over there." Egyptus pointed unenthusiastically at a heap of damaged greenware near his workbench. "The fired fragments can go in a pile near the kiln door. All they're good for now is filling in the doorway." He picked up what was left of a misshapen pot he'd spent a full day making. "Remember this one?"

Nicias nodded, smiling in spite of the sadness he felt. Who could forget that pot? Egyptus had made it on a wager with Philocleon when Hipponous was in the village. Philocleon had watched Egyptus roll a huge stack of wet clay into long coils like he always did. Then, he'd bet the potter he couldn't roll twenty-five coils onto a single pot. Before it was all over, almost every slave on the estate had joined the betting. Egyptus had won the wager, but the pot had ended being one of the strangest shapes ever made.

Egyptus threw what was left of the pot on the pile. "I worked from Selene's fullness to her waning to her fullness again to make that pottery. Now it's all destroyed." He got up and threw the sherds on the pile. Sighing he sat on the ground in front of the kiln.

Nicias moved over next to him. "As soon as I get back from the boar hunt, we'll make another batch."

"Maybe and maybe not." Egyptus opened the sack hanging on his waist and pulled out the pouch full of beads he'd shown Nicias when they'd fired the pottery. He searched through the beads until he found a bright yellow one. "The man who made this bead told me it would protect whoever wore it from harm. I want you to take it with you on the boar hunt. Those twins are evil." He found a leather ribbon, threaded the bead through it and gave it to Nicias.

Nicias slipped the leather strap over his head and slid the bead underneath his tunic. He rubbed the bead through his tunic, his stomach churning. He'd never seen Hipponous so agitated. What was it all about? "I'd better go back to the house," he said. "Hipponous will want me soon." As he stood, he could see the twins entering the door, laughing and joking.

When Homer and Philocleon got back from the pastures, Hipponous, Merops, and the twins had already emptied a mixing bowl of wine. Nicias mixed another, filled two wine bowls and handed them to Philocleon and Homer.

"Sit over here, Philocleon." Merops tapped the empty couch next to him. "We were just listening to my Castor describe a boxing match he had at Thebes last summer."

Philocleon listened to Castor's grisly account for a few moments before he glanced at Homer, grimacing to let him know how disgusted he felt. Homer in turn rolled his eyes toward the courtyard to indicate he wanted to get away as soon as possible. Since the banquet, they'd totally avoided Hipponous by staying out in the pastures testing the horses. They had come in for the evening meal because Hipponous had sent word he wanted them. All they'd been able to find out was that Merops had arrived and there had been some sort of a fiendish exchange out at the pottery kiln.

When Nicias left the dining hall, Philocleon, saying something about talking to the cooks, followed him. As soon as they got out of hearing distance he asked Nicias what had happened. Nicias told him briefly.

"Had Egyptus said something he shouldn't have to them? You know how he is, always carrying on with those crazy stories of his."

"He was with me over by the salt amphorae. He never said a word. For that matter, neither did they, not even to your father. When he told them to put the horses and cart out behind the stable, they went mad."

"What did father do?"

"Nothing." Nicias paused. It wasn't right, talking to Philocleon about Hipponous, but the thought of Egyptus out there picking up the pottery sherds made him less concerned about what was right than he'd ever been in his life. "Your father watched without saying anything. Afterwards, he followed Merops to the house and has been drinking with him and the twins ever since."

Philocleon knew something about the business deal that was to take place after the boar hunt. He also guessed from some of the things Hipponous had said that his father did not expect the arrangement to be an equal one. All at once, his grandfather's words in the crypt came back to him. Whether you want to believe it or not, your father would sell or use anybody if he could gain from it. Was it for his own gain his father had let them destroy all of Egyptus' pottery?

"You'd better go back into the hall." Nicias moved away toward the kitchen. "Everyone's very nervous."

"I'm going, but see to it the cook makes something special for Egyptus. And tell him I'll pay for the pottery."

Nicias nodded and disappeared into the kitchen. Philocleon went back into the dining hall. Waiting impatiently for a break in Castor's unbearably long, bloodthirsty story, he watched his father, wondering, what kind of a man he was.

Hipponous watched his son as he was being watched by him, feeling totally betrayed. While he labored through an evening with these insufferable relatives for Philocleon's sake...after all, who was going to benefit from owning the ship if not his son...the same son who gossiped with slaves behind his back. No doubt criticizing and ridiculing him.

Nicias ordered the cook to send out grout, salted fish, and more cheese and fruit. Hipponous poured a libation to Artemis and spread barley around in her honor when the food came. He hoped the goddess hadn't noticed they'd been eating for some time before he'd gotten around to the libation. "That ox of a cousin even makes me forget the gods and goddesses," he lamented to Artemis under his breath.

Merops ate as much as the others combined, sucking the food with his lips in imitation of the lower classes, feigning innocence whenever Hipponous glanced disapprovingly. Finishing, he turned to Homer. "I have been told by our fine host you are one of the greatest poets in the Aegean. I wonder if you would honor us with the tale of the Calydonian boar hunt. I heard it in Athens for the first time just a short time ago." He smirked at Hipponous as if to say, you see how genteel I can be, just like the rest of you aristocrats.

Castor rubbed his greasy fingers through his coarse black hair. "Tell me uncle, isn't the Calydonian boar hunt the story of one relative taking justified revenge on another?" He filled his wine bowl again, chuckling aloud at the reaction he'd gotten from Hipponous. Immediately he began considering what else he might do to aggravate his uncle.

"Don't forget the revenge Artemis took on the king when she wasn't treated properly." Merops hadn't missed the fact that Hipponous had forgotten to sacrifice earlier. He knew his cousin's meticulous attention to the gods.

Hipponous turned to Homer, "Please do honor us. It is one of my favorites." To Merops, "More food?" Merops would learn about revenge when he discovered too late how empty his silver mine was, he reminded himself. Silently, he vowed a sacrifice for Artemis every day until the rains came if only she would overlook his indiscretion.

Homer hated the epic of the Calydonian boar hunt. He'd never been able to understand why any man would want to hear the saga of how a great and glorious hero like Meleager ended up dying an inglorious death. Still, considering the tension so evident between Hipponous and Merops he decided he wouldn't refuse, as he usually did, to sing it.

Indicating with a sideways glance at Philocleon how he felt, he took the lyre a slave held out to him and began, calling earnestly for the muse, Calliope. When he could feel her sweet presence filling him with the excitement that always came before he was to recite, he began, waiting to see which of the three Calydonian boar hunt legends he had memorized the muse would bring to him that night. It didn't surprise him that she chose the most violent version.

"There once lived in the kingdom of Calydon a king and a queen. When their son, Meleager, was born, the queen was visited by the three Destinies. They told her the life of her child would last no longer than a branch she had burning in her hearth. The queen seized the branch and put out the fire. By keeping the branch from being burned, she got Meleager from childhood to manhood.

"Later, when the king was sacrificing, he neglected the goddess Artemis. Furious, the goddess sent a ravenous wild boar to Calydon. It did so much damage, it finally had to be killed. Meleager organized a hunting party to kill it, including not only such great heroes as Nestor, Peleus, Jason, and Theseus, but also the beautiful Atalanta, daughter of the king of Arcadia.

"The hunting party searched until they found the boar in its lair. But the boar was not to be easily killed. It charged them, chasing Nestor up a tree, running others down. Everyone tried to spear him, but they all failed until Atalanta shot an arrow. Though she didn't kill the boar, she wounded him.

"Much later, when Meleager had succeeded in killing the boar, he gave the head and skin to Atalanta as a trophy for being the first to wound the animal. Sadly, his mother's brothers, angry that he'd given the trophy to Atalanta, took it away from her. Furious, Meleager killed them both.

"When Meleager's mother learned of what he had done, she took the branch she had saved all those years and threw it back into the fire. Meleager was consumed with fire. He died asking why this was happening to him, but even more so, lamenting the inglorious death forced upon him."

Polydeuces clinked his bowl against that of Hipponous as soon as Homer stopped singing. "Here's to poking old bores in the spleen," he said, watching out of the corner of his eye, his father's pleasure with his remark.

Hipponous, determined to let the twins and Merops think they had the upper hand that he might make a better bargain in the end, did not reply but called to Nicias to bring in more wine and water and fill the mixing bowl a third time. He drank his wine and filled his bowl again. Merops did likewise twice more, after which he promptly fell to snoring.

While Nicias stood mixing the last of the wine and water, Castor took a pair of dice out of his girdle. He'd seen how pleased Merops was with Polydeuces spleen-poking remark and he was determined to better his brother. "High man in three throws gets the old slave for the night." He reached over and pinched Nicias' buttocks with one hand and threw the dice with the other. "He looks like he's good for at least one night."

Nicias looked up at Castor in surprise. Realizing the man was serious, he stepped back in horror. Panic overwhelmed him. What could he do? Run? How? He stared at his mutilated foot. His hand went to the bead beneath his tunic.

Philocleon, equally horrified, looked at Hipponous. His grandfather's words raced through his mind. "He'd use or sell anybody."

Polydeuces laughed, his mouth with its missing teeth wide open. He held the dice in the air, threw them on the table. "Eight. That beats your five." He put the dice on the table in front of Homer.

Homer didn't move.

"Not much of a contest here." Castor picked up the dice again and threw them. "Nine. Top that." He handed the dice back to his brother thoroughly enjoying himself. His plan had worked. It was obvious Hipponous was furious.

Philocleon, who had waited quietly for Hipponous to say something, finally lost his patience. "Father, aren't you going to put a stop to this?"

Well aware the situation was rapidly deteriorating, Hipponous snapped back, "Are you telling me what to do in my own house?"

Afraid any outburst on his part would end up being taken out on Homer, Philocleon quenched his anger. He stared at his father but said nothing.

Hipponous had already been pondering the consequences of stopping the dice game when Philocleon spoke up. This is not the moment to risk a major confrontation, he decided. He needed the ship. "There's no harm in a little fun," he shrugged at Philocleon. "Besides, he's only a slave."

"He isn't a slave. He is Nicias," Philocleon insisted.

"He's a slave."

"Grandfather was right. You would sell or use anyone if it suits your needs," Philocleon yelled, standing, his determination to remain silent overcome by frustration and anger.

"Fortunately for you," Hipponous whispered under his breath. "I'm not interested in what your grandfather thinks. Otherwise, I would teach you some respect for your father this evening."

Castor winked and put the dice on the table for Polydeuces.

Surprising both the twins, Philocleon grabbed the dice and tossed them into the fire. "He's my slave and not up for grabs." His voice sounded much calmer than he felt.

Polydeuces staggered to his feet, grabbed Philocleon by the tunic and pushed him toward the hearth. "We'll just see if you are as good at fetching dice out of hot embers as you are at throwing them in."

Homer, pretending to be quite drunk, stood up and staggered across the floor toward the colonnade. In his mind, he and Philocleon had become as inseparable as Achilles and Patroclus. Prepared to protect Philocleon, as he knew Achilles and Patroclus would have protected one another, he grabbed a spear out of the holder standing next to one of the slender columns. Turning, he said in a voice edged with iron, "Let go of him." He walked over and poked his spear into the face of Polydeuces.

Polydeuces dropped Philocleon's tunic, but as he stepped back, Castor lunged forward and punched Philocleon in the mouth, sending him flying backwards across a table.

Hipponous winced. "That's enough. Put the spear back and get some sleep." He was angry. But the boy needed some toughening up if he was going to handle these two. And he wasn't hurt.

Both twins stood, feet apart, fists clenched, and glared at Hipponous. He glared back. At last, Castor turned and went back to his couch. Polydeuces, shaking his fist, walked over and stood over Philocleon. "One day, we'll show you what we do to people who interfere in our business." He kicked Philocleon in the ribs.

Homer pushed the spear he held against Polydeuces' chest. "I'll run you through if you make another move."

Hipponous tried to stand. Too drunk, he fell back against the chair. "I told you to stop," he yelled. Forgetting about the ship in his concern for his son, he threw his wine bowl at Polydeuces. It smashed into the twin's head, the fine silver edge making a deep cut in Polydeuces' face.

Merops, awake again, understood the danger his sons didn't. Castor and Polydeuces had never seen Hipponous in a rage. "It's enough," he ordered, motioning Polydeuces back to his couch. Finding a half-empty bowl, Merops filled it and handed it to Hipponous.

As Polydeuces turned and walked toward his couch, Philocleon scrambled to his feet. Grabbing the spear from Homer, he smashed it down on his cousin's shoulder, drawing blood.

Polydeuces turned, but before he could move, Castor was up, holding him back. He pulled his brother to his couch, poured him another bowl of wine.

"Nobody hits me from behind and gets away with it," Polydeuces told Philocleon. He threw the wine in the fire.

Homer took the spear back from Philocleon and waited to see what Polydeuces would do. Convinced the danger had passed when Polydeuces didn't come after Philocleon, he lowered the spear and taking Philocleon by the elbow, pulled him toward the courtyard. "Come with us," he said to Nicias. "You'll be safe in Philocleon's room."

Dropping on the bed in his room, Philocleon finally spoke. "Mad. Both of them."

Nicias said nothing, but he agreed.

Homer examined Philocleon' lip. "The cut doesn't look too deep." His hands still shaking from the encounter, he took a fresh cloth from the rack above the terracotta tub in the corner and handed it to Philocleon. "Do you think they'll come after us?"

"I don't know."

"We're better off if we all stay together, don't you think?"

Philocleon nodded.

Homer had Nicias make up beds for the two of them on the floor while he slipped back to the dining hall. Both of the twins had fallen asleep. He returned to Philocleon's room. "They're sleeping," he said, dropping onto his bed, the spear within reach.

Nicias went to bed next to Homer. But when the heavy breathing of the two other men filled the room, he was still wide awake, listening.

Six

His cart already loaded, Egyptus waited for Dawn and the appearance of Nicias. As usual, the first rays of her light brought his friend to the threshold of the front door. Egyptus waved and spurred his donkeys forward. Stopping the cart some distance from the house to make certain they couldn't be overheard, he waited for Nicias.

"Are you all right?" He got off his cart when Nicias reached it and looked him over carefully. "I heard about it from the house slaves. Someone should take a bow to those venomous twins."

"I'm fine," Nicias lied. "Just a little stiff from spending the night on the floor." Resting his left hand on the cart for balance, he stretched his right foot up and down and back and forth. After a long silence, he put his foot back on the ground. "You're leaving, aren't you?"

Egyptus nodded.

"I thought you would." Nicias fought against the oppressive sadness he was feeling. He'd known from the first that Egyptus wouldn't stay forever, but why did he have to leave this way?

"I'm only here now because I've been waiting for you." Egyptus took a deep breath. "Come with me. I've been thinking. If you don't have any family left in Argos, you could work with me. We'd never be rich, but we'd earn enough to get along. And you wouldn't have to put up with this." He flipped his hand angrily toward the house.

"Do you really believe Hipponous would just let me leave?" Nicias asked, shocked at Egyptus' innocence. "You forget, I'm a slave, not a free man like you."

"Hipponous won't be up for hours. We could be halfway down

the mountain before he even figured out you were missing."

"Yes, but we would be traveling in a small cart pulled by two donkeys. Hipponous owns the finest horses in Attica. He'd overtake us within a half day."

"We could ride out a little, hide, and wait. After he got tired of looking, we'd leave."

"Where would we hide? The land all around us is owned by friends and relatives of Hipponous. The first man who recognized me would take us captive himself and return us to the estate."

"Risk or not. You can't stay. Not after the way that fiend let the twins treat you." Egyptus set his jaw firmly. He was determined to convince Nicias to run away with him.

"I don't understand it." Nicias looked toward the house. "I've been here since I was a child. This is the first time he's permitted anyone to mistreat me. I'm not saying it's been easy to be his slave. He's demanding, most times totally unreasonable, but never has he laid a hand on me or let anyone else."

"It's the ship he's getting. He struts around the estate like some prize rooster, ordering everyone around. Screaming. Yelling. Talking endlessly about how wealthy he'll be when his first ship comes in."

Nicias sighed. "He's been arrogant since he was a child. But there's something desperate about his arrogance now. It scares me."

"It scares me too. Come with me."

"I can't. The risk for you would be too great."

"I'm willing to take the risk."

"You have no idea what you're saying. After Calonice's funeral, I heard Hipponous out in the courtyard under the mantle of Night. He was bent over in front of the altar of Zeus making one of the most painful cries I've ever heard. After he'd cried for a long while, he stood and swore an oath to take the vengeance of death on anyone who ever tried to take someone from him against his will."

"But Calonice died. Her destiny was decided by the Fates."

"He knew that. I think it was knowing he had no power to change her destiny that made him so angry. He kept moaning about not being able to accept his helplessness against the Fates." Nicias shuddered. "If he ever turned that anger against another man..." He shook his head. "No. I could never let you take that kind of a risk for my sake."

From the frightened tone of Nicias' voice, Egyptus knew he

wasn't going to run away with him. "But what about you? What will happen to you?" he asked, still worried.

"I considered my future carefully while I was lying awake fearing the twins would come to Philocleon's room and take me against my will. My mind is made up. After what happened, I won't stay here. But I need to wait until my leaving won't endanger anyone else."

Egyptus waited for a long while, hoping Nicias would change his mind. Finally he went to the back of the cart and pulled a broken sherd out of his sack. He scratched his name-sign on the sherd and handed it to Nicias. "This is my name. When you get to Sparta…you will look for Bromia, won't you?"

Nicias nodded.

"Take this sherd to the marketplace and show it to the merchants. Someone who recognizes the name will direct you to the shop owned by my uncle Ti. Give him the sherd. He'll find you a place to sleep and give you food until I pass through. When I get there, we'll go to Argos together to find your family."

Nicias took the sherd and looked at it. "How am I supposed to find somebody who can read this?"

Egyptus grinned. "It's the best I can do. I really don't have time to learn how to write Greek before I leave."

Laughing in spite of himself, Nicias hugged Egyptus "I'll miss you."

Egyptus hugged him back. "Promise me you'll come to Sparta."

"I promise." Nicias held the sherd tightly in his hand. "In the meantime, you take care of yourself."

Egyptus climbed onto his cart, snapped his whip and, dropping his wide-brimmed traveling hat on his head, started down the steep path to the main road. At the bottom of the first hill, he turned and waved, whispering an entreaty, "Dear Horus, please give him the wisdom to leave before it's too late."

Nicias hurried to the stable the moment Egyptus went out of sight. The wagons and horses needed to be loaded when Hipponous got up. If Hipponous had to wait around, he might decide to examine the damage at the kiln and discover Egyptus had run out on their agreement.

Before the hawk following Egyptus had circled his wagon and returned to her nest, Nicias had the wagons loaded with bedding, food, and kitchen supplies. He told one of the stable slaves to drive them to the house to wait while he supervised the bridling of the horses the men would ride.

Philocleon and Homer came out of the house first, carrying spears, nets and traveling sacks. They threw their gear into Hipponous' wagon and sat down, prepared to protect Nicias if he needed it. Not much later, Merops wandered out looking like he'd been to the Underworld of Hades and back. Hipponous followed. He loaded his spears and sack into his wagon, mounted his horse and rode over to Merops. "Get the twins."

Merops weighed the advantages and disadvantages of refusing to obey Hipponous. The twins had pushed Hipponous too hard. He'd told them to keep the old prick worried about his son, but he'd never dreamt they'd actually try to hurt Philocleon. From the bitter look in Hipponous' eyes, it was clear their attack had cost Merops his advantage. Better to try to alleviate some of the friction and wait for another opportunity. He got off the wagon and went back into the house.

Hipponous felt certain he'd gained control of the situation once again as soon as Merops returned to the house for the twins without arguing. Determined to push his advantage, he led the group to the northeast as soon as Merops returned with the twins, refusing to speak to any of them, concentrating instead on sending his dogs to savagely kill every small animal they saw along the path.

At the end of a long, silent journey, they finally reached the edge of the forest. Hipponous ordered Philocleon to supervise setting up their camp. Though Philocleon was close to hating his father, the idea of disobeying him hadn't yet occurred to him. Leaving Homer to keep an eye on the twins, he had the slaves build oval shelters out of branches, small ones for each of the hunters, a large one for the slaves. At the same time, Nicias made beds of branches covered with rugs. Hunters and slaves alike fell onto their beds and slept as soon as they were finished.

Hipponous slept little and was up the moment the rosy-fingers of Dawn opened the heavens. He wanted the hunt over with and there was only one way to do that. He woke Merops. "Let's go out and see if there's anything to hunt here." Feeling better after a good sleep, Merops got up and tied on his sandals. Pulling his tunic over his fat belly, he followed Hipponous over to the horses, grinning inwardly. It had occurred to him as he fell asleep that Hipponous would never have agreed to this hunt after what had happened if he weren't desperate.

In the forest the two men sniffed for the distinctive scent of wild pig and, with practiced eyes, searched for evidence of habitation. It only took a short ride. Convinced by both their eyes and their noses there were wild boars in the vicinity, they returned to camp.

"Philocleon and Homer will hunt with me. You can take the twins." Hipponous had no intention of turning his back to either of the twins.

Merops agreed. It would give him a chance to plan.

They woke Philocleon and Homer and the twins. The young men came out of their shelters and joined Hipponous. Silently all six men flexed their spears, examining the shafts for flaws. As each was convinced of the strength of his spear, he mounted his horse and rode it around in a circle, limbering its legs for the hunt. Afterwards they dismounted. Hipponous purified his hands with water and poured a libation to Artemis, promising to dedicate the best pieces of the thigh to her if they succeeded in killing a boar.

"We'll take the northern section of the forest," Hipponous announced as he mounted Pegasus and rode off. Philocleon followed Hipponous into the forest. Close behind he could hear the hoofs of Homer's stallion. He smiled to himself. Hipponous had bragged incessantly about Homer's hunting prowess at the banquet. On their way to the forest, Homer had confessed to him he'd never even been on a boar hunt.

A short way into the forest, the dogs raced past Hipponous barking wildly. They circled a cluster of bushes and waited for the hunters. Suddenly, several small pigs and a full-sized boar raced out of the underbrush. The pigs scattered but the boar, bristles raised menacingly on his back, halted abruptly at the edge of the bush, grunted, and charged the lead dog Wolf. With a sweep of his head, he caught Wolf with one of his tusks and sent him howling to his death. Frightened, the other dogs backed away just long enough for the boar to dart past them into the forest.

All three hunters took up the chase. In spite of the animal's wily dodging and darting in and out of bushes and brush for cover, they managed to stay with him. Then, unexpectedly, he slipped into a ravine and raced down it toward the deepest part of the forest.

Philocleon was the first of the three to reach the ravine. Taken in by the excitement of the chase, he whooped and jumped his mare over the bank of the ravine, plunging his spear forward as he went. A poor stick, it barely touched the neck of the boar. He pulled it back for a second thrust but his mare, missing solid footing on her landing, fell to her knees, sending him flying forward.

Homer jumped his stallion into the ravine between Philocleon and the boar as soon as he saw Philocleon fall, not sure what to do except get himself between Philocleon and the boar. Shaking all over, he prepared his spear to defend, but the boar turned and tore down the ravine in the opposite direction instead.

Hipponous, in turn, jumped Pegasus into the ravine. He raced past Homer and Philocleon, continuing the chase. He could tell from the boar's drooping tail the animal was getting tired. He increased Pegasus' speed, planning to run past the animal and stick his spear in the back of its neck as he passed. As he overtook the boar, the animal surprised him yet another time. It jinked and raced up the side of the ravine. Halfway up the bank, it jumped to the top and, too fatigued to run farther, darted into a bush and prepared to fight.

Homer pulled Philocleon to his feet and helped him back onto his mare. "He's yours." He held onto Philocleon's mare until Philocleon pulled himself together. Then he got back onto his stallion. "Keep your spear ready."

Both men rode up the side of the ravine. At the top they found Hipponous. "He's in there." Hipponous pointed to the bush. "Chase him out."

"I think Philocleon should be the one to get him," Homer said, riding up next to Hipponous. "He made the first stick."

Before Hipponous could tell Homer to mind his own business and order Philocleon to chase the boar out, the animal charged again, straight at Philocleon. His mare, jittered by his nervous reaction, reared. He grabbed her mane instinctively and brought her back down.

"You have to charge him," Homer yelled.

The boar, stopping when the mare reared, charged again. Overcoming his fear, Philocleon tightened his grip on his spear and returned the boar's charge with one of his own. When he got to the boar, he moved his mare to one side. Racing past the animal, he plunged his spear deep into the back of its neck.

"You got him." It was Homer's excited voice.

The boar made one last attempt to run for cover, but before he got more than a few steps, he fell. Blood running down both sides of his neck, he pawed to get back on his feet, snorted, and fell to the ground, dead.

Getting off his mare, Philocleon fought back an impulse to throw up. He walked over and with hands shaking so that they could barely grip, drew his knife. Looking at the boar, which was much smaller than he had imagined when they were chasing it, he tried to take the trophy, but his hands were shaking so badly, he couldn't make the first cut. Soon Homer was beside him, slapping him on the back, congratulating him. Seeing Philocleon's shaking hand, he took the knife from him and cut the head off the boar.

Hipponous jumped off his horse as Homer held up the trophy. He was still angry that Homer had interfered with his instructions to Philocleon on the hunt, but he would tend to that later. For now, he was terribly proud of his son and extremely anxious to get back to see how the twins had fared. "Let's see if Merops and the twins can come up with something better than this, " he said to Philocleon, taking the trophy from Homer.

At the edge of the camp, Hipponous handed Nicias the trophy and ordered him to take two of the other slaves out to cut up the boar and haul it back to the campsite. With his eyes Nicias congratulated Philocleon, but he said nothing.

Hipponous slapped his hip gleefully. "Now let us see what Merops and the twins have killed, if anything." They found Merops with Castor and Polydeuces deep in the forest stirring up a nest of pigs. A small boar raced out of the nest. The three men went after him. Polydeuces quickly rode up beside the animal, but as he sent his spear down, the boar jinked and he missed. Swiftly, Castor came up from the other side. His thrust was strong, but not quite in the right place. The boar continued to run, though slowed by the blood he was losing. Merops took his turn, smashing the boar over the head with a club. The animal staggered and fell.

Merops' slaves were called to take their boar back to the campsite. Waiting for Nicias to prepare the thighs for sacrifice to Artemis, Hipponous described Philocleon's dangerous kill for Merops and the twins, conveniently leaving out the fact that Philocleon had missed on his first attempt to stick the boar. "Bring out your trophy," he said to Philocleon.

When Philocleon placed the head of his boar next to that killed by Merops and the twins, the difference in size was striking. "I knew you had killed a big boar." Hipponous patted his son on the back smiling sarcastically at Merops. "But I really had no idea how big until now when I see it next to this little piglet it took all three of them to kill." With his sandal, he poked at the smaller boar's head.

Watching Merops and Hipponous, Homer decided the tension growing between the two men would probably lead to another confrontation. Determined not to be a part of it, he moved toward his shelter. "I'm going to sharpen my spear point for tomorrow."

"I'll come with you." Philocleon followed him away from the campfire.

"The spear must have gone in that far." Hipponous held his hands apart in front of him. "Philocleon could easily kill anything that got in his way." He looked menacingly at Merops. "It's fortunate he is not easily angered."

Merops acted impressed. Philocleon's pale face told him the kill hadn't been as easy as Hipponous claimed. He simply wasn't as tough as his father, not yet anyway. "You say he killed that boar by himself?"

"That's what I said." Hipponous passed the wineskin to Merops.

"I think my twins could learn from him."

"I'm sure they could."

"Good. Then, I say the three of them should ride together on the next hunt."

Castor laughed and rubbed his hands together. "Good idea. What do you say, brother?"

"Suits me just fine." Polydeuces grinned at Hipponous.

Hipponous, realizing too late he had fallen into a trap, cursed under his breath. He appraised the twins. How capable were they of treachery? Would they go so far as to kill one of their own clansmen? He simply didn't know.

"Who knows." Merops grinned an open mouth grin. "He might even learn a lesson or two from my twins." He could see he had struck the right chord. Hipponous was afraid Philocleon couldn't take care of himself.

"Could be." Hipponous took another long drink of wine. Thinking. Stalling. "There is one problem though."

"What's that?" Polydeuces asked, driving his spear into the head of Philocleon's boar while grinning wickedly at Hipponous.

"With three men chasing a boar, how will we know who actually killed it?" Hipponous faced Polydeuces, hating his smirking face.

"We'll know by whose spear is sticking into the boar." Polydeuces pulled his spear from the boar's head and dripped the blood conspicuously near Hipponous' feet.

"What if there are two spears in the boar? How will we know which one went into it first or which one killed it?"

"We'll ask the boys," Merops said, thoroughly enjoying the squirming.

"How will they know? It's difficult to remember in the heat of the chase," Hipponous scoffed. "We'll need someone to watch."

Merops, in his turn, took a long drink of wine. "If they can't remember, they keep hunting until one of them kills a boar outright. Okay boys?"

"Right," they answered in unison.

Hipponous took another drink. How could he have been so stupid as to let Merops trap him so easily? He raised the wineskin. "To the hunt."

"To the hunt."

As the wineskin went around again, Nicias informed them the meat was ready for roasting. Hipponous stood. "Call Homer and Philocleon." He motioned to Merops to get up.

Hipponous put the thighs for Artemis over the spit, then spread barley in her honor while Merops put meat for their meal to roast and Philocleon mixed water and wine.

At Hipponous' insistence, all six men feasted on Philocleon's boar, together with the other foods brought from the estate. Throughout the meal, Merops and the twins chattered incessantly about a feud they'd had with another ship owner which they'd concluded by stringing the man up on his own ship. The story wasn't true, but Merops could see Hipponous believed it.

Unable to endure listening to them any longer, Hipponous abruptly interrupted Merops, turning to Homer. "I want to hear the story of the death of the great Trojan hero, Hector."

"I'm sorry." Homer looked directly into Hipponous' eyes. "The muse, Calliope, isn't with me." He had no intention of reciting for this group ever again.

Hipponous glared angrily at Homer, all the hostility and frustration he felt toward Merops and his twins suddenly turning into hatred for the poet. "You have treated me with insolence often enough," he said. "I told you to recite."

Homer refused. "I can't recite when the muse isn't with me." He excused himself and went to his shelter, making preparations as soon as he got there to leave Hipponous' estate. His experience since coming home with Philocleon convinced him Hipponous was dangerous.

Every bit as determined as Homer to avoid spending another night with Merops and the twins, Philocleon made his excuse to Hipponous and left the fire. He went to his shelter and threw himself on his bed, falling asleep almost immediately. Much later, he woke groaning aloud over a terrible dream. Sweat pouring from his body onto the bed, he lay for some time listening to see if he'd awakened anyone. Finally convinced no one was awake, he got up and went outside, planning to relieve himself. Much to his amazement, he found Nicias sitting by the fire fingering a bright yellow bead. Not far away his traveling sack sat propped against a tree.

"Have my cousins been bothering you again?" Philocleon asked, sitting next to Nicias.

"No."

Philocleon watched the fire intently. "Remember when I was a boy, how I used to have that dream of falling out of a tree and I'd wake up screaming?"

"Yes. Did you have a bad dream? I heard you groaning."

"I had a terrible dream. I had gone hunting with Atalanta. She killed a boar and I gave her the trophy. Then suddenly, she disappeared and I was being charged by a wild boar just like this morning. I called for help and my cousin Polydeuces came with a club, but instead of helping me kill the boar, he came after me with his club. I tried to run, but my feet wouldn't move. I kept trying and trying and I couldn't move. Just as Polydeuces was ready to club me, I woke up."

"It's pretty frightening killing your first boar."

"Do you think that's why I had that dream?"

"Yes." Nicias didn't know why he'd had the dream, and he didn't like what it suggested.

Philocleon could see Nicias was dressed for riding. He started to ask him when he planned to run, but before he got the chance,

Merops came out of his shelter complaining it was too hot to sleep inside. He wandered over and lay on the ground under a tree.

Philocleon waited for the deep breathing that would indicate Merops had fallen asleep. When it never came, he took a deep breath, looked around and, trying to make it seem like he was having a conversation of no consequence with Nicias said quietly, "You know, Homer and I tested all the horses pretty thoroughly. If I were to take one of them, it'd be the stallion Homer is riding. He's fast and surefooted. In a chase, he'd hold his own." By the time he'd finished his breath was coming in short gasps. He didn't know what his father would do to him if he found out he'd helped Nicias escape. But he knew he was willing to take the risk.

He waited, listening for any movement from Merops. There was none. Still, his uncle's breathing hadn't taken on the evenness of deep sleep either. Sweat gathered again on his entire body.

Moving closer to Nicias, Philocleon pulled a branch out of the fire and sketched the outline of Greece in the dirt. He put an x on the map. "We must be about here." Going over the locations of cities on Na'id-Assur's map in his mind, he scratched a second x on the map. "I'd say a man riding west and then south would reach Argos after Helios had ridden across the sky around eight times." Working carefully, he scratched cross-hatching over a large area. "I'd guess if a man stayed in these parts, he'd be in very thick forest for the first part of his journey. I'd sure hate to look for someone in those trees."

Nicias studied the map carefully. "Where would you say Sparta is?"

"Sparta?" Philocleon was surprised. Hadn't Nicias told him he was from Argos? He put a third x on the map. "Here."

As he pointed, Hipponous came out of his shelter. "I heard someone talking."

Philocleon quickly scribbled out the map and threw the branch back on the fire.

Hipponous walked toward the fire. "What are you doing up?" he asked Philocleon.

Philocleon jumped to his feet and walked over to Hipponous to keep him from observing Nicias too closely. "I think I got too excited over killing my first boar. I couldn't sleep. But I'm tired now. You don't have to worry about me. You can go back to sleep."

Hipponous yawned and walked back to his shelter. At the door he turned and said, "You're going with the twins to the western ravine for you next hunt. Merops, Homer, and I will take the upper cliff." He didn't mention this was the reason he was still awake.

"No!" Nicias screamed silently. Suddenly he understood Philocleon's dream. A bad omen, if ever there was one. Surely Hipponous could see how dangerous a hunt with the twins would be for Philocleon. Nothing could be worth that kind of risk.

Philocleon, still intent on distracting Hipponous from the fire, made no protest. He yawned, saying, "I'd better get some sleep if I'm going to hunt boar again." He waited until he heard Hipponous lie down on his bed, then went to his own, afraid to say more to Nicias. Suddenly, he felt more frightened than he'd thought possible. During his darkest thoughts about his father, he'd never questioned that he would be protected by him. But now, everything had changed. He too was to be sacrificed for Hipponous' gain.

Nicias sat by the fire for a long stretch. He could still see the look of hate in Polydeuces' eyes when he'd knocked Philocleon down. What was wrong with Hipponous? Surely he could see the danger.

Merops got up and wandered back into his shelter. When he was gone, Nicias left the fire and went over to the horses. He paused at the stallion Homer had ridden and patted it on the rear, but he continued to Philocleon's mare. Standing behind her where he couldn't be seen from the shelters, he took the yellow bead off his neck, rubbed it, and whispered. "I hope Egyptus is right when he says you can give protection against evil."

He cut several strands from the tail of Philocleon's mare. Taking the leather thong out of the yellow bead, he threaded the tail strands through it. Then he cut two small parallel grooves in the horse's hoof, placed the bead under the hoof and threaded the tail strands up through the grooves so that they wouldn't get cut when the mare walked and secured them around her ankle. If his plan worked, whenever the mare stepped, she would push the bead into the flesh of her foot. She should be lame before they reached the ravine if the tail strands didn't break.

He picked up his traveling sack on the way back to the slaves' shelter. He couldn't leave now. Philocleon needed protection. He tucked the sack behind his bed and went quietly to sleep, dreaming of Bromia until the cook shook him, saying they needed to prepare the morning meal.

When the hunters were ready to mount, Nicias brought Philocleon his horse. Shock at seeing Nicias showed in Philocleon's eyes, but he said nothing. "Keep the twins in front of you," Nicias whispered and handed him the reins.

Philocleon mounted his horse and followed his two cousins toward the forest. Hipponous mounted his horse as soon as they left camp. "I know a place where there could be a big lair filled with boars. I'll be back as soon as I've looked it over."

"I'll go with you." Merops walked toward his horse.

Hipponous sneered. "You'd slow me up too much."

Merops shrugged. He had warned the twins Hipponous would find an excuse to follow them. "Come," he said to Homer sitting down by the fire again. "We'll have some wine."

Homer watched Hipponous leave, wondering what kind of a man would send his own son out to hunt with Castor and Polydeuces alone. He signaled to Nicias to bridle his horse.

Hipponous rode Pegasus in a wide circle around the path Philocleon and the twins were taking to the west. Once past them he climbed to higher ground and rode back until he spotted them in the forest below him. He drew an arrow from his quiver and placed it into his bow.

Philocleon felt his horse's step fail. She's nervous because I am, he decided. A little farther into the forest, she stumbled. Then she started to limp. Still farther, she could barely walk.

"I have to stop and check my horse," he called ahead to his cousins. "She seems to be going lame on me." Both halted their horses, but neither rode back. Philocleon got off his mare and pulled up her hoof. He found the tail strands secured around her ankle strung through the grooves. When he turned the hoof over, there was the yellow bead he had seen Nicias fingering the night before. His horse's foot had become bruised to the point where she could no longer walk.

"Hurry up," boomed through the trees. "Let's get started."

Philocleon unwound the horse tail ribbon and snapped the bead off it. "My horse must have gotten a pebble wedged under her hoof," he yelled at the path. "It's so bruised she won't be able to continue." He slipped the bead into his mouth, securing it between his teeth and jaw.

Disbelieving, Castor and Polydeuces rode back through the forest to Philocleon, got off their horses, and examined the hoof of Philocleon's mare. Philocleon stepped far enough back from the mare to be able to watch both of them. He clutched his spear tightly in his hand.

"That little bruising won't hurt. Use the whip and she'll straighten out." Castor pushed the mare to see if he could make her walk.

"Not me. I'm not laming one of Hipponous' prize horses. You go ahead. If it isn't too late once I get a new horse, I'll ride out and meet you."

Polydeuces leaned on Philocleon's mare and rested his dark, cold eyes on Philocleon's tense grip on his spear. After a long while he stepped away from the mare and spat. "There's bound to be another chance. You keep that in mind."

Philocleon gripped his spear tighter and waited until the two of them went back to their horses. Patting his mare's head he walked her back toward the campsite, meeting Homer on the path, telling him quickly what had happened.

Hipponous rode back into camp. "Nothing out there worth hunting. Let's try the ridge." He wanted Merops out of camp before Philocleon returned.

Merops didn't move.

"Come on."

"What's the hurry? Have some wine." Merops was curious. Why had Hipponous come back? Something must have happened.

"I want to get some hunting in," Hipponous insisted.

Philocleon walked into camp leading his horse. "What happened?" Merops grinned widely.

"She must have got a pebble or something caught in her hoof. She went lame before we even got started."

Hipponous got off his horse and inspected the hoof. "Where do you suppose she found a pebble in the pine-covered forest?" he asked sarcastically.

"Ask her," Philocleon snapped and walked past Hipponous to his shelter, thanking all of the gods he could think of that his father hadn't noticed the two grooves Nicias had cut into the hoof. Inside his shelter, he took the bead out of his cheek and threw himself on his evergreen bed.

Hipponous sat down by the fire with Homer and Merops. Why couldn't he have left it up to me, trusted I wouldn't leave him to the tempers of his cousins, he lamented. Beasts! He glared at Merops.

"Relax. Remember, we agreed. They're going to hunt until one of them gets a boar," Merops reminded Hipponous. He got up and walked to his shelter. It wouldn't pay to sit and smile in Hipponous' face.

"Don't you have a point that needs sharpening?" Hipponous asked Homer, staring straight ahead, trying to think.

"Yes, I do." Homer was happy to get away from Hipponous even though his wrath had swung back to the twins.

As Helios disappeared below the trees, the twins galloped into camp. They tied up their horses and swaggered over to the fire. "Funniest thing happened." Castor sat down next to Hipponous. Laughing, he grabbed a wineskin and handed it to his brother.

Taking the skin from Castor, Polydeuces began their story. "We were chasing this boar and he ran into a thicket. We thought we had him cornered, but he bolted out of the thicket into a ravine, out the other side and into an open field."

"There was this farmer's slave," his brother interrupted, "standing out in the field. The boar saw him and charged. Sent him flying. While we were distracted by the confusion that followed, the boar got away. Shame, too. It was one of the biggest boars I've ever seen."

"What happened to the slave?" Hipponous already knew.

"Boar killed him," Polydeuces answered.

"There will be trouble with the farmers over this," Hipponous snapped.

"We can handle the farmers," Castor snapped back.

Hipponous got up. "We'll see." He walked off into the forest to wait for the owner of the slave. What else could go wrong, he wondered. Pacing in the forest, cursing himself, Merops, the twins, Philocleon, Homer, and everyone else he could think of – he suddenly realized the twins had actually done him a favor.

"Do you know who killed my slave?" the farmer asked when he got there.

"My nephews." They weren't actually his nephews, but he'd been calling them that ever since they were born. He thought there must have been a reason, but he couldn't remember what it was anymore. It aggravated him that he couldn't break the habit.

"They'll have to pay for the slave." He rode around Hipponous toward the campsite.

"Wait," Hipponous called after him. "I'll pay you for the slave."

The farmer shrugged and turned around.

They made a deal. Several goats for the slave.

"Wait here," Hipponous told the man. "I'll go back to camp and get one of my slaves. He'll take you to my estate for the animals."

Not fully trusting Hipponous, the farmer started to follow him. "I'll ride with you to pick up the slave."

"No. My nephews are not the kind of men to pay for something they've destroyed. It's better if they don't know I've made the payment."

Hipponous went back to camp, picked up one of the slaves, and delivered him to the farmer. He waited until the farmer was well out of sight before he returned to the campsite, emptied the wine-skin, and went to his shelter.

SEVEN

Hipponous rose as Dawn spread her golden robe across the heavens. Anxious to get started, he threw his tunic over his head and slid his feet into his sandals, calling toward the slaves' shelter the entire time for one of the slaves to stir up the fire and get him something to eat. By the time he reached the fire, Nicias stood ready with wheat loaves. "Get everyone up," he told Nicias.

Merops got to the campfire first. "I assume you have a good reason for calling us before Helios has had time to stretch his horses' legs." He took a wheat loaf from one of the slaves, dipped it in wine, and ate. His mouth still stuffed, he sent the slave for another loaf and indicated impatiently to Castor and Polydeuces who'd just come to the fire to take places on either side of him. "Sit."

Castor grabbed a loaf from the slave, tore it in half, handed the biggest half to his father. "What's going on?"

Carefully controlling the anger he felt toward his sons for doing something so stupid, Merops answered, "I suspect it has to do with killing that slave."

Philocleon didn't move from his shelter until a slave had been sent with a firm second message from Hipponous. When he came, he brought Homer with him. They sat across from Merops.

Hipponous paced, concealing his glee over his plan to end the hunt, said with a stern voice, "I had a visitor." He paused for emphasis and stared disgustedly at the twins. "The farmer whose slave got killed by the boar you were chasing came to tell me the owners of the surrounding estates had a message for us: either we leave the forest on our own today or we'll be put out by twenty-five of the area's best bowmen. I told him we would leave."

"I say we stay." Castor threw what was left of his wheat loaf in the fire.

Polydeuces flexed his muscles. "We're up to a good fight."

Determined not to lose the opportunity, Hipponous ignored the twins and concentrated on Merops. "We are six and he has twenty-five men armed with bows. It doesn't take much intelligence – not that we have an overabundance here – to figure out that six, even six of the best, have very little chance against twenty-five." He laced his voice with sarcasm.

"Besides, there wouldn't be six." Philocleon stood. "I'm going to pack my gear." He instructed Nicias to prepare the wagon for the return trip.

Homer left with Philocleon.

Hipponous caught one of the slaves by the arm. "Pull up the bedding." Content things would go his way, he left the fire. Merops would have no choice but to leave now. There would be no more hunting.

Merops sat and thought over his situation. Certainly Hipponous was bluffing. Twenty-five men to roust six – over a slave. Not even thinkable. On the other hand, he and the twins had made their point. Perhaps it was better to leave before the twins did something more damaging. He stood. "Get packed."

Polydeuces pounded one fist into the other. "I'm not letting some farmer chase me out of the forest. Besides, I still have a score to settle."

"You can settle your score later. Right now, we're leaving." Merops walked toward his shelter. "You and your pigheaded bullying have put me at enough of a disadvantage."

When the twins finally threw their spears and traveling sacks into Merops' wagon, the other four men were already mounted. Hipponous barely gave the two of them time to get on their horses before he ordered the slave driving Merops' wagon to head toward Athens. He followed the wagon, leaving Merops and the twins to come when they would.

Philocleon and Homer rode in the opposite direction, toward the estate. Nicias followed behind them in the wagon with the remainder of Hipponous' slaves and the boar Philocleon had killed.

Carefree happiness overtook both Philocleon and Homer as soon as they got away from the camp. Laughing and teasing one another, mimicking the twins and Merops, they chased a deer, then a fox, finally a rabbit, through the dense trees to the edge of the forest.

Coming to a meadow they raced toward the other side. Halfway across the level ground Homer spotted a flock of partridge. He pointed to a large bird. "I was told partridge can only fly twice. Let's find out if it's true." He chased the bird until it flew. When it landed, he chased it again until it flew. The third time he chased it, the partridge didn't fly. Jauntily he slid off his horse and ran after the bird on foot until he caught it in his hands. Handing his captive up to Philocleon, he said, "If only I could fly even once."

Philocleon threw the partridge into the air and watched it glide to the ground. "What would you do if you could fly?"

"Soar with Icarus to the sun god Helios."

"Who's Icarus?"

"He was the son of Daedalus, the Athenian, who was brought to Crete by King Minos to build the labyrinth."

"And?"

"When the labyrinth was finished, Daedalus lost favor with King Minos and he and Icarus got locked up in one of his own towers. To escape, Daedalus made wings for himself and Icarus by welding feathers together with wax. He warned Icarus not to get too close to Helios when they flew from the tower or the wax holding his wings together would melt. They hadn't flown very far before Icarus got so excited he left his father and soared upward toward the sun god. The wax melted and he fell to his death in the sea."

Philocleon searched Homer's face for an explanation. "I don't understand. Didn't you just tell me you would soar to Helios with Icarus if you could?"

"I did."

"But Icarus died."

Homer shrugged. "For me, the idea of dying isn't as difficult as the problem of how much living I can do before I die. Each time I sing the saga of Meleager, it makes me unbearably sad. What could be worse than to die an inglorious death as a young man? But think of it. To die flying steadfastly toward the sun god. What a glorious death!" He mounted his stallion and galloped off with his arms flying out from his sides like wings.

Philocleon raced after Homer, debating whether he thought it would be as glorious as Homer seemed to think to fly to Helios if it meant dying. When he caught up with Homer, the poet was chasing another partridge.

"Fly little Icarus." Homer threw his partridge into the air when Philocleon stopped next to him and watched it sail smoothly toward the horizon, his imagination aglow with an image of himself as Icarus – flying straight toward the chariot of Helios. Daring Philocleon to follow, he mounted his stallion and galloped off toward the trees. How he loved the feeling of freedom that came with racing across the meadow on a fast-paced horse. In a short time he would be free again. Traveling from one festival to another, reciting.

Philocleon galloped past Homer before they reached the trees. "I know where there's a river. I'll race you."

Homer galloped after Philocleon and dove into the river right behind him.

"Narcissus," Philocleon teased when he caught Homer looking at his reflection in the water.

Homer splashed water on Philocleon, leaving him sputtering and coughing. "Better than being Daedalus. At least I'm not afraid to spread my wings and fly."

"Then follow me." Philocleon climbed onto the highest tree hanging over the water and dove with his arms spread like wings on either side of him – somersaulting just before he went into the water. He swam to shore and waded out of the water.

Unwilling to risk such a dive Homer put both hands on his hips and bowed from the waist. "I guess I won't be calling you Daedalus anymore."

"You can call me Gilgamesh," Philocleon informed him.

"Gilgamesh? I've never heard of him. Who was he?"

"Gilgamesh was the king of Uruk, created by the gods when the world was still in its infancy." Philocleon had been practicing for this moment with Na'id-Assur and Qurdi Marduk ever since they first told him the saga.

Using the best of his skills, though he knew they were not those of a poet and surely inferior to Homer's, he told the poet the story of Gilgamesh, from his fight with Enkidu to his battle with the keeper of the cedars, Humbaba, to the killing of the Bull of Heaven, the death of Enkidu, his visit with Utnapishtim, his loss of the thorny plant that would keep men young forever and his return to Uruk.

Then he put Qurdi Marduk's riddle to Homer. "How did Gilgamesh die and still gain immortality?"

Homer turned the saga over in his mind several times before he admitted he couldn't answer the riddle. "What's the answer?"

"I don't know."

"What'd you mean, you don't know?"

"My two Assyrian tutors told me the saga and the riddle, but they won't give me the answer. They insist that learning to read words isn't enough. I have to learn how to reason with the words. I was sure with your help I'd be able to figure it out."

Homer shrugged, throwing both hands into the air. "I'm afraid I can't help you."

Philocleon pretended to be terribly disappointed.

"Why do you want to learn to read anyway?" Homer asked.

"My father thinks it would be useful for the trading business he plans to start when he gets the ship from Merops." Thinking Homer was asking because he was interested in learning to read, he continued excitedly, "If you want, I could ask Na'id-Assur to teach you to read too."

"Why would I want to learn how to read? I'm a poet, not a trader. Besides," Homer swallowed hard, his grey brown eyes imploring Philocleon to understand, "I wouldn't have time even if I wanted to learn. When your father returns from Athens, I plan to leave for Olympia."

Homer's remark pierced through Philocleon like a spear. "Why? Aren't you happy?" Perhaps it was the intoxication of friendship, perhaps the whim of one of the gods, Philocleon wasn't sure, but some way, he'd managed to lull that part of his mind to sleep that told him Homer wouldn't stay forever.

"Of course, I'm happy." How could he explain to Philocleon his intense longing to be back among his own kind again. His need for the excitement of reciting in contests and for hearing other poets recite. Philocleon had never left his father's estate.

"If you're happy, why do you want to leave?" Philocleon's voice had a gentle persistence.

"I'm a poet and I want to learn all the poetry known to man. How can I learn it if I stay here?"

"What about the saga of Gilgamesh? You could learn that."

"The Greeks don't want to hear about Gilgamesh, king of Uruk.

They want to hear about the great Greek heroes of the past. Do you remember when we first met?" Homer felt as sorry as Philocleon, but he was determined to leave.

"Of course. How could I forget, you stumbling down that gangplank, hands and legs flying in every direction." Philocleon mimicked Homer's fall, though his heart wasn't in it.

Homer remembered it too, all too well, though by now it seemed far in his past. "You asked me to tell you my name. I said, 'Remember the gift you promised me and I'll tell you my name.'"

"Yes. And I had to buy you a drinking bowl of wine before you would tell me your name."

"I got that from a poem about the adventures Odysseus had trying to get back to Ithaca after the Trojan war." In spite of his sadness, Homer felt the excitement of the poem welling up inside of him. "Should I tell you about Odysseus?"

"Yes."

"In the most exciting adventure, Odysseus lands his ship on an island where only cyclopes live. He takes his companions into the cave where one of the cyclopes lives, to steal food. The cyclops comes home and, before Odysseus realizes what is happening, traps him and his men inside the cave by rolling a gigantic stone in front of the entrance to the cave. The cyclops keeps Odysseus and his men in his cave, eating a couple of the men for his evening meal.

"When the cyclops leaves, he traps Odysseus and his men inside the cave again by rolling a boulder in front of the entrance. While the cyclops is gone, Odysseus and his men plan their escape. They make a long stake and hide it. When the cyclops returns, Odysseus offers him some of the wine they have brought with them. The cyclops is so pleased with the wine, he decides to do a special favor for Odysseus. He will eat him last. But, to be certain he doesn't eat Odysseus until last, he needs to know his name. When he asks his name, Odysseus says, 'Remember the gift you promised me and I'll tell you my name.' The cyclops promises again to eat him last. Then Odysseus tells the cyclops his name is Outis, which means Nobody.

"That night, Odysseus and his men get the cyclops drunk and when he falls asleep, they blind him with the stake they have hidden. The cyclops screams and cries for help. The other cyclopes come running, but they can't get into the cave because the entrance is blocked with a huge boulder. From the outside they call to him.

'What's the matter? Did someone hurt you?' He answers. 'Outis hurt me.' They reply, 'If Nobody hurt you, then your pain must be the will of Zeus,' and they go away.

"The next morning, the cyclops opens the cave to let out his sheep. He feels among them as they leave to make sure Odysseus and his companions don't sneak out. He does not realize until Odysseus calls to him from the outside that his prisoners have escaped by hiding in the wool under the bellies of his sheep."

Philocleon couldn't help but smile. "Where did you learn it? I haven't heard you recite it before."

"I started to learn it in Ionia, but the poet teaching me couldn't recite all of it. He told me to go to Olympia where he heard there was an old poet who could recite the entire saga." His eyes were snapping with excitement.

"Why were you on that ship anyway?" Philocleon asked. "It wasn't sailing to Olympia."

"I had to leave Ionia in a hurry."

"What happened?"

"I borrowed a man's bed and his wife happened to be in it." Homer laughed and getting up, went to the highest outcropping he could find, ruffled his hair, and with arms outspread, recited what he knew of the return of Odysseus to Ithaca. When he had finished, he turned to the valley below and yelled, "I will be the greatest poet in the Aegean."

Philocleon thought a long time. Not only did he know he couldn't convince Homer to stay, he didn't want to try. He cared too much for him and he longed too much himself for the kind of life he knew Homer would have in Olympia. Yet he couldn't imagine going on with his life without the poet. Then suddenly an idea came to him. Excitedly he called up to Homer, "I won't even try to convince you to stay here if you promise to leave me something when you go."

"But what? Look." Homer pointed at his tunic and sandals. "Everything I have you have given me. I can't give you what was yours to begin with."

"Not everything."

"What then?"

"The saga of the Trojan war. You must give me that."

"But I have. I have recited it for you continuously since I came."

"It's not enough. I want to have it with me when you leave." By now Philocleon was smiling again, knowing he'd stumped Homer.

"You must be the Sphinx," Homer retorted. "For the second time today, you've offered me an impossible riddle. On the one hand you say I can leave and on the other, that my poem must remain with you. Since I am inseparable from the poem, how can I do both?"

"If you don't have the answer," Philocleon said, feeling devious, "I guess I'll have to help you. All I ask of you is that you recite the saga from beginning to end for me at a festival I will convince my father to sponsor. I'll bring Na'id-Assur and Qurdi Marduk, my two Assyrian tutors, to the festival and have them record everything you recite. You see? Then you can both leave me and leave me the poem."

Surprised by the idea, Homer quipped, "I think I shall call you the wily Odysseus from now on."

"Is your name really Homer?" Philocleon had wanted to ask this question for a long time. It was such an odd name for a poet.

"No. I took it when I signed on as a deck hand on the ship in Ionia. It would have been too risky to give the captain my real name. He might have recognized it since the husband whose bed I had borrowed was scouring the city for me."

"Why did you choose Homer?"

"Homer means hostage and I am the hostage of the greatest of the muses, Calliope. Without her to assist my memory, I could never recite the events of the great Trojan war. All at once as he spoke it occurred to him what recording the epic of the Trojan war would mean for the muse, Calliope. It would render her useless.

Philocleon continued to question Homer. "If your name isn't Homer, what is it?"

"I can't let you record the saga," Homer blurted out.

"Why?" Philocleon now saw fear written all over Homer's face. He was amazed, as he'd never seen Homer afraid. Not even when he had stood up against Hipponous and the twins at great peril to himself.

"Don't you see? If I allow you to record the saga, my muse, Calliope, will be rendered useless. You'll be able to read the poem whenever you like. You won't need her presence. Surely she would seek to revenge herself against me if I allowed such a thing to happen."

"She won't know," Philocleon said, a firm plan having developed in his mind.

"How's that?"

"When she hears me reading the saga and she comes to me and asks who tricked her by allowing me to record it, I'll answer, 'Outis'. Then she in her turn will say, 'Well, if Nobody helped you, then having the saga recorded must be the will of Zeus,' and she will go away contented."

EIGHT

Galloping Pegasus up the steep trail to the house, Hipponous felt a surge of the unassailable strength he had known in his youth. Castor and Polydeuces, unaccustomed to riding at the speed he found comfortable, were well behind him. Sending the twins back to the estate with him had been Merops' idea. He wanted to get them started at the mines, he'd said, while he prepared the ship for sailing.

"They won't realize for many seasons the extent to which the contract they signed favors me," Hipponous said, speaking his thoughts, as he often did when a slave was present, to the young slave who had run out to take his horse. Neither expecting nor getting a response he threw his reins to the boy and dismounted. "Put the twins into the small room on the northeast corner of the portico."

"Excuse me, Sir?" The young man looked uncomprehendingly around the empty yard.

Hipponous had forgotten how far behind the twins had fallen. "Unless we are particularly lucky, Castor and Polydeuces will be dragging their tails onto the estate shortly." He pointed toward the trail.

Should he ask them to sleep with the slaves, Hipponous wondered. No, better not. Even they would be smart enough to refuse that kind of insult. Not by much though, he'd wager. Nonetheless, they were going to pay for the insults he'd suffered during their earlier visit.

Walking away from the slave, Hipponous left final instructions. "I want to be informed immediately if they cause even the slightest disturbance." But he wasn't worried. After the ride they had gone through, they'd be entirely too tired to cause any trouble. "And, if they ask, I'm not available."

Seeing Philocleon at the entrance to the house, Hipponous waved. His only regret was that Merops would be dead long before his twins knew the full extent of their father's stupidity. And I, he thought to himself, will never have the pleasure of rubbing it in their face.

Philocleon returned his father's wave, but he didn't walk out to meet him. He could tell by Hipponous' long, bold, strides and his unreserved smile that he was pleased.

Hipponous embraced Philocleon with genuine affection. Now that his business had been transacted so successfully, he wanted to end the quarrel with his son. He would even try to make things up with Nicias. He hadn't missed that in as long as he could remember, Nicias had been the slave to meet him at the stable door. Today it had been one of the young slaves.

Philocleon returned Hipponous' embrace without much enthusiasm. After asking some short, but polite questions about the ship which he knew would enhance his father's mood still more, he turned to the subject foremost in his mind. "Homer is planning to leave. I convinced him to stay until we could have a festival to celebrate the new ship. Did I do the right thing?"

Delighted to be rid of the poet without having to throw him out as he had planned and feeling the hesitancy he sensed in Philocleon's embrace was at least partly deserved, Hipponous consented immediately. "Of course. Send the slaves out with invitations to the neighboring estates and to our friends at Laurion and Sounion. The next time the beautiful moon goddess, Selene, pleasures us with her fullness, we'll have a festival that will still be remembered when my grandchildren wander this estate. Speaking of grandchildren," Hipponous pinched Philocleon's cheek the way he had when his son was a boy, "It won't be long, now."

The pinch, which had thrilled Philocleon as a boy, aggravated him immensely. His anger had not abated like his father's. But he reminded himself, it would not do to risk upsetting Hipponous now when he was in such a good mood. If he got angry and canceled the festival, Homer would have to be sent on his way without a proper farewell. So instead he forced himself to give Hipponous a half-hearted embrace. "Thank you, Father." He smiled. "With your permission, I'll leave you now to prepare the invitations."

Philocleon went to work immediately sending invitations, preparing the estate and slaves for the upcoming event, buying food, and selecting wines. Before he realized it, Selene was a beautiful round disk in the sky, and he found himself directing a steady stream of athletes and spectators to the trees surrounding the farm-yard.

Shelters built out of mud and branches mushroomed into every available space, trees came down for firewood and, as the space most convenient to the food and drink decreased, brawls became as common as the flies that covered the horses' hides.

"Need help?" Homer asked Philocleon as he made final preparations for the games to begin.

"Not unless you can break up the fight down by the stream."

Homer turned just as one of the men who had been fighting was propelled in their direction and landed on a bed of leaves. A rough hand belonging to one of the twins – neither Philocleon nor Homer could tell which – pulled the man up by his hair. "You got anything else to say?" It was Polydeuces. He shook his victim by the hair. "No sir," came the answer. "Good." Polydeuces tossed the man back onto the ground and stalked away.

"It's been this way since the guests starting arriving," Philocleon sighed. "Brawling over space, wine, food, with my cousins always at the center."

"They're getting even with your father for totally ignoring them. Besides they aren't as stupid as your father thinks. Wait until the boxing matches. Who's going to challenge them after watching them knock heads about?"

"I already promised them you'd be the first contender," Philocleon joked.

"Not a chance, but I will compete in the footrace and the horse race just to make sure you get some competition."

"Competition? With that nag you ride."

"You gave her to me."

"That's why I know she's a nag." Philocleon laughed.

"You never know, with the rider she'll have, anything could happen. Which horse are you riding?"

"Pegasus."

"Then I can't win," Homer admitted. "But you'd best be wary.

Remember what happened to Bellerophon when he became too proud and tried to ride Pegasus to the heavens. Zeus sent down a gadfly. The thing stung Pegasus and made him throw Bellerophon. The poor man ended up lame and blind. This, for too much pride."

"I won't be riding to the heavens, only to the sea and back," Philocleon assured him.

"Ah," Homer sighed. "But once you get on a winged steed, who knows where you will want to fly."

Philocleon said no more, but ever since they'd talked about Icarus, he'd been wondering how far he could fly if he tried. He wasn't far from giving it a try.

The two men remained side-by-side, joking, talking, directing the new arrivals and mediating fights as much as they were able until the last cart rolled to its place in the trees. As soon as the beautiful moon goddess, Selene began her ascent into the heavens, the quarrels that seemed so important were forgotten in the preparation of the evening meal. Stewed mutton, roasted duck and pork, fried peppers and onions passed from hand to hand, as did a plentiful supply of wine.

When Selene had sprinkled the earth with her golden light like a maiden dropping flowers and the meal had long since been eaten, instruments carefully placed in the bottoms of traveling sacks and baskets were unpacked and brought to the fires. Encouraged by Hipponous, songs of praise to the gods soon filled the trees. It wasn't long before groups of two and three got to their feet and began dancing around the fires grasping the hands of the men still sitting as they passed them, pulling them up into a chain until every man on the estate except the musicians was dancing.

The dancing continued until Dawn opened the gates of heaven. Then in her soft light men went to their shelters and slept until Hipponous' slaves came around to tell them the festival was about to begin.

So many athletes and spectators had arrived that as Hipponous stood before them, he couldn't control his boasting smile. Before the audience of nearly two hundred men, he ceremoniously sacrificed two of his prize bulls. The thighs he wrapped in fat and burned on a beautiful stone altar built especially for the festival. The remainder of the meat he had roasted over fires built at the four corners of the open space his slaves had cleared for the games.

When the meat was ready, athletes and spectators alike were given as much as they could eat. As they passed from the roasting spits to their grassy seats, they found wheat loaves, baked in the estate kilns, heaped on wicker baskets and wine-filled mixing bowls standing everywhere. Slaves passed constantly among them with greens, cheese and fresh fruit. "This is a meal they are not likely to forget," Hipponous bragged to Philocleon.

Leaving the dogs to fight over the leftover scraps and bones when the meal was finished, Hipponous invited his guests to take their wine bowls and follow him. He led them to the stadium he'd had dug into the hillside behind the stable. He motioned for the guests to seat themselves on the mounds of grass-covered earth left on both sides of the stadium for spectators.

Excessively pleased, both with the number of athletes and spectators who had come and with the fine stadium his slaves had built, Hipponous made his way to the center of the track. He lifted his arms in a gesture most often associated with Zeus. "Silence," he called with the authority that he felt suited his new position as a ship owner. "We are honored to have at this festival one of the finest poets in all of Greece. He will recite each night of the festival from the saga of the great and glorious battle our ancestors won against the mighty Trojans."

Hipponous called for Homer. The poet went to the center of the stadium, followed by Philocleon, Na'id Assur, Qurdi Marduk, and four of Hipponous' slaves carrying couches. Homer had finally agreed to let the Assyrians record the saga, but his decision left him ill at ease. He felt immensely guilty for betraying Calliope. At the same time, he wanted intensely to do something for Philocleon to demonstrate the friendship he'd come to feel.

Homer waited nervously while Na'id-Assur and Qurdi Marduk got their beeswax boards ready, then nodding to Philocleon, he began by making a most earnest appeal to the muse, Calliope, to come to him with her verses. Deep in his heart, he asked her to forgive him.

After a very long pause, he felt Calliope's presence rush through him like a full bowl of fine wine, warming him, giving him an intense desire to sing. At the same time, thunder roared in the distance. Not about to miss any opportunity Hipponous jumped to his feet. "Thunder belongs to Zeus. Listen. He has sent his thunder to praise my poet."

So now, after being mistreated since I came, I am suddenly his poet, Homer thought, listening to the murmurs of the crowd. He felt anger rising. Here he was betraying Calliope for Philocleon's sake and Hipponous was the one benefiting. The anger grew to a crescendo that rocked him. All at once he began singing of great quarrel between Agamemnon, leader of the Greeks, and the bravest of all the Greek princes, the brilliant Achilles.

As had happened before, he saw Hipponous as the haughty Agamemnon and himself as the wronged Achilles. Instinctively, he poured all of his anger into their quarrel, telling his audience how Agamemnon had angered the priest Chryses when he refused to return the priest's daughter in spite of the old man's generous offers of ransom. He related how the Greeks had been punished by Apollo with the plague for Agamemnon's arrogance and how Agamemnon had punished Achilles by taking Briseis from him when he demanded the priest's daughter be returned.

Slashing though the silence he had created with his verses, he described for his spellbound audience death after death among the Greeks as the Trojans hacked them to pieces without the defense of their brave defender and hero, the brilliant Achilles. Gleefully, when he had drunk a full cup of revenge, he ended his singing with the fiery attacks on the Greek ships by the Trojans.

The athletes and spectators were so overwhelmed by Homer's dazzling verses they refused to return to their shelters when the poet stopped singing. Instead they stood and cheered and begged him to continue. All except Hipponous. He had expected Homer to end his singing where he had on the night of the banquet, with the slaying of Hipponous – stubborn in battle. Homer had cheated him of the glory he'd expected and he was furious.

Homer, for his part, reveled in his revenge.

The athletes and spectators were finally convinced to return to their shelters. They slept as best they could, given the noise Castor and Polydeuces made, until Hipponous woke them by announcing the games were about to begin. Homer was one of the athletes who gathered to make sacrifice to the gods at the great altar. Hipponous, having found no way to keep Homer out of the contests without causing unfavorable gossip, announced the first day's contests would include: spear throwing, foot racing, and boxing.

Hipponous led the crowd into the stadium. When they were seated, he held up a finely wrought cauldron. The hemispherical bronze bowl of the vessel rested on three bronze legs, each of which curved outward and ended in a carefully fashioned lion's foot. The rim of the bowl was decorated with an attached ivy vine made from silver taken out of Hipponous' own mines. "First, we will have the spear throwing. The winner will take this beautiful bronze cauldron with him as his prize," Hipponous announced. The murmurs he could hear coming from the crowd were exactly what he'd expected. His pride swelled.

Six men came forward to compete in the spear throwing. Flexing the shafts of their spears and testing their points, they lined up for the contest on the sill of the starting rectangle. The first contestant, a small man from Laurion, prepared for the throw. He ran forward and stopping just at the line, sent his spear sailing through the air. It landed far down the course to the awed sounds of the spectators. Next came a young lad with a powerful build from one of the neighboring estates. He ran with such force everyone feared he wouldn't get himself stopped at the line, but he did. His spear flew out of his hand, up and up and then down, landing well beyond the first throw. The spectators cheered with delight.

The third thrower didn't get stopped on the line much to the spectors' disappointment because he had made an excellent throw. Unhappily, Hipponous disqualified him. The fourth and fifth competitors, young men not yet fully developed, made strenuous attempts, but neither could match the length of the second throw.

The last man to throw was the cousin of one of the nearby estate owners. Rumors started by Hipponous circulated as soon as the crowd saw him that he was training for the games played at Olympia. With a strained yell he ran forward and plunged his spear into the air. It flew up and up, but before it came down, it caught a gust of air and turned just enough to lose some of its momentum, falling short of the spear dropped by the second thrower.

Hipponous was as pleased with the competition as were the spectators. He happily listened to them cheer noisily as the winner came forward with his spear to receive his cauldron. With some prompting from Hipponous, he promised to dedicate the cauldron to Poseidon at the Sounion temenos. The crowd cheered wildly.

Hipponous announced the next contest would be the footrace.

He held up a shield. "This will be the prize of the winner." The shield was made not of ox hide as was the custom, but of wood covered with bronze. A delicately made silver eight-lozenge star had been hammered into the center of the bronze. There wasn't a man in the crowd who wouldn't have been proud to carry such a shield, Hipponous decided from the cheering.

Eight contestants lined up at the sill of the starting rectangle, each poised with one foot before the other, both arms stretched forward. When Hipponous cracked his whip in the air to start the race, dust rose in every direction. Homer and Philocleon were both competing. Running side-by-side, they and the other competitors watched a man with the longest legs they'd ever seen move farther and farther in front of the other runners until there was no contest. He raced over the course and finished by himself.

Although Hipponous was disappointed by the lack of a contest, he was greatly relieved that Homer hadn't even finished near the front of the line. He was determined Homer would not have one of his fine prizes. So he gave the runner his shield, insisting he must have been born a mortal son of the winds, urging everyone to remember where he'd raced first when he won the contest at Olympia.

Boxing, Hipponous announced would be the last event. "And the winner will receive a colt from my finest mare and stallion." He had one of the slaves parade the colt in front of the crowd. It had been curried to a black sheen, its mane, long and finely combed, flowing backward, tail held high in the air.

Many in the crowd would have paid handsomely for such a fine colt. Hipponous, knowing both Castor and Polydeuces would enter this contest, had offered the colt with the hope it would entice some of the other men to challenge either one or both of the twins.

No one came forward except Castor and Polydeuces. Those who might have considered it under any other circumstances didn't when they realized the twins would be competing. At first it looked as though the boxing would be canceled. Then Hipponous, with what he afterwards considered a very real stroke of Hermes' luck, came up with an unusual idea. Why not have the twins box each other?

"No," was their mutual reply. "We have taken a vow to never fight one another. We're too evenly matched and brothers. There could be no winner."

Overjoyed by their reluctance, Hipponous goaded them, saying to the crowd of two hundred, "I say they're afraid."

The spectators, many of whom had taken beatings from the twins, hissed and booed. "Cowards," they screamed ferociously from their seats until Polydeuces, unwilling to carry the label of coward with him to Olympia, offered to fight, planning all the while what he would do to revenge himself on Hipponous when he got the chance. Having no choice, Castor put on his boxing belt too and tied on the leather thongs.

The spectators moved to the boxing arena. The two brothers moved to the center of the crowd. They stood face to face with their fists raised in the air when Hipponous gave the signal to begin. They circled until Castor found an opening in Polydeuces' defense. He came in and hit his brother soundly between the nose and the cheek. Polydeuces fell backwards with a heavy thud. When he finally struggled back to his feet there was blood spurting out of his nose. He circled slowly, sniffing blood, until his opportunity came. He punched his brother at the center of his ribs and watched while his twin in his turn fell backwards and struggled to regain his feet.

Both brothers circled a third time with their fists up, punching at every opportunity. Sweat gathered on their brows. Polydeuces ground his teeth so hard from the exertion that he could be heard all the way to the last row of spectators. It brought no pity from the men watching, only more booing. Castor, again taking advantage of an opening, jabbed Polydeuces in the eye. Before Polydeuces could move, his eye had swollen shut. Squinting and sweating, he lurched forward and smashed his fist into his brother's breastbone. Castor fell backwards.

Hipponous thought the match had ended, but slowly Castor crawled to his feet and the fight began again. They punched without stopping until both were a pitiful mass of bruises and blood. The brutality continued for a long while before the crowd became satiated and started insisting that since neither could win, the fight should be called. Eventually, Hipponous was forced by the audience to stop the fight, calling it an even match, though he was more than a little reluctant.

The spectators, if they'd shown some pity during the fight, were in no mood to befriend the twins when it ended. "Give each half," they chanted. "Cut the colt in half." Hipponous could see their point.

After all of that fighting, to have given each of them a dead half would have suited him fine; that is, if the colt hadn't been one of his prize animals and if he hadn't come up with a better idea.

He called for silence and while two of his slaves poured cold water on the twins, Hipponous went to the barn. Never would he give those two one of his finest colts. Instead he slipped the fine colt he'd chosen into the pen and had two colts he knew to be inferior runners, although they looked as fine as the animal he'd offered, brought out and curried. When they were ready, he presented them to the twins ignoring the fact that neither could stand to accept his prize.

The horsemen among the crowd knew what had happened, but the rest of the crowd didn't. Just as Hipponous had expected, those who knew nothing of horses cheered endlessly over what they considered to be a most generous act, giving two fine colts instead of one, while the horsemen, knowing how difficult it would be to give up one of their prize colts, said nothing. Absolutely delighted with the turn of events, Hipponous called an end to the games and ordered the slaves to begin the evening meal.

The meat from the animals the athletes had sacrificed was placed over four fires, rekindled from the embers still smoldering on the hearths that had burned the night before. When the meat was roasted, it was passed to the crowds along with stacks of wheat loaves and other fine foods. Craters filled with wine were placed everywhere. All of it provided, Hipponous announced, by their generous host. As he'd expected, they toasted him loudly.

Without waiting to be invited, the athletes and spectators wandered over and sat down on one side of the stadium as soon as they'd eaten. Hipponous went to the center of the track. This time he didn't have to introduce Homer. A deep silence fell over the crowd in anticipation as soon as they saw the poet.

Homer began, as always with a most earnest plea to the muse, Calliope, to bring him her purest verses. He waited nervously for the muse. As always, his body slowly warmed, then pulsed with excitement. Just as he began singing, a bird swept across the darkened sky over his head. "Look," Philocleon cried. "An eagle. Homer is surely beloved by Zeus. He has sent one of his eagles."

"It was a hawk, not an eagle," Hipponous insisted to Philocleon. "You're imagining things." He hadn't forgotten his snubbing. The poet was to get no more praise from Zeus.

Surprised and angry, Philocleon turned to the audience. "Was it an eagle or a hawk?"

"An eagle." Most of the men hadn't even seen the bird, but they wanted to believe the poet was beloved of Zeus.

Smiling sarcastically at Hipponous, Homer began his poem where he'd left off the night before by reminding the audience how the Greeks were suffering incredible losses because Achilles, still furious with Agamemnon, had withdrawn from the battle. Grieving with his audience, the silver-tongued poet told them how the greatest of the Greek generals went to Achilles and begged him on behalf of Agamemnon to reenter the battle. How Achilles refused to fight, but after much pleading agreed to let his beloved companion Patroclus enter the battle wearing his armor and driving his divine horses against the Trojans.

Wiping tears from their eyes, Homer's audience listened while he sang of how bravely Patroclus fought, how courageously he drove the Trojans back from the Greek ships, but in the end, was twice wounded and had to fight injured, against the great Trojan hero, Hector. Imagining himself as Patroclus and Philocleon as Achilles, Homer brought such pathos to the epic death of Patroclus, he cried bitterly himself in the end.

The audience wanted to hear more poetry, but most of them were so overwhelmed by Homer's tears, they didn't ask him to sing again. Nor did they complain when they had to watch acrobats for the next two nights while Homer, exhausted and depressed, rested.

"What is it?" Philocleon asked, but Homer had no answer. It was as though all the sorrow he'd ever known had suddenly overwhelmed him when he sang of the death of Patroclus.

On the last day of the festival, Hipponous announced the final contests: discus throwing and horseracing. He led the crowd to the stadium and called for the discus throwers. Holding up an incense burner made of silver from his own mines, he offered it to the winner of the throwing. The burner had a shallow bowl to hold the incense. It was balanced upon the head and upraised arms of a beautiful goddess dressed in a peplos, belted at the waist.

Three men lined up for the discus throwing, one from the village at Sounion, another from Laurion, and a third who was sailing with one of the ships docked at the Sounion harbor. The first man came forward. He made a three-quarter spin and let go. The discus flew for a great distance. The spectators cheered wildly. The second to throw took his turn, but being an unpracticed oarsman, though strong enough Hipponous later acknowledged, he lacked control and his discus flew up into the spectators barely missing the head of one of the men. The crowd booed and was still complaining when the third man stood up to throw. The noise and confusion interfered with the man's concentration and his throw, while respectable, was nowhere near as long as the first throw had been. The winner came to the center and claimed his incense burner, but both he and Hipponous felt cheated by the lack of a contest.

Hipponous had waited throughout the games for the horse race. He pulled out a beautiful dagger and showed it to the audience. The gasps of surprise and awe he had expected escaped almost every pair of lips. He reveled in them. The dagger had been passed down for generations in his family. Some even thought it might have come from the great time of the Trojan war. It had a gold handle formed to look like a braided rope and a bronze blade. Two birds of the finest workmanship, made of gold and lapis lazuli, were inlaid into the bronze blade.

Hipponous smiled to himself. He was getting the best of everything. While those fools watching the games thought he was generous beyond measure, Philocleon was riding Pegasus in the race. His son was the best horseman in the region after himself and Pegasus was definitely the best horse. There was no doubt in his mind but that Philocleon would win the dagger.

The riders lined up. Originally, there had been six, but after the prize was shown, eight more joined the race. Homer was among the original six as was Philocleon. At the sound of the cracking whip, the horses raced off. Hipponous had set up a treacherous track through the trees, to the sea and back again. Before long Philocleon, Homer, and two of the other racers outstripped the rest. They galloped through the woods, taking tree branches and leaves with them as they went. The crowd thundered. Hipponous was ecstatic.

One of the two strangers fell back at the sea. Philocleon jumped a ravine with ease. Homer followed, but the third contestant, not familiar with the terrain, didn't jump his horse fast enough and he and the horse went down. His fall left the contest to Philocleon and Homer. They jested and yelled and raced at speeds that left

Hipponous' heart racing.

As they got toward the end of the course Philocleon took a slight lead. Seeing his chance, he spurred Pegasus forward. Homer, not willing to give up easily, also spurred his horse and gained some again. But it wasn't enough. Philocleon dashed across the finish line half of a horse's head before Homer. The crowd stood and cheered wildly when Philocleon brought Pegasus back to his father to accept the dagger.

As had been the custom throughout the festival, the animals sacrificed by the athletes were roasted for the crowd. They ate the roasted meat together with fruit and greens and wheat loaves. Even before they'd finished their wine and listened to Hipponous' usual boast that called for a toast, most of the men were calling for Homer.

Homer went to his place at the center of the stadium and with a voice stirring inside him like the wind, asked the muse, Calliope, to come to him with her verses. All of the audience waited. "There is Zeus' eagle," someone shouted. Everyone agreed though most of them saw nothing but black-winged Night. As they stood cheering, thunder rolled in the distance. "It's a second sign from Zeus," Philocleon yelled. "Who can doubt Homer is the most beloved of Zeus?"

Silencing the crowd Homer raised his open arms up to Zeus. What else could it be, the thunder and eagles except a sign from Zeus that he approved Homer's allowing the saga to be recorded? Stirred to the very bottom of his soul with the belief he was truly the chosen of Zeus, he began, his voice shimmering so with excitement it sent shivers down the spines of his audience.

He told his rapt audience how Achilles, enraged over the death of Patroclus, returned to the battle. How with relentless fury he pursued Hector, chasing him around the tall walls of Troy until the Trojan was cornered. There under the wall of Troy, the poet told his rapt audience, Achilles killed Hector, afterwards dragging the dead hero's body behind his chariot for all to see, refusing it all human respect until Priam, the great king of Troy and father of Hector, begged Achilles on his hands and knees for the body of his son.

Caressing his words with hexameters as perfect as the breasts of Aphrodite, the brilliant poet told his reverent audience first about the funeral of Patroclus and then about the funeral of Hector. He ended the saga late in the night, hoarse and tired, by standing and reciting the last thrilling line of the poem. "Such was their burial of Hector, breaker of horses."

That night there was no cheering. Overwhelmed, one by one the athletes and spectators got up from their seats and walked past the great poet, each touching his mantle and murmuring praises. Not a man leaving the stadium thought he would ever again experience anything like the recitation Homer had just given.

When the crowd had passed, Homer sat with Philocleon, emptying his own wine bowl. "After a lifetime of reciting poetry, I've finally come to understand what makes a poet great," he confessed to Philocleon. "It's not memorizing the words, but the feelings that go into the words." So simple, but he hadn't known it before. "I've always known anger and expressed it well, but at this festival I came to understand how to feel and express love and pity and sorrow. Our friendship has given me that. Now I think I truly am ready to become the greatest poet in all the Aegean. And it's you I have to thank."

Philocleon smiled even though he was torn between his admiration for Homer, who he decided was the only true hero he'd ever know, and his intense sadness that tomorrow Homer would be leaving him forever. Wanting to do something to seal their friendship forever, the way Gilgamesh and Enkidu had sealed theirs, he took the beautiful dagger he'd won and gave it to Homer. "This is your guest present," he said. "You must take it and promise to never forget my name."

Homer took the dagger and promised.

NINE

Nicias shuddered violently when Philocleon touched his shoulder to wake him. A surprised Philocleon pulled his hand away. "Is something wrong?" Nicias opened his eyes and stared at Philocleon, but said nothing.

Philocleon looked at the beads of sweat covering Nicias' forehead. "Are you sick?" Nicias shook his head. He had been dreaming. He was trying to remember.

"You need to get up," Philocleon said again, shaking Nicias' shoulder gently a second time. Something about the glassy look in Nicias' eyes made him nervous. "Homer is leaving today. We are to accompany him to Corinth."

"The dagger you won yesterday. What happened to it?" Nicias sat up hesitantly.

Surprised again, Philocleon looked at Nicias carefully. "Why do you ask?"

"I was dreaming," was all Nicias said. He got out of bed and dressed slowly, his mind gripped by the dream. In it he was examining the birds on the dagger when suddenly, both of them ripped free of the blade. As he stood there watching the birds fly one after the other toward the mountains, he was overcome with a feeling that something terrible was going to happen. Just as he expected whatever it was to happen, Philocleon woke him. What was it? He asked himself over and over, straining his memory until his head ached wretchedly.

Leaving Nicias to prepare the horses, Philocleon and Homer searched for Hipponous. They found him sitting in his room with an abacus in one hand, a wine bowl in the other. "I've been calculating," he explained to Philocleon, totally ignoring Homer.

Calculating. Yes, he had been calculating...his demise. At the end of the festival, he'd been telling one of his neighbors about his ship and the man had informed him he'd overheard Castor and Polydeuces talking. Merops' treaties to carry goods to the colonies had been lost to the Phoenicians.

The festival had been costly. He hadn't spared any expense to impress his guests. Many of his animals had been sacrificed. His stores of wine and grains greatly diminished. He'd given away three of the family heirlooms: the bronze cauldron, the shield, and the silver incense burner. All this because he was certain he'd be wealthier than ever once he got his ship. Now all was lost. Instinctively his hand went for the silver ring he always wore on his smallest finger. Gone too. He didn't even know when he had lost it.

"I am sorry to disturb you." Homer said, determined to end his stay civilly for Philocleon's sake. It was obvious to Homer from the faraway look on Hipponous' face that his mind was elsewhere. "I'm leaving now and I wanted to say goodbye and thank you."

Hipponous, after some moments, realized Homer had said that he was leaving. Some good news at last, he thought. He looked up prepared to make his goodbye a polite one for Philocleon's sake. His eyes scanned the poet. On his waist hung the family dagger. "What is that?" Hipponous demanded pointing to the dagger.

"It's the dagger Philocleon won in the horse race. He gave it to me as a guest present."

Hipponous turned to Philocleon. "Did you give that dagger to Homer?"

"Yes."

"Take it back." The one heirloom he thought they hadn't lost was the dagger.

"What?"

"I said, 'Take it back.'"

"No. It was a gift. I won't take it back." Philocleon was shocked and embarrassed his father would even suggest such a thing, but he was just as shocked at his own behavior. For the first time ever, he hadn't even attempted to convince or cajole. He'd met his father head on.

"Do you realize that dagger has been passed from father to son in our family since the Trojan war? It's one of our most precious possessions and you have given it to a complete stranger."

Philocleon didn't move. Homer a stranger! What a joke. He knew Homer much better than he knew his father.

Thoroughly exasperated, Hipponous jumped up and threw his wine bowl against the floor, splattering all of their feet with wine and broken pottery.

Hatred swelling within him, Philocleon faced Hipponous. "I won that dagger in the horse race. It's mine to do with as I please." His entire body shook with rage and fear. "If you want it back, you'll have to kill me to get it."

"It's okay," Homer interjected. He took the dagger off the leather rope it hung on and handed it to Philocleon, saying to Hipponous, "I didn't realize it was a family heirloom."

"No." Philocleon handed the dagger back to Homer. "I gave it to you and it's yours." He glared at Hipponous "I'm not a double-dealing Cretan."

Hipponous saw the hate in his son's eyes. It startled and saddened him. He stepped forward to grab Philocleon by the shoulders to try to make him understand, but Philocleon dodged out of his grasp, thinking he planned to force him to take the dagger back, and ran from the room with Homer following. Pacing, Hipponous listened to the two of them arguing in the courtyard. Several times he started toward the door, but in the end he did nothing to intervene.

At last he heard them leave the corridor. "Medusa's curse on that poet." He kicked the broken pieces of pottery. Philocleon had no idea how valuable that dagger was. Or of their financial state. He couldn't force Homer to give the dagger back to him. It was bad enough his eavesdropping slaves would pass the word he'd demanded it back. He felt trapped, the same way he'd felt when Calonice died. Impotent against fate.

"Medusa's curse," he repeated and slammed his fist against the wine-mixing bowl. Reminded of the wine, he poured himself a bowl and drank it down, then threw the bowl against the wall letting the pieces scatter where they would. "Nicias," he yelled and sat down.

After a long silence, one of the kitchen slaves came to clean up the broken pottery. "Where is Nicias?" Hipponous demanded, his words slurred.

"He went with Philocleon and Homer to Corinth. They left right after Philocleon spoke with you."

Hipponous leaned back. At least his relationship with his son would return to normal when Philocleon returned.

"Come with me to Olympia," Homer suggested when they reached the main road to Corinth. "If we sold this dagger, we could live forever." He grinned surreptitiously. "We could have a great time searching for everlasting names like Gilgamesh and Enkidu."

"I can't."

"Why not? Are you afraid of your father?"

Philocleon scoffed. "No. It's my grandmother. I gave her my oath I'd marry Scapha when Persephone returns from Hades' underworld and Demeter causes new shoots to grow in the furrows. I can't break my oath."

"Two seasons will pass before Demeter brings new shoots. You have time to see Olympia. If you like, I'll even return with you to see that you're properly married."

"I don't think your father would allow you to leave," Nicias interjected weakly. "Please. Return and talk with him first."

Philocleon listened to Nicias, but he hated his father at that moment and he wanted desperately to accompany Homer to Olympia. "He'd never agree to it. You know that."

"You coming?" Homer started down the road toward Corinth.

"On your way home," Philocleon instructed Nicias before he raced off after Homer, "stop and tell my grandmother I will most certainly return in time to marry Scapha – just as I promised."

Nicias continued to plead until Philocleon could hear him no more. He couldn't remember ever having been so frightened. Was that the meaning of the two birds in flight in his dream? Homer going to Olympia, Philocleon going with him. But that wasn't the entire dream. A dread filled Nicias. Something horrible was going to happen. He could feel it. But what was it? He turned and raced his horse back toward the estate.

Sweating with heat and anxiety, Nicias stopped the first slave he met on the estate. "Where's Hipponous?"

"In the house."

"Get him." He dismounted and limped toward the front door. Halfway there he met Hipponous. Seeing Nicias' face was enough. Hipponous looked around. Something was wrong. "Where's Philocleon?"

Sweat streaking his face, Nicias looked at Hipponous. Not even trying to hide his fear, he gasped, "He refused to return."

"Are you telling me you have let my son, my only son, run away with that poet?" Hipponous' voice wrenched through his unsteady lips. He was staggering. Pointing at Nicias' foot he continued, "You, of all of my slaves, I have kept with Philocleon because you know best what happens to a young boy who doesn't have the protection of his father." Hipponous' fear and anger intensified as he looked at Nicias' mutilated foot.

"I couldn't stop him," Nicias answered.

"Fool." Hipponous struck Nicias in the face. In all the seasons Nicias had been with Hipponous, he had never struck him.

Nicias, stunned, said no more. What would it help to explain that a slave had no way to force his master or his master's son to do anything against his will?

"Bring two horses," Hipponous shouted toward the stable.

Within moments, the stable hands had two horses ready. Hipponous took one of the horses, Nicias the other. Exasperated, half-drunk and furious, Hipponous led Nicias on a dangerous ride across the countryside, circling the path of the two young men, intercepting them as they rode leisurely ahead toward Corinth.

Stopping his horse in front of Homer, Hipponous called to him, his eyes ablaze with insane rage, "What kind of a man are you that you would accept my hospitality, steal my son, and slink away like a hound? Get down off your horse and let's see if you are as skilled with your weapons as you are with your tongue." He prepared his spear.

No. Father," Philocleon screamed. "It was my idea to follow Homer. Spare him, his life, and punish me."

Homer stared at the ravenous lion aiming his spear at him and considered his possibilities. Schooled as he was in the short but glorious life of Achilles, he couldn't bring himself to run, even though he knew it was the only reasonable course open to him.

Sending an earnest entreaty to Apollo for protection, Homer poked Philocleon's mare on the rear end unexpectedly with his spear, causing her to bolt toward the trees, momentarily out of control. "Do not think I need protection," he cried at Hipponous and prepared his spear. As he spoke, he let his spear fly. It missed Hipponous, but caught Pegasus at the top of his neck. Pegasus reared and Hipponous slid backwards, but he held himself on.

Quickly he pulled the spear from the Pegasus' neck and tossed it to the ground behind him. He hurled his spear at Homer.

The spear caught Homer in the thigh and the strength of the throw knocked him off his stallion. He got painfully to his knees and with both of his hands, tried desperately to pull the gold dagger from its leather holder.

Hipponous dismounted and seeing Homer wounded, charged toward him, thrusting his dagger into the poet's neck when he reached him. Homer gasped and fell forward. He lay in agony at Hipponous' feet when Philocleon returned from the trees.

As soon as he saw Homer, Philocleon threw himself from his mare and ran to him. He took Homer's hand and held it close to his chest, sobbing. The intense emotion revived Homer. He half-opened his eyes. "I would have been the greatest poet in the Aegean," he whispered. "But instead, like Meleager's my life has been snuffed." He gasped for breath bitterly. "I'm going to die an inglorious death here on the road to Corinth."

"No," Philocleon insisted, but he was too late. Life had already left Homer. Throwing himself on the ground at the side of his friend, with both hands Philocleon caught up dirt and threw it over his head. He tore at his face and pulled out his hair. A cry so deep and despairing came from within him it frightened both Hipponous and Nicias.

Nicias started to go to him, but Hipponous stopped him. "Get up," he instructed Philocleon and turned and walked back to examine the wound on Pegasus' neck. He was terribly afraid for his son.

Losing reason to pain and shock, Philocleon pulled his father's spear from Homer and stood. He aimed the spear at Hipponous.

"No!" Nicias grabbed for the spear but he was too late.

"Father," Philocleon cried. "You forgot your weapon."

The spear smashed into the side of Hipponous' head. He fell to the ground at the feet of Pegasus.

Nicias ran to him. "Dear Zeus!" he cried.

Philocleon stood mute for a few moments trying to comprehend what had happened. Gradually, watching the blood run from his father's head, he realized what he had done. He ran to where Hipponous lay. Nicias was tending the wound. "Will he be all right?"

Hipponous pulled Philocleon close to him. Taking his son's

hand in his own, he whispered, "I want to speak."

Philocleon started to pull away, thinking his father was only wounded. "I'll ride for help."

"No. There isn't time. I have little life left, of that I am certain. Sit. Let me speak."

Philocleon sat next to his father.

"I have offended the Mother Goddess, and my untimely death must certainly be her revenge." Too tired to continue, Hipponous rested his head against his son's thigh. His breath came in short spurts.

It sounded so shallow to Philocleon, he turned in a panic to Nicias. "Can you do something?" It was the first time he believed Hipponous would truly die.

Nicias stood staring at the two of them. Suddenly he screamed, "Aeeeeeeeeeee. You see." He pointed hysterically at a snake slithering across the ground. "The snake. It belongs to the Mother Goddess. Your father is right. The Erinyes have taken her revenge."

"What revenge?" Philocleon asked, confused.

"Your father. When he took your mother to Corinth before your birth, he swore an oath to the Mother Goddess that he would return and dedicate a silver statue if you were born alive. When your mother died, he refused. He broke his oath to the Mother Goddess. Now she has taken her revenge." Nicias stood, white and shaking, unable to move.

Philocleon looked at the snake. "How do you know the snake belongs to the Mother Goddess?"

"Why else would a man die in the prime of his life?"

Hipponous opened his eyes again. "Your mother. I loved her. Remember that. Your grandparents are wrong about me. I was going to explain to them right after the funeral, but they were so angry. Time passed and the longer I waited, the more difficult it became. Finally, it was no longer possible." He closed his eyes again. A low moaning sound came from deep within his chest.

Numbed, Philocleon asked Nicias. "What does he mean?"

"Your grandparents never forgave your father for not staying with your mother when she was dying."

"Why didn't he?"

Hipponous opened his eyes and made one last effort to talk. "When your mother's labor continued and the midwives couldn't bring you from her, I spoke with the head midwife. She told me you were wrongly placed in your mother's womb. Either she could live or you could, but not both. I went in and talked with you mother. I wanted her to live. She wanted you to live. In the end, she prevailed. You were to live. She made me promise not to tell your grandparents. If they'd known, they would have insisted she should have been saved..." His voice trailed off.

"All these years grandmother and grandfather thought you didn't love her?"

"They were angry because I left for Corinth before she died. Your mother made me promise to do it. She said she was afraid you would die if I didn't leave to placate the Mother Goddess right away, but I think really she wanted to spare me her death."

Hipponous pulled Philocleon close to him. He could barely whisper. "Killing your father is a crime against the sanctity of the blood of our ancestors. You are surely polluted. You must purify yourself."

Philocleon broke down. "Father, it was done as a senseless act of anger. I did not mean..." He sobbed.

"Listen. You must purify yourself from the bloodguilt. Go to a spring high in the mountains. Wash yourself thoroughly. Then return home and sacrifice an ox to Zeus and a kid to Apollo. Throw the spear on the fire when the thighs have burned. Afterwards, you must go into exile. The shades of my ancestors will be angry. They'll come to my house bent on revenge. You must stay away until they have given up their revenge and gone back to Hades."

"How will I know when they've gone back to Hades?"

Hipponous could say no more. While he was trying to speak, his olive brown eyes slowly misted over and he died.

Philocleon sat motionless, numb. Suddenly he knew what he must do. He stumbled to his feet and rushed to where Homer's spear lay useless. He grabbed the spear near the point, but before he could thrust it into his heart, his hand was stayed by Nicias.

"You must not kill yourself. Someone has to be alive to light the fire for the funeral pyres of Homer and your father." He held the pale, shaking, young man against him, his own heart despairing as much as Philocleon's.

After a long while, Nicias took Philocleon by the hand and helped him on his horse. "Wait here," he said. Gathering up the young body of Homer, he hung it gently over his horse. He returned and picked up the body of Hipponous. Struggling, he got it over Pegasus. Then, taking the reins of all the three horses in his hand, he mounted his horse and began the slow trek back to the estate.

TEN

Only Na'id-Assur and Qurdi Marduk were there to meet Nicias and Philocleon. "What happened?" Qurdi Marduk asked. "One of the neighbors came and told us that Hipponous and Homer are dead. He said he thought they killed one another."

Nicias was surprised to learn that the neighbors thought Hipponous and Homer had killed one another. When he started to tell the two Assyrians the truth, they stopped him. It would be better for Philocleon, they told him, for his rights to the inheritance, if Homer had killed Hipponous.

"I'm afraid all the slaves fled after the neighbor told us about Hipponous," Na'id-Assur informed Nicias.

"Worse, Castor and Polydeuces rushed off to seize the mines," Qurdi Marduk added.

"There's nothing we can do about the slaves or the mines right now." Nicias nodded sadly toward Philocleon.

Agreeing, the two Assyrians helped their pupil from his horse. Qurdi Marduk examined Philocleon's dull eyes carefully. "It's clear," he told Na'id-Assur, "he has slipped into some deep recess in his mind."

"We sent for your grandparents," Na'id-Assur told Philocleon, hoping his desire to see them would bring him out of his stupor.

Philocleon winced. "I won't see them," he stammered. Then, he fell silent again, following them like a dead man to his room.

Na'id-Assur told Alcmena Philocleon didn't want to see her when she arrived, but she rushed to his room anyway. "Nicias told me what happened," Alcmena said, trying to hold back her tears. She kissed his hand. "My beloved Philocleon. I'm so sorry." Philocleon pulled his hand from her. "My father didn't make my mother go to Corinth," he said, staring coldly at his grandmother. The words came haltingly and bitter. "He went to Corinth after I was born because my mother made him promise. She died because she wanted to save me. The midwife gave them a choice. Me or her." He turned from his grandmother. "She died to save me and all these years, you've blamed my father."

Alcmena burst into tears. "Did your father tell you that?"

"Yes."

"Oh please don't be angry with me." Not for a moment did she believe what Hipponous had told Philocleon. But Hipponous was dead now and if Philocleon could find comfort in believing his lies, what could be gained except more pain by trying to persuade him otherwise. "Please forgive me, Philocleon." She took his hand again. "Your father never said anything to me and I loved your mother so much."

Philocleon looked at her. He wanted to hate her, but there was no hate left in his heart for anyone but himself. "I forgive you," he said, breaking into uncontrollable sobs. "It's me I'll never be able to forgive."

Alcmena took him in her arms the way she had when he was a child. "Yes, you will. You will heal. Remember my babies. You will heal." Slowly she rocked him back and forth, singing to him as she had when he was a child. After a long while, he fell asleep.

"It isn't fitting to cremate them together," Daemones insisted to Nicias while they waited for Alcmena.

Nicias was too exhausted and stupefied to argue even though cremating them separately meant he would have to somehow build two funeral pyres instead of one by himself since it was obvious Daemones had no intention of helping. "We'll cremate Hipponous first. There's a cave out in the trees where I can keep Homer's body cool enough that it won't decay until I've had a chance to build a second pyre."

Since Alcmena was the only woman on the estate and she wasn't willing to wash the bodies, Nicias methodically set to work. He placed the bodies of both men on the sacrificial altar built by Hipponous' slaves for the games. After heating fresh spring water in a cauldron over one of the great fireplaces still left from the festival, he washed the blood from each of them and placed unguents in the open wounds.

Feeling a strange mixture of relief and sorrow, Nicias rubbed Hipponous' body with olive oil and wrapped it in white linen. For the first time since Calonice's death Hipponous seemed to him to be totally at peace with himself. Alcmena was wrong. Hipponous had told Philocleon the truth about Calonice. He had loved her. Otherwise, he'd never have let his grief rule him the day he threw the votive of the Mother Goddess into the Corinthian gulf.

Homer's young body, which would have to wait for further attention until Hipponous' funeral rites were completed, he also rubbed with olive oil. Then remembering Egyptus' story about the Egyptians rubbing their dead kings with salt to preserve them, he covered Homer lightly with the brine still left in the two amphorae.

He wrapped Homer's salt-oiled body in linen and laid him out deep in a cave at the back of the house. Retracing Egyptus' description of how the Egyptians buried their dead in mountains made of stone, he covered Homer's body. He knew the stones would protect Homer's body from animals, but he didn't know whether the stone coverings would protect his body from decay. He hoped so. Suddenly, he missed Egyptus terribly.

Alone, Nicias gathered wood for Hipponous' pyre from the piles still stacked around the farmyard. Then he prepared the things they would need for the funeral. Philocleon insisted it had to be a hero's funeral.

When Nicias had everything prepared, he and Daemones brought Philocleon from the house to the yard. Though pale and gaunt, Philocleon seemed to grasp what his responsibilities were. To keep the relatives from finding out exactly what had happened, no one had been invited to the funeral.

Daemones and Nicias placed Hipponous on the pyre. Philocleon asked for the family dagger he'd given to Homer. With it, he slit the throats of several fine goats and sheep, skinned them, and trimming the fat from the meat, placed it around Hipponous' body. Prompted by Nicias, he slit the throats of two of Hipponous' favorite hunting dogs and placed them on top of the sheep and goats, together with two-handled jars filled with honey and olive oil.

Taking the lead on Pegasus, Philocleon led Nicias and Daemones around the pyre three times singing a death lament. He ended the lament by reciting as much as he could remember of the funeral oration of Laius. Like Hipponous, Laius had been killed by his own son, Oedipus.

Philocleon got down from Pegasus and implored Boreas and Zephyrus, the north and west winds, promising fine sacrifices if they would come so his father's body would burn with great speed and a glorious flame. With the dagger, he sacrificed two calves, one for Boreas, the other for Zephyrus.

Finished, he wiped the fresh blood from the dagger and started to put it on the ground next to him when everything that had happened came rushing into his mind, overwhelming him with disgust for himself. He saw Homer, so happy and excited, accepting the dagger as his guest present. Hipponous demanding the dagger be returned. His fight with Hipponous over the dagger. Homer, dying at his father's feet and his father dying from the spear he had thrown.

"No," he screamed. "I am not worthy to see my father's pyre burn." Before Nicias or Daemones realized what was happening, he slashed both of his eyes with the dagger. Screaming with agony he threw the dagger and trying to walk onto his father's pyre, passed out.

"Get the Assyrians," Nicias commanded Daemones, dropping on his knees next to Philocleon. "Dear Zeus!" He cradled Philocleon's delirious head in his hands. "Why couldn't I convince you to turn back from the port that day? What a revenge the Mother Goddess has taken."

"Bring him to our room," Na'id-Assur interrupted Nicias. "Quickly. Qurdi Marduk is already making a poultice."

Qurdi Marduk applied the poultice while Na'id-Assur watched, fear and anger inextricably mixed in his thoughts. "How could my brilliant pupil be so stupid?" he asked Qurdi Marduk. "Putting out his own eyes. What if he dies?"

"From what I can observe," Qurdi Marduk comforted Na'id-Assur. "He will live and his eyes will heal." He sighed. "It's his sorrow I'm not so certain about. That wound is much deeper." He pulled the beeswax boards with the saga of the Trojan war on them from a shelf. "We have to find a way to help him heal the sorrow."

While Philocleon lay treading in and out of despair, Qurdi Marduk and Na'id-Assur copied the saga of the Trojan war from the beeswax boards onto leather hides, making each letter with extreme care so that as they read it to him, they could gently guide his hands over the words.

Under their constant care Philocleon's eyes healed, but the sorrow he felt never lightened. "There are no scars," Qurdi Marduk told him when he'd removed the poultice. "Everything has healed."

"Open your eyes and tell us what you think of our wonderful recording of the saga," Na'id-Assur added, incredibly anxious to see the familiar shy grin that he'd grown accustomed to expecting when Philocleon was happy.

Philocleon opened his eyes, but he saw nothing.

"It can't be," Qurdi Marduk insisted as he fought off tears.

For Philocleon the darkness was not unexpected. While he lay healing, his destiny had become fixed in his mind. He wished he'd been trapped into killing his father by some accident of fate like Oedipus. But he hadn't. It had been his excessive and obstinate pride that had caused him to disobey his father. Like Bellerophon he must pay Zeus' price for obstinate pride. His life would be spent wandering the earth as a blind man.

"Seeing can be done without eyes," Na'id-Assur said, trying to cheer himself and Qurdi Marduk as much as Philocleon. "You will have to learn how to see with your reason."

"I deserved it," Philocleon insisted.

Na'id-Assur took Philocleon's hand. "Right now you're filled with regrets, but your sorrow won't last forever. When you have finished sorrowing, remember – words aren't only for remembering, they are for reasoning. For seeing into the future, for thinking, for deciding what must be done."

Philocleon listened, but he had no interest in what the Assyrian said. What good was a future without Homer or his father?

Na'id-Assur and Qurdi Marduk continued to try to convince their pupil he must begin anew while the wheat in the countryside slowly ripened. At last, despairing of ever changing his mind, they forced themselves to say goodbye. "Though," Na'id-Assur confessed to Philocleon. "I would very much like to wait until you have fully recovered."

They left Philocleon in the care of Nicias. "What will you do?" Qurdi Marduk asked.

"Wait," Nicias answered. He knew from the slave ship, with the passing of seasons, the pain would eventually lessen and Philocleon would begin to live again. If everyone who knew what had happened continued to insist that Hipponous and Homer killed each other, Philocleon could wait as long as he needed. He would inherit the estate.

With Philocleon, Nicias waited through the harvest and the rains that followed. Though he never knew if Philocleon was listening, he talked to him constantly, telling him he must recover and fulfill his father's dying wish to leave the estate until his ancestors had retreated from their revenge.

When the rains ceased and shoots began appearing in the furrows, to Nicias' joy, Philocleon had finally recovered enough to ask about his father's burial. Nicias took him to the family crypt. After purifying their hands with water, they poured libations for both Hipponous and Calonice. "Where are Homer's ashes?" Philocleon asked when they'd finished.

"He has had no funeral," Nicias replied. "I've been waiting for you. I wrapped his body and placed it in a cave."

"Have one of the slaves fetch him. We must build a pyre and celebrate his funeral." Philocleon suddenly felt anxious. During his illness, he'd condemned Homer's shade to wander the earth. Without a funeral, a shade could not enter the Underworld of Hades.

"There are no other slaves. They fled when they heard that you father had died."

For the first time since his father's death, Philocleon thought about his own predicament. "What about the silver mines?"

"They are occupied by Polydeuces and Castor. From what I've heard, it would take a hundred bowmen to dislodge them."

"The treasury?"

"It's safe. I was the only one of the house slaves who knew of its existence."

"What about you? Why haven't you left me?"

"For the same reason I didn't leave you when you needed me on the boar hunt." In all their seasons together, neither of them had spoken of their feelings before. Nicias continued. "When I needed you to protect me from your twin cousins, you did. Only a man loathsome to the gods would refuse his help to someone who had helped him." He squeezed Philocleon's hand. "Besides, I have always loved you as though you were my own son."

At the word son, Philocleon broke into tears. "I'm not worthy to be any man's son. If only you had let me die."

"If I'd let you die, there would be no one to bury Homer. Without burial, the great poet's shade would wander the earth forever, never able to enter Hades. I know you wouldn't want that for your friend."

The two men went to the cave together. Philocleon waited on the cart while Nicias went into the cave and took the stones from Homer's body. The unguents and salt had helped, but Nicias was happy Philocleon wouldn't be able to see his friend. He poured the fragrance he'd brought over the linen and wrapped it tightly around Homer before he carried him out and placed him into the cart.

Lost again in a moment of despair, Philocleon insisted, "Build a pyre for Homer and let me throw myself on it."

"Can you remember back to when you had only celebrated the spring rites seven times?" Nicias asked. "Your father took you from your nurse and gave you to me to raise. You were so frightened and I promised you I would take care of you until you were able to take care of yourself?"

"Yes. But now I will never be able to take care of myself."

"Yes, you will. I've done it and so will you. When I had only seen the spring rites come and go ten times, slave traders attacked my father and me in our olive grove. They killed my father brutally and stole me from the rest of my family, but not before they'd smashed my foot. When my foot healed the captain sold me as a slave to your grandfather. You have no idea how often I wanted to die, but I didn't. Sometimes it's been difficult, but I've managed to take care of myself. You will too."

Philocleon was shocked. "You never told me this. Why?"

"It's a terrible story and there was no reason for you to know. Besides, I didn't want to remember."

"But you could have bought your freedom and returned to your family. Many of the other slaves did."

"Your father wouldn't give or sell me my freedom."

"Why?"

"Because I am a seer. He wanted me near him."

"Then go now. I free you."

"Not until you can take care of yourself. Now you see, you have to do it, for me as well as for you."

Philocleon desperately wanted to give Nicias his freedom. He wanted to do something for someone. How? How could he do it? He searched for a way, thinking of and then discarding one idea after another, until his mind came to rest on Bromia.

"My nurse, Bromia," he suggested excitedly. "If she is still alive and we could find her, maybe I could persuade her owner to sell her to me. Then, she could take care of me and you would be free."

"She's in Sparta."

"Sparta," Philocleon repeated. "How do you know she is in Sparta?"

"Trygaeus told me. He asks all of the drivers who come into the port if they've seen a woman of her description. A man came to the port who had seen her in Sparta."

"Is that why you wanted to know where Sparta was when I drew the map on the boar hunt?" Philocleon was amazed he could have known Nicias all his life and never known about him and Bromia. "Were you going to find Bromia?"

"Yes." Nicias paused before he began. "Bromia and I met here when your father bought her to work as your nurse. We fell in love."

"But why didn't you marry? She could have stayed here with you."

"Your father wouldn't have permitted it."

"I don't understand. I've heard him speak of Bromia. He had only fine things to say of her."

"Yes. But he took her to his bed shortly after she came."

"Grandmother told me."

"Your father never knew anything about Bromia and me. It would have been dangerous if he had."

"I don't understand."

"Your father wasn't a man to believe Bromia would prefer a cripple to himself."

"That's something else I don't understand. If my father truly loved my mother as much as he said he did, it seems strange he would have taken Bromia to his bed so soon and treated her like a wife. Did he ever explain it to you?"

"No." Nicias smiled at Philocleon's innocence. "I'm a slave. He never told me or Bromia. I think he was lonely."

"Lonely." The word stuck in Philocleon's throat. It had never occurred to him, his father could have been lonely. "But he sent her away. How did that happen?"

"I don't know. One day I went to the village and when I returned, she was gone."

"What did you do?"

"There was nothing I could do."

Overjoyed at the prospect of doing something for Nicias, Philocleon felt a little better. "Then we'll do it now. You are no longer a slave. As of now, you are a freedman. We'll find Bromia together, and I'll buy her. Then she will no longer be a slave."

Nicias hugged Philocleon, tears running down his cheeks. Words he had longed to hear for so long were at last spoken. He was free. "First, we have to take care of you. Afterwards, we'll go to Sparta."

"No. First, we must give Homer a proper funeral."

Nicias patted Philocleon on the shoulder. "We'll go now." He felt as though the thunderbolt of Zeus had been lifted from his head as he drove the wagon back toward the farmyard.

By the time they'd reached the house, Philocleon had planned Homer's funeral. "He must be given a hero's funeral," he told Nicias. "We'll put him on the bed where he slept as my guest, collect the treasury, and use the house as his funeral pyre."

Nicias didn't argue since he had a great fear that the angry shades of Hipponous' ancestors might already have moved into the polluted house.

They put Homer into his bed surrounded by skinned sheep and goats, honey and oil. In his hands they placed his much beloved lyre. "Get Pegasus," Philocleon said, remembering Homer's story of Danaë.

"But I saved Pegasus for you. You will need to use him to breed new horses."

"No." Philocleon was firm. "He belongs to our poet."

They sacrificed Pegasus and started the house on fire, chanting the same lament they'd sung for Hipponous. The sorrow Philocleon had spent so long overcoming easily overwhelmed him again, plunging him deep into despair. At the depths of his sorrow, he recited Achilles' lament for Patroclus.

When the fire died, Nicias gathered Homer's ashes and put them in a small covered ceramic jar he'd found among Egyptus' broken sherds behind the kiln. He gave the jar to Philocleon.

"I have no way to honor Homer with games as Achilles did

Patroclus," Philocleon told Nicias. "But I give my oath, I will return his ashes to his family so his grave can be honored by his descendants."

"Where does Homer's family live?"

"I don't know." Philocleon hung his head, suddenly hit by the reality that his noble gesture could not be fulfilled as Homer had told him nothing about himself. "And I honestly don't have any idea how to find out."

"What about Delphi?"

Philocleon knew where Delphi was from his lessons, but he knew nothing more. "What's at Delphi?"

"It's the home of Apollo's oracle. You could ask the oracle how to find Homer's fatherland. I went there with your father before his marriage to your mother. He wanted to know if the marriage would be auspicious."

Philocleon vaguely remembered his father telling him about Delphi. "What was the oracle's answer about the marriage?"

"His lot wasn't drawn so he never got to ask Apollo. I'd say it was generous of Apollo to spare him that knowledge. Most times, it's best to not know the future."

Nicias felt confident Philocleon's future was assured. To prevent Merops from claiming Hipponous' estate, Alcmena and Daemones had decided to keep the circumstances of Hipponous' death secret. Philocleon had agreed to appoint Daemones guardian of his estate until he returned. He had objected to the arrangement at first but Nicias had convinced him, it was the only way he could leave the estate with impunity to bury the ashes of Homer.

Without regrets, the two men poured a libation to Hermes and set out on their long journey to Delphi, stopping high in the mountains to burn the spears that had killed Hipponous and Homer as Philocleon had been commanded to do. Afterwards Nicias sacrificed a goat and helped Philocleon bathe in the blood to purify himself.

Part II

ELEVEN

"That has to be Delphi up ahead," Nicias announced as they rounded the last curve before the sanctuary. High up in the hills among the olive trees he could see the temple of Apollo, a rectangular building with columns. Down the road ahead of them sat the village of Delphi, its streets jammed with mules, horses, carts and men. "If the number of men I can see from here is any indication, I'd say we aren't the only ones who have come to consult the oracle," he observed, more to himself than to Philocleon.

Philocleon straightened from his hunched position, but said nothing. This was his first journey away from home and, he was trying to prepare himself.

Accustomed to silences when Philocleon lapsed into long periods of thought, Nicias didn't describe the temple during their ride to the village as he would have liked. Rather, he hummed the tune to a funny little song Bromia had sung to Philocleon when he was a child, pleased when it made Philocleon smile. The village was even more crowded than it had seemed from the road. Nicias tethered the horses at the first inn he found. "I'm going to ask about a room," he informed Philocleon. "You wait here."

Given all the strangers wandering the street, Nicias felt guilty about leaving Philocleon by himself, but this would be his first walk through the front door of an inn as a free man. He wanted to do it alone.

Happy to be sitting on the street where the noise kept his mind from dark thoughts, Philocleon listened to the jostling and banter of the men around him. Soon he joined in, exchanging jibes with a couple of men standing near the cart, then applauding when the men around him did. "What are we cheering?" he asked when the noise died down.

"A magician," a man answered who sounded as though he had seen about the same number of seasons pass as Philocleon.

"A good one?" Philocleon asked.

"Good enough to have tricked a bronze piece from most of us standing here," someone else added. "Care to try your luck?"

"As you can see, Hermes hasn't exactly been sitting on my shoulder," Philocleon answered, indicating his blindness. But there was no self-pity written on his face.

"We need some men for dice," a husky voice called from across the street.

"We're going to play dice," a man standing next to Philocleon said. "You want to come along?"

Philocleon shook his head. Though he really would have liked to get into the game, he didn't think he should leave the cart without Nicias being there. So he stayed where he was and listened. It wasn't long before he had turned the listening into a game. He would concentrate on a single voice and try to figure out what kind of a man belonged to it.

"We must be the favorites of Hermes today," Nicias told a smiling Philocleon when he got back to the cart. "We got the last room in a good inn. According to the innkeeper there won't be a room to be had in the entire village no matter how poor the quality when Helios drops below the trees." He helped Philocleon to the ground while they waited for the innkeeper's son to come for the cart and horses.

"Over here," Nicias called to the boy when he came around the corner of the inn.

The boy walked over, jumped onto the cart, and grabbed the whip. "I'll meet you at the stable."

"Wait," Nicias said, taking hold of the side of the cart.

"Why? Your friend want to ride?"

"No." Nicias reached into the back of the cart and pulled out the wooden box containing Philocleon's treasury. "I want to take this one with me." He slipped a small bronze piece into the boy's hand. "When you have the horses bedded down, bring the rest of the gear to the inn."

The boy threw the bronze piece into his cheek. Examining the box Nicias held, he said, "I'd keep a close eye on anything I didn't want to lose if I were you. It's not just the suppliants that show up for the oracle. We get our share of thieves, too."

"Thanks." Nicias tightened his grip on the box.

"If you need someone to watch your room, ask my dad. I have an older brother." He snapped the whip and disappeared behind the inn. Nicias hoisted the box of treasures onto his shoulder. It was the first occasion he'd had since Philocleon had given him his freedom to hire someone to do something for him. "Feels good," he admitted to Philocleon as he led him toward the inn. "Being called your friend instead of your slave."

"You didn't have to tell me that. I already knew it."

"How?"

"Your voice has been different ever since I gave you your freedom. More alive. And your step is lighter, even younger." Philocleon smiled to himself, pleased with his observation.

Nicias chuckled. "You mean I'm getting younger instead of older like most men?"

"Something like that," Philocleon answered, following him through the inn door, knowing from the tone of Nicias' voice he'd been right about him.

Inside the room Nicias put the box of treasures on the floor and opened it. "It's all here," he exclaimed happily.

"What's all here?"

"The treasury. I shouldn't have left it in the cart with you." He'd been so anxious to get to the inn, he'd forgotten all about the treasury. He refused to think of their predicament if they'd lost it. "The innkeeper says you have to be care..." Before he could finish something caught his attention. He looked at the door.

"I have your gear." It was the innkeeper's slave.

Nicias shoved the box under his bed. "Do you always open a man's door without knocking?"

The man shrugged and dropped the traveling sacks on the floor. "You told the innkeeper's son you wanted the gear."

Nicias closed the door as soon as the man was gone and locked it. He emptied his traveling sack and loaded Philocleon's treasury from the wooden box under the bed into his sack: gold and silver vessels, jewelry, fibulae, daggers. The sack was heavy, but he fastened it onto his back anyway.

"What are you doing?" Philocleon asked.

"Strapping your valuables to my back." There might not have been enough in the treasury for Hipponous' extravagant lifestyle, but there was plenty for the two of them if he didn't lose it. "I didn't like the way that man was looking around the room just now."

"Why? What did he do?" Philocleon had taken note of the man's voice. It sounded honest enough to him.

Not wanting to worry Philocleon unduly and anxious to try out his new freedom in the tavern, Nicias murmured, "Nothing really," but he took the sack anyway.

At the tavern they learned that the oracle would be held when the waning moon goddess, Selene, had grown into a full circle. "You watch," the man said who'd told them about the oracle. "You'll see the prices double. Right before the oracle they'll triple or quadruple. The Delphians are a greedy lot."

"Aren't you a Delphian?" someone piped in.

"How else would I know?" He threw back his head and laughed. "I've got barley cakes for sale right now at a good price. If I were you," he nodded toward Nicias. "I'd buy one before the prices go up."

"Don't buy from him," someone else warned Nicias. "The priests won't accept any but the ones sold at the altar. You'll buy one from him now and still have to buy one at the ridiculously high temple prices when you get there."

"He's right about prices though," the innkeeper said from behind the bar. "As the village fills up, prices will get higher."

"And yours won't?" someone yelled across the room.

The innkeeper winked. "More wine?" he asked Nicias.

Nicias nodded.

"Fill mine too," Philocleon said.

Nicias clinked his bowl against Philocleon's. "When the beautiful Selene is full again, we'll be toasting the price we're paying right now." It was the first time he'd drunk a toast with Philocleon. He liked the feel of it.

"Better yet, let's be drinking to throwing the Delphians out of Delphi and creating a pan-Hellenic village for the suppliants," a Boeotian suggested from the corner. Bowls went into the air and voices cheered.

The drinking and toasting to throw the Delphians out of Delphi continued until the beautiful moon goddess evolved into a full disk again. When she first appeared as a disk, Philocleon and Nicias sat, as Nicias had predicted, with the same group of men, toasting the prices when she was waning in Zeus' sky. They complained bitterly as usual, but everyone was too euphoric to really care. The proclamation they'd all been waiting for had finally come down from the sanctuary. The casting of the lots would be right after Night gave up the sky to Dawn.

Had it not been for the fight that broke out in the street in front of their inn, Nicias and Philocleon would have probably stayed in the tavern until Helios arrived. Instead, they went with the rest of the men who'd been eating and drinking in the tavern to see what the noise was about.

"I caught him in my room stealing, and I intend to make him pay with his skin," a big man with a scruffy beard told the crowd that was gathering. He was dragging a scraggly young slave who looked enough like the slave who had brought their gear to their room to convince Nicias he was related to the innkeeper's slave.

"We'll see about that," his captive said, biting the big man hard on the hand, sending him into a fit of threats and curses. Before anyone realized what had happened the thief slipped from the man's grip and ran down the street.

As men gathered to go after the young thief, Nicias took Philocleon by the arm and headed for their room, boasting just a little to Philocleon about how pleased he was he'd had enough sense to keep the treasury with him.

Philocleon made a mental note. He would have to listen more carefully in the future. He had listened carefully to the voice of the slave who brought their gear and he'd judged him to be an honest man.

Still awake when Dawn appeared in the heavens, Nicias got up and woke Philocleon. Expecting they would be two of the first to the sanctuary he was shocked to find the street already filled with men when they got to it. Pleading silently with Apollo he took Philocleon's arm and led him slowly along amidst a massive crowd to a small outcropping just below the sanctuary.

"Before we go to the temple of Apollo we have to cleanse ourselves in the Castalian spring," he told Philocleon, weaving a path for the two of them among the huge crowd of men already gathered at the spring.

"What's the Castalian spring?"

They had been told about the spring by several men during their stay in Delphi, but Nicias wasn't surprised that Philocleon didn't remember. Since they had come to Delphi Philocleon had been so immersed in his thoughts that he only half-listened to what people said.

"The Castalian is the sacred spring of Apollo. Don't you remember? It begins high in the mountains and ends in the Castalian pool." He guided Philocleon's hand along the natural rock basin, then to the cold stream of water flowing from the side of the outcropping into the basin.

Philocleon kept his hand under the water until his fingers began to tingle toward numbness. Still he was reluctant to pull it away. After so long being barely aware of his surroundings it thrilled him to feel something so acutely. Gradually, as the tingling moved up his arm, he became aware that Helios felt hot on his back. It felt so good to him, feeling again, he wanted to shout. Eventually, with his tingling hand, he followed the cascade up to the bedrock. Feeling carefully with his fingers, he asked, "Does the water flow from the rock through lion's heads?"

"Yes." Nicias held a bowl under the cascade and filled it. "Some say they can see the past and the future when they drink this water." He handed the bowl to Philocleon.

"And what about you? Can you see the future?" Philocleon held the bowl in both hands for a moment before he drank the water.

"I'm not interested in looking into the future," Nicias answered, his face sternly fixed. "It's too frightening." Though he knew the Delphic priests required everyone who visited the oracle to drink from the spring he put the bowl away without using it. He wasn't about to risk another premonition. He hadn't recovered from the horror of the last one yet.

On that note of decision, Nicias returned to the task of getting Philocleon ready for the oracle. "You have to bathe in the spring water," he said. As he poured water over Philocleon's head and shoulders he silently implored Apollo to show some pity when it came to the drawing of the lots. Philocleon had aged enough since the death of his father and Homer to pass for a man who had participated in the harvest festival fifty times. His hair had grayed. His skin had become drawn and wrinkled. There was no longer any tone in his muscles.

"My mother," Philocleon suddenly asked. "Was she as beautiful as grandmother says she was?"

"She was very young when she died, but I think she would have been beautiful." For Nicias beauty required maturity.

"Was she as kind as Bromia?" Philocleon conjured a picture in his mind of Bromia's warm smile. He imagined that he felt her gentle touch.

"I'm sorry but I really don't know what to tell you. I didn't see your mother very often. She was mostly in the women's quarters. When she did come to the portico or courtyard she rarely spoke. Yet from the things I know, I believe she was kind. Why are you asking?"

"I've been thinking. Grandmother says Scapha is as beautiful and kind as my mother was. I know she's right in one sense. Scapha is beautiful. But do you think she will be kind enough to marry me now that I'm blind?"

Nicias didn't lie. "I can't say what Scapha will do. But I think it would be better if you didn't worry about things like that right now. You need to concentrate on the oracle." Philocleon wasn't the only one with doubts. Nicias was struggling with some of his own. He and Philocleon had agreed to go to Sparta to look for Bromia when they left Delphi. He'd lost count of how often he'd asked himself during their stay in Delphi whether Bromia would still want him.

Finished with Philocleon, Nicias stepped into the basin and rinsed himself completely. The pool was so crowded when he finished and stepped out of it, men were fighting for a spot. He tried not to think about the odds for Philocleon's lot being drawn. Rather, he concentrated on entreating Apollo once more to intercede as he walked Philocleon to the sanctuary.

At the gate they stopped and waited with the other suppliants, watching from below while the priests chased the birds from the temple of Apollo and sprinkled the entire temenos with water. "They get the water from the sacred stream that runs beneath the temple," one of the Delphians told Nicias as the gate was opened.

Nicias and Philocleon entered the sanctuary amidst the crowd of suppliants and started up a small winding path the priests had named the Sacred Way. Nothing in his life had prepared Nicias for the things he saw. "You just wouldn't believe it!" he exclaimed to Philocleon. "Gold and silver vessels, many times larger and more beautiful than your father's finest silver crater. Beautifully decorated tripods everywhere." Awed at every turn in the path, he did his best to describe each object as they passed it.

Halfway up the hill, Nicias stopped. "There's a shrine here with a statuette of Apollo," he told Philocleon. "It's looks just like a man. He wears his hair over his shoulders like yours was before you cut it for your father's funeral. He's muscular. The artist has even carved the fingers and knees with such likeness you'd think it was a real man." He took Philocleon's hand and helped him feel the statuette.

"Is he smiling?" Philocleon asked when his fingers reached the statuette's lips.

"He certainly is!" Nicias traced the lips with his own fingers, feeling suddenly very hopeful and happy. He patted Philocleon's shoulder vigorously. "Apollo is smiling on you. I can feel it."

They walked on, Nicias continuing his descriptions while he repeated the stories he'd heard in the village. "Over there on our left is the platform of the Delphic sibyl. They say she comes and gives prophecies from that platform. During the rains when Apollo abandons the sanctuary and returns to the land of the Hyperboreans, Dionysus comes to Delphi and his maenads dance on her platform."

They walked past the platform to a small outcropping. "Here is the place where Apollo shot the Python with his arrow. They say the Python guarded the sanctuary for the Mother Goddess until it was killed by Apollo."

"Where is the Mother Goddess now?" Philocleon asked.

"She has a temple below the sanctuary. The women still go there to sacrifice before childbirth."

Philocleon winced. It seemed wherever he went he was reminded of his own mother.

Quickly Nicias patted his arm. "Today you must not allow bad thoughts to enter your mind. You must look forward instead of backwards. Apollo awaits you."

Philocleon nodded, forcing himself to concentrate on what lay ahead of them.

Walking around the final curve, they came to the temple of Apollo. Nicias stopped Philocleon at the base of the temple. "We have to wait here until the priests determine whether Apollo is in the Pythia," he said. "If he is, they'll cast lots."

Guessing from the noise that they were surrounded by a large crowd of men, Philocleon asked, "Are there as many men here as it sounds like there are?"

"I'm afraid so."

"Then my lot will never be drawn." He fought hard against disappointment.

"Wait and see." Nicias squeezed Philocleon's hand. "Remember, Apollo is smiling on you."

"What of the other men who passed the statuette?"

"It wasn't the same," Nicias lied. "I saw a special smile when you were there."

Philocleon didn't believe Nicias, but felt better knowing Nicias was so confident.

They waited until a priest came out of the temple and stood in front of it. A nervous silence fell over the crowd as he announced that he would see whether Apollo was in the Pythia. He told them the Pythia had bathed in the Castalian spring, and he warned anyone there who hadn't done the same to withdraw from the drawing of the lots. "First, the Pythia will drink water from the sacred stream which flows below the temple. Afterwards, she will chew laurel leaves. If Apollo shows us a sign he is willing to enter her, she will mount the sacred tripod and the oracle will begin."

He motioned toward the temple and a young novitiate came from the interior leading a kid with one hand, carrying a gold rhyton made in the shape of a goat's head in the other. The rhyton had been filled with water from the Castalian spring.

After an entreaty to Apollo, the priest sprinkled water from the rhyton onto the kid's nose. Breathlessly, the crowd of suppliants waited. Suddenly, the kid shivered, head and all four legs. Men jumped into the air, hugged one another, slapped their thighs, screamed, and clapped. Apollo was in the Pythia. The oracle would be held.

The Delphians, who always had first rights to the oracle, lined up at the three steps leading to the temple platform. Behind them the novitiate placed the statesmen who had been given special privileges. The remainder of the men were told to put their name or sign on a clay tablet and place it in a crater brought to the edge of the platform by the novitiate. Those men whose names or signs were pulled from the crater could proceed to the altar.

Philocleon put his name on the clay tablet Nicias held for him. Together, they took it up the three steps to the crater. As Philocleon's hand opened to let his tablet fall, it shook uncontrollably. He felt Nicias stir next to him. "Apollo is certainly with you," Nicias whispered, convinced the uncontrollable shaking was a good omen.

When there were no longer any men waiting to drop in lots, the priest went to the crater and began pulling clay tablets from the heap piled inside, reading the name or showing the sign on each tablet as he drew it. With each name, Philocleon's chest tightened until he could barely breathe. Just when he was convinced he would burst from the tension he thought he heard his name. He gasped. "Was it my name?" he timidly asked.

"It certainly was." Nicias grabbed Philocleon and hugged him tightly to him. "Thank you, Apollo," he whispered toward the temple. "When I find my home, you will endlessly smell the smoke of sacrifices made in your name."

"A hecatomb of oxen from me when I return home," Philocleon added, hugging Nicias in return.

Nicias, following the novitiate, took Philocleon up the steps of the temple to the altar in front of the entrance. They went to the table standing to the side of the altar and bought a barley cake for a price as exorbitant as they'd been promised at the inn. "You have to dedicate the cake before you are allowed to enter the temple," the novitiate informed them.

They placed the cake on the altar. Afterwards, the novitiate led both of them to the front the temple. There, with the assistance of the priests and the representative from his district, Philocleon bought a goat and sacrificed it to Apollo at the temple hearth.

"Over there." The priest who was putting the goat's thighs on the hearth pointed to benches along the temple wall. "And remember, any ill-spoken words uttered in the temple will not be looked upon favorably by Apollo."

Nicias couldn't see the Pythia and he didn't dare ask where she was for fear his question might displease Apollo. He'd heard in the village that her tripod was in a crevice below the temple. Silently he searched the room with his eyes, but he saw nothing.

As both men sat breathing heavily from the tension and

excitement, a priest stepped from behind a purple cloth hung at the far end of the cella and asked their purpose. With shaking hands, Philocleon gave his question to the priest, written down as prescribed by the rules of Delphi. The priest stepped behind the purple cloth and read it aloud. "What is the fatherland of the great poet, Homer?"

From somewhere behind the purple cloth came a series of high-pitched shrieking sounds, followed by guttural moaning. When the moaning had subsided into a low groan, the priest stepped from behind the purple cloth. "Apollo says you must go to Ios," he told Philocleon. "There you must seek not the fatherland of Homer, but his motherland and the land of his mother's father."

Philocleon covered his face with his hands and moaned, a mixture of relief and sorrow.

"Quiet," the priest commanded.

"Come," Nicias whispered, taking Philocleon by the hand.

Philocleon followed him without further sound, his mind racing.

"What's wrong?" Nicias asked once they were outside the temple. He looked carefully at Philocleon's pale face. "Aren't you happy? We've found Homer's birthplace. I thought that was what you wanted?"

"It was and I am happy," Philocleon answered. "It's just that for a moment I started thinking about making the journey to Ios with Homer's ashes. Do you remember? Homer and I were going on a journey together when I refused to turn home with you." He moaned again. "If only I'd known then what kind of a journey it was to be."

"I don't remember. I was so worried, I wasn't really listening to you. What journey did you plan?"

"Na'id-Assur and Qurdi Marduk," Philocleon explained, "had told me the story of king Gilgamesh and his friend Enkidu. It was my desire to go with Homer, like the two friends, Gilgamesh and Enkidu, in search of everlasting names that made me decide not to return with you. Don't you see? If I'd returned, Homer and my father would be alive." His face paled again with nervous bitterness.

"You have to stop remembering," Nicias said firmly. "Try to concentrate on thoughts of keeping your promise to return Homer's ashes to his family."

Philocleon agreed to try, and as he fought to leave the past behind and think about burying Homer's ashes, a remarkable realization flooded him. Homer's life didn't have to end like that of

Meleager – with an inglorious death. He, Philocleon, Homer's closest friend, was capable of changing everything. All he had to do was answer Qurdi Marduk's riddle. If he could figure out how Gilgamesh both died and gained immortality, then Homer's death could become as glorious as that of Achilles.

TWELVE

Philocleon felt the lingering sense of guilt he had brought with him into the sanctuary dissipate as they walked back down the Sacred Way. He hadn't thought about the future since he had watched both Homer and his father die. Now, he excitedly thought about nothing else, about finding Bromia, Nicias' family, Homer's birthplace. Fervent hope edged back into his life.

Hope was also foremost in Nicias' mind as he walked sideways down the Sacred Way toward the gate of the sanctuary, his right hand gripping Philocleon's arm tightly, his left extended in front of him to keep people from running into them – hoping they would stay alive long enough to reach Sparta.

Shortly after they had arrived in Delphi, while Nicias was standing outside the inn, the owner of a fishing boat had come into the village from the port looking for men who wanted to cross the Gulf of Corinth. On an impulse of desperation to see Bromia he had signed himself and Philocleon up for passage on the boat. They were scheduled to leave when Helios dropped below the trees. When he had made the agreement, getting on the boat hadn't seemed so difficult. Now, with the moment so close, the thought terrified him.

"Watch where you're going!" An old man gave Nicias a shove.

Catching his balance, Nicias squeezed Philocleon's arm to reassure him. "We're almost to the cart."

From the noise and pushing, Philocleon could tell the path had gotten more crowded with men. Every shore of the Aegean must be represented here today, he decided, listening to the many accents and dialects that were being spoken. He felt a surge of gratitude that his lot had been drawn.

Somewhere outside the temenos a baby cried, interrupting Philocleon's thoughts. He tried not to listen. It cried again. A scene imagined over and over during his illness crept into his imagination. He saw himself as a newborn cradled in his dying mother's arms, crying fiercely as though he somehow sensed her inevitable death, his father standing at the end of the bed watching.

Despair suddenly overwhelmed him, robbing him of the hope and gratitude he'd felt since they arrived in Delphi. If only his mother had let him die, he wouldn't be here now, knowing he had killed both his parents.

"Here's the cart." Nicias helped Philocleon up and took the reins from the young boy he'd hired to watch it. He climbed on, pulled the heavy sack from his back with one hand and tossed a bronze piece to the boy with the other. From the stone cold expression on Philocleon's face, he knew Philocleon was remembering again. He guided the horses down to the harbor road, turned and followed its winding path into the thick olive groves that filled the land between the sanctuary and the seacoast. Attempting to distract Philocleon, he took a deep breath of the air. "Smell. The olive trees are beginning to bloom."

Philocleon breathed deeply but the fresh scents that came with each breath didn't comfort him. Instead, they reminded him of his home – his father taking Pegasus out after the rains. "Did you hear that baby cry when we were in the sanctuary? Father always wanted grandchildren. Now that I'm blind, I won't be able to do even that for him."

"Why do you say that?" Nicias was confused. "What does blindness have to do with having children?"

"I'm certain Scapha won't want me now."

Nicias understood. He put his arm gently around Philocleon's shoulder. "You can't be certain about that. Do you remember when I told you about my first meeting with Bromia?"

"Did you tell me?"

"It was when you were very sick."

"I don't remember."

"She was standing in your father's courtyard with her owner. Your father was trying to decide whether or not to buy her to take care of you. She was the most beautiful woman I'd ever seen.

Blessed by Artemis, she was tall with dark brown hair and unblemished white skin. I fell in love with her the moment I saw her.

"Up until then I had lived with my foot, not thinking much about it, knowing it was there, but not really thinking about what it meant. But that horrible moment when Eros shot me with his arrow, I felt mutilated. In my heart I knew no woman so beautiful could possibly love a man with a foot like mine.

"I stood in the corner of the courtyard looking at her, my foot hidden behind the altar, praying to Zeus, Apollo, Athena, all the gods and goddesses that your father wouldn't call for me. I didn't want to walk in front of her with my hideous foot.

"My prayers didn't help. Your father called for me. He wanted wine to celebrate the agreement with her owner. I felt her eyes turn on me as I limped across the courtyard. I decided, no matter what happened, I wouldn't look at her. But she was so beautiful I couldn't help myself. When I looked into her eyes I expected to see nothing but disgust. Instead, she looked at me with such quiet gentleness, my hands began to shake and I spilled wine all over your father's feet. He screamed at me. Never had I wanted to run and hide so badly."

Philocleon smiled, relaxing a little again.

"I didn't see her again until much later when she was down at the stream washing out some of your clothes. I wanted desperately to talk to her, but I was afraid. When I got to the stream she stopped her washing and sat up on her knees and watched me. Then she did the last thing I expected. She smiled. I got so flustered I stepped into a hole with my bad foot and fell. I expected her to laugh. She didn't. She asked if I'd hurt myself. 'Cripples never hurt themselves,' I said, making a silly face. 'We're used to falling.'

"She stood and came over to me, took my foot in her hands and examined it to see if I had injured it. No one had ever touched my crippled foot. I was so shocked I jerked it away. 'We aren't ever going to get to know one another,' she said, 'if you insist I can't see past your foot.'

"And she didn't. She never saw me through my foot." He patted Philocleon's hand. "Remember, there are all kinds of women. You always hear about the cruel ones because most men like to moan about their lot in life. But I'd say there are many more kind and generous women than cruel ones. Don't you go giving up on Scapha without giving her a chance."

"You really think she might still have me?"

"I can't say for certain whether she will or not. But I can say for certain you shouldn't jump to any conclusions. Wait and see what she says before you worry."

"I will." Hope crept once more into Philocleon's life. He began again to think about the future, about Bromia, of how happy it would make him to help Nicias find her. He even allowed himself to think what it might be like to return home and find Scapha waiting for him.

Nicias relaxed. The softened expression on Philocleon's face told him all he needed to know. The boy's mind had turned once again to more pleasant thoughts. It had been a long struggle but gradually the long periods of despair had begun to be replaced with longer and longer periods of peace. He'd heal.

Feeling content with Philocleon's peace, Nicias spoke no more. He let the horses pick their own way down the road and returned to his own memories, remembering as he had ever since they got to Delphi, the soft touch of Bromia's hands on his skin working their way down his body. Caressing him. Exciting him.

When they finally reached the port his visions of Bromia had come close to overcoming Nicias' anxiety about the boat. He stopped the horses by the dock and waited. He'd had a terrible battle convincing the fisherman to haul the cart and horses across with them. If there hadn't been so few people interested in traveling before the final celebrations at Delphi, the fisherman would never have agreed. As it was, they'd had to pay plenty.

"Wait over there." One of the oarsmen directed Nicias to a place on the other side of the gangplank. "When we're ready I'll let you know."

Nicias guided the horses around the gangplank and halted them. Gingerly, he looked at the boat he was going to board shortly. It left his stomach churning, his heart beating so hard he could feel every beat in his head. He looked away from the boat and didn't dare to look back. He knew he'd change his mind if he did.

"What's the sea like?" Philocleon felt a surge of excitement pulse through his body. How he had dreamt of this moment when they had gone to the port village to buy supplies, of his actually boarding a ship. In his dreams he had always been standing on deck captaining the ship as she sailed from the harbor. Well, things were different now, he decided, refusing to let go of his hard-won hope.

Nicias examined the sea. "There aren't any white caps on the waves. Must be gentle out there." He tried to swallow, but his mouth was totally dry. The hold below the deck of the slave ship flashed before him. He remembered a gale throwing all of them around in the hold, into one another and the walls. He and the other boys were screaming, not because they were being thrown around, they were used to rough treatment, but because they knew the door to the deck was locked from above. If the ship went down, they would go down with it.

"Bring her over," the oarsman shouted.

Philocleon waited for the cart to move. When it didn't, he reached over and shook Nicias' arm gently. "The fisherman's calling us."

"I heard." Nicias wiped sweat from his forehead.

"Are we waiting for other carts to get on the boat?" Philocleon asked when the cart didn't move.

"No." Nicias took another dry swallow, looked up and saw the oarsman waiting for him to bring the cart. His legs shaking, he got down and led the horses slowly up the gangplank. At the top, one of the deck hands took the horses from him. "You can sit over there." He pointed to a row of benches aft.

By the time they reached the benches the old excitement Philocleon had known watching ships in the harbor had overwhelmed him. "Is she a big ship?" he asked excitedly.

"No. It's a small fishing boat."

"What does she look like?" He persisted in imagining a huge ship like the one Homer had come on.

"The little fishing boats we used to see in the Sounion harbor. One sail, not much more." Nicias sat Philocleon down. "You have to rest now. We have a long ride ahead of us when we get to the other side."

Out of respect for Nicias' fear of the sea – which he'd learned about from a long discussion they'd had about the slave ship, Philocleon didn't ask the questions running wildly about in his head. He stretched out on the bench as Nicias had suggested and waited, certain something adventurous was about to happen. In a short while, the fisherman was yelling and cursing at his oarsmen to get to their oars and move the boat out. Amidst the heavy grunting of overworked men, Philocleon felt the boat bump away from the dock. He was greatly amused. Some adventure. The sea was so calm there wasn't even a ripple of excitement to be felt. "It's interesting," he said to Nicias though it was Na'id-Assur and Qurdi Marduk he had in mind, "how nothing in life ever turns out the way you expect it will."

As soon as the boat moved, Nicias sat down on the floor in front of Philocleon, leaned his head against his knees, and closed his eyes. He didn't open them again until he heard the fisherman order his oarsmen to take the boat as far into shore as they could get it.

When the boat came to a halt, Nicias helped Philocleon back onto the cart and led the horses off the boat. On dry land, he climbed onto the cart himself and without once looking back, urged the horses forward as fast as the busy port would allow, away from the sea, straight through the port town without stopping, to the road.

The sense of urgency that had prompted him to board the fishing boat heightened even more when they reached the road. Relentlessly, he kept the cart rolling toward Sparta. They rose with the beautiful rose-colored Dawn, ate their meals in the cart, stopped only to water the horses and relieve themselves. They slept in the cart, halting only when Night made it impossible to continue on the steep, winding road.

So preoccupied was Nicias with getting to Sparta, he didn't see the budding trees, the freshly turned ground, or the farmers out planting. He was barely aware when they had to stop, unable to move because the cart was surrounded by sheep being driven by herders to the high pastures. Under different circumstances, he would have noticed the cart was often followed by wolves.

Philocleon, understanding Nicias' unwillingness to talk, spent the journey listening to the sounds around him, smelling the scents in the air, guessing to himself what they were. Fighting off the bouts of depression that came upon him whenever a sound or scent brought him memories of his father or Homer, he managed to renew his spirit until he became once again totally committed to living.

They reached Sparta just as Helios began his ride from the sky. Giving in to Philocleon, Nicias got them a room at one of the inns before he went to look for Bromia. "You need to rest and eat," Philocleon insisted. "It'll keep you from losing your judgment if things don't go as you expect." He thought about telling Nicias how he'd decided that nothing ever went the way you expected, but he didn't.

Though Nicias would have preferred to skip the evening meal, he ate with Philocleon. Afterwards, he took Philocleon to their room and helped him into bed. "I'm going out to see if I can find the estate where Bromia lives," he said heading for the door a bundle of nervous energy.

"It would be better to sleep first," Philocleon said, but he didn't argue, knowing how anxious Nicias was.

Nicias left the room and went to the marketplace. Where should he ask, he wondered. Thinking of nothing better to try, he started at the vegetable and fruit stalls, moved on to the fish stalls, then to the craftsmen. He gave the name of the man who owned Bromia to everyone he met. All people did was shrug and shake their heads.

Sweating from exhaustion and nerves, he sat down at the marketplace fountain and rinsed his head and chest. He'd never been so close to breaking down. "What if I don't find her?" he said aloud.

"Find who?"

Nicias looked up. Standing in front of him was a filthy woman in rags. She smelled so bad she took his breath away.

"Find who?" the woman repeated.

He didn't answer. The woman, the smell, the exhaustion. He was too weary to speak. Philocleon had been right. He should have rested first.

She shrugged and walked away.

He took a drink of water. Something about the smell of the woman struck him...what was it? It hit him. She smelled like she'd slept in a load of goat dung. The haulers. He jumped to his feet. Why hadn't he thought of the haulers before? Trygaeus had told him one of the men who delivered salt had seen her. He rushed toward the portico. Rounding one of the stalls, he came upon the ragged woman again. She was sitting on the ground clutching herself, surrounded by a group of young boys. They were throwing rocks at her and poking her with sticks.

"Stop it," he screamed, the woman suddenly becoming Bromia as a small girl in his mind, being beaten up by boys from her village. He grabbed one of the boys, then threw him against a stall, brought his closed fist down on his head.

A stick came crashing down on his shoulder from behind. He whirled around and caught a second boy by the wrist, yanked the stick from him and threw it. "Leave her alone," he hissed as he shoved the boy down on the ground.

The boy crawled to his feet. "Let's get out of here," he said to his friends. "This man's as funny in the head as she is." They ran away.

Nicias stood for a moment trying to figure out what had happened. The woman, as terrified of him as the boys, got to her feet and started wailing.

"Look, I won't harm you," Nicias said, trying to soothe her. But she wouldn't stop wailing, and he couldn't get out of his mind the picture that Bromia had drawn of her as a ragged child being beaten by the village boys. "Oh, Bromia," he moaned. "Where are you?"

"You look like you need a bowl of water." A thin man with grey hair handed him a bowl. "I saw what you did. She's not like the rest of us. Never has been since she was a child, but that's no reason for the boys to beat on her." He turned to the woman. "Go away now."

Nicias drank while he watched the woman wander off toward the vegetable stands talking to herself. "Where will she go?"

"Someone will give her vegetables. Then she'll sleep under one of the stalls."

Nicias handed the empty bowl back to the man. "I'm looking for someone," he mumbled, trying to regain his composure.

"Maybe I know him."

"Is it possible?" Nicias repeated the man's name and all the information he had about the estate.

"Can't say that I've ever heard of him, but I can take you to someone who might be able to help you."

Nicias followed the man, thankful for his help since most stalls were closing and he couldn't see any haulers. At the back of the market they took a path to a group of small dirt hovels. Calling ahead the man went inside one of the hovels and told Nicias to follow him.

An enormous woman sat on the dirt floor. She didn't bother to look up. "What'd you want?"

"He's looking for someone," the man said. He turned to Nicias. "She used to be one of the most popular hetaerae in Sparta. There isn't a man between here and the sea she hasn't had at least once."

Looking at her Nicias found it difficult to believe she could have ever had a single man, let alone most men, but he repeated the name of Bromia's owner and the information he had about him nonetheless.

The woman spat on the floor beside her. "I know him."

Nicias waited breathlessly.

The woman said no more.

"She wants payment," the man volunteered.

"Oh, yes. Of course." Nicias pulled open the leather bag tied around his waist and dumped everything in it on the floor. "It's all I have."

She picked the bronze pieces up one at a time, smelled of them, bit them, and scratched each one with her broken and filthy fingernails.

Nicias controlled an urge to shake the information out of her. "It's all I have," he repeated. Suddenly he wondered what was to prevent her from keeping the bronze pieces while refusing to tell him where Bromia's owner lived. She probably doesn't know, he thought, close to hysteria.

When she was through testing the bronze pieces, the woman threw one to the man who'd brought Nicias. "Take the southernmost road out of town. Follow it to the ravine. Turn north at the ravine and follow the path over the hillside to the first main road. Stay on that road until you see a house. It's his house." She dropped the bronze pieces down her dress and said no more. Didn't even look up or answer when Nicias thanked her.

When they got back outside, it was raining. Nicias thanked the man and walked slowly back to the inn letting the cool rain soothe his aching body. He couldn't help remembering the beautiful hetaera who had caused so much trouble at the estate. Did they all end up like this?

Philocleon was awake, sitting up on his bed when Nicias got back to the room. "Where have you been? I've been worried."

"I've been looking for someone who could tell me how to find the estate where Bromia is," Nicias answered, tired enough now to know he'd have to sleep before they went to find Bromia.

"I know you went to find Bromia. What did you find out?"

"It's to the south," Nicias answered falling on his bed, sleeping almost immediately.

Philocleon fell asleep too, suspecting Nicias would be up before

Dawn had even begun to think of her morning journey.

Philocleon was right. They were up before Dawn had stirred from her soft bed. He insisted, in spite of Nicias' desire to leave immediately, that Nicias go to the baths and the barber. Afterwards, together they bought a new white linen tunic. "Remember, she hasn't seen you in many seasons," Philocleon reminded Nicias.

Nicias wished Philocleon hadn't reminded him. Now that he knew where she was, the nagging fear she might not want him any longer surfaced again in his thoughts.

They took the first road running out of town. Sensing a tension in Nicias he hadn't known before, Philocleon said none of the things he was thinking.

They hadn't gone very far before Philocleon felt the cart turn around. He was certain they were returning exactly the same way they'd come. He must have gone too far, he decided, not wanting to disturb Nicias.

They continued in the same direction they'd come from for some time and then Philocleon felt the cart turn completely around again. "How far is the estate?" he asked. "I thought it was only a short distance."

"It's farther than we thought," was all that Nicias said.

When they'd continued their drive for some distance, Philocleon felt the cart turn completely around again. "Are you turning the cart around?" he asked Nicias.

Nicias didn't reply.

"Nicias. Are you turning the cart around?" He reached out and grabbed Nicias' arm.

Nicias still didn't answer.

"You are. You have been driving back and forth in front of the estate, haven't you?" Philocleon laughed. But feeling Nicias tense up next to him, he quickly added, "I'm not laughing at you, just the situation. You're afraid to drive into the estate, aren't you?"

Nicias laughed. "So what if I am?"

"But what are you afraid of?"

"What if she's married?"

"Did she promise not to marry?"

"Yes."

"Then she won't be."

"What if she doesn't want me anymore?"

"Why? Have you grown ugly since I lost my sight?"

"I don't know. Maybe."

"What has changed? You have a tail now? Horns maybe?" He felt of Nicias' hair. "I don't find any horns."

Nicias laughed again. "No. It seems I'm as handsome as ever."

"Then what is it?"

"I know it's ridiculous. It's just that I've never had to think about what I would do if something has changed, if she doesn't want me anymore. All those seasons of dreaming, but I knew they were dreams. What will I do, now that I'm actually here and not dreaming, if she doesn't want me?"

Philocleon answered honestly. "I have no idea what we'll do, but I can tell you it won't change anything if you wait. Besides," his mood lightened again. "How could she not want a handsome man like you?"

Nicias sighed, built up his courage, and turned the horses around. "It isn't far to the estate." He urged the horses forward.

"Why do I think you're laughing quietly?" Philocleon asked.

"Because I am."

"What's so funny?"

"I am."

They arrived at the estate as Night began gliding across the sky. Nicias drove up to the house and stopped the horses. He looked carefully around. First, he surveyed the stables and the other outbuildings, places he knew she wouldn't be. Only after searching them thoroughly did he finally turn toward the house. He didn't see her. He felt both relief and anxiety. The one thing he hadn't considered was what he would do if she wasn't on this estate.

"What's happening?" Philocleon asked over the barking of the dogs gathering around the cart.

"Nothing yet," Nicias answered.

They waited and after some time, the estate owner rode out of the trees accompanied by several more barking dogs. He was met by a group of squealing children, obviously curious, but afraid to come away from the house until they saw him. Together they approached the cart. "Are you looking for me?"

Philocleon introduced himself and Nicias. "Actually, we're looking for a slave named Bromia. We were told she might be working here on your estate."

"Why do you want Bromia?"

"If you agree, I'd like to purchase her. She was my nurse as a child and now that I am blind, I wish to have her services again."

There was a pause while Philocleon and Nicias held their breath. "I'm prepared to pay top rate," Philocleon inserted into the silence. "I know she is probably one of your best slaves."

After another silence which the owner created to see if he could get any further concessions, he finally said. "We can talk." He sent one of the children for Bromia.

Philocleon felt Nicias stir next to him. "Get me out of the cart," he instructed Nicias, wanting to give him and Bromia as much privacy as he could.

Nicias helped him down from the cart and guided him toward the estate owner. "Come." Philocleon said, taking the owner's arm. "Let us discuss this matter privately."

Nicias waited alone. He wiped his sweaty palms against the new tunic. His eyes searched the lines of the house with some hesitancy. After what felt like a terribly long wait to him, he saw the familiar form of Bromia in the doorway of the house.

She was still tall, straight backed, not stooped like most of the other women slaves he knew. Her hair, exactly the color he remembered except for a few streaks of grey, hung in those familiar waves down the side of her face and fell onto her shoulders.

Nicias ran his thumb and forefinger nervously up and down on the side of his lips. So many seasons since he'd seen her and yet, as he stood there looking at her, he felt as if nothing had really changed. In many ways she looked as though she had just stepped out of his room at Hipponous' estate.

After some moments, Nicias realized Bromia hadn't moved. Her eyes. Were they the same? Deep brown, velvety soft. He knew she was waiting in her quiet way for him to let her know what he was thinking. She's as nervous as I am, Nicias thought. But how can she be? Haven't I come all this way for her? But does she know I've come for her? No. Of course she doesn't. Philocleon, afraid her owner wouldn't part with her if he knew the purchase was to secure her for Nicias, had decided instead to tell the owner he wanted to buy her to care for him. Does she think that? That I have just come along?

Nicias looked at his sandals. I should have rubbed them, he

decided. They're all dusty. He bent down and began rubbing them frantically. While he rested on the knee of his good leg cleaning the dust off his sandals, he felt the presence of Bromia. At last Nicias looked up. His eyes met the quiet gaze of love he had become so acquainted with at the estate. "Bromia," he finally managed to say. "I have come for you."

Bromia smiled. She stepped toward him. "And, I have waited for you."

Nicias stood up. There was no passionate embrace as he had imagined over and over again in his dreams. She simply reached up and took his arms in her hands just above the elbows and holding herself at arm's length, ran her hands up to his shoulders, back down his arms and took his hands. She walked forward then, wrapping his arms around her as she came.

Nicias tried to speak, to say all of those things he had rehearsed over and over, but no words came. Instead, he stood holding her and whispering her name over and over. "Bromia. Bromia. Bromia."

THIRTEEN

Nicias opened his eyes. Helios' light was already shining through the open window onto the bed. He'd slept past the rising of rosy-fingered Dawn for the first time since his childhood. It felt strange, being in bed when Helios was shining, but he felt no inclination to get up. Sighing, he moved closer to Bromia. By now he should have gotten used to having her with him. Yet, the first thing he did whenever he woke was reassure himself she was actually there in his bed. Still asleep, she snuggled into his arms and rested her head on his chest, her soft breath stirring the hair around his left nipple.

He buried his face in her hair, greedy for the rich perfumed scent he'd become accustomed to finding there. She stirred, turned more tightly into him. He kissed her forehead. She opened her eyes, smiled, nibbled his nipple. He picked up a few strands of her hair and twisted them in his fingers, kissed them. She turned her face up toward him so that he could take her chin in his hand and kiss her lips gently. She ran her hand along his ribs, across his stomach, down his thigh. Goose bumps followed her hand on his skin. He kissed her face, her neck, her breasts. She caressed his chest and stomach with her hand, kissed his ears and neck. With her tongue, she traced his lips. Opening his mouth to her exploring tongue, he rolled onto her.

They kissed, long and deep, holding tightly to one another. After a long while, he entered her pulsating softness, spreading turbulence through both of them. They moved up and down together, slowly at first, then with total abandon until suddenly, Bromia exploded. Writhing and screaming as the rampant sensations raced through her, she sent Nicias plunging into a frantic explosion of his own. Moaning, he collapsed into her arms.

Stroking her hair, Nicias rolled back onto his side. Eventually he fell asleep. Bromia curled once again into the niche his body created, remembering how she'd silently worried all the way to Sparta that things might not work out for them. Now, resting her head on his chest, listening to the even breathing sleep brought, she wondered how that worry could have even crossed her mind.

When Nicias woke for the second time, Bromia was already gone. He got up, washed himself with the lilac water she'd poured into a bowl and left on the table beside their bed. He put on his tunic and sandals and walked down the portico to Philocleon's room. Gone too. With Bromia, no doubt. They were almost inseparable.

Feeling happier than he'd thought possible, Nicias returned to the room, pulled open his traveling sack and searched through it until he found the pottery sherd Egyptus had given to him the day of the boar hunt. 'Give it to my uncle, Ti,' Egyptus had said. 'He'll give you a place to sleep and food until I get to Sparta.' It was time to look for Ti. He didn't need food and he had a place to stay, but he'd sure like to see Egyptus or at least get a message to him.

Assuming Ti was a potter like Egyptus, Nicias circled the marketplace and cut into the stalls near the back where the craftsmen were gathered. He made his way slowly around the leather workers, through the bronze workers, to the pottery stalls. Finding a group of potters sitting together at the first stall, he handed the sherd to one of them. "Do you know where I can find this man's shop?"

The potter looked at the name scratched in hieroglyphics, shook his head, and passed the sherd on. The next man did the same, as did the next and the next until the sherd reached a red-haired Macedonian at the far end of the group. He threw it back to Nicias. "Try the Egyptian selling beads." He pointed toward a group of stalls beyond those set up by the potters.

Nicias found the Egyptian and held out the sherd. With a crippled hand he took the sherd and saying nothing, got up and walked away. He returned with two young girls. "Daughters help find." He motioned for Nicias to follow them.

The two girls took Nicias behind the pottery stalls, through the bronze casters to a small hill behind the market. Winding their way around carts and mules, they led him up the hill. From the path, Nicias could see that most of the hillside was covered with pottery kilns.

"In there," one of the girls said, stopping in front of a small hut. She held out her hand.

Nicias flipped her a small bronze piece and ducked through the door. Blinded by darkness and smoke, he stayed at the doorway until his eyes adjusted enough for him to see that there were two people in the hut, a man and a boy. Scanning their small, dark-skinned faces, black hair and black eyes, Nicias knew he was in the right place. They both looked so much like Egyptus, the man had to be Ti; the boy, his son.

Although neither the man nor the boy said anything to him about entering, Nicias sensed it was expected and walked in. Smiling his most gracious smile at the two inquisitive but quiet faces, he looked around the hut seeing immediately he'd been wrong about Ti. This was no pottery workshop even though the center of the hut was filled with a small circular furnace built out of mud brick covered with mud plaster. The top of the furnace was flat, not bee-hive-shaped, and there was no opening for the smoke which was pouring out of holes cut into the furnace walls. The whole thing wasn't much more than waist high. Nothing at all like the kiln he'd helped Egyptus build.

The boy, bare except for a faded red loincloth, sat at the back of the furnace. Nicias recognized what he was doing from the times he'd helped Egyptus fire the pottery kiln. Obviously it was the boy's responsibility to stoke the fire. He walked closer to watch, smiling at the youngster. "I'm a friend of Egyptus."

The boy broke into a wide grin, but said nothing. From the other side of the furnace, Ti said something to the boy Nicias couldn't understand. Still grinning, the boy hurried to a stack of branches piled from floor to ceiling along the front wall of the hut, pulled a few down, returned, and stuffed them into the stoke hole, sweat pouring off his body.

Curious as to what they were making if not pottery, Nicias walked around the furnace to the front. The heat in the small hut was stifling. So was the smoke. He wiped his face and arms with the skirt of his tunic and blinked to clear his eyes.

The front of the circular furnace had two rectangular wings

attached to it at right angles. Ti sat on the dirt floor between the two wings, his legs crossed in front of him. Nicias held the pottery sherd out to him and asked about Egyptus. Ti looked at the sherd, shrugged, and pointed to a three-legged stool behind him.

From the stool Nicias could see there was an opening into the wall of furnace directly in front of Ti. A ceramic pan filled with a thick liquid sat in the opening. Ti stirred it constantly with a wooden paddle. "What are you making?" he asked.

When no answer came, Nicias decided to leave and come back when Ti wasn't so busy. But just as he stood, the boy brought Ti a basket of...what? They looked like clubs: long wooden handles with mallets on the end. Were they weapons? No. Not possible. The mallets weren't made of stone as they'd need to be for weapons. They were gourd-shaped mixtures of straw and manure.

The boy picked up one of the clubs by the wooden handle and rested it on a small tripod near Ti. After stirring the thick liquid one last time, Ti picked up a wooden stake and put it into the liquid. He turned the stake around, gathering the liquid on the end as he went until it formed a large glob. He pulled the glob of liquid out of the pan and as it oozed from the stake in a long thread, he wound the thread around the mallet like a snake. Nicias waited for the liquid to run off the mallet onto the dirt floor, but it didn't. Too thick, he decided.

Overcome with curiosity, he sat back down again and leaned forward so far he almost toppled the stool. He could feel the heat from the thick liquid, whatever it was, on his face. When there was no more liquid on the stake, Ti put it back into the pan and turned it until he had another glob. As the liquid fell slowly from the glob into a long thread, Ti wound it around the mallet. He kept repeating the maneuver until the entire mallet was covered with the liquid.

The boy picked the liquid mallet off the tripod when Ti had finished covering it and, holding firmly to the wooden handle, put it down on an over-turned ceramic pot. He flattened the bottom by pressing it against the pot. Then he ran a little water around the edge where the wooden handle met the heavy liquid mallet and tapped it. The handle fell away from the mallet. He threw it into a pile of handles at the back of the hut.

Ti rolled another glob of the liquid on his rod. The boy pulled out a second club and they repeated everything they'd done the first time. Nicias moved closer to the furnace and watched them. They covered a second, then a third and a fourth mallet.

As soon as Ti ran out of the thick liquid, the boy took the mallets they'd made and put them inside the rectangular wing of the furnace. At the same time, Ti pulled a cool mallet out of a basket sitting on the floor and gave it to Nicias.

Examining it, Nicias easily figured out what it was. Not a mallet, but a small cup. Surprised, he rolled the cup over in his hand and held it up toward the fire to get a better look at it. "Would you look at that?" he said excitedly, holding the cup first one way, then another. At the very edge of the rim, he could see the light coming through the cup. "I'm a friend of Egyptus," he said to Ti. "He told me about these." So this was how Egyptus knew about cups you could see through made of sand and limestone and salt. Smiling happily, he handed the cup back to Ti. "What do you call it?"

Ti didn't understand what he'd said, but he refused to take the cup back. Instead, he pushed it back toward Nicias and indicated he was to keep it. Nicias took the cup and thanked him profusely even though he could see Ti understood nothing of what he said. "Egyptus tell me about," Nicias said, pointing to the cup. He pulled the sherd from his leather bag and showed it to Ti. "Egyptus. Friend."

Smiling and bowing Ti said something to the boy who left the hut and returned with a bowl of fresh water for each of them. Nicias drank the water and repeated. "Egyptus. Friend." He pointed to his heart and clasped his two index fingers together. "Egyptus and Nicias friends."

Ti took the sherd from Nicias, turned it over in his hand and nodded.

Nicias pointed to the sherd. "Message for Egyptus."

Frowning, Ti showed the boy the sherd. Nicias indicated he needed something to scratch with. The boy brought him a pointed tool. He scratched his name and Argos on the sherd and handed it back to Ti. "Please give to Egyptus," he said, feeling more than a little doubtful and silly.

Ti took the sherd a second time and looked at the names scratched on it as did his son. They talked to each other. Then, they looked at Nicias and waited. Unable to explain any better, Nicias thanked them again and moved toward the door. They hadn't thrown the sherd away. He could at least hope they would save it and show it to Egyptus when he came through.

Nicias slowly made his way back down the hill anxious to find Philocleon and Bromia. They were at a tavern near the inn eating figs and drinking wine. Placing the cup dramatically into Philocleon's hands, Nicias asked, "Do you remember when Egyptus told me he'd seen a man make cups you could see through out of sand and limestone and salt?"

Philocleon felt the cup. "Yes."

Nicias poured wine from their mixing bowl into the cup and handed it to Philocleon. Both men laughed as Philocleon lifted the cup toward Nicias, then drank.

Nicias accepted the cup back from Philocleon and held it up against the sun so Bromia could see through the edge. He filled it again and handing it to Bromia, told her the story of Egyptus and the cups you could see through.

"Where did you get it?" Philocleon asked, sorry he hadn't been with Nicias.

"From Egyptus' uncle, Ti." Nicias described everything he'd just seen for the two of them.

Examining the cup carefully, Bromia asked, "When will Egyptus be here?"

"I don't know. I couldn't understand anything his uncle said and he couldn't understand anything I said. I left the pottery sherd for Egyptus. I can only hope he gets it."

"Will he come to you if he does?" Bromia asked, curious about the potter.

"Absolutely," Philocleon answered for Nicias. "Did you tell him to come to Argos?" he asked Nicias. Up until this moment, he hadn't said anything about moving on toward Argos, wanting to give Nicias and Bromia time together, but now he was suddenly anxious to get started. "I for one am ready to go in search of your family."

"So I am." Nicias said, sensing Philocleon's urgency. "Now that I've seen uncle Ti."

Bromia smiled at Nicias. "I can think of nothing I'd like more than seeing the estate I've heard so much about."

"I'm glad," Nicias said. "Because I'll feel like we really belong to one another when we're together on the estate."

Philocleon sighed happily. He'd brought Nicias and Bromia together. He was terribly pleased it had worked out so well for them. But now he felt it was time to get on to the burying of Homer's ashes. Once they got to Argos, he and Nicias could continue on to Ios while Bromia waited at the estate.

FOURTEEN

A strong feeling of familiarity pulsed through Nicias as he turned the horses onto the road leading to Argos, but he couldn't remember enough to get himself to the estate. "I know it's somewhere near here," he announced to Bromia and Philocleon, his eyes searching the countryside ahead, hoping something would stir his memory. "But I can't remember how to get to it."

"Ask him," Bromia suggested, pointing out a swineherd driving three pigs down the road in their direction.

"Stay on this road 'til you come to a fork," the swineherd told them when they stopped him. "Keep to the left at the fork. You'll come to a bridge. Cross the bridge, you'll see a small hut on your left. Just beyond the hut is the path up to the estate. You know the family?"

"Yes. I'm related." Nicias suppressed an urge to tell the swineherd who he was. It would be too disappointing to have the news reach the estate ahead of him. "But I haven't seen them in many, many seasons."

"You'll get a fine welcome, I'd say. They're one of the nicest families in this area."

"Do you know them?" Pride surged through Nicias.

"The little hut you'll pass. Mine. I rent land from the master of the estate."

Before Nicias could ask any more questions, one of the man's pigs bolted down the road. He went running after the pig waving his stick in the air and threatening the animal with butchering right there on the road when he caught it.

"He said master of the estate," Bromia observed. "If it's still your family estate, your sister must be married."

"I'll bet I'm an uncle," Nicias added gaily.

They followed the road to the fork, turned left and crossed the bridge. Just beyond the small hut they found the path. Nicias stood as soon as they got onto the path and looked as far into the distance as his height permitted. It wasn't long before the estate came into view. He sat down and took Bromia's hand. "It's our estate, all right."

"Are you frightened?" Philocleon asked.

"No. Just anxious. My mother's dead, I'm certain of that. But what about my sister? Do you suppose she's still alive?"

His question was answered almost as soon as it had been asked. When they came bumping through the gate into the farmyard, two young girls ducked past them into the house. Shortly after, a short, small-boned woman with the same rich brown eyes as Nicias' came to the door.

Bromia smiled, hugging Nicias' arm. "She has to be your sister. She looks so much like you."

"I think you're right." Nicias stopped the horses near the house and got out of the cart. He hurried toward the woman. "Evadne?"

Evadne turned pale, braced herself against the doorpost. It couldn't be. He'd been dead for many seasons. Her daughters had told her someone was coming who looked like her. She had expected a relative, but not Nicias. But it had to be Nicias. Who else could it be with that foot? She took a very deep breath to calm herself and went gingerly out to meet him.

"Evadne?" Nicias repeated, his voice hoarse with excitement.

"Nicias?"

"Yes."

She ran up and threw her arms around him. "We'd heard you were dead."

He hugged her, picking her small body completely off the ground. "Dead. Why on earth did you think I was dead?"

"It's quite a story." She turned excitedly toward the house. "Girls, come meet your uncle." She hugged him again. "It's you. Really you."

Both girls came shyly out of the house and stood next to their mother. "This is Clymene," Evadne said, putting the smallest girl's hand in his. "And this is Themis." She handed him Themis' hand.

Nicias stood for a moment and admired them. They both had their mother's brown eyes and small features, but their skin wasn't the deep olive of his family. It was lighter. "Dear Father, Zeus. I have nieces," he said, tweaking Clymene's blushing cheek. "Such pretty ones too." He hugged them both.

Not letting go of either niece's hand, Nicias turned again to Evadne. "What about Mother?"

"She died several seasons ago."

"I was afraid she'd be gone."

"She believed right up to her death, in spite of what we'd heard that you were still alive."

"Who told you I was dead?" Nicias was curious and surprised they'd heard anything of him.

"As I said, it's quite a long story," Evadne answered, glancing toward Bromia and Philocleon still waiting in the wagon.

"Dear Zeus," Nicias said, taking the two girls in one arm and Evadne in the other and walking them to the wagon. "I got so excited about finding you, I totally forgot to introduce you to Bromia and Philocleon."

When they'd all met, Evadne hurried her daughters off to the stable. "Tell Molus to go to the village and find your father. More than likely he'll be talking with the grain merchants. When Molus finds him, he's to tell him to hurry home as my brother Nicias is alive and has come back to us."

Evadne waited until the girls had disappeared through the stable door. Then taking Bromia's arm she walked her toward the house. "Now tell me all about how you came to know Nicias?"

"We met on the estate where he was enslaved."

"So, my handsome brother did all right for himself in spite of what had happened to him," Evadne said, assuming Bromia was the daughter of the estate owner.

"I don't remember a statuette of Poseidon at the entrance," Nicias said, interrupting the two women. He described the small figure to Philocleon.

Evadne smiled. "Most things you see you won't remember. We've rebuilt much of the estate since you were a child." She sent the slave who met them at the entrance for wine and food, then walked them down the long corridor connecting the main door with the interior courtyard. "One thing you will remember though, I think, is the pool."

"I spent half my childhood in this pool," Nicias informed Bromia and Philocleon at the edge of the pool. He pulled off his sandals and waded in. "Was it always this small?"

"Yes," Evadne answered. "But it looks smaller now than it did when you were a child because the courtyard has been enlarged. We'd planned to enlarge the pool too, but mother insisted it had to be left exactly as it was when you were taken from us."

Nicias looked around the courtyard. Pointing to the room directly in front of him, he said to Bromia. "My room used to be right there."

"That's the dining room now," Evadne explained. "The sleeping rooms are on the other side of the portico." She pointed to a row of rooms opening off the portico behind Nicias. "The one in the corner was mother's. We gave her that room because Helios favors it during the day. She spent the last years of her life sitting contentedly in her room weaving in the light of Helios."

Turning from Nicias to Bromia and Philocleon, she continued, "Mother loved to weave. When we were children she used to have the slaves set up her loom out here by the pool. While we splashed around in the water, she'd sit and weave and tell us stories. Do you remember? " she asked Nicias.

"Of course. I also remember some very stern spankings when I piddled in the water and a certain sister tattled to mother." Grinning, he scooped up a handful of water and pretended he was planning to splash Evadne.

Evadne laughed. "I also remember a brother who did his share of tattling." She ordered the slaves to bring couches and place them around the pool.

Nicias stepped out of the pool, slipped back into his sandals, and sat down between Evadne and Bromia. "How wonderful of you to have kept the pool for me."

"It was mother's insistence, I have to admit." Evadne handed Bromia a bowl of wine. "He's nothing like the bigger brother I remember, though he still teases."

Nicias took a bowl of wine from Evadne and gave it to Philocleon. "Remember when I told you about all those times Evadne crawled up on my lap pretending she was going to give me a big hug and then, suddenly, she'd pull my ears half off."

"Did I do that?" Evadne laughed.

"What's so funny?" Themis asked coming across the courtyard. She'd changed from the short green peplos she'd been wearing when Nicias arrived into a long, red one and combed both her and Clymene's hair into curls.

"Your uncle is tattling on me," Evadne answered. "Did you get Molus off to find your father?"

Sitting down next to Philocleon, Clymene answered. "He's on the road right now. Were you born blind?" she asked Philocleon.

"Clymene!" Evadne exclaimed, embarrassed.

"It's all right," Philocleon answered. He could tell from Clymene's voice she was young. Probably hadn't seen the four seasons pass much more than nine or ten times. "No, I wasn't born blind."

"What happened to you?" Clymene asked, ignoring her mother's disapproving look. "I saw a blind man once in Argos and his eyes didn't look like yours. They were kind of milky."

Nudged by Evadne, Themis jumped up and grabbed Clymene by the arm. "Come on, we have something to do."

"What?" Clymene asked surprised.

"I'll tell you when we get there," Themis answered, pulling Clymene firmly away by the arm.

"Really, I don't mind," Philocleon said, catching his breath from the heavy perfume Themis had put on. "You smell like a flower," he said to Themis, guessing she had seen the changing of the four seasons about four times more than Clymene. "I'll bet you're as gentle and pretty as a flower too."

Embarrassed and excessively pleased, Themis pulled Clymene from the courtyard. "Come on."

"They're very nice girls," Bromia assured Evadne. She'd was already working when she was Clymene's size. She was taking care of Philocleon at Themis' size. How wonderful it would have been to have had the chance to be a child.

"You still haven't told me why you thought I was dead," Nicias said, bringing Evadne back to the discussion of the family.

"A man. Actually a sea captain told us you were on a ship that sunk."

"How did he hear such a thing?"

"Simo, that's my husband, will be here soon, and he'll never forgive me if I tell you the story before he gets here. He loves to tell it himself. Do you mind waiting?"

"No, of course not."

"Good." Evadne poured more wine. "While we wait for him, you must tell me everything that's happened to you."

As they sat, watching Helios disappear and the stars slowly appear in Zeus' blue heaven, Nicias, with the help of Bromia and Philocleon, told Evadne about his life on the slave ship, his eventual sale to Philocleon's grandfather, the long seasons on the estate, his experience as a seer, the unwillingness of Hipponous to free him after his seeing experience, the death of Calonice, the arrival and departure of Bromia, his experiences at Delphi, and finally his and Philocleon's rescue of Bromia.

"You were a slave?" Evadne asked Bromia unable to hide the shock she felt at the idea of her brother bringing a slave into her house as his wife.

Bromia nodded, but said nothing. It hadn't occurred to her Evadne would think she was anything else.

"But she's no longer a slave," Philocleon said emphatically. He guessed from Evadne's silence, she was more impressed with the fact that Bromia had been a slave than that she no longer was one. He felt compelled to defend Bromia. "And even if Bromia were a slave, I don't think it would make any difference."

"You're quite right, I just meant that...." Evadne began explaining, sensing she was about to get a lecture from Philocleon. She looked to Nicias for help, but got none. "I mean, slaves aren't..." She refused to look at Bromia.

"Since my eyes have gone dark," Philocleon continued, "do you know what I discovered? Without my eyes to tell me who is richly dressed and who is poorly dressed, I can't tell which men are aristocrats and which ones are slaves."

Evadne was displeased, but she said nothing.

"In Delphi," Philocleon continued, hearing Nicias breathe a definite yes to what he'd said. "There was a young slave who stole from a man in our inn. You remember, don't you, Nicias?"

"Yes."

"It was wrong for that young slave to steal. But if you ask me, the priests at the temple of Apollo, who are all men of aristocratic birth, are worse. They don't steal from just one man as the slave did, but from all of us when they ask many times over the rightful price for a simple cake to dedicate at the altar. I don't think they're any better than the slave. Only richer. You know what I think? I think if you take away an aristocrat's fine possessions, you have a slave and if you give a slave possessions, you have an aristocrat."

Evadne looked from Philocleon to Nicias to see how Nicias would react. He showed no signs of displeasure. "Are you saying you think it's all right for slaves to associate with aristocrats?" she asked as shocked by Philocleon's remark as she had been by finding out Bromia had been a slave.

"I can't say about all slaves." Nicias put his arm defensively around Bromia's shoulder. "But if Bromia were a slave, which she isn't, she'd still be running my household."

"Look at me," Philocleon went on, his voice shaking from the excitement of hearing himself actually state the ideas he'd been formulating since they'd left Delphi. "I was born to one of the most aristocratic families in Attica. Yet I was capable of a most treacherous deed." He reached out for Bromia's hand. "Bromia was born a slave and I've never even so much as heard a treacherous word from her."

Bromia squeezed Philocleon's hand while she looked shyly at Evadne. "I've said treacherous things. You may not have heard them. But I've cursed people and I've wished people dead."

"Was my father one of them?" Philocleon asked.

Bromia didn't answer. What could be gained by going over it all now?

"I wouldn't blame you if you hated him." Being with Nicias and Bromia in Sparta, knowing how happy they were together, Philocleon was convinced his father had been wrong to keep them from marrying. Now, feeling suddenly overwhelmed by the possibility their happiness could be at risk again, he felt an intense urgency to make Evadne see his point. "It's the man that counts, not his birthright. "Take me, for instance. For all my lineage, I am guilty of..." His voice trailed off. Admitting to his horrible crime was turning out to be much more difficult than he'd thought it would be.

The silence held for several moments before Bromia took his hand again. "You don't have to talk about it."

"I want to." Philocleon answered. He'd been thinking about it since Sparta. "It's the only way for me to come to peace with myself." Slowly, he told Evadne and Bromia of the things that had led to his blindness. He finished with the words he'd been rehearsing for his confession before Scapha. "I hope you won't hate me for what I've done."

"Certainly not," Bromia said quickly.

Evadne wanted to utter something comforting, but the intensity of what she was feeling kept her from saying anything at all. Bromia a slave. Philocleon a young man who had killed his father.

Nicias stood and helped Philocleon gently to his feet, amazement written all over his face. When had Philocleon grown so wise? "We've had a long journey," he said. "I think we should all get some rest."

Evadne took Philocleon to a guestroom, Nicias and Bromia to the corner room where their mother had spent her last seasons weaving. "If only she'd known you were alive before she died," she repeated to Nicias, leaving the room thinking how much Bromia's presence would have angered their mother.

Nicias and Bromia's bed consisted of a thick, soft fleece on a wooden frame. A coverlet made by Nicias' mother lay folded on the fleece. Her loom, untouched since her death, sat majestically in the corner where she had used it. Nicias went over and sat on her stool. He ran his fingers over the loom trying to remember her.

She was small like his sister with the same olive skin, but her hair had never been black like Evadne's. It had been light brown like the two girls' before it had grayed. And her eyes were deep greenish, not fully brown. The family's brown eyes had come from their father. What else could he remember? She sang much of the time, old songs taught to her by his grandmother about the noble maidens of her youth. And he could remember her dancing, holding his and Evadne's hands, leading them around the courtyard.

"She must have been happy," he told Bromia. "I remember her laughing a lot. Once I caught my father kissing her." He smiled, remembering his father's hand under her gown, his mother twisting and teasing.

"Come." Bromia took him by the hand and led him to the bed. "Put your arms around me," she said, pulling the coverlet his mother had made over them. "How terribly happy you must be you've found your family."

Nicias took her in his arms.

"When I was Clymene's size," Bromia confessed, "I used to

pretend I'd been born to aristocratic parents and that I'd fallen out of their carriage when I was a baby and they hadn't noticed until they were many stadia down the road. When they came back I was already gone, picked up by the wretched woman who found me. They searched, but they never found me. I convinced myself that unexpectedly my father would come riding through the village where I lived and recognize me. I knew he'd be furious. The woman who'd stolen me would be severely punished and I'd be taken home to live with my real parents. It was a good dream."

In reality, she had been exposed at birth, according to the woman who took her in, left under a bridge by the river. She'd lived with the woman who plucked her from beneath the bridge until she was Themis' size. Then she'd been sold as a slave.

Nicias pulled her tightly to him. "There's no need to think about the past anymore. Now at last we are both free to live as we choose."

"Yes," she answered, resting her head on his chest. "I never truly thought I'd be free." He seemed so happy she decided not to mention how Evadne's reaction to finding out she'd been a slave frightened her. Eventually, comforted by Nicias' strong arms, she fell asleep.

Both were still asleep when Simo came home and found Evadne in the kitchen making barley cakes. "Molus didn't find me right away. I came as soon as I could." He kissed her on the cheek, being careful not to disturb her work. "It has to be a real occasion when you're in the kitchen doing the cooking yourself," he teased her, leaning on a table next to where she stood. He waited for her to talk. Evadne always took to the kitchen when something was bothering her.

"He's been a slave in Attica since he was taken from us," she said, filling a small pan with barley. Holding the pan over the cooking fire, she told him the story of Nicias' life. "It's so sad. All of us mourning him as dead when he was so close."

When the husks had steamed off the barley, she ground the pearl barley that was left and molded it into a paste, using honey. "He has a young man with him…and a woman," she continued, trying to make her voice casual. While she made the barley paste into cakes and put them over the fire to roast, she told Simo about Bromia and Philocleon.

"Well, who'd have guessed his life would be so complicated," was all Simo could say when she'd finished telling him Bromia had been a slave and Philocleon had killed his father.

Waiting for the cakes to roast, she shredded cabbage, pounding it with vinegar, honey, coriander leaf, rue, mint and asafetida. She put down the cabbage. "Oh, Simo, I don't know what to do. I've never had a slave in my house before. If Mother were alive, she'd never forgive me."

"Your mother isn't alive and you've had plenty of slaves in your house." He walked over to the fire where the barley cakes were roasting.

"Not as a guest."

"Besides, Bromia isn't a slave anymore. She's a freedwoman."

Evadne felt cheated. All these seasons she'd waited for Nicias and now that he'd come...

Back at the counter, Simo tasted the cabbage, ignoring the troubled look in her eyes. "It's very tasty."

Evadne sighed. "I don't like it. I think we should talk with Nicias."

"I think you should let Nicias decide for himself what he wants." Simo could hear his voice was too harsh, but he couldn't stop himself.

"But if we don't say something right away, she'll settle in with him." She'd decided to ignore the nastiness in his tone.

"Is that so terrible?"

Evadne looked away. "It isn't that she's not a nice person. I like her and she's mannered and polite, but..." She stopped. What was the use? Simo had left the kitchen.

"He's gone to the stable," the slave Evadne sent to look for Simo told her when she returned. "He says you're to send for him when Nicias and the others are ready to eat."

Nicias didn't appear in the portico until Helios had ridden high into the sky. He found Bromia and Philocleon with Themis and Clymene by the pool. Philocleon was telling the girls the story of Homer. "Soon," he said, when he heard Nicias' voice, "Nicias and I will have to leave for Ios to bury the ashes of the great poet."

Clymene groaned. "But you just got here." Seeing Nicias, she ran to him. "Uncle, you won't leave us, will you?"

Nicias, saying nothing, took her by the hand and led her back to Philocleon and Themis. "And what kind of adventures have you been telling my two young nieces?" he asked Philocleon.

"The story of the Trojan war," Philocleon answered. "And of Homer. But don't worry. I've only told them the parts of the legend small girls should hear."

"Good," Nicias said, hugging Bromia. "Has Simo returned?"

"I'll get him," Themis volunteered.

Nicias followed her into the kitchen. He kissed Evadne. "Where's Simo?"

"In the stable. I've sent a slave to get him." She considered speaking with Nicias about Bromia now that they were alone in the kitchen, but changed her mind when she saw Simo coming across the yard. He could be very touchy about slaves, as he'd demonstrated earlier. This was not the moment to get him started.

Simo hugged Nicias with genuine affection. "I've heard all about you."

Nicias hugged him in return. He was much shorter than Nicias had expected. Only about a head taller than Evadne. He had the same light brown hair and pale skin as the girls, but his eyes were a deep blue. "And, since I've come, you'd be surprised how much I've learned about you," he teased Evadne.

Simo made a point of hugging Bromia enthusiastically before he clasped Philocleon's arm at the wrist and held it affectionately. Taking a couch next to Nicias, he asked about their journey from Sparta and gave them the details of his trip from the village. Nicias liked Simo immediately.

As soon as they'd been served their morning meal, Nicias gave vent to his curiosity. "Evadne told me you thought I was dead, but she made me wait for you to tell the story."

Themis and Clymene both squealed with delight. "Do tell us father," Themis said. They'd heard the story often enough, but they never tired of it.

Simo shifted uncomfortably and slowly finished chewing his barley cake. He loved telling the story as much as Themis and Clymene loved hearing it, but he'd never been quite honest in the way he'd told it. Should he tell it truthfully now? No. He loved Evadne too much. "To understand you have to hear it from the beginning," he told Nicias.

"I want to," Nicias assured him.

Clymene climbed up on Simo's lap, settling in for the story by snuggling against his shoulder. To his amusement, Simo saw that

Themis had found a way to sit next to Philocleon. Only a few seasons ago, she would have been fighting for a place on his lap.

"I was born on an estate way north of here, the only son of a wealthy landowner," he began. "One day my father asked me to accompany one of our herders to a nearby village. We were ambushed by the very same captain who stole you from this estate. He and two of his men sat on a boulder that was hidden by the branch of a tree. When I rode past them, one of them hit me over the head with a stone. Another did the same to the herder. They took me and the goats with them to the ship. I never did find out what happened to the herder, but I think they must have killed him because he didn't return to my father's estate."

Nicias gasped surprise. "The very same ship? It can't be! Did you hear that?" he asked Philocleon and Bromia.

They both nodded, their interest perked.

Philocleon could hear from the little he'd said, Simo was going to prove to be a great storyteller. But there was something about the way Simo told the story that puzzled him.

Simo waited for everyone to quiet down, having enjoyed his surprise as much as he thought he would. "After the captain had me, they threw me down into the same rat hole where you were. Like you, I sat in the dark eating the scraps that were thrown down to me, drinking stale water from a pail that was lowered once a day. Every once in awhile the captain had me brought out of the hold. It wasn't long before Helios blinded me so that I couldn't keep my eyes open on deck; and my legs were so weak, I couldn't stand. 'Are you ready to obey commands?' the captain asked whenever I was on deck. At first I refused, but it wasn't long before all I wanted was to be out of that hold. I told him I was ready to do anything if he'd let me stay on deck."

Nicias nodded knowingly, remembering clearly how much he'd hated that hold. He looked at Simo's foot which hadn't been mutilated, but said nothing.

"I'll get to that in a moment," Simo said understanding what Nicias' thoughts were. "Anyway, when I agreed to work, the captain turned me over to an oarsman everybody called Fox. At first I thought Fox had seen about the same number of spring rites as I had because he wasn't much bigger, but when we got out of the captain's sight and I took a close look at him, I could see he had seen many more seasons pass than I had. He instructed me as to how to serve the captain his meals.

"It didn't take long before I understood why I'd been given the job. Always it was the same. The captain drank more wine than a maenad at a Dionysiac ritual. Before he finally passed out, he'd lose his temper any number of times, and I would take the same number of beatings.

"Fox taught me all the tricks he knew to avoid the captain's blows. In fact, that's how he got his name from the crew, being so sly in avoiding the captain's whip. When he could find a way, he helped me serve the captain's meal, but mostly I was on my own, taking one good beating after another.

"While I kept the captain's wine cup filled, he had the crew, which wasn't much more than a handful of men who drank as much as he did, sail around stealing boys. When the captain needed more wine or food or supplies, he'd pull into a port and sell some of the boys. Then we'd go off for more.

"After I'd been on the ship for three seasons, while I lay half crazy with the pain on the floor of the captain's kitchen from a beating I'd taken, all the boys except for me got together and overpowered the drunk crew. They jumped ship and disappeared into the port village. The first I knew anything had happened was when Fox rushed into the kitchen and grabbed me. He put me into a cupboard and told me to stay there no matter what happened until he came for me.

"When the captain found out about the escape, he took his whip to everyone he could reach. Luckily, he was too drunk to reach most of the men because they were all too drunk to run. If he'd gotten to them, there wouldn't have been anyone left to sail the ship.

"From the cupboard where he'd hidden me, I heard Fox tell the captain I was still with the ship. He took a good rap before he got away from the captain, but he never told where I was. Later when the captain had finally sobered up, Fox brought me out. By then, the captain needed me to help sail the ship, so he threatened me with punishment for hiding, but he never did do it.

"We sailed back to ports on the Mediterranean where we had been before and the captain and two of his men started stealing boys all over again. But after the mutiny, the captain decided to smash one foot on every boy to keep him from escaping. It made them less able to work, but he didn't care. He simply kidnapped twice as many. Fox saved me from the foot smashing by convincing the captain I'd stayed on the ship out of loyalty.

Nicias sucked in his breath with disgust. "So that's why he did it," he said softly.

"Good old Fox. Whenever the captain was too drunk to notice, he'd slip into the hold under the deck and clean and treat the boys' feet with whatever he could find. Some died, but Fox kept many of them alive." Simo paused. "He treated you when the captain stole you. Do you remember him?"

Nicias nodded his head. "I remember Fox, but I don't remember you."

"I was moved from the hold to the floor of the kitchen after the mutiny. The captain didn't want me talking to any of the other boys. He was afraid I'd tell you about the mutiny and you might get ideas."

"Whatever happened to Fox?"

Simo poured himself another bowl of wine. "I'm coming to that." He wasn't about to alter his story now that he'd started. "Not long after the captain had sold you, I overheard him talking to his first mate. He was telling the mate that with your father dead and you gone, he'd decided to go back to the estate to see how well protected your mother was. The next thing I knew, we'd docked in a cove down the shore from your father's estate. I was called into the captain's cabin and told I was to go to the estate as a beggar and find out how much protection your mother had.

"I went, following the first mate. With a swat to the head, the mate reminded me he'd be watching and any attempt to escape would end in my being cut to pieces and fed to the dogs. The captain had promised him the ship if they took the estate.

"I went to the gate, and trying to think what I should do, sat down alongside two other beggars. It wasn't long before Evadne came to the gate. She gave each of us bread and a big bowl of fresh water. When the other two had eaten, they left. I stayed, still trying to think what to do. After a while Evadne returned and asked if I was still hungry. Thinking of nothing better to say, I said I was."

Simo stood and, still holding Clymene, put his hand on Evadne's shoulder. "When Evadne came back with food, I blurted out I wasn't really hungry, but I was there because I had some news for her mother about you. Would she please take me to your mother? She told me to wait and left. I was so scared. I expected her to return with your mother's brothers and kill me for sure.

"She returned and took me to your mother who was waiting for me in the little room near the kitchen. It was obvious she was terribly afraid of me. Her hands were shaking. She was pale. I threw myself at her feet and explained that I too had been taken captive from my home by the captain. I told her of his plan to come and take her and the estate, though I knew in my heart it would be your sister and not your mother he would take.

"She called Evadne into the room and had me repeat the story. It was Evadne who came up with the plan. When I went back to the ship, I had news for the captain. I explained that in a stroke of Hermes' luck, I'd gotten a chance to talk with the daughter of the house. Though she wouldn't let me far enough into the house to see anything, when I told her that I'd met an oarsman who had news of her son, she asked to see him.

"The captain, dressed as an oarsman, accompanied me when I returned to the estate. He brought the first mate, thinking to take him inside and make a finish of things right away if there wasn't much protection, but I insisted the mate stay outside the gate. Otherwise, I assured the captain, the woman who was head of the house would become suspicious, and he would never get inside.

"There was a terrible argument between the captain and the mate when, not trusting the captain, the mate refused to wait outside. When it was over, the mate was lying on the ground, the captain's spear through his heart. 'Get rid of him,' the captain told me. Terrified, I carried the mate's body away from the gate and put it under a bush. I left the spear in the body. The captain was so anxious to get inside, he didn't bother to send me back for the spear when he realized I'd left it.

"When Evadne came to the gate, I told her I had the oarsman with me who knew something of her brother. I watched her eyes, and I could see she was as terrified as I was, but she told him to follow her. She led him to the great dining hall. Your mother was sitting on one of the couches. She invited the captain to recline on another one and ordered a slave to bring him wine. He dropped his sword and shield on the floor next to him and accepted the bowl of wine. As fast as he drank, your mother offered him more wine. After a while when your mother was certain his wits were dulled, she called Evadne into the room. 'Lazy child,' she scolded. 'Here we have a guest and you have not had the man's weaponry put up. What kind of hostess will he think I am?'

"Evadne returned with a slave. Bloated by your mother's attention, the captain let them take his sword and shield.

At the dining room door, Evadne gave his sword and shield to me. I slipped on the shield and took up the sword, looking so pale and frightened that for a moment she became afraid I couldn't carry out the plan."

"I told him that afterwards," Evadne interrupted.

Simo chuckled. "Evadne returned to the couches and requested your mother's appearance in the kitchen, mumbling something about a problem with a cook. Your mother, calm as Athena, stood and told Evadne to lead the way. 'No,' the captain insisted, taking Evadne's hand. 'Surely you don't need two women to handle the cooks. Leave your lovely daughter here to pour my wine.'

"I panicked. Our plan had failed. Evadne would be left in the room with no protection. But your mother, having lost one of her children to the captain, had no intention of losing the other. With a show of strength I wouldn't have believed possible had I not seen it with my own eyes, she walked behind the captain, picked up a candlestick, and smashed it down on his head."

"We used to tease her about that," Evadne added, smiling. "She said she didn't know herself where the strength came from. Suddenly, it was just there."

Simo continued, sitting again. "The captain slumped forward, stunned. I ran into the room and yelled at your mother and Evadne to leave. As soon as they were safely out of the room, I went toward the captain wearing his shield and sword. Cursing, he got to his feet, rubbing his head from the blow your mother had given him, and staggered toward me. He thought I had brought him his weapons until I pointed the sword at him.

"The sword shook so that he could see the end bobbing up and down. Taking too much confidence from my fear, he lunged toward me, his hand out. I held my breath and swung the sword. It cut his arm, just at the wrist, disabling it from use. He cried out in pain and stood there looking at me. Suddenly, he seemed to realize I meant to kill him.

"He circled around me looking for a chance to grab me. I circled with him, fearing for my life with every step he made. Then he lunged forward again, trying to duck under the sword and grab my legs. I swung the sword down. It caught him on the shoulder and made a very deep cut. He fell to the floor.

"Too weak from the loss of blood to get back onto his feet, he offered me the ship and Evadne, even half the estate, if I'd let him live.

"'Not even if Zeus himself ordered it,' I said and I brought the sword down on his neck as hard as I could. Blood spurted all over my legs. I dropped to my knees, weak with the sight of a man dying, and passed out."

"Then what happened?" Simo asked Clymene.

"Grandmother offered to let you choose any one of the vessels in the family treasury you wanted as a reward."

"Right. I didn't take anything, though. I thought being rid of the captain was reward enough." He took Evadne's hand. "And I had another type of reward in mind.

"I returned to the ship and told Fox what had happened. With the help of the other boys, we threw the captain's drunken crew overboard. Fox and I took the boys home, hiring oarsmen to replace the boys as they left. Fox knew sailing and, as it turned out, was one of the shrewdest traders to sail the Mediterranean. We sailed until we'd amassed a fortune. Afterwards, we set sail for Argos again. I asked your mother's permission to marry Evadne. She agreed. After we were married, I stayed on the estate and Fox sailed our ship until he died."

Simo kissed Clymene on the cheek. Then turning to Nicias he said, "The only thing I knew about you was that you'd been sold. I had Fox search for you. He was told by a sea captain you'd escaped from the estate where you were living and had set sail for Sidon on a ship that sunk."

"Never," Nicias said emphatically. "I've only been on the sea once since the ship. That trip across the Gulf of Corinth to get Bromia I told Evadne about. I have terrible dreams even talking about the sea. I only agreed to sail across the Gulf to get to Bromia faster." He shivered with disgust. "I'll never step onto the deck of a ship again as long as I live."

"Except to take Homer's ashes to Ios," Philocleon added, realizing when Nicias sighed as the words left his lips that they would not be making the trip to Ios together. "At least I don't know of any way to get to Ios by land," he added, not knowing what else to say.

A long silence followed during which Nicias signaled to everyone to say nothing. When the right opportunity came along, he'd tell Philocleon he wasn't going with him to Ios.

Bromia finally broke the silence. "Why don't you tell Simo about Homer while Evadne shows Nicias the estate," she suggested to Philocleon.

"I'm coming with you," Clymene told Nicias.

"All right." Nicias took her hand. "First, I'd like to see the stables." He waited for Bromia to stand. When she didn't, he asked, "Are you coming with us?"

"I'm sure she'll be more comfortable here," Evadne interjected.

Bromia avoided Evadne's gaze. "I'll wait here."

Philocleon told Simo about Homer, but his heart wasn't in it. His story always ended in Ios. Without Nicias' help, how would he get to the island?

Fifteen

Shivering, Philocleon sat up, found the coverlet at the bottom of his bed and pulled it over him. He'd been awake for some time listening to the wind. It sounded sinister, stirring through the trees. Winter had come and gone three times since Homer had died. He'd promised his friend he'd bury his ashes and here he was, still living with Nicias.

Outside his window he could hear the slaves arguing on their way to the barns. One of them had stubbed his toe on a stone. It sounded as though he thought his threats and curses could pulverize the stone. Just like home, Philocleon thought. Home? What home? He was no closer to home than he was to burying Homer's ashes.

I must go to Ios, he decided, getting up. He'd known since they arrived Nicias wasn't going with him when he left the estate even though Nicias had carefully avoided telling him so. His fear of moving on without Nicias had immobilized him long enough.

Nicias was sitting in the courtyard when Philocleon found him. "Do you remember what happened three summers ago?"

"Yes."

"I haven't buried Homer's ashes and I'm no closer to getting home than I was when I started. Would you do something for me?"

Nicias braced himself. The moment had come when he'd have to tell Philocleon he wasn't going with him to Ios. "You understand that I care a great deal for you..." he began.

Philocleon interrupted him. "Nicias. I've known for a long time that you weren't coming with me when I left the estate."

"You have?" Nicias paused, trying to find a way to explain how he felt to Philocleon. "It's not that I don't want to go with you, it's just that..."

"I understand. This is your home. You've waited most of your life to find it. Now you're here with Bromia. I can't expect you to leave. I haven't stayed on at your estate because I thought eventually you'd agree to come with me but because I didn't have any plan for proceeding by myself. Ever since the breezes began to blow, I've done nothing but think. I finally have a plan. Will you take me to the great tomb in the north? They say one of the great heroes is buried there."

"Yes, but why?"

"I've been told many go to this tomb to petition the gods in Hades' Underworld. I will ask them to send my father's shade to me. If his shade comes, I'm going to ask it for advice." It was a reasonable choice. Since he'd been a child, either Nicias or Hipponous had guided him when he needed to make decisions. Now that Nicias was no longer available, it was only logical he should turn to his father.

"What makes you think your father's shade will advise you?"

"When I was a child I heard my father tell one of the neighbors how he had gone to this tomb as a young man and gotten advice from the shade of his father."

The idea brought great relief to Nicias. Though he remained steadfastly determined not to accompany Philocleon to Ios, he had been uneasy about the decision ever since he'd made it.

Philocleon listed the things he'd need. "I'd like to leave as soon as possible."

"We can have everything ready in a horse's whinny, if this is what you want." Nicias felt pleased to be able to help. Besides, it eased his guilt for refusing to go to Ios after all the kind things Philocleon had done for him. "You go to the kitchen and tell Evadne. I'll get the slaves started preparing the wagon."

Evadne was waiting for Nicias when he came from the barn. "The food you wanted is packed," she announced and smiled what looked to Nicias like a genuinely happy smile. "I sent it to the wagon with one of the slaves."

"You seem pretty anxious to be rid of us," he said jokingly, wishing he really was joking. She'd been quiet and ill humored for so long, her sudden happiness made him nervous.

"No, I'm not,"Evadne answered. "I'm just happy Philocleon has made his decision, and I'd like to help if I can." Still smiling, she went to her room, leaving Philocleon and Nicias to eat and finish their preparations by themselves. As soon as she heard the two men leave the house, she sent one of her slaves to find Simo. "Tell him I'd very much like to speak with him."

"I'm always happy and 'curious' when you very much want to speak with me," Simo said laughingly when he got to the room, wondering why he'd brought such a strong sense of foreboding with him.

As she began, she sat on a chair next to the window impatiently watching Bromia and the girls wander off toward the fields. "We need to talk with Nicias."

"About what?" Simo pulled up a chair and sat down opposite her. "How lovely you look with Helios shining through your hair." He reached over and stroked her hair.

She took his hand and kissed it, hoping to win him over just a little before she started talking. "If Philocleon is truly preparing to leave the estate we must talk Nicias into sending Bromia with him. It would be dangerous for him to travel to Ios by himself." She kept her voice even and casual, trying to make Simo think the idea was something she'd just thought of when Philocleon announced he was leaving.

"Why would Nicias do something like that? He just found her." Simo began to understand why he'd had such a bad feeling coming to the room.

"Philocleon will need someone to look after him. I'm sure Nicias feels somewhat responsible for him."

Simo examined her face carefully. It had a deceptively innocent look. "I don't think Nicias would permit Bromia to leave the estate without him for any reason. Haven't you been watching him? He loves her."

"Nicias is free now and there are many available women in Argos. He doesn't need to settle for a slave." Evadne sighed. She'd waited patiently for this opportunity.

"Bromia isn't a slave! I've told you a number of times. She's a freedwoman! Further, I don't think Nicias wants one of your Argive women. He loves Bromia."

"He thinks that now, but after Bromia is gone he'll forget her easily enough." Hadn't her mother told her many times real love was impossible between aristocrats and slaves.

"Evadne, a person doesn't forget someone he's loved for his entire life." Simo felt his temper rising.

"People of our class never truly love the lower classes. We, that is, men enjoy them for physical pleasure, but they never really love them. Once Bromia is gone, Nicias will forget her."

"I don't think so. In fact, I agree with Philocleon. Give a slave possessions and you have an aristocrat. Take away an aristocrat's possessions and you have a slave. Underneath it all, we aren't much different."

"Who told you Philocleon said that? You weren't here when he said it."

"Themis. She and Clymene hid in the dining room and listened to everything that was said. Themis was quite impressed with Philocleon and Bromia."

Evadne felt betrayed. Themis hadn't said anything to her. "Themis and Clymene are too small to hear such things."

Simo took a firm hold of Evadne's hand. "Listen to me. You like Bromia. You've said yourself, she's polite, she's clean. She's good to and good for Nicias. The children love her. Every time I turn around I see Clymene cuddling up next to her, asking for a story."

"That's why I want her out of here. She's grown too close to the children. I don't want her influencing them." Hadn't her mother insisted the great danger of letting the lower classes into your home was their influence on your children?

Simo sighed. How could this woman who was so kind and gentle in other ways be so unreasonable about this? "What is it about Bromia that bothers you so?"

"She was a slave. There's no place for a slave in our home."

"What about Nicias? Wasn't he a slave?"

"He wasn't born a slave. He was born with all of the qualities of an aristocrat. Circumstances forced him into slavery. That's different from Bromia. She was born a slave – with all the vulgarities slaves are born with."

"Exactly what are the vulgarities Bromia has that offend you so?"

"I want you to talk to Nicias. Ask him to send her with Philocleon."

"No. If you want her to go with Nicias, you talk to him."

"Why do you always do this? Take the side of every slave and freedman or woman who comes up against me?"

"I don't always. I only take their side when you're being unreasonable." He started to walk away, but stopped midway across the room, his temper flaring. "Besides, I think you know perfectly well why I take the side of slaves and freedmen."

"I don't want anyone from a lower class living in my house."

Those were the same words he'd heard her mother repeat more times than he cared to count. Wasn't Evadne's attitude toward the lower classes his fault too? He should have told her long ago. He walked back and took Evadne's chin firmly in his hand and forced her to look directly into his angry eyes. "If you don't want anyone from the lower classes living in your house, then I think you have some serious thinking to do."

"What do you mean?"

"I'm going to tell you the story of my capture by the slave captain again, but this time I'm going to tell it to you as it actually happened."

"I already know that story." Evadne suddenly felt very uneasy. What did he mean – as it actually happened.

"Oh, but you see, I changed the story a little for your sake. I wasn't the aristocratic son. I was the herder. The captain and his men killed my master's son and took me. When I came to you, I took his identity. I wasn't a slave, but I was a freedman, the same as Bromia."

Evadne pulled away from him. "I don't believe you. You're just telling me that because you want to force me to change my mind about Bromia."

"Did you ever wonder why I didn't go home to collect my father's fortune after I'd freed myself?"

"No!" Suddenly, Evadne felt angry and helpless.

"Well, your mother did. I didn't go home to collect my fortune because there wasn't one."

"You lied to me!" Evadne stood, furious with herself for forcing this confession out of Simo.

"Yes! Would you have accepted me as your husband if I'd told you the truth?"

Evadne didn't answer.

"You see. I have my answer." Simo walked to the door.

"Mother knew?" Evadne asked.

"Yes. When I asked her permission to marry you, she asked why I hadn't gone home to live with my father. I told her the truth."

"Why didn't you tell me? You had no right to keep it from me!"

"It was your mother's idea. She didn't think you were strong enough to know you'd married someone beneath you."

Evadne stared at him.

Softening, Simo returned to her side. "I'm sorry you found out this way. I hadn't meant to tell you, ever." He reached over and touched her cheek.

"Don't touch me."

Angry again, Simo went to door, paused only long enough to hurl a few final words at Evadne. "Since you are incapable of truly loving someone of a lower class, I assume you won't miss me."

At the stable, Simo ordered his cart and, whipping the horses, raced down the path to the main road. Without knowing what he would do, he turned the horses toward the village.

Not strong enough? Evadne thought. I was strong enough to help kill the slave captain, to keep the estate going for mother until Simo returned, to bear two children, but I wasn't strong enough to be told the truth about my own husband. She got up and went out to see if she could find Nicias. She needed to talk to someone.

Nicias was no longer on the estate. He and Philocleon were already following the old road north toward the Greek tomb. Since this was to be their last trip together, he described everything he saw to Philocleon. First there was the temple of Hera, situated high in the cliffs over the Argive plains. Then there were the many villages they passed through, and finally the acropolis near the ancient tomb.

"All I can see from the road is a wall surrounding the acropolis," he told Philocleon. "It's made of boulders that look to be wider than a man is tall. I've heard men say only the cyclopes would have been strong enough to carry boulders that size up there. They also say the palace where king Agamemnon lived was inside those walls. I'm told there isn't anything left of the palace."

"What happened to it?"

"The elders in the villages say it was invaders from the north that destroyed it."

"But if the walls were so strong, how did they get into the palace?"

"I don't know. It happened so long ago, I don't suppose there's a man alive who remembers."

Nicias stopped at the foot of the acropolis and tethered the horses. He decided not to walk Philocleon up to the palace as the hillside was steep and there was no longer a path through the thick underbrush. Instead, finding a path around the lower side of the acropolis, he went directly to the tomb that men said belonged to Agamemnon, a large rectangular opening cut into the hillside below the acropolis.

He helped Philocleon feel his way into the entrance and lit a torch. They walked down the narrow corridor of the tomb to the interior. "It has the shape of a rainbow," he informed Philocleon taking him to the center of the tomb and helping him sit on one of many stones placed around a circular pit.

Awed by the strange echoing of his words off the tomb walls, Nicias sat quietly next to Philocleon for a few moments before he returned to the wagon, untied the black lamb they'd brought with them, pulled a sack filled with pottery jars from behind the seat, and hoisted a bundle of branches onto his shoulder.

"It's all ready," he whispered when he'd deposited everything next to Philocleon.

"Ready, ready, ready," bounced gently off the walls, sending shivers up Nicias' spine.

Philocleon was barely aware of the echoing, though under different circumstances it would have fascinated him. He was too concerned with performing the rites perfectly so that the gods of Hades' Underworld would listen to him.

When he asked for it, Nicias gingerly gave Philocleon the dagger he had used to put out his eyes. Much to his surprise and great joy, Philocleon took hold of the dagger with a steady hand.

Meticulously, Philocleon spaded up a pit with the dagger. When he was finished, he threw the dagger into the pit and covered it with a mound of earth. Ignoring the gasp of disbelief that came from Nicias when he discarded the gold dagger, he poured the contents from the pottery jars over the pit. The first jar contained milk taken from a snow-white goat. The second jar contained honey. The third, water drawn from a sacred spring. Finally he spread barley.

His voice trembling with emotion, Philocleon addressed the gods of Hades' Underworld. "I have brought you a flawless black lamb. If the smoke from my sacrifice pleases you, send up the shade of my father." With Nicias' help, he lit a fire, slit the lamb's throat, wrapped the best pieces of the thigh in fat and set them over the fire to roast.

Philocleon called into the pit when Nicias told him the thighs had thoroughly roasted. "Father. I have done as you instructed. I washed in the sacred spring high in the mountains, burned the spear that caused your death and made sacrifices to our ancestors. With Nicias' help, I gave you a hero's funeral and buried your ashes in the family crypt. If I have pleased you, do me the honor of speaking to me in my dreams."

Without saying more, Philocleon lay down and waited for sleep to come to him. Nicias lay next to him, falling asleep only after his own worries had numbed him. He woke, feeling damp and chilled. Getting up, he rekindled the fire and waited impatiently for Philocleon to wake.

"Did your father's shade come to you?" he asked as soon as Philocleon stirred.

"No." Philocleon sat up and went over the dream again in his mind so he wouldn't forget it. "It was a very strange dream. I expected to speak with my father's shade, but it was Na'id-Assur and Qurdi Marduk who came to me."

"What did they say?"

"I asked them why my father's shade hadn't come. They said because my father wouldn't be of any help to me in deciding what I must do."

Surprised, Nicias asked, "What do you think they meant by that?"

"What's even more strange. It didn't seem as though Na'id-Assur and Qurdi Marduk were actually talking to me. It was as though I was telling myself my father couldn't help me, only the words were coming out of their mouths."

"Why do you think that?" Nicias always felt nervous about rituals that took strange turns.

"Because they were telling me exactly what I've been thinking these last seasons. Somehow, I knew my father wasn't the one to help me, but I wanted to try anyway." Now that he thought about it, how could his father help him? There was no doubt in his mind; his father wouldn't approve of anything he'd done thus far: freeing Nicias, buying Bromia and freeing her. His attitude toward slaves and aristocrats would infuriate his father. What's more, he had no regrets and no plans to change his mind. As things stood, there was no place for his father's beliefs in his life anymore. So how could he be of any help?

Nicias sighed unhappily. "I'm really sorry."

"Don't be." Philocleon's understanding of the dream was growing. "Though I've finally come to realize I won't have you or my father to advise me, I'll still have Na'id-Assur and Qurdi Marduk." He smiled a knowing smile. "Of course, their advice is much more difficult to follow than yours or father's since it is always for me to reason and think and decide for myself."

"What will you do now?" Nicias was still worried though he could see Philocleon wasn't.

"Return to the Simo's estate and figure out how to get to Ios."

"You do understand...." Nicias began. "It isn't that I don't want to go to Ios with you. It's just that..."

"Don't worry about it," Philocleon reassured him. "It's as clear to me as to you that Bromia needs you more than I do right now."

"What do you think I should do about Evadne?" As soon as he'd asked the question Nicias realized with amusement he and Philocleon had exchanged places.

"Nothing."

"You mean you think I should continue to let her treat Bromia like a slave?"

"I don't think she will for long." Philocleon had figured out what it was that had struck him about Simo's storytelling the first time he told the story of his capture. Although subtle enough so that it required the kind of precise listening Philocleon had taught himself after becoming blind, Simo used some words and phrases that were more common among freedmen than aristocrats. "I think Simo is a freedman himself."

Nicias was shocked at first, but the more he thought about it, the more he became convinced Philocleon was right. "Do you think Evadne knows?"

"No, or she wouldn't act the way she does. But you've seen how Simo takes Bromia's side in every way. Sooner or later, I think he'll tell her. How can she continue to hate Bromia if Simo is a freedman?"

"Do you think I should talk to Simo?"

Philocleon shook his head and stood. "I think you should let them settle it. They'll tell you if they want you to know." He smiled wryly. "I know a lot about obstinate pride. Evadne will come around, but she'll have to do it in her own way."

Nicias felt as proud of Philocleon as he would have had he been his own son. "How wise you've grown," he murmured. Taking Philocleon's arm, he led him from the tomb feeling he no longer had to worry about him. "You remember when I told you that you'd be able to take care of yourself? I was right. You don't need me anymore."

Philocleon nodded. It was true he'd changed a great deal since the death of his father. He didn't believe any more that his fate was to be the same as Bellerophon's even though he was blind. He'd buried that thought when he threw the dagger into the pit. It wasn't pride, though he was proud enough, that made him disobey his father. It was a desire to learn about the world outside their estate.

Nicias said no more. As they drove toward the estate, he could see Philocleon was deep in thought, and he himself had a number of things to think about, for instance, exactly why he had this strange feeling he was about to see his friend Egyptus again.

"Maybe because you were about to see me again," Egyptus suggested when Nicias told everyone at the evening meal he'd had a feeling that he was going to see Egyptus all the way home from the tomb.

"What brought you?" Nicias asked excitedly. "My scratchings on the sherd I left with your uncle Ti?"

"He gave it to me when I stopped in Sparta to make a cartload of pottery. Now I'm on my way north to sell the pots I made. Your sister has been kindly entertaining me while I waited for you."

"Did you introduce him to Bromia?" Nicias asked Evadne more harshly than he'd intended.

Evadne shifted uneasily on her couch. "Yes."

"She went to get the little cup my uncle gave to you," Egyptus added, grinning. "So tell me. Do you still think I have sand and rocks in my head?"

Evadne stood. "I'll send in more wine." She left the three men and went into the kitchen.

Bromia returned with the cup and gave it to Nicias. He filled it with wine and handed it to Egyptus. "To friends who have heads made of sand and rocks and limestone."

Both men laughed. Nicias told Egyptus everything that had happened after he'd left the estate. "So Philocleon came here with me. Soon, he'll be leaving to bury the ashes of Homer."

"Where will you go in the north when you leave here?" Philocleon asked Egyptus. He'd been thinking while the two men were talking.

"Wherever I can sell my pots."

"What about Attica?"

Egyptus thought about it. "I might go there, why?"

"I've an idea. If you were to go to Attica, you could stop at my estate and use the clay you found there to make pots."

"It's a good idea," Egyptus said. "I found some of the best clay I've seen on your land. Do you suppose the kiln we built is still standing?" he asked Nicias.

"It was when we left the estate."

"If you go to Attica," Philocleon persisted in his thoughts, "I'd like to send a message to my grandfather with you."

Nicias and Egyptus both grinned. "So; now I see why you're so willing to let me use your clay," Egyptus said. "What is the message you want me to deliver?"

"It's actually not a message but a request. I want to know whether he stills plans to have Scapha marry me."

Egyptus thought a while. There wasn't any reason for him not to go to Attica. "All right. I accept your offer to use the estate clay and I'll take the message for you, but how will you get the answer?"

"I was hoping you'd bring it when you come back this way to see your uncle in Sparta." Philocleon smiled to himself, hearing in Egyptus' breathing the potter's surprise at how well he'd worked out his plan. "Besides, I was hoping I could get you to take me to Ios."

"You've thought of everything," Egyptus teased. "I'll tell you what. I'll agree to take the message to your grandfather. Beyond that, I can't promise."

"If you can't come back yourself with the answer," Nicias suggested, "send Trygaeus' son. He can be trusted."

"Yes. Tell Trygaeus I promise to pay him well. Maybe he could take me to Ios and then we could sail together to the Sounion port," Philocleon paused, "that is, if you can't make it back."

"Here's my brother-in-law," Nicias interrupted, seeing Simo out in the corridor.

"Simo," he called. "Come and meet my friend Egyptus."

Simo had told himself he was coming home to pack his belongings when he left the estate, but he knew even then that wasn't the reason. He had come home, hoping to talk with Evadne. His mother-in-law was a fine woman, but she had been wrong about him and Evadne. He had turned out to be the one who wasn't strong enough, not Evadne. He had been too weak to tell Evadne the truth about his lineage. Instead, he had sat by and let his mother-in-law use all of her influence to convince Evadne there was no place for the lower classes in their home. It had been his mother-in-law's way of making certain the exception she had made for him didn't become a way of life for the family. And he had let it happen.

"Evadne," Nicias called to the kitchen. "Have another bowl sent in. Simo is home."

Evadne's heart raced. She rushed to the kitchen door and watched Simo walk into the courtyard. "Take a bowl to Simo," she told a slave.

Nicias introduced Simo to Egyptus. "He's on his way north with a load of pottery," he explained.

"I've asked him to go to our estate in Attica," Philocleon added, intent on getting his message to his grandfather.

"What's in Attica?" Simo asked politely, watching the kitchen door.

"My grandfather," Philocleon said and repeated his idea of sending a message.

"You should send Scapha a wedding gift," Evadne suggested walking back into the room. "It would be a way of letting your grandfather know you plan to honor your father's pledge. Committing yourself to marry someone is a very important decision. Once you've made the commitment, you have obligations to that person, no matter what happens." She glanced at Simo. There were so many things she wanted to say.

"She's absolutely right," Simo said, searching Evadne's eyes to see if there was a message for him in what she'd said.

"I could send her one of the fibulae from my treasury," Philocleon suggested.

"You could, but I think I have a better idea, if you don't mind," Evadne continued.

"What is it?" Simo asked, watching Themis and Clymene come into the courtyard.

"Bring me the wedding gown I've been weaving," Evadne told Themis.

Nicias looked at Bromia. With his lips he mouthed. "What's happened?"

Bromia shrugged casually to indicate she didn't know.

Evadne took the rectangular linen cloth Themis brought to her and wrapped it around her daughter, expertly pulling the two corners up over Themis' shoulders from the back and fastening them at the front, creating a peplos. "I was making this for Themis, but she's only seen the spring blossoms a few times. I'll have time to make her another before she weds."

"It's beautiful," Simo said.

Evadne showed them the embroidered gold and green meander pattern she'd begun around the outside edge of the violet peplos. "Inside of the meander, there's supposed to be a row of rosettes, then another meander, then rosettes."

She handed the dress to Bromia. "I thought, maybe...if we worked on it together, we could finish it before Egyptus leaves. After all, if you're going to live here, you'll want to learn where everything is and how to use it." She looked at Simo. It was the only way she could think of to tell him how she felt.

"After we finish the peplos," Bromia suggested, "if Egyptus hasn't left, maybe we could make a shawl for Philocleon's grandmother." She reached out and took Evadne's hand.

"What a wonderful idea," Nicias added. He went over and picked Evadne up and hugged her. "Thank you," he whispered in her ear before he put her back down in front of Simo.

Simo stood for a moment. Then he threw his arms around Evadne and kissed her.

Tears gathering in her eyes, she scolded Simo for kissing her in front of the children and told Nicias to pour more wine. Nicias did as he was told, handing each of them a bowl.

"To wonderful wives," Philocleon proposed, lifting his cup. "Especially Evadne."

"To wonderful wives," Simo repeated.

"To strong wives," Evadne said and lifted her bowl to Simo.

"How about to finding a wife?" Egyptus said.

"And a husband," Themis added.

"She wants to marry you," Clymene said to Philocleon. "She thinks you're so wooooooonderful!"

"I do not," Themis yelled, chasing after Clymene to cover her embarrassment.

Laughing, Evadne told everyone to return to their couches. "It's time for us to eat as a family."

At the end of the meal, Themis asked Philocleon to tell them the saga of Gilgamesh and the riddle. "He and I have been trying to figure it out since he got here," she announced.

"You never told me about Gilgamesh," Clymene wailed, feeling totally betrayed.

"I'll do it right now," Philocleon said, helping her onto his lap. "Once there was a very fine, but unruly king named Gilgamesh. To keep Gilgamesh out of trouble the gods made a companion for him named Enkidu. The two men went off together in search of enduring names. While the two men searched they killed the guardian of the forest, Humbaba, and insulted the goddess, Ishtar. For these crimes the gods decreed Enkidu must die. After his death, Gilgamesh searched to the ends of the earth for immortality, but he failed to find it. He did find a thorny plant that would have kept men young forever, but he lost it trying to bring it back to Uruk. So, he had to return to his kingdom with nothing. When he got there, he looked his kingdom over, and weeping, wrote the story of his search on stone. When death approached him, he, like his friend Enkidu, lay down and did not rise again.

"Now," he said, hugging Clymene and smiling in the direction of Themis. "Let me put Qurdi Marduk's riddle to you. If you answer it, I'll buy you anything you want when we go again to the village. How was it that Gilgamesh died having lost the thorny plant of immortality and yet gained immortality?"

While the others tried to answer the riddle, Philocleon considered Gilgamesh. He'd always thought of the king as being very much like Achilles, but today, telling the saga, he'd found a very profound difference. Where Achilles was interested in fighting in Troy to gain glory for himself only, Gilgamesh had lost the thorny plant trying to bring it back to Uruk to share it with all the men in his kingdom.

SIXTEEN

Egyptus pulled his cart to a halt in Daemones' yard. Furious with the pack of dogs that had chased his donkeys all the way from the main road to the house, he jumped off the cart, his whip ready, roaring, "Get out of here." He cracked the whip in the air. One of the dogs lunged at him. He drove it back. "A plague on you." He snapped the whip again, forcing the entire pack back a few paces. Patting his donkeys on the rear end to calm them, he prepared for a second attack.

Suddenly, the lead dog turned and ran into the trees taking the remainder of the pack with him. Egyptus moved quickly to check his donkeys for damage, but before he got a chance the dogs were back, barking and snapping. A tall, statuesque woman followed them out of the forest. She had a quiver thrown over her shoulder, a bow in her hand.

Stopping a few paces from him she called the dogs to her. "Are you looking for someone?" she asked.

Egyptus nodded, but he didn't answer. He was too busy staring. Watching her walk out of the forest, he'd thought she'd lived almost as long as he had. Now that she was standing in front of him, he could see she hadn't seen the four seasons change much more than sixteen or seventeen times.

"Sit," she commanded. The dogs fell to the ground at her knees. She repeated her question. "Are you looking for someone?"

She was wearing a green tunic, cut off at the knees. Never before had he seen a young woman outdoors with so little cover. Even more shocking, her soft brown hair wasn't held by a net as was proper. It hung loose, freely curling down the sides of her tanned face and spilling onto her shoulders. Philocleon hadn't described Scapha, but who else could it be?

"They won't hurt you," she said, assuming it was out of fear of the dogs he remained speechless.

"I'm not afraid of them," Egyptus said, at last able to concentrate on what she was saying instead of what she was wearing. He stepped away from the cart. Instantly the dogs were up again, barking and snapping. He froze. He wasn't afraid of them, but he wasn't interested in a fight with them either.

She calmed them a second time. "I'm still waiting for your answer." She fingered her bow and fixed her impatient velvet brown eyes intently on him. "And I'm beginning to lose patience."

"I've come to see Daemones." He was amused that someone who'd seen so few seasons pass would attempt to frighten him.

She looked him over carefully. He was clean. He didn't look dangerous. Still, she didn't recognize him and she was alone with her aunt and uncle, both of whom were unable to defend themselves should his intentions prove unscrupulous. "He isn't well. What do you want with him?"

"I have a message from Philocleon."

"Describe him."

"Who? Daemones?"

"No. Tell me what Philocleon looks like so I can be sure you really do know him."

Misunderstanding the seriousness with which she viewed the interrogation, Egyptus couldn't resist teasing her. "He's short with warts all over his face."

She moved into a shooting position and pulled an arrow from her quiver. "Get out."

"What?"

"I said, get off the estate." She placed the arrow in her bowstring and pointed it at him.

Egyptus stepped back and put his hands out in front of him, palms out. "Wait. I was only joking. I meant to be funny." He described Philocleon carefully, including even the dimple in his chin and the blisters on his left foot. "Of course, you wouldn't know about the blisters," he said, trying to establish some good will between them with a little light-hearted banter. "He got them walking around Nicias' estate with me."

She examined him thoroughly again. He didn't look dangerous. And he had described Philocleon perfectly. It would probably be safe to take him inside. She lowered her bow.

Assuming the lowering of her bow was an indication he'd established some trust, Egyptus continued to try to win her confidence. "I think you must be Scapha."

"I am." Without bothering to ask who he was, she turned and whistled shrilly toward the stable. Moments later a slave appeared and unhitched Egyptus' donkeys.

"Come with me," she said ordering the dogs with her hands to stay where they were.

Egyptus pulled his traveling sack from the back of the cart and followed her, as curious as he was amused.

Scapha went directly to the courtyard. Daemones was lying, as usual, curled up on a couch in Helios' light. "Uncle," she said rubbing his shoulder lightly. "Someone's here to see you."

"Who is it?" Daemones mumbled without opening his eyes.

"You haven't told me your name," she said to Egyptus without turning around.

"Most people call me Egyptus."

"The potter who worked on Hipponous' estate?" she asked.

"That's right."

"It's Egyptus," Scapha told Daemones.

Daemones neither opened his eyes nor spoke.

"He isn't ready to wake up," she explained, turning to face Egyptus.

He stood staring at her.

"I'm not what you were expecting, am I?" she asked.

"Well, not exactly. Not that I'm not pleased with what I've found." He'd thought she would be small and feminine, though he had no idea why.

Scapha was not small nor was she feminine, her face had strong features, attractive, but firm and solid. He could see finely toned leg muscles below her short gown. And she was tanned from the sun, not pale like most women he knew. "I mean, I thought you would be somewhat...smaller."

"Everyone expects me to look like my aunt." She called toward the interior of the house. "Aunt Alcmena. Come out here for a moment. Philocleon has sent someone with a message."

While Scapha put her bow and quiver on a bench near Daemones, Alcmena burst into the courtyard. She stopped to catch her breath. "I ran all the way from the kitchen."

"Perhaps you should sit down," Scapha suggested.

Alcmena sat heavily on a couch. "You have news of our Philocleon?" she asked Egyptus eagerly.

"He is well and sends you his love."

"Where is he?" She wiped her face with a kerchief. She'd gained considerable weight since Philocleon left. It wasn't so easy for her to run now.

"At the moment, he's in Argos with Nicias and Bromia."

"Bromia? Why ever is he with Bromia?"

"She was his nurse as a child and..."

"I know who she was," she snapped, using the tone of her voice to express how she felt about Bromia.

Puzzled by Alcmena's attack of Bromia, Egyptus continued. "It seems Nicias and Bromia had been in love since they met without Hipponous knowing it. Philocleon helped Nicias find her." He continued, making it clear with the tone of his voice how he felt about Bromia. "If you want the truth, Nicias and Bromia treat Philocleon a whole lot better than Hipponous ever treated them."

"Aunt Alcmena." Scapha went over to kneel in front of her. "How often have I told you it isn't fair to blame Bromia. She was Hipponous' slave. There wasn't anything she could do when he took her to his bed. Think how miserable she must have been, loving Nicias and being forced to attend the bed of Hipponous."

"I know," Alcmena answered quietly, feeling guilty for what she'd said. "I only wish it would have been otherwise."

"If it's any help," Egyptus added, not having known about Hipponous' use of Bromia before, but even more determined to help defend her, "If she'd had a choice, she'd never have gone to Hipponous' bed." He continued by telling Alcmena what a fine woman Bromia was.

Leaving her aunt to Egyptus for the moment, Scapha returned to her uncle. She took both of his hands in hers. "Uncle, did you hear that? Philocleon is in Argos with Nicias."

"Who?" Daemones opened his eyes and looked puzzled.

"Philocleon."

"Who's that?"

"Your grandson. Don't you remember? Hipponous' and Calonice's son."

"Oh yes." He paused for a moment. "Where is he?"

"He's in Argos with Nicias, Hipponous' slave. You remember him?"

Daemones shook his head. "Who?"

Scapha smoothed his hair and returned to Egyptus. "He's not the same as he was before Hipponous died. Something went out of him after Philocleon accused them of lying about his mother's death..." She stopped, not knowing how to continue without upsetting her aunt.

"I can see." Egyptus pulled the beautifully wrapped wedding peplos out of his traveling sack. "Philocleon sent this with me."

Scapha opened the package. "Oh, Aunt, look." She carefully removed the peplos from the wrapping and laid it out on Alcmena's lap.

Alcmena examined the material, meticulously running her fingers over the weaving to test the quality. "It must have taken someone with considerable skill a long time to make this," she concluded.

"Bromia and Nicias' sister, Evadne made it," Egyptus explained. Turning to Scapha, "Philocleon hoped your uncle might accept it for you as a pledge of his intention to honor his father's wedding pledge to your uncle."

"It would be perfect wedding dress," Alcmena said. "Show it to your uncle."

Scapha took the peplos over and held it up in front of Daemones. "Uncle, look at the beautiful peplos Philocleon sent to me."

Daemones glanced vaguely at the peplos. "Who died?"

"No one died. It's a wedding peplos. Philocleon sent it to me."

"Who's Philocleon?"

Scapha kissed Daemones on the head. "He's your grandson. Remember. Calonice's son."

"Oh. Where is he?"

"He's in Argos with Nicias, Hipponous' slave. Can you remember him?"

"No."

Egyptus waited until Scapha had given the peplos back to her aunt. Even though it was obvious the decision would be made by Scapha and Alcmena on behalf of Daemones, he put the request to Daemones in exactly the manner it had been given to him by Philocleon. "I'm to ask whether you plan to honor your pledge to marry Scapha to Philocleon. He requests that you send Trygaeus' son to Nicias' estate in Argos with his answer."

"I...that is." For the first time since they'd met, Scapha was clearly flustered. "Trygaeus' son is getting military training in Athens."

Not believing her, but ever more curious, Egyptus offered another suggestion. "Perhaps you have a slave you could trust to deliver the message."

"Just now we can't afford to send a slave. I need, that is, my uncle needs every slave he has to work on the estate."

"What about one of Philocleon's slaves?"

"He doesn't have any slaves. They fled after, well, you know." She glanced at her aunt. "We've been using our slaves on his estate and just now we can't spare a single one." She thought about telling him the real reason, but decided against it. If things worked out, she'd tell him.

"Maybe when your slaves aren't so busy, you could send one," Egyptus suggested, deciding Scapha's hesitancy and discomposure were probably due to her not yet having decided whether she wanted to marry a blind man. "I don't think Philocleon is expecting an answer immediately."

"Yes, that's it. We'll send one a little later," she said returning to Alcmena to help her fold the wedding peplos again.

Alcmena stood. "I'll put this away."

"Before you leave," Scapha prompted her, "don't you think you should ask Egyptus to stay and rest a few days? He has come a long way to deliver Philocleon's message to uncle."

"Yes, of course. I'll have one of the slaves prepare a guestroom for you if you'd like to stay. When it's ready, I'll send her in to pick up your traveling sack."

"Thank you. I'd very much like to stay." Smiling, Egyptus took the shawl Evadne and Bromia had made for her out of his sack. "It's for you, from Nicias' sister and Bromia."

Alcmena accepted the shawl. Embarrassed about the hostile remarks she'd made about Bromia, she mumbled something about wine and hurried from the courtyard.

Scapha filled a cup of wine for Egyptus as soon as the mixing bowl arrived. Before she had a chance to hand him the cup, Alcmena was back in the courtyard. She handed him a finely crafted gold cup with two handles. "Please give this to Philocleon." She hesitated, then handed him two shawls. "For Evadne and Bromia. Please thank them for the shawl they sent me. I'm afraid mine aren't nearly as fine. My eyes aren't what they used to be."

After a long, admiring inspection of the cup and shawls, Egyptus packed them carefully into his traveling sack. It didn't occur to him until Scapha pointed it out that he'd just made a commitment to return to Philocleon on their behalf.

"As long as you've agreed to take the cup to Philocleon for my aunt, there's really no need for me to send a slave with my uncle's reply. When you give Philocleon the cup, tell him my uncle plans to honor his pledge," she said casually. "I may have a message for him, too, if you don't leave too soon."

"And what might your message be?" Egyptus asked, amused at how easily she'd trapped him into carrying the message. Still, he didn't mind. He'd planned to return to Argos anyway the next time he went to Sparta.

"More wine?" Scapha asked. There was something about him, his passionate defense of Bromia, his teasing of Scapha, his way of talking with her aunt, that made her feel she could trust him, but she wasn't ready to talk yet.

As she poured wine, Egyptus examined his wine cup. A fine vessel, he decided. Perfectly fired and only a little clumsy in shape of the foot. He recognized the clay as coming from Philocleon's estate. Scapha must have given another potter permission to use the clay bed. Anxious to let her know he had gotten rights to the clay bed from Philocleon, he held his cup up and examined it for her benefit. "When I left Argos, Philocleon said it would be all right if I stayed on at his estate a while and fired some pottery. That is, if the kiln is still standing or if I can rebuild it without too much difficulty."

"I think you'll find the kiln in excellent condition." Feeling a little shy, Scapha nodded toward his cup. "What do you think of it?"

"It's very nice." He drank the wine. "Who made it?"

"I did."

"You? I don't believe it." He'd never known of a woman to make pottery of that quality before.

"Why not me?" she asked defensively. "The kiln was sitting around and we needed some dishes, so I experimented until I figured out how to fire it. I had to try it a few times, but I managed, eventually."

Feeling bad he'd offended her with his outburst, Egyptus quickly apologized. "I'm sorry if I made it sound like I thought you couldn't have done it. I was just a little surprised. Women don't usually make pottery." He looked at the cup again carefully. "This is a fine piece of pottery."

"After you've slept off your long journey, I'll take you over to Philocleon's estate and you can see the kiln,' she suggested, forgiving him.

"I'd like that."

His voice sounded so enthusiastic, Scapha couldn't help smiling.

"Look at that." Egyptus grinned at her. "You do know how to smile."

She continued to smile in spite of her best efforts to stop while she waited for him to finish his wine. When his wine cup was finally empty, she quickly called for a slave. "He'll take you to your room now. I must go to the kitchen and give the cook instructions for the evening meal. I want it to be very special." She stood, leaving him no choice but to follow the slave. In his room, Egyptus fell asleep wondering what was going to happen at the evening meal. The mention of a message for Philocleon earlier together with her telling him she wanted the evening meal to be very special made him certain Scapha had more planned than eating.

Still curious, he woke when a slave touched his shoulder lightly. She bathed him and dressed him, then she led him to the dining room where he found Scapha waiting for him with her aunt and uncle.

Scapha was dressed in a peplos, belted with a fine embroidered girdle. She had on earrings, rings, bracelets and a silver necklace. "You're a different person," Egyptus said, folding his hands behind his back, waiting for her to invite him to join them.

"I'm dressed differently, but I'm still the same person. Don't be afraid." She pointed to the couch next to hers. Why was it, she wondered, that men always assumed if you liked some of the same things they did, like hunting, you couldn't possibly like being a woman.

"Actually I was more frightened when I first came," he teased sitting down next to her. "Arrows pointed at my head terrify me."

She handed him a cup of wine, then lifted her own in a toast. "Fear is a good thing in a man. It makes him sensible."

"And in a woman?"

"It depends on what she's afraid of."

Egyptus waited to see whether Daemones or Alcmena would object to Scapha's behavior. He'd never seen a woman propose a toast with a guest present before. Neither of them seemed the slightest bit interested in what she did. They were concentrating on the last of their wine.

"They always eat before I do," Scapha explained as Egyptus sipped his wine. "That way uncle can get down to the business of really sleeping instead of wasting his time taking naps. Isn't that right, Uncle?" she asked him affectionately.

Daemones smiled benignly.

"Come on," Alcmena said. "It's off to bed." She helped Daemones up and leaving with him, wished Scapha and Egyptus a pleasant meal.

Scapha waited until her aunt and uncle were out of hearing distance, then she moved directly to the subject she wanted to discuss with Egyptus. The rains would soon come. To be successful her plan needed to be executed before the rain destroyed the cliff paths. "Does Philocleon know the silver mines were taken by his twin cousins?" She motioned to a slave to bring in their meal: fresh partridge, squirrel, rabbit, leeks with eggs, cabbage, wheat loaves, and fruit.

Distracted by the wild game, Egyptus didn't answer her question. Instead, he asked one of his own. "Do you have brothers?"

"No." What a peculiar question, Scapha thought until she saw him staring at the game. She picked up the breast from a partridge and handed it to him. "I hunted for it."

"What don't you do?" Once again Egyptus could not conceal his surprise.

"I detest weaving."

"That's impossible. All women love to weave," he said, half-joking, half-serious. Certainly all the women he knew loved to weave.

"Not this one." She took an egg from the plate, put it on a wheat loaf, added lentils and ate it, waiting for him to argue about women and weaving. When he didn't, she repeated the question she'd just asked. "Does Philocleon know the twins took his silver mines?"

"Yes. They were taken from him before he left Attica. But he doesn't know what has become of his ship."

"No one knows what happened to the ship. Castor sailed off in it with a load of silver right after they confiscated the mines. He never returned. Everyone thinks he drowned at sea."

"Then Polydeuces must have the mines."

"Yes." Scapha leaned forward, her breath catching in her throat. "One of his slaves escaped and came here to me. Polydeuces badly mistreats the slaves. They are ready to revolt."

Egyptus nodded knowingly. "I would have expected Polydeuces to mistreat his slaves."

"With help, I could retake the silver mines." Scapha tried to sound calm though her heart was beating ferociously. She was testing him.

"You?" How often could this woman amaze him, Egyptus wondered.

Scapha looked carefully at Egyptus. Was he teasing her again? No. She could see he didn't believe she could retake the mines. "I didn't say I could do it by myself," she continued, trying to keep her voice from sounding too disappointed. "I said I would need help."

Egyptus returned her gaze for some moments before he understood what she was up to. "Oh no," he said. "I wouldn't be of any help. The one thing I never learned was the use of a sword or spear."

"You wouldn't need to know how to use a weapon. There are plenty of farmers willing to provide the bowmen I'll need. Polydeuces regularly raids the surrounding estates for the meat and vegetables he puts on his table and everyone here wants to be rid of him. There's another kind of help I'd need."

"Whatever it is, I wouldn't be able to do it. I've made plans to be out of here as soon as I can make a load of pottery. Besides, your aunt and uncle would never agree to let you attack Polydeuces. I'm sure of that." It was obvious they let her do as she chose, but even they must have some limits.

"My aunt and uncle don't know anything about my plan," she said. "Besides, how could they stop me? Uncle is too feeble and aunt wouldn't know how."

"Well, somebody should stop you."

"Why?"

"Why? Because, I've had some experience with Polydeuces and Castor. They are dangerous men."

"I know. That's why I need someone I can trust to help me." She'd hoped his experience with the twins would make him more willing to listen to her.

"You can trust me. I'm telling you truthfully. I'm not interested in any scheme to retake the mines from Castor and Polydeuces."

"All right. You don't have to help me. But will you at least listen to what I'm proposing?" She hadn't been able to talk about it to anyone, and she desperately wanted to discuss it.

"No, I won't. And you need to forget about it completely."

"I thought you were Philocleon's friend."

"I am."

"Don't you understand? I'm doing this for Philocleon."

"Look," Egyptus made a point of keeping his voice fatherly. "I think your idea is noble. I'm certain Philocleon would be very proud of you. But you're a woman. It isn't the kind of thing a woman should be involved in."

She poured each of them more wine. There was no point in arguing with him. She'd made a mistake. He wasn't going to help her. Raising one of the cups she had made herself, she smiled. "To women who weave."

He raised his cup in return. "And to men who are afraid."

"Is Philocleon as afraid of danger as you are?" she asked, actually curious.

"Probably not. Since he's only seen the four seasons pass twenty-three times and I've seen them pass twenty-nine times."

"I don't understand."

"Fear is something you learn. The fewer seasons you've seen, the less experience you have and the less fear you have."

She shrugged. She was plenty afraid. But she wasn't going to let fear stop her.

"Have you ever seen a man die, his head split open and his brains spilling out on the ground, or maybe his heart pierced through with blood running all over everything?"

Scapha tried not to look impatient. "I've killed a lot of animals. I know what blood looks like."

"It's different when it's a man. And what about you? Would you mind having an ugly scar running down your face? Polydeuces isn't the kind of man who'd give you any special consideration. If you go into his mining camp, he'll kill you the same as any man. That is, if he doesn't decide to take you captive and use you for other things."

Scapha got to her feet and prepared to leave the room. She was furious. "What makes you so sure I can't take care of myself?" She'd spent the last four seasons doing nothing but preparing herself for this fight. She could shoot a bow as well as any man.

"Scapha. I'm not trying to demean you. I'm only trying to get you to think a little. Taking the mines away from Polydeuces may sound easy, but it won't be."

"I know that." She walked to the door of the dining room. "Anyway, let's just forget all about it. I'll take you over to Philocleon's estate after the morning meal and you can get started on your pottery."

Egyptus had no choice but to follow her from the dining room though he'd have liked to stay. He could see he hadn't convinced her. She was pretending she wasn't angry, but he knew she was. Maybe he should have listened to her plan.

"I'll send a slave for you when I'm ready to leave," Scapha said, leaving him outside his door.

"Thank you." But what point was there in listening? Any plan she had to take the mines back would be too dangerous. Someone needed to make her understand that. I'll make it up to her, he decided as he crawled into bed exhausted from their argument. I'll teach her some pot-making tricks when we get to the kiln. It'll get her mind off the mines.

When they reached the kiln after the morning meal, he kept his promise to himself. The first thing he did when they finished examining the kiln was ask her if she wanted him to show her how to improve her pottery. When she agreed, he took a wad of clay from the pile in front of the kiln and showed her how he shaped the foot of a cup.

"Tell me about Philocleon," Scapha said, smoothing out her first cup with his help. "We've been promised to one another since we were children, but I really don't know much about him. I've seen him many times at festivals and parties, but I've never been allowed to talk privately with him."

"What do you want to know about him?"

"Has he become helpless?"

"You mean because he's blind?"

"Yes. There are plenty of unscrupulous men who will take a man's land from him if they are stronger than he is. Two seasons ago a man and his sons came from Athens and took our neighbor's estate from him just because he had no sons and was too feeble to defend his rights."

"I don't think you'll have to worry. When I left Philocleon, he had a long list of things he planned to learn how to do before he moved on."

"Good." She took another wad of clay and concentrated on making a cup until she heard a soft whistle come from behind the stable. She handed the cup to Egyptus. "I'll be right back."

Egyptus watched her race into the trees behind the kiln. Though she tried to keep him from seeing what she was doing by ducking behind an outbuilding, the man she was meeting was not fast enough and Egyptus saw him.

"Who was that?" he asked when she returned and sat down next to him.

She took her half-finished cup from him. "You remember I told you that one of the slaves had escaped the mines and come to me?"

"Yes."

"The man you saw was that slave."

"What did he want?"

"To talk to me."

"About what?" His voice sounded more demanding than he'd intended.

"Look. You said you wouldn't help me. Fine. You don't have to help. That doesn't mean I can't look for someone who will."

"I thought we settled it. You're not going to try to recapture the mines."

"You may have thought you settled it, but you're not my father or my husband, though you act like you think you're both. You have no right to tell me what to do."

"I wasn't trying to tell you what to do. I was just trying to make you see how foolish what you're planning is." He felt angry and hurt.

"See. There you go. Telling me what I'm planning is foolish

when you don't even know what I'm planning." She was as angry and hurt as he was.

Egyptus threw the pot he was making back onto the clay pile. She was right. He wasn't her husband or her father. And Philocleon hadn't asked him to look after her. Still, someone had to. Perhaps if he listened, he could dissuade her. "You're right. I shouldn't have decided your plan wouldn't work without even knowing what it is. Why don't you tell me what you have in mind right now?"

Scapha debated. What would be the point in telling him? He'd listen, then try to talk her out of it. "Why should I tell you? You'll be against it, no matter what it is."

"No, I won't," Egyptus lied.

She put down the cup she was working on. She'd try once more to persuade him to help her. "The escaped slave has a friend inside the mines. We call him Clidus. We were talking just now about how we could get a message to Clidus."

"Why do you need to get a message to Clidus?"

"He needs to know I plan to light a fire on Mountain Lion Ridge when my bowmen are going to attack the front gate."

"Why?"

"When Clidus sees the smoke from the fire, he'll know the attack is about to begin and he'll distract Polydeuces and his overseers from the front gate by starting a ruckus inside the camp with the other slaves."

"I don't see how it can work. Even if the slaves can distract Polydeuces and his overseers for a while, with no weapons..."

"Let me finish. As soon as the bowmen have attacked, the slaves will go to the back of the compound. I'll be waiting for them with a wagon load of swords and spears."

"How will you get the wagon into the compound? It must be surrounded by a tall fence."

"I won't. There's a rise in the hillside behind the compound. I'll drive the wagon up on it and throw a rope over the fence. Clidus will scale the fence with the rope. When he gets over the fence, I'll have a plank waiting for him in the wagon. He'll set the plank between the wagon and the fence and use it to carry up the weapons."

"How do you know there's a rise in the ground behind the compound?"

"I've been to the mines."

"You went to the mines?" Egyptus shook his head in disbelief. "What if Polydeuces' men had caught you up there? Do you have any idea what Polydeuces would do to you if he held you captive?"

Scapha shrugged. "I would dress as a slave and go into the mines with the message for Clidus myself, but Polydeuces would recognize me."

"What do you mean you'd go into the mines?"

"Polydeuces is constantly looking for slaves to replace those that are dying. That's how I'll get someone inside to give my message to Clidus. One of my neighbors will take him to the mines and sell him."

"And?"

"Once my man gets inside the camp, he'll have until Helios has ridden across the sky three times to find Clidus and tell him about the signal."

"How do you know you can trust Clidus?"

"Why wouldn't he help me? It's his only chance to get Polydeuces out of the mines."

"If something went wrong?"

"Nothing can go wrong. I've thought this through very carefully."

Egyptus looked at her. She no longer seemed as naive and amusing to him as she had yesterday. Her plan was risky, but it wasn't foolish. "I have to admit, you've thought it through, but I simply don't understand why you are so intent on recapturing the mines."

"I'm not intent on recapturing the mines. I'm forced to recapture them. When Hipponous died, he was deeply in debt. His creditors couldn't be paid because the slaves, afraid of the vengeance of his ancestors, fled. That left no one to do the farming. Philocleon and Nicias abandoned the animals when they left. Most of the creatures wandered off or were stolen, leaving nothing to sell.

"Hipponous' creditors are threatening to band together to take Philocleon's estate as payment. Normally it would be my uncle's duty to protect Philocleon's estate. You've seen him. If they grab Philocleon's estate and my uncle doesn't stop them, they'll take his estate as well.

"Once they take my uncle's estate, do you think my fate will be any different than if Polydeuces captures me? I can't fight all of

Hipponous' creditors. They are too many and too powerful, but I can recapture the mines and pay Hipponous' debts."

Egyptus sat and thought about what she'd said. From the first mention of her plan he'd thought she was acting naively and foolishly, when in fact he'd been acting that way. Teasing her. Ordering her around. Acting so superior because he'd seen a few more seasons pass. Not even guessing how desperate her situation was.

"I know what I'm asking is dangerous," Scapha continued. "I've asked you because I can't risk telling anyone from this district about my situation. If I did, my predicament would certainly become known to the wrong people. I know I can trust you because you're a friend of Philocleon."

Egyptus sighed. "Let me think about it."

Scapha stood and whistled for her horse. "When you've thought about it, come back to the estate and tell me what you've decided. I'll be waiting."

As soon as she was out of sight, Egyptus pulled his traveling sack from his cart and carried it to the hut where he had lived when he had worked for Hipponous. He had been in such a hurry to teach her pot-making tricks, he hadn't bothered to look inside the hut when they arrived.

He dropped the sack on the floor and sat down. Someone had been living in the hut. There was fresh fruit piled on the shelves and a wheat loaf and a jar of wine on the table. More than likely it was the escaped slave, he decided as he poured himself a cup of the wine.

He took his wine to the door and looked out. There was plenty of clay stacked up in front of the kiln and an ample supply of wood behind it. With some hard work, he could have his cart filled with pots and be on his way before the beautiful Selene waned into a crescent. Certainly that would be the sensible thing to do. Why was it then that the sensible thing to do seemed so wrong? With the arrival of Dawn I will begin my pot making, he finally decided. When I'm finished, I'll make my decision.

Much to his frustration, it wasn't until he put the last pot onto his wagon and covered it with straw that he finally made up his mind. He would help her. He still had all the sensible reasons for not getting involved in the plot to retake the mines, but sitting here working on his pots, he had been flooded with too many emotions to be sensible.

Whenever he had sat down to make pots, he would remember Nicias building the kiln, helping him find the clay, feeding wood into the stoke hole, teasing him about the number of snakes he could get on a pot, refusing to believe his stories. Then he would remember him coming from the house after Castor and Polydeuces had thrown dice for him, his shoulders slumped, his foot aching, embarrassed, hurt.

He had fired the kiln twice during his stay. Both times he'd worked himself into a rage remembering the day Polydeuces and Castor had ridden their cart through his pottery, destroying all his fresh-made pots then coming back to smash the fired ones. Philocleon had been good to him even if Hipponous hadn't. He had even had a special evening meal sent out and paid him for all his lost work.

His thoughts moved to Scapha. So few seasons passed, so intent. She had no idea what she was up against. He would never have been able to talk her out of going into the mines, even if he wanted to, which he didn't anymore. She was right. Her fate would be as bad if Daemones lost Philocleon's estate as it would if Polydeuces trapped her.

He took a deep breath as he got onto his cart and turned it toward Daemones' estate. In spite of his fear, he couldn't help but smile. Philocleon was getting himself quite a wife.

Turning his cart onto the path that led to the estate Egyptus let out a shrill whistle. He got his answer from somewhere deep in the trees. Just as he had expected, it wasn't long before the dogs came racing out of the trees, Scapha behind them.

As soon as he told her he would go into the mines, she went to work sending messages to the surrounding farmers, conferring with the escaped slave, getting the wagon loaded with spears and swords. By the time Helios had crossed the sky twice, Scapha had everything ready.

They ate one final evening meal together, going over all the plans. Afterwards, Egyptus went to his room. While Night ruled the sky, he petitioned, one after another, the gods of his Greek mother and Egyptian father. When Dawn appeared in the sky, he hadn't slept. Tired and shaking with fright, he put on the worn-out tunic Scapha had sent to his room.

He met Scapha at the barn. She instructed one of the slaves to rub enough dirt on him to make it appear he'd been hiding in the forest. Then she showed him how to make Clidus' name sign. Egyptus could see she was as nervous as he was.

Trying to smile bravely, Scapha poured a libation to Hermes. "Dearest Hermes, if ever I have sacrificed to you, remember me now. Give Egyptus the ability to trick Polydeuces, and I will sacrifice two of my finest white goats when it's over."

"It's time," a man Egyptus hadn't seen before said. "I'll bring the wagon around."

"He's my neighbor," Scapha explained, tying a rope around Egyptus' wrists. "He'll take you to the mines."

"Why do I have to be tied up here?" Egyptus had never had his wrists tied together before and he didn't like the way it felt.

"Polydeuces usually has at least one of his overseers out searching for cattle. If he should happen to see you without your hands tied and you turned up later at the camp with them bound, it would be dangerous for both you and my neighbor," Scapha explained.

Egyptus suddenly remembered all of his logical reasons for not doing what he was doing. "I'm to be in the mines until Helios has crossed the sky three times, starting now, and not one horse's whinny longer, right?"

"I'll be outside the camp at the beginning of Helios' fourth ride," she assured him. "Don't worry. Everything will go exactly as I promised." She followed the wagon to the end of the yard. "Be careful," she called. "Come back."

On a ridge above the mines Egyptus realized fully for the first time exactly what he had gotten himself into. From his perch he could see that the slaves were lined up across the compound. Many had open sores blistering on their backs. He watched an overseer bring a whip down on the back of a boy with a crushing blow. "Just so you won't be lazy today," the man said, sniggering as the boy fell and dragged himself to his feet again. Farther down the line another overseer kicked a miner.

Just as he turned to tell Scapha's neighbor he'd changed his mind, one of Polydeuces' overseers came riding up to them. "Move," he said pointing toward the camp, his sword drawn.

Polydeuces came to the gate when the overseer called in to report that he had prisoners. Ares' own war-thirsty eyes could not have looked more bloodthirsty, Egyptus thought.

"My man tells me you were spying," he snapped.

"No sir," Scapha's neighbor said quickly. "I came to sell this slave."

Polydeuces walked up to Egyptus and poked him in the groin with his spear. "Aheeeeee," Egyptus cried out in pain and fell writhing from the wagon to the ground. He considered begging the neighbor to tell Polydeuces he wasn't a slave after all. But he knew it was too late. He was trapped. All he could do now was hope everything went as Scapha had planned.

"Get up." Polydeuces put the tip of his spear on Egyptus' neck. Egyptus somehow managed to scramble to his feet. He tried hard not to show the hatred he felt. Sadly, he thought, I'll be dead before Helios has ridden across the sky three times. He wanted to run, but he knew he'd be killed before he'd gone two steps. Smashing the butt of his spear down on Egyptus' shoulder, Polydeuces ordered his overseer to take him inside the compound. Stumbling through the gate Egyptus did something he'd never done to another living man. Using carefully learned words from his mother, he called the death curse of the Erinyes on Polydeuces. "As you were conceived by the Mother from the drops of blood shed by Oceanus, when his own son, Cronus, cut off his testicles, so I call on you to suck the blood of Polydeuces, to drag him into Hades, to punish him for the blood he has shed," he whispered.

Inside the compound the overseer untied the rope. "Get over there." He shoved Egyptus toward a shaft that had been dug down into the mountain at the back of the camp. "You're working in this one." He handed Egyptus a pick.

Egyptus took the pick and went to the edge of the shaft. He looked down, but it was impossible to see the bottom. "What do I do?"

"You see that?" The overseer pointed to a pallet suspended over the shaft by a rope. "Your job is to go to the bottom of the shaft and fill it." He shoved Egyptus toward a rope ladder that had been loosely attached to the side of the shaft with wooden spikes.

Hesitantly, Egyptus made his way down the ladder, stepping onto the ground just before the pallet came crashing down into the pit. He ducked and covered his head. The pallet swung to a stop at the bottom, missing him.

When he uncovered his head and looked around, he saw there was another man in the shaft. It made him feel better. "My name is Egyptus," he said.

"Don't talk, work," came roaring down the shaft together with a rock that missed Egyptus' head, but gashed his shoulder open. He winced from the pain, but he didn't dare to cry aloud for fear of bringing another rock down, this time on his head.

He hadn't worked long before his shoulder began to ache so much that he thought he'd never move his arm again. I have to do something, he thought. He looked up. The overseer could hear from above, but he knew from his own attempt to see to the bottom that the man couldn't actually see what was going on down below. Using one weary arm to keep the rhythm going so there would be no suspicion above, he scratched Clidus' name sign on the wall under his partner's lamp.

The man looked at it and continued to work. Egyptus waited. When permission to crawl back up the ladder was called down to them, he scratched the name sign off the wall and followed his partner up the ladder.

Hungry and worried about the unwillingness of his partner to help him, Egyptus waited with the other men for something to eat. The porridge the cook was making smelled so foul it made him sick to his stomach. Someone finally motioned for him to get in line. Following the other men, he grabbed a bowl from a stack on the ground and dipped it into the big kettle the cook had placed in the middle of the compound. He sat down on the ground, held his breath, and drank the entire bowl of porridge at once. When he finished, he saw that the man next to him was staring at him. "It helps if you don't have to smell it," Egyptus whispered.

When they finished their porridge, the slaves stacked their bowls up again and went to the shelter where they all slept together so they could be watched. It was a thatch building with branches spread out on the floor for sleeping. More tired than he'd imagined possible, Egyptus dropped onto some branches and slept.

Before long he was awake again, his shoulder wrenching in pain, his stomach demanding food. He tried to sit up and he couldn't. It hurt his shoulder too much. As he lay wondering if he would die, Helios began his journey across the Zeus' sky.

Rolling carefully to his side and using his uninjured arm, he managed to get himself to his feet without damaging his shoulder any further. He followed the other men into the yard of the compound and grabbed a loaf of wheat loaf. It smelled as bad as the porridge had. He forced himself to eat it anyway. He would need as much strength as he could get to survive the work he would be expected to do.

"Line up," one of the overseers commanded before most of the men had eaten. Egyptus got into the line. He concentrated on staring at his toes while the overseers walked up and down the line. Though his shoulder ached unbearably, he didn't move. Behind him, he heard a whip snap. A man screamed.

"You looked like you might be feeling lazy today," one of the overseers sneered.

Egyptus heard Polydeuces. Keeping his head down, he watched with a guarded sideways glance while Polydeuces pranced out of his shelter. He was dressed in a white tunic and a panther fur mantle. The giggle of a woman followed him out of the shelter. He carried a wineskin and a big piece of cheese, eating and drinking and belching as he walked down the line. Egyptus silently repeated the curse his mother had taught him.

"Are you hungry?" Polydeuces asked one of the young slaves.

"No sir," the boy answered without looking up.

"Good." Polydeuces took the cheese he held in his hand and dropped it on the ground at the boy's feet. When the boy didn't move, he squashed the cheese into the ground with his sandal.

"Polydeuces," the woman in the shelter called. "Come on, I'm hungry."

Polydeuces waited for the roasted quail he was having for his morning meal to be carried past the line of men before he went laughing back to his shelter.

Egyptus was sent to the same pit he'd worked before. He struggled down the rope ladder, hanging desperately onto the rungs with his uninjured arm. His spirits remained low until he finally got to the bottom. He had a new partner. Quickly, he scratched Clidus' name sign on the wall of the pit.

His partner looked at the name and nodded.

As Helios continued across the sky Egyptus felt more and more uneasy. Scapha's bowmen were going to attack and there would be no distraction from inside the mines. This man wasn't going to help him find Clidus either. What if there wasn't any Clidus? What if Polydeuces had invented the whole thing? Sent the slave out to trap Scapha into an attack? What if his partners were spies?

No. They couldn't be spies. If he'd been reported by his partner, he'd have been punished. What was it then? He concentrated. After a long while, he figured out what must be wrong. What chance would there have been for Clidus to show any of the other slaves his name sign? It probably wasn't that his partners were unwilling to help him. More than likely, neither of them knew what he wanted. He picked up a large stone and held it above his head. Hoping the stone would prevent his voice from traveling to the top of the shaft, he said quickly to the man. "I need to find Clidus." He pointed to the name sign. "Clidus."

The man nodded. "Clidus," he whispered. Then he looked at the name on the wall and shrugged.

That's it, Egyptus thought. He doesn't recognize the name sign. He scratched it out feeling jubilant that he had finally gotten his partner to understand.

As the day wore on, his jubilant mood disappeared. His shoulder ached unbearably. By the time Helios had dropped below the big shade trees, he could barely lift the shovel. As he stood struggling to keep himself moving he saw that the man in the shaft with him had increased his work to keep the pace steady. He's covering for me, Egyptus thought. He wanted to cry. He wanted to sit down and sob his thankfulness, but even in his depressed and tired state, he realized they would both be beaten, he and the man who was helping him, if he made any noise. So he bit his lip until it bled, and kept himself moving until the work ended.

When they came to the surface and sat in their appointed places to wait for the evening porridge, Egyptus fell asleep sitting up. When he woke, he was standing in line, held by two of the slaves. "If they see you're down, you'll be thrown out of the compound, left to starve or be killed by some animal," a man whispered, handing him a bowl of porridge.

"I can't," Egyptus said. Even the smell made him sick. He turned his head away, but the man pushed the bowl to his lips.

"You must," was all the man said. He held the bowl until Egyptus drank everything in it. Afterwards, he helped the unsteady potter to his spot in the shelter.

Egyptus slept even less than he had during the last visit of Night. The pain was worse and he knew he had to move quickly. He had to find Clidus, but how? If he crawled around among the slaves asking, he'd certainly be killed.

By the time Dawn appeared, his muscles were so stiff, he had to be helped up by one of the other slaves. Two men got him into the compound yard. They grabbed a piece of bread for him. He ate it without arguing and got in line.

Everything was the same as it had been his first time in the line. One or two of the slaves were singled out for beatings while Polydeuces walked among them with his cheese and wine.

The smell of the cheese made Egyptus want to beg for food. He forced himself to keep quiet by swallowing. Not now, was all he could think. Somehow, concentrating on swallowing, he got through the inspection.

He was assigned to the same shaft. Crawling down the ladder, he became convinced he wouldn't come up from the shaft again. He clung to the ladder. I will fall, he thought and they will leave me at the bottom to die. His foot slipped near the bottom, but a hand reached out and steadied him.

"Quickly, when?"

Egyptus paused, then realizing what had been said, answered too loudly. "When Helios begins his next journey. The signal is smoke on Lion's Ridge."

He had barely gotten the words out when a voice thundered from above. "Get back to the surface." Egyptus looked up and saw the overseer. "You," the overseer yelled, though he couldn't see Egyptus. Petrified with fear, Egyptus started the climb back up the ladder.

As soon as he got to the top a whip lashed across his neck and shoulder. The force of the blow knocked him to the ground. As he lay there, he felt blow after blow until he could feel no more. In his mind, he drifted off to the Nile. There he saw his mother standing in the middle of the water beckoning to him. "I'm coming," he whispered deliriously to his mother.

At last the blows stopped. The overseer ordered him taken back to the shelter. "I should have killed you," he whispered. "If Polydeuces finds out I've let you live, we're both dead men."

Egyptus slept until Night descended. When he opened his eyes, he found a wheat loaf beside him. The overseer sat beside him. "Eat," he commanded. Egyptus did as he was told and went back to sleep.

When Dawn greeted the camp, Egyptus staggered, helped as he had been the morning before, into the compound. He refused to eat, but he took his place in the line, his wounds festering. He prepared to ask the Erinyes to curse himself as well as Polydeuces – for stupidity. Then he saw smoke on the ridge. He laughed hysterically and pointed. One of the overseers ran toward him. As the overseer reached for Egyptus, Clidus screamed out in faked pain and fell on the ground. Quickly the other men joined in. The overseers came from everywhere, their swords swinging at anything they could reach. In the midst of the confusion, Scapha's bowmen broke down the front gate.

"Cover the gate," Polydeuces yelled running from his shelter. As he raced toward the gate an arrow pieced his arm, causing him to drop his sword. Egyptus, too weak to run or fight, stood watching. He saw that the arrow had come from Scapha's bow. He gathered all of his strength and yelled at her. "Get out of here. Go to the back of the compound with the weapons or we'll all be killed." He somehow got to her wagon.

Scapha grabbed him and pulled him up next to her. "You rest," she said maneuvering the horses back through the gate. She raced the horses to the back of the compound and stopped them on the rise. Quickly, she threw the rope over the fence. "Clidus is coming," she assured Egyptus. "I can hear him on the fence."

A head appeared at the top of the fence. "He's not Clidus," Egyptus screamed frantically. "He's an overseer."

Scapha grabbed her bow and took aim. She hit the man in the face and he fell backwards.

"Quickly," she said to Egyptus. "Help me get the plank up to the fence."

Somehow finding the strength, he helped her. "What now?" he asked.

Without bothering to answer she skimmed up the plank to the top of the fence still holding her bow. The man she'd shot lay dead on the ground, but one of the other overseers was keeping the slaves away from the fence with his sword. Taking aim, she shot an arrow at the overseer and sent him crashing to his death.

A roar came up the rope with Clidus. She met him at the top of the fence with a load of weapons. He threw them to the ground. The slaves passed them around and the armed men went back into the compound. She brought another load and Clidus threw them. When the wagon was empty, Clidus left.

"It's done," she said to Egyptus, sitting down next to him pale and shaking. "You were right. Killing a man isn't the same as killing an animal, even when the man is someone who deserves to die."

Egyptus wanted to answer, but instead, he slumped to the floor of the wagon.

She washed his wounds with water and applied the herbs she had with her in the wagon before she drove back to the front gate.

The fighting continued until someone yelled that Polydeuces was dead. Hearing it, his overseers broke rank and ran, but they were outnumbered. Even the woman Polydeuces kept, who had hidden under the furs in the shelter, was dragged out and stabbed.

When the killing ended, the slaves and the bowmen poured through the gate. Scapha signaled to her farm slaves to come down from their hiding place in the mountain. They brought two white lambs. The slaves who weren't injured cared for the wounded, applying the herbs she carried in her wagon while the bowmen slaughtered the lambs. Scapha announced that those slaves who wished to do so were free to leave. Those who wanted to stay and work should see Clidus.

Leaving the slaves and bowmen to celebrate their victory, Scapha drove Egyptus back to the estate. She had her slaves carry him into the house and put him to bed.

When he woke, his wounds had been washed and cared for. "How long have I slept?" he asked.

"Helios has crossed the sky twice and Night has visited us once," the slave answered. "I'll tell the mistress you're awake now."

Scapha came to him. "How do you feel?"

"Foolish," he answered, some of his old self returning. "Only someone very foolish would have undertaken such a task."

"It's lucky for me that I found you," she teased in return. Then she became serious. "Philocleon and I will be indebted to you forever."

Egyptus smiled and slept again. When he woke the next time, the evening meal was ready. The slave who had been waiting for him to wake bathed him and led him to dining room where Scapha sat with Daemones and Alcmena.

Scapha offered him the couch next to hers. She poured him a cup of wine, then lifted hers. "To men who are afraid." Alcmena and Daemones lifted their cups too.

"To women who are brave." He lifted his cup to her and to Alcmena and Daemones.

"To men who are brave," she continued.

"And to women who know when to be afraid," he added.

Laughing, Scapha handed him a package.

Inside the package, he found a fine woolen mantle decorated with an intricate pattern he often put into his pottery.

He turned to Alcmena. "It's wonderful!"

"Scapha made it," Alcmena informed him.

"But you don't weave," he teased Scapha, watching her slowly blush.

"I didn't say I didn't know how to weave. I said I detested weaving. As we both know, there are some circumstances which merit doing even those things we detest." She'd actually made the mantle for Philocleon, but she knew she'd have time to make him another. "Wear it for your wedding. The woman who marries you will be fortunate."

Egyptus could feel he was blushing. "I will, but where will I ever find a wife as fine as the one I'm going to tell Philocleon about?"

Scapha laughed. His wounds were beginning to look better already. It wouldn't be long until he'd be leaving. They'd certainly miss him. Still, she couldn't be totally sorry. His leaving would bring Philocleon closer to home.

SEVENTEEN

"Where is my gold cup from Alcmena?" Philocleon asked, feeling around in the wooden box that held his treasury.

"Here." Bromia guided his hand to the corner of the box where she'd placed it.

Philocleon picked up the cup and traced its profile with his finger. Achilles had buried the ashes of Patroclus in a golden jar. He was returning the ashes of Homer to his family in the two-handled gold cup Alcmena had given to him.

"And here's our other hero," Bromia informed Philocleon trying to sound more cheerful than she felt.

"I came to see if you're ready," Egyptus said quietly, not wanting to disturb them. "We have to leave soon. Our ship sails when Helios drops below the trees."

Philocleon put the gold cup back in the treasury. "Where's Homer's saga of the Trojan war?"

"It's going with you," Nicias assured him. "I put it into one of Egyptus' wide-mouthed craters. He's holding it."

"Then everything's ready." Philocleon closed the lid on the treasury.

Egyptus motioned to the slave waiting at the door to take the treasury from the bed. "I'll wait for you at the cart. I've got a few more things to take care of before we leave."

"How long do you think it'll take to sail to Ios?" Philocleon asked Nicias.

"I don't know. We can ask Simo. If he doesn't know, you can ask the captain when you get on board. It isn't part of his normal route, but I'm sure he'll know."

The captain, a friend of Simo's, had agreed to collect Philocleon and Egyptus in the cove below the estate and drop them off on Ios during a cargo run between the coast and Cyprus.

"If I remember the geography Na'id-Assur taught me, I'd guess Helios will not cross the sky more than five times before we arrive," Philocleon decided. He sat down on the edge of the bed. "I've done more planning than sleeping in this bed. Trying to figure out how to get to Ios. Deciding what to do once I get there. It's almost impossible to believe I'm actually on my way to find Homer's family instead of dreaming about it."

Bromia sat down next to him and took his hand. "Before you know it, you'll be home again."

He put his arm around her and rested his cheek on her head. "I have to admit, I'm a little frightened. This will be my first trip without Nicias." He held her close. "Life away from you and Nicias. I can't imagine what it will be like."

"He'll miss you terribly and so will I. But remember, you'll have Scapha. She'll more than make up for us."

Philocleon kissed her on the forehead. "No one will ever make up for you and Nicias."

"Promise me again you won't forget to send us word when you arrive in Attica. We'll both feel much better when we know you're home safely."

Philocleon smiled in spite of the sorrow he felt. She'd reminded him so many times he'd lost count. "I won't forget. I'll let you know the moment I get to the estate." He squeezed her hand. "What about you, will you be all right?"

"She'll be fine," Nicias answered for her. He sat down on the other side of Philocleon and put his arm around both of them. "I've noticed whenever we are all together, Evadne always takes a place next to Bromia. Many times I've seen her smile at Bromia like they were sisters."

"We work together in the spinning room often now. We're becoming quite good friends," Bromia added.

Philocleon smiled. "Good. It makes it easier for me to leave if I don't have to worry about you."

"All you need to worry about is getting back to Scapha," Nicias assured him. "I promise you I'll take care of Bromia."

Philocleon blushed. "I know you will." Deciding to break a

solemn promise he'd made to himself the day they went out to the estate to find Bromia, he told Bromia how Nicias had driven back and forth in front of the estate.

"You never told me about that," Bromia teased Nicias.

Nicias cuffed Philocleon playfully on the shoulder. "You shouldn't have either."

"We have to leave," Egyptus said quietly from the door.

"We'll be right there," Nicias answered. Gently, he helped Philocleon to his feet. "I guess this is it."

Fighting back tears, Philocleon threw his arms around Nicias. "I'll miss you."

"I'll miss you, too." Nicias hugged Philocleon hard. "I feel like I'm losing my son." Tears rolled down both his cheeks. "You won't forget to be careful."

"I won't. And, don't forget, I'll have Egyptus with me."

"I'm thankful for that," Nicias said, kissing Philocleon on both cheeks. He wiped the tears from Philocleon's face. "I know he'll take good care of you."

"We'd better go," Bromia said, taking Philocleon's arm.

Nicias hesitated for a moment, going over in his mind whether he'd forgotten anything he wanted to say. They'd talked so much since Philocleon decided to leave, he couldn't think of anything else to say. Taking Philocleon's other arm, he started for the door, "Come on. Let's get this sailor off to sea."

Simo, Evadne, Themis and Clymene were waiting for them in the courtyard. Themis and Clymene ran to Philocleon as soon as they saw him. He took Themis in one arm and Clymene in the other and hugged them. "And now it's time to say goodbye to the two most beautiful girls in Greece." He had a picture of each of them in his mind, made up from the sound of their voices and the things they'd told him about themselves and each other. He was convinced they were both beautiful.

"Don't get caught by any slave traders," Clymene warned him seriously.

"Clymene," Themis said, looking to her parents for help. "What a thing to say."

"It could happen," Philocleon joked. Still holding Clymene, he pinched her cheek. "But don't you worry, I'll be careful."

When Themis hugged him, he kissed her cheek, sensing she was blushing.

He hugged Simo and then Evadne. "Promise me you'll come to Attica one day and bring Nicias and Bromia with you. I have so much hospitality to repay."

"We promise," Evadne assured him.

"And, we'll bring the answer to the Gilgamesh riddle when we do," Simo added.

"That was a wonderful farewell banquet you gave for me," Philocleon continued, trying unconsciously to find ways to delay his departure. They'd eaten more specialties than he could name and drunk the best wine from the estate. Then they'd danced around the pool in a circle holding hands until Dawn had visited the courtyard. "I'll never forget it."

"The cart's ready," Egyptus said, stepping up to the door.

Philocleon waited until they'd all said their goodbyes to Egyptus, then he kissed and hugged each one of them again before he let Nicias take him to the cart.

"Don't forget to tell Trygaeus about the captain. And don't forget to send word when you get home." Nicias hugged him one last time. He put his cup from Ti into Philocleon's hand. "I want you to have this for your wedding."

Philocleon started to object, but before he could say anything the cart was rolling away from the estate.

"They're all waving at you," Egyptus told him.

Philocleon waved in return as he wiped tears from his cheeks.

Partly because he was excited, but mostly to keep Philocleon from feeling too sad, Egyptus started to chatter. "Neither man nor beast will be hungry for a long time from the look of things. Both will be as well fed as a man I once saw in Egypt. He could balance six wine cups on his belly when he was sitting upright – not that he sat upright very often." He chuckled.

Philocleon chuckled too just as the wagon suddenly lurched. His fingers tightened around the seat. "What was that?"

"I think the fat man just hiccuped and sent the six wine glasses rolling," Egyptus answered.

Together, they laughed. The wagon rambled on and so did Egyptus. It would be fun traveling with Egyptus, Philocleon decided. "I want you to know how much I appreciate your agreeing to take me to Ios," he said when Egyptus finally paused.

"It's not really much out of my way." He had been offered workspace and the use of a kiln in exchange for a fourth of the pots he made by a potter from Rhodes he had met in Sparta on his return trip to the estate.

"But it'll slow you up," Philocleon continued. He had offered to pay Egyptus' passage to Rhodes, but Egyptus had refused. Philocleon had already given him a fine silver fibula and dagger for what he had done in Attica. He thought that was enough.

As the path leveled out, Egyptus stood and watched for the shoreline. When it came into view, he waved his wide-brimmed hat and yelled, "Hey down there."

"What is it?" Philocleon asked.

"I can see the ship. She's a beauty." The long sleek ship, already rolled into the water, rocked gently three stadia below. The captain's sailors, waiting for them, were squatted in groups of three and four along the shoreline throwing dice. Egyptus described the ship to Philocleon and added, "If we're lucky with dice, we might even come off the ship with some extra bronze pieces in our possession. Now, what would you say to that?"

"I'd say I'd like it."

"Bring the cart on board," one of the sailors yelled when they came into sight.

Two sailors held the gangplank. Egyptus jumped from the cart and taking one of the donkeys by the bridle, led the pair up the rough, unsteady board, onto the ship.

"Over there." The sailor pointed to a wooden railing. "Tie the donkeys down good and the cart too."

Egyptus led the donkeys to the railing. While he carefully lashed both cart and donkeys, the captain ordered the sailors on the shore to break up their dice game and come on board.

As the last man had stepped onto the deck, the two men steadying the gangplank grabbed the uneven board and shoved it onto the ship. They threw the stern cables onto the ship and jumped on board themselves.

The captain, already aft, called for the mast and the sail. Keeping himself and Philocleon out of the way, Egyptus described to Philocleon how the crew pushed the fir mast up, some securing the bottom amidships in a box while others ran ropes from the top of the mast to the bowsprit and then hoisted the sail upward, fastening it when it reached the top.

The oarsmen rowed the ship away from the shore. When the sail caught the wind, it billowed out and pulled the ship forward, cutting a deep wave in the sea as it went. Philocleon's heart beat with excitement when he felt the change as the ship rounded the edge of the cove and sailed onto the high seas. This was how he imagined it would feel.

As excited as Philocleon, Egyptus grabbed his friend's arm and took him aft as soon as the captain indicated they could leave the cart. "The captain's pouring a libation to Poseidon," he told Philocleon. They sat down next to him and listened gaily to the sailors. When the ship fell on course and the sailors weren't needed anymore, one of them took a pair of dice out of his pocket. "You game to lose some bronze pieces?" he asked Egyptus and Philocleon.

Both men got into the circle of players and stayed there until well after Night had descended. When the sailors finally went to their bunks and Egyptus led Philocleon to the cart, they'd played more games of dice than any of them cared to count.

"I've never seen anyone with as much luck as you," Egyptus complained jokingly to Philocleon when they reached the cart, "except maybe for Hermes."

Philocleon shook his leather bag and smiled. "Whenever I went with Nicias to the Sounion port village, I'd dream of sitting on the deck of a ship throwing dice with the ship's crew."

Egyptus made up their beds in the back of the cart using the fleeces Evadne had sent with them. He helped Philocleon, then climbed up himself. Exhausted, both men fell asleep.

The ship, bathed in Selene's full glow, sailed smoothly toward the islands until without warning, a howling gale came swooping in from the north, buffeting the ship one way and another. While the sailors fought in vain to steady their course, Egyptus jumped up and held tight to his donkeys to calm them. He threw a rope to Philocleon. "Tie yourself to the wagon."

"What about you?" Philocleon sat up.

Egyptus loosened the rope securing the donkeys. "I'll take the other end of the donkeys' rope."

Rain fell, blotting out the land and all sense of direction as the winds spun the ship around in the waves. A gust caught the sail and ripped it apart as the sailors were lowering it. The mast snapped almost in half, falling so that it hung like a broken tree limb swinging to and fro over the heads of the oarsmen. The oarsmen rowed frantically to keep the boat from capsizing.

Philocleon clutched the cart tightly, ducking his head between his arms to protect it from falling wood, his heart racing, partly from fear, partly from the thrill. The ship tipped leeward and a huge wave smashed across it. He lost his grip. The knot he'd made gave way. "I'm going overboard," he screamed, grabbing for the rope.

Egyptus abandoned his donkeys, caught Philocleon by the tunic and pulled him back to the cart. "Hang on," he yelled pushing the loose end of the rope into Philocleon's hand. Fighting to keep himself from going overboard, he secured Philocleon to the cart.

He turned to his donkeys. "No," he cried as both donkeys washed overboard.

"What is it?" Philocleon asked.

"I lost the donkeys."

Back and forth across the water the boat careened, tipping one way, then the other, until everything not completely secured was tossed into the sea. The captain gave up trying to call commands and secured himself to the broken mast. The sea raged on while the oarsmen and the captain alike pleaded with Poseidon.

When the wind finally abated and the rain slowed to a drizzle, the number of men on board had halved. Some of the captain's best men were gone, washed overboard to the bottom of the raging sea. The men still on board searched the ship in the foggy darkness for oars and anything else they might use to row.

They floated on whatever course the waves took them until the dark rain clouds finally lifted and the heavy drizzle ceased. When they finally saw the glow of Selene's fullness again, no one knew how many times Helios had ridden across the sky or where they were. All the captain could do was watch for land with his crew.

Hope had nearly ceased when one of the sailors aft broke into a triumphant yell, "Land ahead."

Egyptus rushed Philocleon to the prow of the ship along with the rest of the crew. "It's Crete," the captain announced. He'd sailed the coast of Crete many times before. He divided the oars that were left among the crew, gave one to Egyptus and took one himself. Heaving and pushing, cursing and groaning, they pushed forward until the ship grounded.

"You two," the captain ordered, pointing to his two strongest oarsmen, "follow the land and see if you can find help." He ordered the remainder of the crew to busy themselves uprighting the cargo while he examined the ship to determine how much damage had been done.

The two oarsmen the captain sent to look for help still hadn't returned by the time Night swooped down upon them. Drenched and exhausted, Egyptus and Philocleon lay down on the deck with the rest of the crew and waited. Under the light of Selene the two oarsmen returned with help from a nearby village.

Once the villagers had gotten all the men and the cargo from the ship to land, Egyptus borrowed a donkey from a villager. As he harnessed the donkey and prepared his cart for the trip into the village, the captain briefed the crew. He'd had time to examine the damage to the ship, he told them, and they could expect to be in port long enough to see Selene wane to a crescent ten times before the ship could be repaired.

EIGHTEEN

It was almost time for the evening meal, and as Egyptus had hoped, most of the inn regulars were gathering in the courtyard to talk a bit before they ate. "They're potters all right," he said happily to Philocleon after examining their hands. He had chosen this inn at the center of the potters' quarter hoping to meet someone who would rent him some space and the use of a kiln while they were on Crete. With some of Hermes' luck and a little persuasion, he would own a pair of donkeys again by the time the captain got the ship repaired.

Pausing for a moment to decide which of the men in front of him looked approachable, Egyptus suddenly realized Philocleon was no longer holding onto his arm. He turned. "Philocleon?"

"I'm afraid the brazen young woman who stole your friend is my daughter," a short, balding man with broad shoulders informed him.

Looking in the direction the man pointed, Egyptus spotted Philocleon across the courtyard. He was standing with a young woman who didn't resemble the man who claimed to be her father at all except that she was short. She had turbulent red hair that looked as if it had never seen a comb, while what was left of her father's coarse dark brown hair was neatly pulled into a braid at the back of his head. His skin was dark. Hers was fair and covered with an array of fascinating freckles. His eyes were brown. Hers could only be described as a sparkling, mischievous green.

"She takes after her mother," the man said having guessed at the reason for Egyptus' surprised look. "Her mother wasn't Greek, as you might have already guessed. Are you new or have I just not seen you before?"

"We were on the damaged ship that's anchored up the coast."

"I heard about the storm. According to the gossip in the marketplace, the captain saw half his crew sent to the bottom of the sea."

"Together with the sail, most of the mast and my two faithful donkeys." Egyptus felt guilty he was so concerned about his donkeys when so many men had drowned, but he'd had those donkeys since they were born.

"I know how treacherous Poseidon can be. I lost my wife in one of his storms."

"I'm sorry. Here I was worrying about my donkeys."

"Don't apologize. It happened long ago when my daughter was still as small as a kitten. How long until your ship is repaired?"

"According to the captain, quite a while."

"Then I'd imagine we'll be seeing a lot of one another. My name's Sosias."

"Everyone calls me Egyptus."

"If I'm not mistaken, you're a potter."

"I am."

"If you're looking for a spot in the market, I have some extra space. And you can use my kiln if you like." Sosias paused, grinning at Egyptus' surprised look. "I'm not so generous as you might think. I saw some of the pots you carried into the inn this afternoon. They interest me."

As Egyptus prepared to thank Sosias, they were interrupted by his daughter. She threw her arms around her father's neck and kissed him on both cheeks. "We're going over to Meton's." She smiled at Egyptus. "My name is Delphium." She hugged Sosias again. "And this is Philocleon."

"That's my daughter," Sosias informed Egyptus with unabashed pride as they watched Delphium and Philocleon disappear around the side of the inn. "You may as well eat with me. My guess is you'll go hungry if you wait for your friend."

"Who is Meton?"

"A poet," Sosias answered and led the way from the courtyard into a tavern.

"If you're hungry, we can eat when we get to Meton's," Delphium informed Philocleon as she led him around the outer edge of the marketplace to a small enclave of houses built into the hillside behind the main portico. She couldn't wait to introduce him at the house. It must have been decreed by the Fates, she decided. A blind man steps on her foot. He stops to apologize and they start talking. Who could have guessed he would turn out to be a man who had known one of the poets they had heard about. At the far end of a row of houses, she finally stopped. "Meton, are you home?"

"Come in if you have wine," a deep voice said from inside.

"Something even better." She pulled the rug aside that hung in the doorway. "This is Philocleon," she said to the three men seated on the floor. She turned Philocleon toward them. "These are the men I was telling you about. This is Meton."

Meton wiped his sweating hands and his broad, flaccid face on his dirty tunic before he stood and clasped Philocleon's wrist. "We've been arguing," he explained to Delphium, feeling compelled in spite of Philocleon's blindness to make at least a half-hearted attempt to smooth the mass of straw brown tangles that covered his head. He always ran his hands wildly through his hair when he argued. His beard hadn't fared much better. It twisted like an uncut straw field from his face to the middle of his chest. He hadn't had a bath in days and he smelled. His slovenly appearance was as always, revolting. But as Delphium had said many times, who could resist him in spite of it all, as long as he had those incredibly seductive burnt-almond eyes?

"And here's Xanthias."

"We haven't been arguing," Xanthias insisted, clasping Philocleon's wrist. "As usual, Meton has been arguing and Cario and I have been listening."

Philocleon tried to guess what Xanthias was like. Meton's plump hand, hot and enthusiastic, had drawn a firm picture in his mind, but Xanthias' hand was more difficult to decipher. It was firm, but it definitely lacked the exuberance of Meton's. He guessed Xanthias was tall and thin and somewhat reserved. And meticulous in his dress and personal habits Delphium told him later when he asked her. And, she added, though he wasn't handsome, what he lacked in looks he made up for in neatness and careful dress.

"And I'm Cario," the third man in the room said. He too stood and clasped Philocleon's wrist. Cario possessed naturally all of the handsome features Xanthias coveted and Meton insisted on ignoring. He had a sculpturesque face with an ideally proportioned nose, high cheekbones, and wide deep-violet eyes.

"You wouldn't know it," Delphium informed Philocleon, helping him sit on one of the torn rugs thrown on the floor. "But they really are devoted friends. Where's Iris?" she asked Meton.

"She went for wine."

"She went and came back," Iris said from the doorway. She came through the door balancing a jug of wine on her left shoulder.

As Philocleon was soon to find out, Meton, Xanthias, and Cario argued constantly about Iris. Meton insisted her long and slender legs, sumptuous hips and breasts were her best quality. Xanthias preferred her face which he described as a perfect oval encased in a bed of soft, tawny curls, ornamented with deep pink sensuous lips and startling hazel eyes. While Cario claimed to be the one who most loved her alert mind and quick wit, he was the first to admit he hadn't missed any of her other qualities.

Iris sat next to Philocleon. "We're all poets."

Before Philocleon had a chance even to say, "Hello," Cario dropped to one knee in front of Iris and recited a short poem he'd been practicing.

"It's much better than it was, don't you think?" Iris asked the others.

"It still needs work, but I feel I'm closer to 'perfection' now than I've ever been," Cario answered for the group, lightly running his finger over Iris' breast as he said, 'perfection'.

They all laughed.

"What happened?" Philocleon asked.

"Nothing," Iris answered. "Cario is being silly."

"What about you Xanthias?" Meton asked. "What do you have for us?"

By the time Xanthias finished his poem, Delphium was fairly bursting to spring the surprise she had brought them in the person of Philocleon. "Tell them about Homer," she said excitedly to him.

Pleased to find people who were almost as interested in Homer as he was, Philocleon told them about the poet being thrown off the ship in the Sounion harbor, how he'd recited in the tavern and had finally come home. He ended his story by telling them about Homer's saga of the Trojan war, leaving out the details of his death.

"Where is he now?" Iris asked.

"He died in a spear fight," Philocleon answered.

"We know some verses from that saga," Cario said, scratching his head as he always did when he was trying to remember.

"Oh – oh. Beware," Xanthias said. "Cario's thinking. Look at his hands."

"Meton, you remember, don't you? The old poet who'd come from Ionia for the festival in Cnossos recited from that saga. How did it go? 'Sing goddess, the anger of Peleus' son'..."

"I remember lots of wine and beautiful women and handsome men." Meton raised and lowered his eyebrows at the group.

Ignoring Meton, Cario moved over and sat next to Philocleon. "Recite something for us."

Philocleon began reciting the scene of Patroclus' death which was the only part of the saga he could remember completely, but his voice trembled so badly when he came to Hector's death threats to Patroclus, he couldn't finish. "I'm sorry," he said.

"Don't be sorry," Cario said, putting his hand on Philocleon's shoulder. "Poetry is like that." He thought it was the poetry that had upset Philocleon.

Philocleon took a deep breath and calmed himself. "Anyway, it doesn't matter that I can't finish because I have the entire saga recorded on leather."

"You have what?" Meton asked. He'd never heard of anyone recording poetry.

Philocleon told them the story of the festival his father had given. How he'd convinced Homer to let Na'id-Assur and Qurdi Marduk record the saga.

All five of the poets spoke at once. As usual, Meton's voice surfaced above the others. "What are we waiting for? Let's go get the saga."

Cario jumped up and pulled Delphium to her feet. He kissed her long and passionately on the lips. "What a surprise you've brought us." Smiling at the passionate response he'd gotten, he pulled Iris to her feet and kissed her just as passionately.

Iris in turn pulled Philocleon up and kissed him passionately. "Take us to your room."

Trying not to show how much Iris had shocked him or how much her throbbing warm breasts had excited him, Philocleon took her arm. Outside the house they all linked arms and walked back to Philocleon's inn, taking turns reciting lines from a poem they had just learned.

Xanthias anxiously helped Philocleon find the crater holding the saga once they got to his room.

"Give it to Meton," Delphium said when Philocleon pulled the poem from the crater.

"He's the only one who can read," Xanthias explained.

Meton danced wildly around Philocleon's room, holding the poem at arm's length above his head as soon as he'd seen it. "Make sacrifice, my fair poets. The gods have favored us. When we get back to my house, we will celebrate the greatest festival of our lives."

Cario and Delphium broke into a song of praise everyone sang at the harvest festival. They put Philocleon between them and led the others out of Philocleon's room, down the corridor, out the door and into the street dancing the harvest dance.

Once they reached the street, Iris insisted they needed a procession to properly carry the saga back to Meton's house. They formed a line, Meton first, carrying the poem above his head, followed by Cario, Iris, Philocleon, Xanthias, and finally, Delphium.

As soon as they'd walked through the door of Meton's house, their solemn procession broke into a wild celebration. Xanthias poured a libation to Apollo and filled the wine cups. They emptied their cups toasting Homer. Afterwards, Meton took his place at the center of their circle with ribaldrous pomp. Invoking the muses, he began the poetry festival he'd promised.

When Egyptus learned Philocleon hadn't returned by the morning meal, he asked Sosias where he might be. "It's not that I'm thinking to stop him," he explained. "It's just that I feel somewhat responsible."

Sosias assured him he didn't have to worry. "I heard him come into the inn with Delphium and her poet friends. They took something from his room and left again. No doubt they're still at Meton's. When they're working on poetry, they sometimes disappear for as long as it takes the olives to ripen."

As they walked through the marketplace, Sosias introduced Egyptus to the other craftsmen, announced the potter had been on the ship anchored down the coast and waited patiently while everyone asked questions about the storm.

"Now you know everyone," he told Egyptus when they reached his stall. "No one will question your being at my stall. We watch out for each other." He showed Egyptus where to put his sack full of pots. "You've been working in Athens?" he asked, pulling one of the pots from the bag.

"A couple of times during the rains," Egyptus answered. "How do you know this is Attic pottery?"

"A man from Athens came through. He had the same kind of pottery."

Egyptus looked down the row of pottery stalls. There wasn't any Attic work. "If you want, I'll teach you how to make the Attic style."

Sosias winked. "You didn't think I invited you to work at my stall because I liked you?"

Egyptus laughed. It was obvious to him Sosias did indeed like him. "I really couldn't imagine any other reason."

As the two men finished unloading Egyptus' sack and exchanging information about pottery, one of the leather workers hurried past Sosias' stall. "Here she comes."

Egyptus looked up. Most of the men around them had left their stalls and were rushing toward the back of the marketplace.

"It's Myrrhine," one of the men told Sosias as he walked past him. Sosias looked up, but made no motion to follow the other men.

Egyptus wandered over and stood at the edge of the crowd. They were watching a woman walk down the hill behind the marketplace, followed by two slaves. She was dressed in a pale blue linen peplos embroidered with a white dove.

"Come on over here and I'll crush that dove for you," one of the men at the front of the crowd yelled when she got to the bottom of the hill.

"That's the Athenian, Theopropides," a man standing next to Egyptus explained.

The woman said nothing to defend herself against the rude remark of Theopropides, but neither did she lower her eyes as she passed him. Without so much as pausing she walked past the crowd of men, her dark eyes raw with anger and hatred.

"Pandora," Theopropides hissed.

"Hey Theopropides," someone goaded from the back of the crowd. "Your Athenian stick too short for a good Cretan woman?" He held his hand under his tunic and thrust his body back and forth. "Maybe you need help."

"We know a good bull you can borrow a prick from," two men

added with a sneer.

Theopropides whirled around and smashed his way through the crowd toward the two men. Both of them turned and ran before he could catch them. "We'll see who's in need of a prick when I catch you," Theopropides yelled after the two men. "You prickless Cretans."

No one else in the crowd dared say anything, but it was clear to Egyptus as he returned to Sosias' stall they all felt the same as the two men who had run away.

"One time he'll catch one of them and there will be plenty of blood spilled," Sosias said, still not looking up.

Egyptus was curious. "Doesn't the woman's husband mind having all these men gather to watch his wife? Yell at her? You'd think he'd keep her at home."

"Her husband's been dead for many seasons," Sosias replied.

"How did it happen?"

"He was a sea merchant. One day his ship sank with him standing on the deck." He paused and looked in the direction Myrrhine had just passed. "He left a fleet of ships and plenty of merchandise. Theopropides has a mind to get his hands on those ships."

"She's a beautiful woman," Egyptus observed. "Surely her brother could find someone suitable if she's set against marrying the Athenian."

"She has no family. No father or brothers to give their permission. Her guardian is an uncle who seems willing to leave it up to her as long as she supplies him with plenty of wine. So far she hasn't shown any interest in marrying any man."

"Every woman wants to be married. It's the natural order of things." He still remembered the anxiety in his father's house until his sisters were promised to suitable men.

"Maybe you should tell her that." Sosias grinned. "Besides I hear she didn't care much for marriage."

"Do you know her?"

"Not me. But my Delphium knows her. They worship the Mother Goddess together."

"Are you saying there's some connection between worshipping the Mother Goddess and not wanting to get married?"

"You don't know anything about the Mother worshippers, do you?"

"Not really."

"They believe in communal living of men and women, as it was when the Mother Goddess ruled the earth. They see no need for marriage. Many of them, like Myrrhine, see no need for men, except when they want to have children."

"Does Delphium feel that way?" Egyptus was shocked. He'd never heard a man talk so casually before about women not needing or wanting men.

"Delphium believes in communal living, but not in separating herself from men." Sosias returned to his work. "But then, her peplos doesn't hide the kind of scars Myrrhine's does."

Egyptus had more questions, but he could see Sosias was anxious to end their discussion of Myrrhine, so he returned to their examination of pottery and talked no more of her, though he made a mental note to ask Philocleon about her the next time he saw him.

It wasn't long before he got his chance. Walking past the portico, he spotted Philocleon in one of the taverns. "What are you doing out alone?" he joked, sitting down. "I haven't seen you without Delphium since we got here."

"I'm waiting for Delphium and Iris," Philocleon answered and called for the young serving boy to bring a bowl of wine for Egyptus. "They went with Myrrhine to one of the caves sacred to the Mother Goddess."

"What do they do in the caves?" Egyptus sipped his wine.

"They learn how to perform the rituals of the Mother Goddess from the sibyls who hide in the mountains."

"Why do the sibyls hide?"

"There are many men who don't want the Mother Goddess worshiped anymore. They demand that all people worship Zeus and the Olympians."

"Is that what you do at Meton's every night? Learn the rituals of the Mother Goddess?" Egyptus was curious again.

"Sometimes, but most of our time is spent reciting and learning poetry." Philocleon leaned forward. "I took Homer's saga of the Trojan war to Meton's house. Everyone has learned it. We go regularly to the portico and recite. We make quite a spectacle, the six of us. Now Delphium got the idea we should write a saga of our own."

"What's your saga about?" Egyptus leaned back and put his hands behind his head. He enjoyed hearing about the things that went on at Meton's house though he had no interest in being a part of them. He much preferred making pottery to listening to poetry.

"It isn't really our saga. We've taken some stories they already knew and added to them. It's about the return of Odysseus to Ithaca after the Trojan war."

"Odysseus?"

"He was one of the heroes from the Trojan war. Delphium and Iris want to add legends from the days of the Mother Goddess to the saga of Odysseus. That's the reason they go with Myrrhine to the caves."

"Are you writing poetry too?" Egyptus asked.

"No. I'm not a poet, but they say I'm a great storyteller. I told them about my visit to the ancient tomb and the next thing I knew, they had Odysseus calling up shades from Hades' Underworld in their saga."

Egyptus smiled and shook his head. "You're quite the group." He then ordered some figs.

Philocleon took a handful of figs. "And I told them the saga of Gilgamesh. They're helping me solve the riddle of immortality when they aren't arguing about the saga. Meton thinks it's impossible to change things in life. Delphium believes passionately he's wrong. You can change things if you really want to."

"What do you think?"

"I agree with Delphium. The more I think about my father and his extravagant living..." He paused, thinking for a moment about his father's banquets. "We also talk a lot about Scapha."

"You do?" Egyptus was now entirely curious. When he'd come back to Argos with the story of Scapha's heroic capture of the silver mines, Philocleon had listened quietly, but instead of being overjoyed as Egyptus had expected, he'd said nothing. "What do you say about Scapha?" he asked casually.

"Mostly we argue. It's the only thing the five of them aren't divided over. It's all of them against me. They say I'm wrong not to accept Scapha the way she is."

"Don't you?"

"In my mind, I've always had this idea that Scapha would be like my mother and Bromia. Quiet and reserved. Keeping to herself in the women's quarters. Coming to me when I called. Having our children. Maybe even willing to sacrifice her own life if she had to for an only son. Scapha doesn't sound like that at all."

Egyptus shook his head and grinned. "Scapha is nothing at all like that, but she's the most wonderful woman I've ever met."

"Who's the most wonderful woman you've ever met? My Delphium?" Sosias sat down with them.

"She's certainly wonderful," Egyptus said enthusiastically, a little because he knew how much Sosias thought of her, but for the most part because he believed it. "But right now we were talking about Scapha, the woman Philocleon's going to marry. He thinks she won't act enough like a wife."

"Do you mind about Delphium?" Philocleon asked Sosias. "I mean about her being so, well, so independent."

"Mind?" Sosias smiled. "Why should I? I raised her to be independent. Look, my wife died because I wasn't strong enough to hold onto both her and Delphium when we were in a shipwreck and she was too afraid to hang on for herself. Do you have any idea what it feels like to lose someone you love for such a stupid reason? I didn't want that for Delphium. I wanted her to learn to look after herself – not that I wouldn't be there to help her if she needed me and I could do it – but just in case I couldn't help. And to tell you the truth, I like it better now that she can. Occasionally when her old dad needs some help or encouragement, she's there for me too. Besides, she's more interesting and fun than most of the women I see – even if she doesn't always do what I think she should."

Egyptus smiled and waved as Delphium walked toward them. "Your father has been telling us all about you."

"You're bragging about me again," Delphium teased, kissing his blushing forehead.

"Only a little," Sosias smiled proudly.

She took Philocleon's arm and helped him to his feet. "Do you mind if I leave you with Egyptus?" she asked Sosias. "Iris and I have just returned from the cave of the Mother Goddess and we have so many things to tell the others."

"Mind?" Sosias asked and kissed her. "As I've told you often enough, potters are much better company than poets." Winking at Egyptus, he drank what was left of Philocleon's wine while Delphium led Philocleon off to Meton's.

Egyptus ordered two bowls of wine and more figs. Sosias took one of the bowls of wine and a fig before he turned to what was on his mind. "I've been thinking, Egyptus. We really don't need two of us at the marketplace stall. What if we were to load the cart with pots and have you take them into the villages to sell? I think we could double our trade without much trouble."

Feeling the sense of excitement he'd always known before a long selling trip, Egyptus drank down his wine. "There's nothing I'd like more now that I have donkeys again."

They spent the remainder of the Night's darkness making plans. As soon as they had finished the morning meal, they went to the kiln and loaded Egyptus' cart with pottery. By the time Helios was beginning his journey over the mountains, Egyptus was on his way to the nearest village.

When Helios had ridden across the sky fourteen times, Egyptus was on the same path coming back to the village. He'd already sold all the pots. Thinking about where he would go on his next trip, he came upon the woman from the marketplace walking along the road to the village. She wore the same pale blue peplos with the dove embroidered on it. Why would she be out walking by herself, Egyptus wondered. He hurried his donkeys so that he could catch up to her. "Do you want a ride?" he asked.

"No." Myrrhine continued walking.

Egyptus kept pace with her. "You won't come to any harm from me," he said. "And you look awfully tired."

"Aren't you the potter who works with Sosias?"

"Yes."

She had been walking a long time and he was right, she was exhausted. She knew Sosias. And she'd heard many good things about this potter from Delphium.

"You'll come to no harm," Egyptus repeated.

"I am tired."

Egyptus stopped the cart and she got on next to him.

After a long silence during which Egyptus' curiosity continued to grow, he nodded toward some pottery fragments she held in her hand, hoping to get her to talk. "Where did you get them?"

She started to answer him, but changed her mind. Even if he was a friend of Sosias, he could be one of those who wanted the Mother Goddess worship totally stopped.

"Do you mind if I see them? It's always interesting for a potter to see someone else's pottery."

She handed him the fragments. They made up the bottom half of a doll. One of the detachable legs was missing. He looked the doll over carefully. "What's it for?"

She shrugged, took the fragments back and put them into her girdle. If he knew about the Mother Goddess, he'd know what they were.

"Did you make the doll?" He was determined to get her to talk to him.

"No. I found the fragments in a cave. The doll was probably made before I was born."

"Where's the cave?"

"In a mountain."

"Which mountain?"

"The mountain where the Mother Goddess hid Zeus from his father, Cronus."

"I guess I'm not sure what you're talking about."

"Do you know about the hiding of Zeus?"

"Not really. My mother was Greek and she taught me about the Erinyes, but mostly I worship my father's Egyptian gods."

"Are you interested in knowing about the Mother Goddess?" She'd just come from celebrating one of the important rituals of the Mother. If she could make him understand...

"Yes."

"Before the world existed, our Mother came into being," she began, repeating the words of the ritual. "She was all that was. She divided the sea from the sky and danced upon the waves. Her swift dancing caused a wind to gather behind Her. When she rubbed the wind between her hands, it became a great serpent. She took the great serpent to her and they mingled in love. Soon after, a great egg grew within her and she became a dove. The dove-mother brooded over the egg until it was ready. Then out of the egg came all things: sun, moon, stars, earth, mountains, rivers, and all living creatures.

"Later, the Mother took her first born, Oceanus, and she coupled with him and had many children. But Oceanus was jealous of his children and took each one as it was born and hid it in the Mother's womb. At last the grieving Mother made a plan. She fashioned a sickle. Of her children, only her son Cronus was brave enough. He took the sickle and when Oceanus lay with the Mother, he grabbed his father and cut off his genitals and threw them into the sea.

"Cronus then came to rule over the gods and he took his sister Rhea to be his wife. But he, like his father, was jealous of his children and made Rhea swallow each child as it was born. At last, Rhea appealed to the Mother for help. When Rhea's next child was born, she called him Zeus. The Mother took Zeus and hid him in a cave. He stayed there until he grew strong and returned to overthrow his father, Cronus. From that time on, Zeus has ruled over gods and men."

"That was very brave of the Mother," Egyptus said when she'd finished. "It must have been dangerous for her to disobey Cronus."

"Except," Myrrhine continued, growing angry, "Zeus is ungrateful. He has long forgotten the help of the Mother. Now his followers no longer worship her as they should. Only a few of us are left and we are persecuted by the worshippers of Zeus. We must go quietly, slyly to the Mother's cave to worship. It isn't right!"

Egyptus looked carefully at Myrrhine for the first time. She didn't look as young or as beautiful to him now as she had in the market. But Sosias had been right about her husband. He could see the edge of a deep scar at the neckline of her peplos.

She saw him staring at her. He'll think I'm mad like most of the other men in village, she decided, but she didn't care. She had just come from the cave of the sibyls and she was angry. "Don't think that I blame only the male priests of Zeus. The women have done their part as well. Look at Delphi. When Apollo came to the sanctuary of our Mother Goddess and overthrew the Python, he gained power over the sanctuary. But, where would his priests be today without the priestess? They have no method for making Apollo's wishes known except through the priestess. If she had refused to become the slave of Apollo, the Mother Goddess wouldn't have lost her power at the sanctuary. In our time, the priestess parades around Delphi, taking for herself the glory that belongs to the Mother."

She paused and smiled what looked to Egyptus like a very ominous smile. "I have heard from one of the believers that, even now, the priestess is not allowed to speak directly to the suppliants. Her words are interpreted by the male priests of Apollo. How long will it be until they embellish and change the things she says to suit their own needs? What glory will she have for herself then? She will be nothing more than this doll." She pulled the pottery sherds out of her girdle and waved them in the air. "The priestess should have gone to the sanctuary below the temple of Apollo and stayed with the Mother Goddess."

Egyptus waited a long time after she'd finished speaking to see if she would say more. When she didn't, he spoke. "I heard a man who came from across the Mediterranean talking in the portico in Athens. He told us the Mother Goddess wasn't the first to exist, but a god they called Yahweh. He said Yahweh created the sun and stars, earth, rivers and everything else we know, even man. He even created woman from the rib of man. The man he called Adam and the woman, Eve. They were happy until the woman, tempted by a snake, ate from the forbidden tree of knowledge and brought sorrow and pain upon the whole world."

"The man tells this to discredit the Mother Goddess," Myrrhine insisted. "The snake is sacred. He was first created by the Mother Goddess from the winds. He helped her to create the remainder of the world. She created man. How could it be otherwise? She was here when there was nothing else. She brought forth life out of her body. I have heard in many places men are destroying her sacred temples, taking her land from her followers. These men are too evil for words." She sighed and refused to say anything more. At the edge of the village, she insisted Egyptus let her off the cart.

As soon as he'd tethered the horses, Egyptus went to find Sosias. He found him sitting in the courtyard of the inn with Philocleon. "Theopropides calls her Pandora," he said to Sosias and Philocleon when he'd finished telling what had happened on the road. "It seems strange. Both Eve and Pandora brought evil upon mankind in the same way. Eve, because she was curious about the tree of knowledge and ate from it. Pandora because she was curious and took the lid off the jar in which Epimetheus kept hidden illness for the minds and bodies of men. Do you suppose women aren't supposed to be curious?" he asked half-joking, half-serious.

"At least that's what some men think," Philocleon answered. "You remember how I told you we all go to the portico to recite the saga of the Trojan war? Delphium and Iris are often treated very rudely in the portico."

"Why do they go to the portico if they're treated rudely?" Egyptus asked.

Philocleon smiled. "They're curious."

"You don't mind if Delphium is curious, do you?" Egyptus

turned his questioning to Sosias.

"It wouldn't matter if I did mind. But I don't. Now I think it's time for us to forget about Myrrhine and get ourselves something to eat."

Egyptus did forget about Myrrhine, but not until he was walking with Sosias to their stall after the evening meal. He was soon reminded again. One of Myrrhine's slaves was waiting for him with a package. "My mistress sends this to you to show her gratitude."

Egyptus opened the package. "Look at this," he said to Sosias. Myrrhine had sent him a white linen fillet for his hair decorated with an embroidered snake.

Neither man realized Theopropides had been watching until the Athenian grabbed Egyptus by the front of his tunic and shoved him up against the stall. "You wouldn't be thinking of interfering in my business, would you?" he asked.

"No!" Recovering from his surprise, Egyptus began to assess the danger. He looked for Sosias, but he couldn't see him.

"Maybe you'd like to tell me why you got a gift from the woman I mean to have?" Theopropides shoved him tighter into the stall.

"I gave her a ride back to town. She'd gone for a walk in the countryside and she was very tired. She sent this to thank me." He held up the fillet for Theopropides to see.

Theopropides yanked the fillet out of Egyptus' hand. As he stepped back preparing to rip it in two, Sosias came up behind him. He laid a heavy wooden club on Theopropides shoulder. "Give it back." When Theopropides didn't move, he tapped the club. "Give it back."

Theopropides threw the fillet on the ground at Egyptus' feet. Sensing that Sosias would use the club, he walked away, threatening over his shoulder. "You'd better learn to stick to your own affairs..."

Egyptus picked the fillet up from the ground and brushed it off. "I'm scared," he admitted and told Sosias about the recapture of the mines. "I don't want to go through something like that again."

"You won't have to," Sosias assured him. "I'm here."

Egyptus folded the fillet. "You can't be with me every time I'm in the marketplace."

Sosias thought about it. "You're right. And I can't rely on the others to protect you when I'm not here. Maybe it would be better if you stayed out in the countryside for a while. Theopropides has become so obsessed with having Myrrhine, there's no way of knowing what he might do if he caught you by yourself."

"What about you? If I leave, you'll be here alone."

"I can take care of myself." Sosias pulled a knife out of a leather bag hanging on the back wall of his stall and showed it to Egyptus. "I've dealt with men like Theopropides before. Besides, I'm well known and liked by the other craftsmen. We protect one another." He put the knife back into the leather bag. "Now, let's go up to the kiln and get your cart loaded."

When they'd loaded the last pot into the cart, Sosias told Egyptus about a friend of his in another village. "Go to him. He'll give you a bed and a place to work until it's safe to return here."

"Leave some of the fired pots in the kiln," Egyptus said, getting onto the cart. Theopropides spends much of his time in the taverns. If I'm near, I'll slip in. If he isn't here, I'll take the pots. That way, you'll know I'm around."

"I will," Sosias said waving. He stood and watched until he could no longer see Egyptus. He felt lonely. It'd be a long time before they'd be sitting around sharing a bowl of wine again. Walking slowly back to his stall, he decided he'd go to see Delphium to cheer himself up.

"Father." Delphium jumped up and ran to the door when he called in. She hugged and kissed him and told Xanthias to pour some wine. "Sit here," she said, throwing a clean rug on the floor next to the one she'd been sitting on. "What brings you to Meton's?"

"Nothing special."

Cario stoked the fire while Meton roasted peppers over it and Iris went for wheat loaves. When everything was ready, they sat around the hearth and ate. Sosias told them about Egyptus' meeting with Myrrhine, the fillet, and Theopropides' threat.

"Will Egyptus be all right?" Philocleon asked, alarmed.

"I'll take care of Theopropides," Sosias assured him.

"And we'll help if you need us," Meton added. He pointed to the three swords hanging on the wall by the door. "Xanthias," he said. Xanthias jumped up and he and Meton held a mock sword battle, knocking over the little furniture they had in the house before it had ended.

Sosias was certain neither of them knew how to use a sword, but he joined the others in noisy cheering when the battle ended with both of them claiming victory. Cario, for his part, recited a battle scene from the Trojan war during the fighting.

"Ignore them," Iris said. "Listen to us." She and Philocleon sang a song they'd composed.

"The best is yet to come," Delphium insisted. Repeating it exactly as Myrrhine had told her, she told them how the Mother Goddess had created the world.

By the time Sosias left Meton's house, he no longer felt lonely. Instead, he felt like singing, which he did, all the way to the inn.

Delphium waved until her father had disappeared into the marketplace. When she returned to the fire, Meton was pouring wine. She drank, smiling to herself over the sight of her father so happily singing his way through the marketplace. Suddenly, she felt impulsive. She grabbed Philocleon's hand and led him into one of the bedrooms.

"Take off your tunic," she whispered as she dropped hers on the floor. "All the talk and wine, I feel like I belong to Aphrodite tonight."

Pleased and surprised, Philocleon pulled off his tunic. Delphium pushed him down on the bed and lay on top of him. She kissed him, not gently as he had expected, but forcefully and passionately. Up and down his body she went with her tongue. Taking him over and over, as he later described it, into the Elysian fields.

When Philocleon woke, he found Delphium still lying on him. "I'm going to sacrifice a hecatomb to Aphrodite," he said, kissing her hair.

"So am I," she said, kissing him in return.

He ran his hand over her shoulders. They felt strong to him. "What color is your hair?"

"Red."

"Red?"

"My mother was from the north."

"What about your eyes?"

"Green."

He ran his hands over her thighs and her buttocks. They felt firm and narrow.

"I'm shaped a bit like a man," she said.

Philocleon thought of Egyptus' description of Scapha. "I wonder. Are all women who are, well, more likely to think and act like men more likely to look like them too?"

Delphium laughed. "It won't be long, I'm certain, until you'll spend some time with Iris. You won't find a woman who is stronger of will, softer of body. Her cheeks are like the petals of flowers. Her breasts soft and full. Her lips like the nectar of Zeus. And as you already know, she has one of the best minds in the Greek world." She kissed him and got out of bed.

Selene was but a sliver in the heavens when Delphium spent the night in Philocleon's bed. By the time the goddess had waxed to fullness, Philocleon had discovered Iris' soft, full breasts for himself, and he agreed with Delphium. Iris was as sensual and soft as Aphrodite, but no less forceful than Delphium.

"You don't mind that I've been in each of your beds?" he asked as the three of them shared their morning meal. It was Meton, Cario, and Xanthias' turn to trade work for food.

"We live as the Mother Goddess intended, sharing everything," Delphium answered.

"I don't understand," Philocleon said.

"Look," Iris said "If I tell Delphium she can't go to your bed if I've been there, I'm attempting to enslave her. If she agrees, soon she'll tell me I can't go to Meton's bed if she has. So, you see. If we enslave someone else, we also enslave ourselves. And that isn't the way of the Mother Goddess. She wanted everyone to live equally in peace and harmony. Do you understand what I'm saying?"

Philocleon thought about it. "No. I don't see."

"You said yourself you never knew Nicias as a person until you freed him even though you spent most of your seasons with him while he was a slave. Wasn't that a form of slavery for you?" Iris asked. "Since you value him greatly now."

"Yes, but I could have gotten to know him if I'd made the effort."

"Maybe," Delphium said. "But I don't think we'd be talking with you as we are now if we were your slaves."

"And," Iris added. "It isn't just slaves. Would your father have killed Homer if you hadn't been enslaved?" A short time before he'd told them how Homer died.

"How was I enslaved?"

"You were as enslaved to your father as Nicias was. Otherwise, he'd have let you go to Olympia with Homer."

"There are all kinds of ways to enslave people," Delphium said, standing.

"We don't believe in any of them. Especially those that attempt to enslave women." Iris stood too. "Now, we must go to meet Myrrhine. We're making plans to go together to a ritual of the Mother Goddess." She took Philocleon's hand. "We'll take you to the portico and you can listen to the mischief the poets offer."

They left Philocleon at the portico and went with Myrrhine to the ritual. When they returned to the village, they continued their discussion with Philocleon about slavery. Meton, Cario and Xanthias joined in, and so did Sosias, who had come to tell them he had a feeling Egyptus would stop at the kiln some time after the evening meal.

Sosias was right. Egyptus drove into the village just as they finished their evening meal, loaded his cart with the pottery Sosias had left, and hid it in the trees. He walked back to the kiln and found the jar of wine Sosias always left for him in the kiln.

As he sat drinking the wine, he heard two men talking behind one of the kilns up the hill. He recognized one of voices. It was Theopropides.

"Well, what have you found out?" Theopropides demanded.

"She'll leave when the market opens."

"How do you know?"

"You told me to watch her and to ask around. I've been watching and asking."

"Where will she go?"

"How should I know? You paid me to find out which path she'll take out of the village, not where she'll take the path."

Theopropides snickered. "When our Myrrhine, goddess of the high and mighty, begins her walk up that mountain path, she'll have more than her thoughts of the Mother Goddess to accompany her." His laugh was sinister. "And you'd better be right about the path she's planning to take."

"I told you. We go out the old road. Follow it to the fork. Stay to the right on the fork. Around a curve, and there's a huge boulder." He snapped his fingers. "Once she walks around that boulder..."

Sweating with fear and anger, Egyptus waited until he heard Theopropides leave before he slipped down the hill to the market place. Cutting quickly through the stalls, he made his way to the inn. He couldn't find Sosias. Meton's, he decided. Maybe he's there.

"Come in if you're bringing wine," Meton called from inside when he heard Egyptus at the door.

"Excuse me," Egyptus said as soon as he got through the door. "Do you know where Sosias is?"

"Is it you, Egyptus?" Philocleon asked from the bedroom.

"Yes. Quickly. I must find Sosias."

Throwing on their garments, Philocleon and Delphium came to the fire. Iris was sitting with Meton. There was something about the urgency in Egyptus' voice that frightened them.

"I heard Theopropides, the Athenian, talking to a man up by the kilns," Egyptus said. "He knows Myrrhine plans to walk to the cave of the Mother Goddess. He plans to lay in wait for her along the mountain road."

"We must warn Myrrhine," Delphium said, running for her sandals. "Xanthias, Cario," she called into the other bedroom. "Come quickly."

"We can warn her," Iris said, "but she won't stay home. The ritual of the Mother Goddess is too important to her." She looked inquisitively at Egyptus. "Theopropides didn't know Delphium and I are to be on the walk with her?"

"I don't think so. He didn't mention it."

"You can't go," Xanthias insisted, slipping into his sandals.

"Let's go and speak with Myrrhine," Cario suggested.

"It won't help," Iris repeated.

"Wait," Philocleon interrupted. "I have a plan. Egyptus and I could take you two and Myrrhine to the cave in the cart."

"How will it help to have all of us in the cart?" Delphium asked. "We aren't any match for Theopropides."

Philocleon continued, the plan materializing in his mind as he spoke. "While we take you and Myrrhine by a different route to the cave, Meton, Cario, and Xanthias can circle through the mountains on the back roads to the place where Theopropides and his men are waiting." He turned toward Meton. "You can disarm them and hold them until we are safely beyond their reach."

"It could work," Delphium said. "What do you think Meton?"
"Where will Theopropides and his men be hiding?"Meton asked Egyptus.

"You know where the old road forks?"

"Yes."

"You follow the fork to the right."

"All right."

"Then the road curves and there's a big boulder on the left-hand side."

"I know it."

"Theopropides and his men will be hiding behind the boulder."

Meton pulled their three swords from the wall. Throwing one each to Cario and Xanthias, he said, "Let's get the horses."

"I'll take the women on the road that cuts through the trees," Egyptus said. "It'll take longer, but it should take us well around the boulder. If they should happen to escape you, they'll still have trouble trying to find us."

As the three men raced from the house, Egyptus gave instructions to Delphium and Iris. "You take Philocleon back to the inn. I'm going for the cart."

Watching carefully for Theopropides, Egyptus picked his way through the marketplace to the small wooded lot behind the kiln where he'd hidden the cart. He drove his donkeys along one of the back roads of the village to the inn. In the stable, he unloaded the pottery and filled the back of the cart with straw. He had the women get into the back and hide in the straw while he helped Philocleon up onto the seat and climbed on himself.

When she understood the danger, Myrrhine agreed to ride with them in the cart, though she would have preferred to walk with the cart following her.

By the time Helios appeared, they'd circled around the place where Theopropides and his men were waiting. Still, Egyptus didn't feel relieved. He kept pushing forward even when he could see his donkeys were tired.

By the time Helios dropped below the trees, they were at the entrance of the cave belonging to the sibyls of the Mother Goddess. There were many women already gathered, preparing the ritual barley.

Relieved, Egyptus jumped from the cart. "I'll take the cart down the path and watch for Theopropides," he said to Delphium. "If he comes, or anyone else, I'll signal with a scream of an owl. Do you think you could take Philocleon with you? If I should need to try to protect you, it would be difficult to have him with me. And being blind, he couldn't watch the ritual."

The three women conferred. "He can come with us," Myrrhine said.

Taking his arm, Delphium led Philocleon into the cave. "Where should I have him wait?" she asked Myrrhine.

"In the small room at the back where we keep the tablets."

Delphium took Philocleon to the room as she'd been instructed. Spreading a fleece, she told him to sit down. "You must stay here," she instructed. "I'll bring wax to fill your ears."

Philocleon put his hands on the cave wall to drop himself onto the cave floor. As he reached the floor, his hands ran across some clay objects. Feeling, he asked, "What is it?"

"The clay tablets," Delphium answered.

"What are they?"

"They hold the ancient rituals recorded by the sibyls many years ago. When the turmoil began which ended with the overthrow of the Mother Goddess by Minos, the followers of the Mother brought them here. We use them to learn the old rituals. Without them, we wouldn't know how to follow the rituals."

When she left, Philocleon began thinking about the Mother Goddess and her rituals. Instinctively, he ran his fingers over the incised letters on the tablets. He couldn't follow them. The language must not be the same, he decided and continued fingering them.

Delphium went to the center of the cave. The other women were already gathered around the sacred hearth. They joined hands and began chanting, circling together around the fire.

Though Philocleon couldn't hear the chanting, he could feel the rhythm of their pounding feet in the ground. As he sat wondering about their ritual, fingering the tablets to see if he could understand anything written upon them, the answer to Na'id-Assur and Qurdi Marduk's riddle about Gilgamesh suddenly came to him! Forgetting where he was, he stood and shouted for Delphium and Iris, breathless with excitement. So simple. Why hadn't he thought of it before?

Someone put her hand over his mouth. "Quiet," she said harshly, pushing him back down onto the fleece. "You're in the cave sacred to the Mother Goddess."

"I'm sorry," Philocleon whispered and said no more, though he was desperate for the ritual to end so that he could tell the woman what he'd discovered.

When the pounding on the cave floor ceased, Delphium came

and removed the wax from Philocleon's ears.

"I have the answer," he blurted out.

"Quiet," she commanded. "You can't speak in here. Your voice will disturb the memory of the Mother Goddess."

Disappointed, Philocleon said no more.

"We're ready," Delphium told Egyptus when she and Iris and Philocleon reached the cart.

"Where's Myrrhine?"

"She's going with one of the other women to her village. The woman has brothers who worship the Mother Goddess. They'll take Myrrhine to her house and stay there to protect her."

"I'll take the same road back to the village we came on," Egyptus told them. "If for some reason Theopropides and his men escaped Meton and Cario and Xanthias, they won't be likely to find us."

"What's that?" Delphium asked, her face suddenly pale with fright.

"Horses," Egyptus said. "Get in the cart." He jumped on, pulled Philocleon up and whipped his donkeys as fast as they would go toward the cave to warn the other women.

It wasn't long before the horses were no longer in the trees. They were galloping down the path behind them. Egyptus snapped his whip over his donkeys. They'd have to make a run for it.

"Wait," Xanthias called, as he and Meton and Cario overtook the cart.

"I didn't realize it was you," Egyptus explained when he'd halted the donkeys.

"We've been searching for you," Meton said, his voice shaking. There was no sign of his usual humor. "We wounded Theopropides and killed one of his men."

"What?" Delphium asked.

"There was a fight," Cario said breathlessly. "We all pulled our swords, thinking to keep them confined, but before we knew what had happened, they came after us. One man is dead. The others escaped with Theopropides. But Xanthias wounded Theopropides."

"He's in the village now paying men to come after us," Xanthias added.

"What will we do?" Delphium asked.

"We went to your father," Meton explained. "He has arranged to have a fishing boat waiting for us down the coast. Under cover of dark-winged Night we are all to board the boat. Your father will be waiting on board with our things."

"Then what?" Iris asked.

"My uncle has a house on Chios," Meton answered, trying to sound more confident than he felt. "We can go there, at least for now."

"What about Philocleon and Egyptus?" Delphium asked.

"They have to come with us. Theopropides knows they took Myrrhine to the cave." To Philocleon and Egyptus, he said, "We can drop you off at Ios."

"Homer's ashes and the saga. My cup from Nicias," Philocleon said. "I can't leave without them."

"Sosias is bringing them and as much of the pottery as he can carry."

Taking paths hidden by the trees, they made their way to the appointed place on the coast. "That's the boat," Meton said, pointing to a small fishing craft.

They crept down the coast and boarded the boat. When they were safely on board, Sosias helped the fisherman put up the sail. Quietly, they stole away from the shore.

NINETEEN

Though he couldn't see the man sitting in front of him, Philocleon was convinced from the man's deep voice he had to be a very large person. "You're certain you've never heard of him?" he asked.

"I'm certain," the man answered. "Now if you'll excuse me, I have cattle that need tending."

"But..." Philocleon described Homer for the third time. "He was about my height, had golden-brown hair, grey-brown eyes, and the most gifted voice you could imagine."

Indicating to Egyptus he wanted Philocleon out of his courtyard, the man sighed, repeated, "I told you I don't know any poet, nor have I ever seen a man who meets your description."

"I don't know his real name, but I think his mother might have named him Perseus. At least he told the saga of Perseus and Danaë all the time. You had a daughter who died, didn't you? Did she have a son?"

"Get out," the man snapped. "I told you I don't know the poet you're talking about. My daughter is not dead. She went to live with relatives of ours in...in Smyrna."

Egyptus helped Philocleon to his feet. "It's no use."

"But he's our last hope," Philocleon insisted. "We've been to every other estate on the island." He could hear it in the man's voice. He was lying. Either he was the grandfather or he knew who was. "He knows something. I can sense it."

Frightened by the frustrated anger spreading from the farmer's wide-set grey-brown eyes to his broad nose and wide lips, Egyptus resolutely escorted Philocleon from the courtyard whispering, "If he does know, he isn't going to tell you. And he's becoming very angry."

"Are you suggesting I forget about this man even though I haven't found Homer's family and I know he knows something he isn't telling me?" All the frustration he'd been feeling since they arrived in Ios came out with the question.

"I don't know what else we can do. We've been to every house in the village, every estate on the island. There's no one left to ask."

"The old weasel knows something," Philocleon repeated, but he knew as well as Egyptus it wouldn't help to stay and question him.

"Let's go back to the village," Egyptus suggested trying to make his voice sound hopeful. "I'm sure we'll think of something to do if we just give ourselves a chance."

During the long ride back to the village, Philocleon mentally reviewed the things he'd done to find Homer's family. He was convinced he'd left nothing undone. Still, he hadn't found a single trace of the family, except for the last farmer, who wasn't going to tell him what he knew.

"What are you thinking?" Egyptus asked, interrupting Philocleon's thoughts.

"That I should have thought to ask for more than Homer's land of birth at Delphi."

Both men fell silent again until Philocleon, feeling the cart begin the bumpy trek down the cliff overlooking the port village, came up with an idea. "Stop the donkeys," he said gaily to Egyptus. The most obvious solution had suddenly occurred to him. Just because he couldn't find Homer's family, that didn't mean he couldn't bury the poet's ashes on Ios.

Egyptus pulled his donkeys to a halt. "What is it?"

"I know what to do."

"I knew you'd find an answer if you really thought about it. What will you do?" Egyptus was pleased to see Philocleon so happy.

"I'll bury the ashes myself."

"On Ios?"

"Yes. On Ios. Right here overlooking the sea. Homer loved the sea. Choose a place you think would make a good burial."

Egyptus looked around. "There's a clearing about halfway down the cliff with a perfect view of the sea."

"Good. When we get back into the village, we'll find the best builder on the island. I'll have him build a hero's tomb for Homer on the spot you've chosen."

Pleased, the two men returned to the village. "Is there a builder on Ios?" Philocleon asked the innkeeper before he and Egyptus had even carried their gear to their rooms.

"I should guess so. My brother, Pheres." He took Egyptus outside and showed him a house built on a cliff overlooking the western end of the village.

Egyptus recognized the house. When they'd visited it to ask the family if they knew Homer, it had looked to him as if the owner was one of the wealthiest men on Ios. "Tell me, what would be the shortest way to get to your brother's house? We were there, but we came in from the other side."

"Take the path that runs west behind the marketplace. Follow it up the cliff and you'll find his estate. If you get lost, ask for Pheres. Everybody knows him."

"I'll come with you," Philocleon said, when Egyptus was ready to leave for Pheres' estate.

"I think you should stay here and think about the kind of tomb you want. I'll bring him back."

Philocleon agreed and while Egyptus took the cart back up the cliff behind the marketplace, he sat down to plan Homer's tomb.

Egyptus explained the purpose of his visit to the slave who met him at the front door. "I've come for a friend of mine. He wants to talk with your master about building a tomb."

The slave took him to the courtyard. "Wait here, I'll fetch my master."

Egyptus found a stone bench and sat down.

"Who's the handsome stranger in the courtyard?" someone asked from behind Egyptus.

Quite unexpectedly, Egyptus felt a flutter in his stomach at the sound of the words, 'handsome stranger.' He turned and searched the shadows of the portico until he found the source of the intriguing voice. It came from a woman about his own height, having lived fewer seasons, though, he decided, as his eyes moved over her peplos, up her delicate hands and arms to her face. "I'm Egyptus," he said.

Embarrassed to be overheard, the woman rushed from the portico into a room.

"Wait," Egyptus said, jumping up. Without thinking, he dashed after her. Racing down the portico, he ran headlong into a man. "Sir, I'm sorry," he stammered, stepping back, checking to see if he'd done any damage.

"Exactly where did you think you were going in my home?" The man wasn't much taller than Egyptus but the broad shoulders and muscular arms of a builder made him seem taller.

"Sir, I," Egyptus stuttered. "Nowhere. That is, I apologize. I mean, I saw." He gave up.

"What is it you want?"

"I've come to speak with the builder, Pheres." He'd already figured out that the man in front of him was Pheres.

"I'm the builder you're looking for. And I'm not accustomed to men running around in my house without being invited."

"There was a young woman in the portico. She asked who I was and..." Egyptus looked at the floor. He hoped Pheres would tell him who the woman was, though he was certain without being told she was his daughter.

"What is your business?"

"I've come for a friend. He'd like to speak with you about building a hero's tomb."

"Here on the island?"

"Yes."

"Who's the hero? It certainly isn't anyone from Ios. I know everyone on the island and no one's done anything heroic that I know of. Is it that poet you've been asking about?"

"I think it would be better for you to talk to my friend about everything. He's at the inn. If you'd be willing to accompany me, I'd be happy to take you to him."

Pheres decided he was curious enough to make the trip into the village. "Wait here. I'll get my mantle." He started to leave, then turned around. "Perhaps it would be better if you waited at the front door."

Desperate for a second glance at Pheres' daughter, Egyptus hesitated.

"The door," Pheres repeated.

"Yes, Sir." Egyptus turned and walked back to the door. When he turned around, he saw that Pheres' daughter had come out of the room she'd disappeared into earlier. She was standing at the other end of the corridor that connected the courtyard to the front door.

"I'm Egyptus," he said knowing she couldn't hear him, but wanting to say something, anything, to keep her from leaving the corridor. There was something about her hazel eyes. He couldn't stop staring.

She smiled, but she didn't dare to speak. Her father had forbidden her to come out of her room until he had left with the handsome stranger. When she had asked what the stranger wanted, he had told her nothing that should concern her. She'd come out anyway for a second look. She waved at Egyptus, then hurried away. Her father wouldn't be happy if he caught her disobeying him.

Reluctant though he was to leave when Pheres returned with his mantle, Egyptus followed him out of the door.

Pheres called for his horse and told Egyptus to lead the way. During the entire trip to the village Egyptus considered how he might ask Pheres about his daughter. In the end, he didn't have the nerve.

"I want you to build an altar for me," Philocleon said as soon as Pheres had been seated. He explained about the Delphic oracle. "Apollo, through the priestess, told me to come to Ios to the father of Homer's mother, but I've not been able to find a single man or woman who knows of him, so I've decided to leave his ashes buried here in a hero's tomb."

"Do you have plans for this tomb you want built?" Pheres looked Philocleon over carefully. He couldn't decide how long he'd lived. In some ways it looked like he'd seen the seasons change twenty-four or five times, yet his grey hair and sober face were those of a man who'd seen many more seasons.

Not realizing Pheres was scrutinizing him, Philocleon continued enthusiastically. "Yes. Well, I don't exactly have plans, but I know what I want built. I want an altar surrounded by an enclosure wall. The side of the enclosure that faces the sea I want to be a row of columns. The other three sides, I want made of intertwined branches. I want the altar placed at the center of the enclosure. It should be built of wood and covered with finely worked sheets of bronze. I will bury my friend's ashes under the altar. His saga, which I will dedicate to Apollo, will be kept in a stone box on the altar."

"Saga?"

"It's a poem about the Trojan war."

"Where do you plan to build this altar?" Pheres approved of the idea.

"I wish to buy land on the cliff behind the marketplace. Egyptus will show you the exact place."

"The land will be expensive."

"I'm prepared to offer these." With Egyptus' help, Philocleon pulled a fine gold fibula and a bronze cauldron from his traveling sack.

Pheres examined the two objects carefully. "I should say with these pieces, you'll get the land you want."

"Would you speak with the owner for me?"

"I will. And what will you be offering me for building the altar?"

Philocleon took a silver incense burner inlaid with gold from the sack and handed it to Pheres. "This will be yours."

Pheres fingered the incense burner. "Where would a young man like you get such a finely made object?" he asked.

"From my father's treasury. He owned one of the largest estates in Attica until his death."

"I see." Pheres was impressed; he couldn't deny it. "I'll return with plans for the tomb shortly. In the meantime, I'll send the landowner down to talk with you." He examined the incense burner one more time before he left.

As soon as Pheres was out of hearing distance, Egyptus burst out with what was on his mind. "When I went to his estate, I saw the most beautiful woman ever to live." He paused, trying to control the emotion he felt. "She must be Pheres' daughter. You have to help me find a way to meet her."

"So," Philocleon smiled. "You've been struck by the arrow of Eros."

Egyptus blushed. "Pierced through to the bottom of my heart." He told Philocleon what had happened at the estate. "I looked such a fool chasing his daughter down the portico, I can't approach him myself. But he might listen to you."

Philocleon felt as happy as Egyptus felt desperate. He'd never known Egyptus to be so impassioned. "When Pheres returns, I'll speak with him. Of course, I can't promise he'll listen to me either."

"Speak to him. That's all I ask."

"She must be beautiful for you to be so anxious."

"She's beautiful all right, but it wasn't her beauty that caught my eye. It was…it was something else. Her smile maybe. Or the brazen way she looked at me with those soft hazel eyes of hers. Oh, I don't know."

"Don't worry about it. If Pheres agrees to let you meet her, you'll have plenty of time to decide what it is that infatuates you."

Egyptus thanked Philocleon again as he stood. "I need to do something or I'll go mad waiting for Pheres to return. If you don't need me, I think I'll go into the marketplace to see if I can find someone who'll rent me some space."

"Go. If I need you, I'll send one of the innkeeper's children to look for you."

After Helios had crossed the sky five times, while Egyptus worked in his newly found stall in the marketplace, Philocleon met with Pheres and the owner of the land he wanted to buy. The land purchase and the plans for the tomb were finalized. Philocleon invited Pheres to join him for the evening meal to celebrate.

When Pheres arrived for the evening meal he found Egyptus on the couch next to Philocleon. So, he decided, taking the couch on the other side of Philocleon, there's to be more on the agenda than a celebration.

"You know my friend Egyptus," Philocleon said, ordering wine and food from the waiting innkeeper.

"Of course." Pheres accepted a bowl of wine. "I hear from our potters you've already established yourself in the market."

"I've gotten myself a stall and a kiln." Egyptus tried to sound casual though he was desperately intent on impressing Pheres.

"He's already got contracts with merchants on three of the nearby islands," Philocleon added. "When we were on Crete, he had more business by himself than all the other potters together."

"You're exaggerating," Egyptus said to Philocleon, but he was thankful for the help.

Pheres sat back and listened to the two young men, Philocleon bragging about his friend, Egyptus, obviously proud, but embarrassed.

Finally Egyptus got up his courage to say what he'd wanted to say to Pheres. "Sir. About that incident in your courtyard. I hope you realize I meant no harm to your daughter. It's just I was so taken with her, I didn't stop to think."

Pheres smiled. "A man who has evil intentions doesn't usually chase my daughter in the light of Helios and then stumble around over his tongue apologizing when he's caught." He liked Egyptus. There was something about the potter's industriousness and honesty that appealed to him.

"Thank you sir," Egyptus said, pouring Pheres another bowl of wine with shaking hands.

"I understand your daughter is very beautiful," Philocleon added, moving to the subject he wanted to discuss.

"Most of the men on the island seem to be of that opinion," Pheres said. "But she has other qualities I think are more important."

"What are they?" Egyptus asked eagerly.

"She isn't silly. She doesn't spend her time gossiping. She's interested in many things."

Egyptus felt his heart beating beyond control. He wanted to ask what she was interested in, but he didn't dare. He was afraid Pheres might think he was too forward.

Pheres looked at Egyptus who was trying so hard to seem calm when he was obviously a mess of nerves. It reminded him of how he felt when his father went to arrange for his marriage with his wife, Halia. How he'd worried. "It seems my daughter has some interest in you as well," he told Egyptus. "She's asked about you several times."

"She has?" Egyptus could barely control his excitement.

"Go ahead," Philocleon whispered.

"Would you mind, sir, if I sent her a small gift?" Egyptus handed Pheres a small covered jar he'd spent considerable time making. "I made one for your wife too, with your permission." He handed Pheres a second covered jar, just as carefully made.

As Pheres admired the jars, Philocleon asked their question. "Is your daughter promised to someone?"

"Not promised, but I've discussed marriage with one of the men from the island." He handed the jars back to Egyptus. "Idas. I'm sure you met him when you were inquiring after your poet friend."

"You don't mean the man who owns the estate next to yours?" Egyptus blurted out. "He's seen more seasons pass than Philocleon and me together."

Pheres nodded. "His estate is one of the largest on Ios after mine and he's one of the ruling council members of the village."

Egyptus' hopes began to fade. He could never compete with a man that wealthy and important.

"To tell you the truth, my daughter's not too happy with the idea of marrying Idas," Pheres continued.

"What is her name?" Egyptus asked, desperate for anything he could learn about her.

"Charis."

"Charis," Egyptus repeated. "It's a lovely name."

"If she isn't promised to this Idas, I would like to ask you to consider my friend, Egyptus," Philocleon persisted.

"I like Egyptus," Pheres told Philocleon. "But I'm a practical man and Idas is one of the wealthiest men on the island."

"I doubt he's as wealthy as Egyptus," Philocleon countered.

Egyptus stared at Philocleon. Since when could a stall in the marketplace compete with an estate the size of that owned by Idas?

Pheres was as surprised as Egyptus. "How's that?"

"Egyptus owns an extremely rich silver mine in Attica."

Egyptus leaned forward. "Wait a moment," he said to Philocleon.

"You wait a moment," Philocleon said, smiling. Then to Pheres. "I will send you proof he owns a silver mine. When you receive the document, examine it. If it's in order, and you approve, give Egyptus some consideration. That's all I'm asking."

"I will." Pheres was truly impressed.

"Good," Philocleon said, pleased the matter had been settled. "Now, tell me. When will you be able to begin construction of the tomb?"

"When Helios has left chariot tracks in the sky twice."

The three men spent the remainder of the evening meal discussing the tomb. When Pheres stood to leave, Egyptus stood too and held out the two jars he'd made for Charis and her mother.

"You bring them with you."

"I don't understand," Egyptus said.

"I'd like you and Philocleon to come to my estate for your next evening meal. You can bring the jars with you and deliver them yourself."

Shocked by the invitation, Egyptus put the jars back on the floor, almost dropping them and walked Pheres to his cart.

When Pheres was no longer in sight, Egyptus rushed back into the dining room. "What have you done?" he asked Philocleon. "Telling Pheres I own a silver mine."

"You do. You own one of mine."

"No. I can't do that." He sat down next to Philocleon. "Look, I appreciate what you're trying to do for me, but I can't accept one of your silver mines."

"I wouldn't have even one silver mine if it weren't for you."

"Scapha is a very determined woman," Egyptus said honestly. "If I hadn't come along, she'd have found someone else."

"But you did come along. And you told me yourself, she is very successful with the estates. I have no intention of living the extravagant life of my father. Surely, we can spare one silver mine." We, Philocleon thought. It was the first time he'd thought of himself and Scapha together. He was surprised at how good it made him feel.

Egyptus knew he should protest further, but he also knew his one chance to win Pheres' permission to marry Charis rested totally with his owning the silver mine.

"We'll go together to the portico and find an advocate who can prepare the document for us," Philocleon said, rising. "When it's ready, I'll send a copy to Pheres."

Egyptus took Philocleon to his room before he went to his own. He sat on the edge of the bed in his room. What had happened to him, he wondered. It wasn't that long ago he'd never even thought of marriage. Now, suddenly, it was all he wanted. He got up and went to the window. Soon Selene would be a full round disk. Perfect for marriage.

He lay down on the bed. When he met Charis, what would they talk about? He had talked with a lot of women, but never one he had wanted to marry before. He went over the conversations he'd had with women. Maybe he could borrow from them. No. None of them seemed right. He rolled over and tried to sleep. He couldn't.

He got up and paced in his room. He had started thinking about marriage when he had seen how happy Nicias and Bromia were. In Crete, out on the road, he had thought about it constantly. Settling down. Having someone to come home to. It would be nice. He didn't have Sosias to talk with anymore. Soon Philocleon would be gone.

"Wake up." The innkeeper's son shook Egyptus' shoulder. "Your friend is waiting for you."

Egyptus opened his eyes. When had he fallen asleep? "Tell him I'm coming."

Philocleon insisted they go immediately to the portico and get the agreement transferring the silver mine started.

When Helios had dropped below the trees, they were picked up at the inn by one of Pheres' slaves. Pheres himself waited for them at the gate. "You're to come with me," he told Philocleon. He sent Egyptus with a slave to the women's quarters.

When Philocleon arrived in the dining room, he found there were other guests. "They're the members of the island's ruling council," Pheres explained. "Idas. You know of him. He owns the estate next to mine. Antiphus. He owns most of the ships docked in the harbor. And Thyestes. He owns the estate you visited last on your journey."

"I'm happy to learn from Pheres you've found a solution to burying your friend's ashes," Thyestes told Philocleon with exaggerated kindness.

"Thank you," Philocleon said. He considered asking one more time about Homer but changed his mind. "And please forgive me if I seemed a little too persistent when I visited your estate. It was the disappointment."

"Don't worry. A man's loyal devotion to a friend is something to be pleased with."

As Pheres led Philocleon to his couch, Egyptus entered the room. From the glow on his face, Pheres assumed all had gone well with Charis and Halia. He introduced Egyptus to each of the men before he assigned him a couch for the meal.

Egyptus paused momentarily before Idas. The man had lived even more seasons than he'd remembered. He was nearly bald with wrinkled skin and little beady eyes. He felt repulsed by the man, livid that he might put his veiny hands on Charis.

"Now I must confess," Pheres said to Philocleon as the slaves brought wine. "The ruling council members have not come by accident. We have something we wish to discuss with you."

Idas spoke as the chief of the council. "First, we want to say we approve very much of your plan to build a hero's tomb for your friend Homer. Your friendship, as Thyestes said, is commendable. As the ruling council we would like to know what your plans for endowing the tomb are. If you plan to leave the saga of Homer at the altar, there will be a need for a sibyl to attend the tomb."

Philocleon nodded. He'd already thought about that. "I plan to endow the tomb with funds from my silver mines."

"Good," Idas answered and thought to himself how well his plan was working. "If you would like, as the ruling body of the island, we could take responsibility for selecting a sibyl from among the island virgins to serve at the tomb."

"I'd be most grateful," Philocleon answered and began to tell them about Homer and the saga.

"If you would allow me to interrupt you for a moment," Pheres said to Philocleon when it became obvious to him Philocleon intended to speak at length about his friend. "I'd like to make a sacrifice to Apollo in honor of your dedication to him."

"I'd be most pleased," Philocleon answered.

Pheres had a lamb brought to the courtyard. With Egyptus' assistance, he slaughtered the lamb and put the thighs on the fire to roast for Apollo, the remainder of the meat on the spit to roast for his guests.

"I'll take the list of island virgins to the temple of Apollo at Delos," Idas told Philocleon when Pheres had completed his sacrifice. "As is always done, I'll request that the priests in the temple ask Apollo's assistance in choosing the virgin to become the sibyl."

"We could also arrange to have one of the priests come for the dedication of the tomb," Pheres added. "Would you want us to do that?" he asked Philocleon.

"I would very much like that." Philocleon answered, feeling very pleased.

While they waited for the lamb to roast, the council members talked with Philocleon and Pheres about the design of the tomb and with Egyptus about his ever-increasing business in the marketplace. Afterwards, Philocleon finished his description of Homer and his saga.

Egyptus continued to speak with them, though he was hardly aware of what was said. When the musicians were called at the end of the meal, he barely knew he'd eaten. He tried listening to the music and to Philocleon when after the meal he recited from the Trojan saga, but all he heard were the words Charis had spoken to him. It wasn't until he heard Pheres tell Philocleon he'd see him when Helios rode into the sky that Egyptus fully realized he was standing at the front door.

"You'll bring him up to the site, won't you?" Pheres asked.

"Yes, sir."

Pheres put his hand on Egyptus' shoulder. "I talked with Idas. I told him I've decided that you shall marry Charis."

A fierce sensation raced through Egyptus' entire body. Had he heard correctly? "Did? That is...I thought I heard you say?"

"You did," Pheres laughed. "Now get into the wagon and go home. You look like you need to sleep."

When they were out of sight of the estate, Egyptus threw his arms around Philocleon and whooped. "I'm so happy, I could fly from here to the market," he said. "You've done this for me. How can I ever repay you?"

"You already have," Philocleon laughed.

Egyptus stood in the wagon and called to the stars, telling them of this happy event. He thanked all of the Egyptian gods and with Philocleon's help, the Greek gods as well. He promised Egyptian and Greek gods alike more sacrifices than they'd ever known.

When Egyptus rose to greet Dawn, he was even worse. Frenzied with happiness, as he called it. He took Philocleon up to the site of the tomb and returned to his stall where he tried to work, but mostly he dreamed until Helios rode below the trees when he went to visit Charis and Halia. Afterwards, he went back to the tomb site to take Philocleon back to the inn.

Philocleon was as excited as Egyptus. He gave his friend an account of everything Pheres had reported doing. Before returning to the inn, they walked slowly through the site together, Philocleon running his fingers over everything Pheres had built, Egyptus eagerly repeating every word Charis had said to him.

Egyptus continued to take Philocleon to the tomb as soon as Helios appeared in Zeus' blue sky and pick him up when Helios rode below the shade trees, until, well before Philocleon expected it, Pheres announced the tomb was complete. "Come to the inn tonight," Philocleon said to Pheres when he'd recovered from the excitement. "We'll share the evening meal in celebration and I'll give you the incense burner."

"I'll come for the incense burner," Pheres said. "But I can't stay for the evening meal. Idas has called a special meeting of the island ruling council. I have to attend."

When Egyptus came to fetch him, Philocleon insisted they walk through the entire tomb so that he could touch every part of it. Overjoyed that his promise to Homer would finally be fulfilled, he returned with Egyptus to the inn, gave Pheres the incense burner and spent the entire evening meal reciting from the saga of the Trojan war for the men gathered at the inn. He wanted them to know about their wonderful poet.

Accompanied by Dawn, the two friends began preparations to bury Homer's ashes. Taking a pot from Egyptus' stall, they went to a spring hidden in the trees behind the village. They undressed and bathed, filled the pot with water from the spring and took it back to the marketplace.

In the marketplace, they bought milk from a pure white goat, a jar of the finest island honey, a pure black lamb, and a sack of barley. They carried the water and the other things they'd bought, together with Homer's ashes, to the altar. Philocleon placed the two-handled gold cup containing Homer's ashes on the altar. He spaded up a circular pit under the altar, carefully placed the gold cup in it and covered it with black dirt.

Taking up the other jars, he poured the milk, the honey, the spring water, and finally barley over the pit. With the help of Egyptus, he slit the lamb's throat and let the blood drain into the pit. They wrapped the thighs in fat, and as they began burning, Philocleon sent Egyptus away. "Come get me for the evening meal," he instructed.

Smelling the smoke from the thighs, Philocleon called to the gods of Hades' Underworld to send up the shade of Homer. He sat in front of the tomb and waited. Unexpectedly, he felt the air around him stir. It could be the sea breeze he thought, or the fire or, it could be the shade of Homer coming through the pit. The longer he sat, the more convinced he became that it was Homer's shade he was feeling.

"Come sit with me, my friend," he said, "if you are truly here." I'd like to tell you what I've done and see if it pleases you." He explained to Homer's shade how he'd gone to Delphi to inquire after his homeland. "The oracle said to come to Ios and to look not for your fatherland, but for your motherland and your mother's father. I've searched the island, but I haven't found your grandfather as the priestess instructed I would. So I've had this hero's tomb built instead that you might be honored forever here on Ios where you were born."

Breathing deeply to keep his voice even, he told Homer's shade the tragic story of how he had killed his father and blinded himself, of his journey to Delphi, his journey with Nicias to find Bromia and then to Argos to find Evadne and Simo, the trip to the tomb of an ancient hero, the shipwreck and his life in Crete.

Barely able to contain his excitement, he asked, "Do you remember how Gilgamesh returned from his journey to the gates of Uruk in despair over his failure to discover the means to immortality? Poor Gilgamesh! His despair was misguided. Though he didn't realize it, he actually had discovered the means to immortality.

"It came to me the day Egyptus and I took Myrrhine and Iris and Delphium to the cave of the Mother Goddess. The women put me in a small room at the back of the cave during the ritual dancing. The ancient clay tablets on which the sibyls had written the rituals of the Mother Goddess were in the room. Sitting there fingering the clay tablets, trying to understand them, I answered Na'id-Assur and Qurdi Marduk's riddle." He paused, expecting Homer's shade to gasp in surprise.

"Gilgamesh gained immortality by recording his story on a stone. Do you see, my dear friend? We haven't forgotten Gilgamesh because we have his saga. Though his body no longer exists and the monuments he built are gone, he will be with us forever. He found immortality, though he didn't realize it.

"Because we recorded your saga, I will be able to keep my oath to you. I'll use your saga to make you immortal. Your tomb will soon be dedicated to Apollo by his priest from Delos. Afterwards, I will dedicate your saga at the altar. From then on, men from all over Greece will come to see and touch it. Your death will no longer be inglorious. You will have an enduring name!"

Philocleon sat quietly listening for a sign from Homer when he'd finished. Hearing rustling behind him, he felt assured Homer's shade was still in the tomb. Just as he was about to remind his friend of how thoroughly they'd tricked the beautiful muse Calliope, he felt someone sit down next to him. "Homer. Is it you?" he asked.

"No. I'm not Homer," a voice Philocleon didn't recognize said. "I am a priest of Apollo. My sanctuary is on the island of Delos and I've been asked by the village ruling council to dedicate this tomb. I understand you are the generous young man who has had it built."

"I am. It's to honor my friend, the greatest of all poets, Homer. Just now I was speaking with his shade."

"I know. I heard you as I approached. I'm told you've promised to endow a sibyl to care for the saga. A list of the island virgins was brought to me. I have asked Apollo which among the virgins he favors and he has chosen the young virgin, Charis."

"Charis? Pheres' daughter, Charis?" Philocleon was shocked. He hadn't even imagined she'd be considered.

"Yes."

"The council made a mistake when it gave you Charis' name. She can't be the sibyl." Philocleon jumped up. "A sibyl has to remain a virgin and Charis has already been promised to my friend in marriage. You have to return to Delos and consult Apollo again."

"It's a great honor to be chosen by Apollo. And once the god has spoken, no mortal can ask him to reconsider. Charis will be the sibyl." The priest stood. He was angry. Now he understood why Pheres had insisted he come up to the tomb and talk with the donor. Why hadn't Idas warned him?

"Was it Idas who brought the list of names to Delos?"

"Yes."

"Did he also tell you he'd asked for Charis in marriage?"

"No. Though I don't see that it matters. Apollo has spoken."

"I withdraw my endowment. I won't pay for a sibyl to tend Homer's saga if Charis is to be the sibyl."

"I'm sorry you feel as you do," the priest said, walking to the colonnade at the front of the enclosure. "But the dedication will be made as scheduled. Idas, who apparently could see you might be mean-spirited, has promised to endow the tomb should you refuse." He'd been promised a third of the endowment if Apollo chose Charis and it mattered not a wit to him whether he got it from Idas or someone else. "I'll see you at the dedication."

Philocleon listened to the priest leave. He refused to accept that Apollo's decision to have Charis was final. There had to be something he and Egyptus could do. But what? Anxiously, he considered alternatives until he came up with one he was certain would work. Idas had most certainly bribed the priest. Why couldn't they bribe him with more gifts? He'd offer his treasury to the priest. Surely his possessions were valuable enough to get one of the other women chosen as the sibyl. Except he'd told Egyptus to come get him for the evening meal and from the feel of the air, he was sure it wasn't even time for the noon meal. By the time Egyptus came for him, it might be too late.

He remained at the center of the tomb for some time, trying to decide what to do. All at once, it came to him. He'd have to go and find Egyptus. But how? He was blind and he was halfway up the cliff, incapable of going anywhere by himself. He realized that though nothing held him inside the tomb, he felt as trapped as if he'd been tied there. For the first time in his life he understood what it truly meant to be a slave. He was as surely the hostage of blindness as Nicias had been the slave of his father. It was frightening and demeaning and he made up his mind he would not remain a hostage.

Groping his way from the altar to the enclosure wall and following it, he got himself to the colonnade. Shaking with terror, he stepped through the colonnade trying to remember where the path was. As he walked slowly in what he thought was the right direction, his foot caught on a stone and he fell forward, smashing his head into a fallen tree. Using the tree, he crawled to his feet, his nose bleeding and his face scratched. It's no use, he decided, sitting down, holding his head back to stop his nose from bleeding. He'd never get to the bottom by himself. He might as well wait for Egyptus to come after him.

After a long while his nose stopped bleeding. He stood again. Sitting there, thinking about the life he was resigning himself to if he gave up the struggle to get to the bottom, he started to fear staying on the cliff more than he feared the horrendous walk to the bottom. He knew he'd never find the path, but he'd developed his sense of hearing acutely. He could listen for the sea and keep moving toward it until he got down the cliff. Gingerly, he took a few steps. Suddenly, he plunged forward. Pain tore through his left arm. It felt like he'd broken it.

Frustrated and angry, he crawled around on the ground until he found a stick. He got back to his feet and holding the stick out in front of him, edged forward again. He thought of Nicias. Always there when he needed him. His head banged into a branch. He sat down for a moment, too frightened to move. Too frightened to stay. He made a vow. There would be no slaves in his house! Life as a slave was intolerable. Why hadn't he realized this before? When he'd told Evadne all of his discoveries about aristocrats and slaves, why hadn't it occurred to him to abolish slavery? Because he'd never truly understood the terror of helplessness before. Even when he'd freed Nicias, it had been for the pleasure of making himself happy, not because he understood what Nicias had lived through.

He stood again, and concentrating on keeping the stick out in front of him, made some small progress down the cliff without falling. He thought about Charis and Egyptus, so happy together. What about his father and mother, he wondered. What was their life together like? Had his father insisted his mother obey him? Do things exactly the way he wanted them done as Delphium and Iris had argued was likely. Certainly his grandfather hadn't been much different from his father in that way. The memory of his grandmother telling him how his grandfather had exposed all her girl babies was still vivid in his memory.

He wouldn't enslave Scapha the way his grandfather had enslaved his grandmother. If she had girl babies and she wanted to keep them, he wouldn't take them from her. Why anyway should any man be allowed to take a woman's baby and expose it? Further, he decided, remembering the good times he'd had with Delphium and Iris, Scapha could eat in the dining room whenever she wanted, whether there were guests or not, just as she was used to doing with his grandmother and grandfather. She could hunt and make pottery if she wanted to. What did he care?

And his children. They would be special. He'd find someone to teach them to read, boys and girls alike. But more important, as Na'id-Assur and Qurdi Marduk had taught him. His children would not learn just to recognize and repeat words, they would learn to reason with the words they learned.

Gradually, the ground felt as if it was leveling out. Could he have reached the bottom? A branch scraped across his leg, leaving a long, bloody scratch. He cursed the tree, wishing desperately Egyptus were with him. No. He realized. He'd really rather have Scapha at his side.

"Here, let me help you," one of the leather workers said, running up to get Philocleon when he came toward the marketplace. "What happened? You're a mess."

"Don't worry about me," Philocleon said. "Help me find Egyptus."

The leather worker got him to the inn. "What happened?" Egyptus asked when he saw Philocleon. He helped him inside.

"Have you heard?" Philocleon asked, sitting down on his bed, terribly weak now that he'd made it down the mountainside.

"Yes. How did you find out?"

"The priest of Apollo who is going to dedicate the tomb came up to see me. Have you gone to see Pheres?"

His voice shaking with emotion, Egyptus told Philocleon he'd been turned away at Pheres' gate.

"Why?"

"He doesn't think it would be right for me to visit the house now that Charis is to be the tomb sibyl. I don't know what to do." He saw that Philocleon was close to fainting. "I'm going to send the innkeeper's daughter in to bathe you and dress these wounds."

"We'll go to see the priest of Apollo. I'll offer him my treasury to change his mind." Philocleon was prepared to ignore his wounds.

"It's not possible. He's with Idas."

"We have to do something."

"I know we do, but what?"

Philocleon tried to stand, but he couldn't.

Concerned again for his friend, Egyptus insisted he lie down. "I'm going for a walk to try to think of what we can do," he told Philocleon as the innkeeper's wife and daughter entered the room. "I'll return as soon as your wounds have been cleaned and dressed. Then we'll decide."

Philocleon fell asleep after he had been bathed and drunk the herbal mixture the innkeeper's wife gave to him. Dark-winged Night had descended by the time he woke. He sat up. "How long have I slept?"

"A long time," Egyptus answered. He'd come back from his walk and found Philocleon sleeping. He'd been pacing next to his friend's bed ever since trying to come up with a plan. He had none. "Soon Charis will become the sibyl of the tomb," he said, walking over to the window. He leaned his head against the frame and looked out at the black sky.

"Idas went to Delos with the list. He bribed the priest, I'm convinced of it," Philocleon said.

"So is Pheres, but there was nothing he could do. When Idas returned with the priest and announced the selection, Pheres objected. Idas insisted they put it to a vote by the ruling council. Pheres was the only one who voted against selecting Charis. He's unhappy, but he's not willing to go against the wishes of the council."

"So Idas not only bribed the priest of Apollo but the entire council as well."

"So it seems," Egyptus said. He dropped his head in his hands. "What will I do now?" He couldn't imagine his life without Charis.

"Reason," Philocleon answered. "We can't rely on the priest for justice, so we'll have to trust our own good judgement." As he spoke, a plan began emerging. Within moments, he knew what they had to do. "Come, Egyptus, quickly," he said. "Take me to the tomb."

"What? Do you realize it's black out? Selene has disappeared totally from the sky. You're already bruised and scratched almost beyond recognition and I have more important things on my mind than going back up to visit the tomb." Truthfully he thought the blows to Philocleon's head must have left him a little delirious.

"We must move quickly," Philocleon said as undaunted as if Egyptus had said nothing. "We're going to burn down the tomb."

"What? You've watched the seasons pass many times while you tried to get to Ios. Why do you want to burn the tomb down? And ask my help when I am losing my beloved Charis?" He started to leave the room, his anger over Philocleon's insensitivity growing.

"Wait! Listen to me. If there is no tomb, there is no need for a sibyl. Don't you see?"

"I see, but..." Egyptus took Philocleon's arm. "I see! I see! I see!"

Egyptus left Philocleon at the altar when they reached the tomb while he gathered wood. Philocleon stirred the dirt in the pit with his fingers. "My dearest friend," he said to Homer. "Please forgive me. I'm burning down your tomb. Don't be disheartened. I promised to dedicate your saga to Apollo and I will." He piled the wood Egyptus brought to him under the altar and waited while Egyptus placed stacks of wood at intervals along the entire wooden enclosure and between the columns. Saying a final goodbye, Philocleon started the fire.

When they got back to the inn, most of the villagers were getting up to watch the blaze. Idas stood at the center of the group. "What's going on?" Idas demanded of Egyptus and Philocleon.

"I had a visit from Apollo," Philocleon answered. "He told me that I must make an even greater sacrifice than I had already made by building the tomb. In fact, the only sacrifice great enough, he said, was to sacrifice the entire tomb in his name. He wanted to smell the smoke all over Olympus."

"Apollo will certainly take revenge on you for mocking him," Idas threatened, knowing he'd been beaten. He wasn't willing to rebuild the tomb just to prevent Egyptus from marrying Charis. In fact, when he'd offered to endow the tomb, he'd never expected to have to do it.

"And what about you?" Philocleon asked in return. "Do you think Apollo won't take revenge on a man who bribed one of his priests? And what will the council say if I tell them about your bribery?"

Pheres stepped up to the three men. He'd just arrived from his estate. He tried not to show how pleased he felt. "I think we should all go home."

Idas stepped back. "I'm not done with this yet."

Philocleon turned toward Pheres. "You need to call a council meeting. Idas and I have something to tell them, don't we Idas?"

Idas, unwilling to face bribery charges, answered, "I'm asking for a meeting tomorrow. I think we should reconsider our vote to provide a sybil for the altar."

Pheres slipped his left arm through Egyptus' right and his right through Philocleon's left as Idas stomped away. He walked the two men toward the inn. "Idas is not a foolish man. I'm certain the council will change its vote."

Philocleon felt relieved. "Now that Charis is free, don't you think we should have the wedding?" he asked Pheres, determined to act before Idas had time to come up with a new plan.

"Selene will reappear as a full disk soon and Selene at her fullest is most propitious for a wedding," Egyptus added mischievously.

Pheres dropped their arms and looked at them. "You've been plotting more than the burning of the tomb." He laughed, pleased with the idea of his daughter being married to a man with a silver mine. "I think you're right. When Selene returns as a full disk, we'll have the wedding."

When Selene waxed into a full disk, Pheres sent his youngest son up into the mountains to the sacred spring to draw two urns of water. One urn was brought to the house for Charis to bathe with, the other was delivered to Egyptus for his ritual bath.

Egyptus and Philocleon were already awake when the urn was delivered. One of the innkeeper's daughters was called. She bathed

Egyptus in the water from the sacred spring and oiled his skin until it glistened. Teasing him, she curled his hair and tied it with the white linen fillet Myrrhine had given him. She put his carefully cleaned sandals on his feet and tied them, slipped a white linen tunic over his head, and placed the exquisite woolen mantle Scapha had given to him over his shoulders. "Tell Philocleon I'm ready," he instructed when she'd finished.

Philocleon came to the room dressed in his finest linen. "How do you look?" he asked.

"I wish you could see me. The mantle Scapha gave to me must be one of the finest ever made."

Philocleon felt the mantle as he handed Egyptus a silver fibula from his treasury.

Egyptus hugged Philocleon and waited for him to pin the shoulder of his mantle. He looked at himself in the bowl of spring water he'd saved especially for this moment. "I look like a god," he told Philocleon.

"Good. Because we must leave for your wedding."

Laughing and joking, the two got into the carriage Pheres had sent for them and rode to the estate. They were met at the front door by a group of young women who led them into the courtyard singing praises to Hymen, goddess of marriage.

Egyptus looked for Charis as soon as he stepped into the open space. She stood across the courtyard dressed in a long, flowing peplos of yellow linen fastened at the shoulders by the two silver fibulae Philocleon had sent to her as a gift. Her hair was filled with yellow flowers tied with white ribbons. A small white veil sat lightly on her flower-strewn hair, fell partly over her face, draped onto her shoulder. "She's beautiful," he whispered to Philocleon.

"What does she look like?" Philocleon asked.

"I can't say," Egyptus whispered back.

"Why?"

"She's coming over here. I can't breathe, let alone speak."

Charis placed a garland of flowers on Egyptus' head while her attendant placed one on Philocleon's. Silencing everyone, Pheres ordered his slaves to bring a white kid into the courtyard. He examined it for flaws, then held its head back and slit its throat. He cut the best pieces of the thigh from the animal, wrapped them in fat and placed them over the fire. Spreading barley, he called to Zeus,

Hera, Apollo and Artemis, each in turn, invoking them to consecrate the marriage and bless it with fertility.

One of the slaves brought in a mixing bowl Egyptus had made for the occasion. Pheres mixed water and wine and filled two goblets. He gave one to Egyptus and the other to Charis. Cheered on by the family, they drank their wine. One at a time, each member of the family took a goblet and toasted the couple. The singing of praises to Hymen began again and Halia ordered the servants to bring in sesame cakes and sweets.

Before Egyptus and Charis found time to speak for a moment, the many guests invited for the banquet began filling the courtyard, congratulating Pheres and Halia, teasing Egyptus, complimenting Charis. They drank and danced until the animals were roasted and Pheres announced that they were ready for the banquet and everyone crowded into the dining room.

Egyptus drank so many toasts that he could barely stand when Halia announced it was time for the procession to the bridegroom's house. Somehow he managed to pour a libation, though to which god he wasn't certain. With the help of Pheres, he got to the marriage cart and climbed up onto the seat between Charis and Philocleon. Overcome with happiness, he threw his arms around Charis and kissed her. When it finally occurred to him all the noise he was hearing was due to his kissing Charis, he pulled away, grinning awkwardly at her.

Charis smiled and took his hand lightly in hers. "You're going to be asleep when we get to our house," she whispered. This was the closest she'd ever been to Egyptus and she liked the feelings it was arousing in her.

"No, I won't," he promised.

Halia, as was her duty, took the bridal torches to the hearth and started them on fire. She took her place behind the carriage and the others fell into line behind her, the musicians in the center of the group so that everyone could hear them. As they approached the door to the couples' house, Charis' attendants ran ahead and covered the entrance with wreaths.

Egyptus and Charis entered the door to their new home together, a large house given to Egyptus by Pheres as the dowry. They ate fruit, to bring fertility, Halia said, and drank wine. Amid cheering and singing, they entered the bridal chamber. The guests were ushered out of the house and Philocleon took up his post outside the door to keep everyone out.

Egyptus locked the door to the bridal chamber. "I don't really think we'll need it locked," he said, trying to find something to say.

Charis took off her veil. "Listen to them."

Outside they were singing and dancing and the smaller boys, encouraged by the bigger ones, were yelling suggestions at the window as to what the couple might be doing.

Egyptus sat down on the edge of the bed. "You're very beautiful," he said.

They both blushed.

"I hope you didn't mind that I kissed you out there."

"No. In fact, I liked it."

"You did?"

She came over and sat next to him. "Yes." She ran her hand through his hair. Ever since she'd first seen him, she'd wanted to touch his hair.

He kissed her again.

All at once their wedding clothes were flying in every direction and they were in bed.

"They're not interested in us anymore," Philocleon told the crowd when there was a pause in the singing. "We may as well go back to Pheres'."

"To Pheres," one of the cousins yelled.

Amid hoots and obscene gestures, the group left the married couple to themselves and returned to Pheres' courtyard. When Helios rose in the sky most of them were still there, drinking wine.

Philocleon went to the village after the morning meal with one of the villagers who had attended the wedding. Tired from the celebration he fell into bed and slept until he was awakened by Egyptus.

"Charis and I want you to come and stay with us," Egyptus said. "There's no reason for you to live at the inn now that I have a house."

Philocleon hugged Egyptus. "Now that you're married, I won't be staying on Ios any longer. I haven't completed my journey. I promised Homer I would dedicate his saga to Apollo. I don't dare to rest until I've done it. Since we burned down the tomb, I've been thinking what I must do."

"Will you build another tomb?"

"No. I'll leave his ashes buried where they are on the mountain overlooking the sea. But his saga I must dedicate to Apollo as I promised. My journey will end where it began, at Delphi. I'll return to Apollo's sanctuary and leave Homer's saga with the temple priests. There it will remain forever at the center of the earth with the omphalos."

Twenty

"We're here!" announced the cocky young man Philocleon had hired to drive him from the port to Delphi as he pulled his mules to a jerky stop and slid jauntily off the cart.

Philocleon was flooded with memories as he had made his way to the gate and hired a guide. Smiling sardonically he silently followed the guide up the Sacred Way, remembering how his first time in Delphi he'd been convinced his blindness had resulted, like that of Bellerophon, from Zeus' severe punishment for his obstinate pride. No longer. Now he believed his blindness hadn't been caused by Zeus, but by himself. By the dagger he'd put to his eyes of his own will. Why would Zeus – who didn't punish the priests of Apollo for robbing people with their exorbitant prices for cakes or for accepting bribes to select a sibyl – bother with punishing him for wanting to go and see the world for himself? No. His blindness was his own. It had nothing to do with Zeus.

He fingered the well-worn leather copy of the Trojan war he carried. Though he was still determined to dedicate the saga at the temple of Apollo for Homer and though he still loved the saga and would miss having it with him, he no longer saw himself as having anything to do with Achilles or Patroclus. After all, wasn't the entire purpose of the Trojan war to take booty and punish Paris?

For him, it was still Na'id-Assur and Qurdi Marduk's Gilgamesh he most wanted to emulate in his life. Like Gilgamesh, he would devote his life to making an enduring name for himself. But he wasn't interested in doing it by killing Humbaba or insulting Ishtar, or traveling across the abyss. No. He wanted to be like Gilgamesh when the king decided to take the thorny plant of youth back for the men in his village.

Someday, he and Scapha would travel. They would sit in porticos and he would talk about what he had learned. He would try to convince others to worship Reason instead of their frivolous gods and goddesses. With the help of Reason, he'd show them it was wrong to have slaves and expose babies and he would make them understand how much better it would be for everyone if they gave up their clan rivalries and extravagant lives and dedicated themselves instead to the public good.

"We're at the temple, Sir," the guide informed Philocleon, interrupting his thoughts.

"Have we already passed the statuette of Apollo?"

"Yes. I told you about it. Didn't you hear me?"

"No."

"Do you want to go back to it?"

"No. I don't think so." What he had to say, he could say to the priest.

"You have to buy a cake and dedicate it at the altar," a young novitiate informed them as they started up the steps of the temple platform.

Smiling, Philocleon paid the high price and left the cake on the altar. At the temple, he was stopped again. "What is your reason for visiting the temple of Apollo?" a priest asked.

"I have come to give a gift to the priests of Apollo."

The novitiate pointed to a small room at the back of the temple. "Take him over there," he told the guide.

"I understand you wish to make a dedication." A young priest walked sulkily into the room several moments later. It wasn't fair. He was always the one chosen to take care of the petty requests of the people. Just because he wasn't from Delphi.

"Yes." Philocleon began his explanation, handing the saga to the priest. "I came here long ago to ask Apollo where I might find the fatherland of Homer, the greatest of all Greek poets. I wanted to bury the poet and dedicate his saga to Apollo in the land where he was born. Apollo told me through his priestess to go to Ios and look not for Homer's fatherland, but his motherland and the land of his mother's father."

The priest waited, barely listening to this blind man who had lived more seasons than he cared to imagine, refusing to look at him.

Instead, he examined a small tear in the hem of his tunic, preparing in his mind the reprimand he would give the woman who took care of his garments when he saw her. Had he bothered to look, he would have seen that although Philocleon's hair was still grey, his muscles had begun to regain their tone and the wrinkles were beginning to disappear.

"I went to Ios and I searched everywhere for his mother and his mother's father," Philocleon continued, "but I couldn't find either, so I buried his ashes on the island, but I wasn't able to leave his saga."

"I still don't understand why you've asked to see me." The young priest moved around the room, tapping the saga impatiently with his fingers.

"Please allow me one more moment," Philocleon pleaded. He wanted to explain fully. "Homer died because of me. When I was yet more boy than man, I put Na'id-Assur and Qurdi Marduk's riddle of immortality to him. He died because I decided to disobey my father by accompanying him to solve the riddle. When he lay dying, I promised him I would find the answer to riddle and when I did, I would bestow immortality upon him."

The priest yawned and sighed loudly. "You must understand I have duties."

"The saga you have in your hand. It's going to bestow immortality on Homer. You see, it's recorded. Now men will remember Homer and his poem forever." He'd planned to explain about the saga of Gilgamesh, Na'id-Assur and Qurdi Marduk's riddle, but the impatient priest cut him short.

"Tell me what it is you want."

"To dedicate to Apollo Homer's saga of the Trojan war."

The priest looked at the saga Philocleon had given him for the first time. Soon, he was reading it, line by line. Never had he seen such fine poetry. "Are you the poet Homer?" he asked without looking up from the poem.

Philocleon didn't answer. He'd already explained to the priest.

"Who are you?" the priest asked, but already he'd lost interest in the man sitting in front of him.

"I am Outis," Philocleon answered, smiling to himself. But the priest paid no attention to his clever answer. Nor did he notice when Nobody got up and left the room. By the time he looked up from the poem, Philocleon had passed through the gate of the sanctuary and gone to the Castalian spring.

He pulled Ti's cup from his traveling sack and filled it with the spring water. Nicias had told him on their first visit that the men who drank from this spring could often see the past and the future. He'd seen enough of the past. Now he wanted to see the future.

He drank greedily and waited. His insight came, not as he'd expected – as a flash of some future event, but rather as a vague realization that his ideas would some day be common among the men of Greece. If men began to record their poetry, he realized, soon they would record their thoughts and ideas as well. Men who recorded their ideas could never be held hostage by Memory as Homer had been. They would be free to think. Reason would replace Memory in their hearts.

Suddenly, overwhelmed with a desire to see Scapha, he packed the cup in his traveling sack and told the guide to take him back to his wagon. Climbing impatiently onto the wagon seat, he heard a large crowd talking at the gate to the sanctuary. "What's going on?" he called.

"They're carrying an inscription toward the gate," someone answered.

"What does it say?"

"KNOW THYSELF."

Philocleon laughed – a long happy laugh – as the young driver started the mules toward Attica.

Bibliography and Notes

Iliad and *Odyssey*

There are many translations of the *Iliad* and *Odyssey.* Recommended for their ease of reading are *Homer: The Iliad* (translated by Robert Fagles, Penguin Books, 1990) and *Homer: The Odyssey* (translated by Robert Fagles, Penguin Books, 1996). Extensive discussions of the controversies surrounding Homer are found in the introductions to both translations and in *Homeric Questions* by Gregory Nagy (University of Texas Press, 1996). The oracle, "Happy and ill-starred..." quoted in the foreword was taken from *The Delphic Oracle* by H.W. Parke and D.E.W. Wormell (Basil Blackwell, MCML VI, p. 394).

History

Two series of taped lectures produced for the Teaching Company's Great Courses on Tape are highly recommended for their scholarship, insights, and accessibility: *The Iliad of Homer* and *The Odyssey of Homer,* presented by Professor Elizabeth Vandiver, Northwestern University, and *Ancient Greek Civilization, Parts I and II,* presented by Jeremy McInerney, University of Pennsylvania.

Greek Myths

Excellent modern translations of the ancient myths are published in Robert Graves, *The Greek Myths 1 and 2.* (Penguin Books, 1955, 1960, reprinted several times). It should be noted that in some of the details the myths included in the novel vary from the myths which are now included in all surveys of Greek myths. This was done because it is the author's opinion that many versions of these myths probably existed before their codification by writing led to an official version.

Gilgamesh

Unlike the *Iliad* and the *Odyssey* which passed from the ancient Greeks to the modern world in pretty much complete form, the *Epic of Gilgamesh* has come into existence through a series of excavations in which tablets and fragments written in more than one language were recovered in various locations. The narration included in the novel is not intended to be an exact rendition of the Gilgamesh epic, but rather a general summary of the story. For an exact translation of the extant tables upon which the story of Gilgamesh is based, see R. Campbell Thompson *The Epic of Gilgamesh*. (Luzac & Co., 1928). An excellent account of the excavation of the tablets recovered in Nineveh is published in Sir Ernest Wallis Budge *The Babylonian Story of the Deluge and the Epic of Gilgamesh* (revised by C.J. Gadd, British Museum, 1929).

Characters

Alcmena: Mother of Calonice. Mother-in-law of Hipponous. Grandmother of Philocleon. Wife of Daemones. Aunt of Scapha.

Bromia: Slave of Hipponous.

Calonice: Wife of Hipponous. Daughter of Alcmena and Daemones. Mother of Philocleon.

Cario: Friend of Philocleon, Delphium, Meton, Xanthias, and Iris.

Castor: Son of Merops. Nephew of Hipponous. Brother of Polydeuces. Named after the legendary hero.

Charis: Daughter of Pheres and Halia.

Clidus: Slave in silver mines.

Clymene: Niece of Nicias. Daughter of Evadne and Simo. Sister of Themis.

Daemones: Father of Calonice. Father-in-law of Hipponous. Grandfather of Philocleon. Husband of Alcmena. Uncle of Scapha.

Delphium: Daughter of Sosias. Friend of Philocleon, Meton, Xanthias, Cario, Iris and Myrrhine.

Egyptus: Egyptian potter who works for Hipponous.

Evadne: Sister of Nicias. Wife of Simo. Mother of Themis and Clymene.

Halia: Wife of Pheres. Mother of Charis.

Hipponous: Father of Philocleon. Son-in-law of Alcmena and Daemones. Husband of Calonice.

Homer: Eighth century poet?

Idas: Island landowner.

Iris: Friend of Philocleon, Delphium, Meton, Xanthias, Cario, and Myrrhine.

Merops: Cousin of Hipponous. Father of Castor and Polydeuces.

Meton: Friend of Philocleon, Delphium, Xanthias, Cario and Iris.

Myrrhine: Woman who worships the Mother Goddess.

Na'id-Assur: Assyrian tutor of Philocleon.

Nicias: Slave of Hipponous. Philocleon's pedagogue.

Pegasus: Hipponous's horse. Named after legendary horse.

Pheres: Husband of Halia. Father of Charis.

Philocleon: Son of Hipponous. Master and friend of Nicias. Friend of Homer and Egyptus. Grandson of Alcmena and Daemones. Fiancée of Scapha.

Polydeuces: Son of Merops. Nephew of Hipponous. Brother of Castor. Named after legendary hero.

Qurdi Marduk: Assyrian tutor of Philocleon.

Scapha: Fiancée of Philocleon. Niece of Alcmena and Daemones.

Simo: Husband of Evadne. Father of Themis and Clymene. Brother-in-law of Nicias.

Sosias: Potter. Friend of Egyptus.

Themis: Daughter of Evadne and Simo. Sister of Clymene. Niece of Nicias.

Theopropides: Athenian.

Ti: Uncle of Egyptus.

Trygaeus: Friend of Nicias.

Xanthias: Friend of Philocleon, Delphium, Meton, Cario, and Iris.

Mythological Events and Figures

Achilles: Hero in the Trojan war. Fought with the Greeks (Achaeans) against the Trojans.

Agamemnon: Supreme commander of the Greek (Achaean) army.

Aphrodite: Greek goddess of beauty, love and reproduction.

Apollo: Greek god of reason. Associated with music, archery, medicine, the care of flocks and herds, and the oracle at Delphi.

Artemis: Virgin huntress. Twin sister of Apollo.

Assyrians: Lived in Mesopotamia. Dominated area from about 1400-1600 BCE.

Atalanta: Famous huntress.

Athena: Daughter of Zeus. Goddess of war. Patron of the arts and crafts. Personification of wisdom.

Bellerophon: Later legend said that he performed magic with the help of the winged horse, Pegasus. Incurred wrath of the gods when tried to ride Pegasus to heaven. Was driven mad and died a wandering outcast.

Calliope: Muse of epic poetry.

Castor and Polydeuces: Twin brothers of Helen. Castor famous for taming and mastering horses. Polydeuces for boxing.

Calydonian boar hunt: Hunt during which Meleager got into an argument and killed his mother's brothers.

Danaë: Locked up by her father when he was told by an oracle that she would give birth to a son who would slay him. Visited by Zeus as a shower of gold. Gave birth to Perseus.

Dawn: Goddess of the morning.

Delphi: A major oracle center in Greece.

Delphic Oracle: Revelation of Apollo through the Pythia.

Demeter: Corn-goddess.

Enkidu: Friend of Gilgamesh.

Erinyes: Greek spirits of vengeance.

Gilgamesh: Mesopotamian hero.

Hades: Reigned over the dead in the Underworld.

Hector: Trojan hero.

Helen: Wife of Greek king, Menelaus. Kidnapped by Trojan prince, Paris. Her kidnapping was said to be the cause of the Trojan war.

Helios: Greek sun-god. Greeks believed he drove his cart from east to west across the sky every day.

Hermes: Son of Zeus (and Maia). Messenger of the gods. Patron of wayfarers, travellers, and thieves.

Horus: Egyptian god. King of the earth.

Icarus: Flew too close to the sun with wax wings his father had made for him to escape from Crete. Drowned when the wax melted and he fell into the sea.

Ishtar: Mesopotamian goddess.

Medusa: Changed by Athena from beautiful maiden to cruel monster with hissing snakes for hair. Killed by Perseus.

Meleager: Son of the king and queen of Calydon. In later legend, it was believed that his life was guaranteed by the Fates as long as a particular firebrand was not burned. His mother pulled the firebrand from the fire and kept it until he angered her by killing her brothers during a quarrel after a boar hunt about his having given the boar's head to Atalanta. In revenge, his mother threw the firebrand into a fire and he died.

Menelaus: Greek king whose wife, Helen, was kidnapped by the Trojan Prince, Paris. Brother of Agamemnon.

Mother Goddess: Term used in the novel to represent Gaia or Ge, a personification of the earth, daughter of Chaos and the wife of Uranus (Heaven). Delivered the oracle at Delphi until Apollo killed the Python.

Narcissus: Beautiful boy who fell in love with his reflection in a pool. Pined away when he couldn't embrace his reflection and died.

Night: Goddess of night.

Odysseus: Greek (Achaean) hero of the Trojan war. Hero of the *Odyssey*. Through misfortune, takes years to return to his home.

Oedipus: Oracle predicted he will kill his father and sleep with his mother. Tried to avoid, but didn't. Blinded himself when he learned of his deeds.

Olympus: Highest mountain in Greece. Home of the Greek gods, often referred to as the Twelve Olympians.

Paris: Trojan prince who kidnapped Helen.

Patroclus: Friend of Achilles. Killed by Hector.

Persephone: Daughter of Zeus and Demeter. Believed to live half year in Hades and half year on earth. Associated with change in seasons.

Perseus: Son of Zeus and Danaë. Placed in a trunk and set out to sea with his mother when his grandfather learned of his birth and didn't believe she had been visited by Zeus. Rescued and raised by a tyrant. Killed Medusa.

Polyphemus: Cyclops Odysseus encounters on his way home.

Poseidon: God of earthquakes and the sea.

Priam: King of Troy. Father of Hector and Paris.

Pythia: Priestess of Apollo at Delphi who delivered the oracles. Took her name from the Python, a guardian serpent, believed by the Greeks to have lived near the site of the oracle before it was killed by Apollo.

Selene: Moon goddess.

Sumer: City-states of the Sumerians. Developed between 3500 and 2800 BCE along the rivers of southern Mesopotamia (modern Iraq).

Trojan War: A battle fought between the Greeks and their allies (Achaeans in Homer) against the Trojans, a people who may have lived in modern Turkey.

Zeus: King of the gods. Governed the universe. Attribute is the thunderbolt. Ruled the sky and weather, hospitality and the rights of guests, and punishment of injustice.

9 780967 347110